Behold the Marshal

R.W. Hamilton

PublishAmerica
Baltimore

First printing

ISBN: 1-4241-7459-7
PUBLISHED BY PUBLISHAMERICA, LLLP
www.publishamerica.com
Baltimore

Printed in the United States of America

This book is dedicated to Dale Mix, a Yale scholar and friend who introduced me to the rich history of the Plantagenets over a chess game.

Foreword

In her fifteenth year Eleanor of Aquitaine married King Louis VII of France, as was proper custom for noble ladies. The enormously wealthy province of Aquitaine was her dowry and the chief reason for the union. The union failed to produce the needed male heir with the dull and pious Louis. Several daughters and a failed crusade left them with a strong distaste for the other's company. The marriage was dissolved. After a clandestine affair, which some say preceded the annulment, she married the dashing Count Henry of Anjou. She was his senior by eleven years. Two years after the marriage he was crowned King of England.

The marriage had profound consequences giving the ambitious King Henry II control of Anjou, Normandy, and Aquitaine. Most of France was now under the rule of the Plantagenets and not the French king. The Queen bore the lusty King Henry four sons: Henry, Richard, Geoffrey and John. Bright and educated, far beyond that of most ladies, Eleanor was behind many of the struggles for the next thirty-five years as she tried to secure an inheritance for her sons. Much of what we know comes from the songs of minstrels and courtiers.

The struggle between these two enormous personalities led to a marriage that was in name only. Henry sought comfort in numerous affairs. Eleanor was left to her own devices which were considerable. Into this bubbling caldron of political intrigue came a handsome young knight errant of incredible skill and valor. He would play a dominant role in the lives of King Henry, Queen Eleanor and their sons. Time and again his life would be threatened by the constant changes in political power. His steadfast loyalty and fighting prowess would make him a legend and take him from obscurity to eventually become acting King of England. Sadly his story has been lost to all but a few. It is a story that begs to be told. The year is 1220.

Chapter 1
A Troubadour's Story

A dozen men are seated in a small tavern on a street called the Shambles in York, England. The chill of the early fall has caused many to seek a brew and warm fire in this establishment. They are having a pint with a group of townspeople when the door opens. In shuffles an old man dressed in what appears to be fine, but worn, clothes. Hanging from a strap on his back is a lute of fine quality, but also old, like its owner. His hair is white and thin. He has a careworn face, but seems to be at peace with his condition as he grins and smiles at the patrons. He sits down on a bench where he can be seen by all and, extending both arms in a beckoning gesture, invites everyone to gather round him. He begins to speak.

"I am Lewellyn, a poor singer of songs. By a strange twist of fate, which can be viewed as curse or a blessing, I became sirrah for one of the greatest men of our age. His passing one year ago left me in service to his jealous son, a son who saw little gain in having an aged entertainer in his household. Thus I will spend my declining years telling my stories in taverns for whatever largesse the locals will provide. I have seen what few have seen and even fewer are willing to tell." He pulls at the strap until his instrument is cradled gently in his lap.

Many in the establishment ignore the speech. However some of the patrons are listening. It is a hopeful sign. He clears his throat and raises his voice, "'Tis a tale of the great Eleanor of Aquitaine and the intrigues of her court. It spans the reigns of many great Kings and I, Lewellyn, knew them all."

Several in the tavern now scoff and laugh at the claim. One man with soot-stained skin and the acrid smell of fire betraying him as a charcoal maker snarls, "Piss on you. You tell stories that praise our betters who care nothing for us. Be gone, beggar, before my foot feels the need to test your old bones." He waves his mug in a dismissive gesture.

The old troubadour stares angrily and icily rebuffs the attempt to silence him. "It is true of those who practice the craft in tapestry-covered halls, but no so I. Even though they know what I know they pretend they do not for they fear the headsman's ax. At my age the ax offers relief not fear. If my story does not exceed your expectations you have my leave to do as you will. Greater men than you have had at these bones and your threat is feeble." His courage intrigues the patrons and he continues uninterrupted. "Each man, be he peasant or king, seeks to be more than he is, and therein lies the wonder or tragedy of our lives. Stories of those who succeed give us hope; stories of those who fail give us warning. Tonight I will share a story of both and each may decide which speaks loudest to them. My master was not of royal blood, and yet, through deeds of valor none can match, he ruled England for three years and saved for all time the right of a free man to a fair hearing as written in the Great Charter. Pray let me share the glorious events in the life of the greatest of all knights in Christendom. A reputation so singular he was 'The Marshal' and this troubadour was by his side for sixty-two years."

The tavern grows silent at this extraordinary claim. It cannot be! They cast skeptical glances at each other. Few believe the old one could possibly prove this boast. One man in the back cries out, "You think us fools to believe such a boast."

The troubadour nods and responds, "A fair challenge! I offer this as proof." He holds his instrument above his head. "Keeper, can you read?"

The tavern keeper responds, "Aye."

"This instrument is of the finest quality. No wandering beggar would possess one and this one bears the name of its previous owner—Sir Bertran de Born! The name engraved on the back." Again a surprised silence grips the gathering as the keeper inspects the proffered evidence and nods affirmatively. Having roused the curiosity of the patrons the troubadour smiles, his eyebrows raise gently and he says, "I can be encouraged to tell this amazing story for only small token of appreciation." Again the throng begins to mutter.

Tom, the town blacksmith, sneers and shouts, "I work all day for what you want for words. My purse remains shut. Your proof; clever fakery."

It prompts the old one to add in an almost mocking tone, "'Tis a dull evening and I ask for naught but the price of a flagon of ale. For this pittance your ears will hear what only a few have heard." He smiles and extends his hands in a pleading gesture.

One man, prosperous by the quality of his cloak and broad belly, nods to affirm the old one's logic. He looks at his friends, then the troubadour. He rises to his feet and laughingly he makes an offer. "Why not? Conversation this evening has been a stale repetition of last night. A mug of ale is cheap enough. If this one proves to be an uninteresting liar then we will amuse ourselves by hurling insults and scraps of this bad food at him." They all laugh and he continues. "Either way it will provide us with an entertaining evening. Bring the ale. I will pay to amuse you all," he shouts magnanimously. The patrons cheer the gesture. The troubadour seems satisfied. He nods, smiles and prepares his instrument.

Old Lewellyn closes his eyes and with knurled fingers begins picking out a beautiful tune on his instrument. As his fingers dance effortlessly across the strings they see his talent is far greater than they expected. A serving boy adds a log to the fire and pauses to listen briefly to the sweet sound that is beginning to fill the room. The old troubadour hums gently and starts casting a spell over the surprised gathering. Before the night ends they will be amazed and puzzled by the story they are about to hear.

It was the 27th day of March, year of our Lord, 1168. I was just a boy in the service of the great Queen Eleanor. I was one of the many who helped make life enjoyable for our betters. A woman of exceeding beauty and a will of iron, she had been married to the Kings of France and England.

The morning gave promise of a fine spring day after a rather harsh winter. The Queen, in residence at Lusignan Castle, recently captured by her husband, would certainly be anxious to make the most of the change in weather. She paced the halls with an air of excitement. Those in service waited for the commands that would spill out once she had reached a decision as to how this day should unfold. She wore a bright red gown and her head covered by a white wimple that framed the ivory skin of her face. The Queen was in her forty-sixth year and it is not false flattery to say she looked half the age. It was rumored in the scullery she started each day hanging from a bar suspended above her bed as a method of maintaining her youthful appearance. If this was true, it was having the desired effect.

She was busily raising King Henry's brood and trying to ignore the strain on her marriage as she and Henry grew increasingly more estranged. Preparing a group of spoiled children for their royal responsibilities was her main task. Her passion for King Henry had long since waned. He was off on another of his many "diplomatic" missions of peace to Poitiers. To put it plain, he was trying to seize more land from the weak-willed King Louis VII. He had left his trusted military commander, Earl Patrick, in charge of his family's safety.

As she entered the gathering hushed. No one could dominate a room like the beautiful Queen Eleanor. She was a petite woman, but her dark eyes blazed with the fire that revealed her enormous talents. All bowed awaiting her wishes. Finally the decision was announced.

"We wish to spend the day hunting," the Queen said as she scanned those gathered in the great hall. It was issued as a command not a request.

The Earl grumbled, "As your Majesty wishes." He clapped his hands and began planning the party to include himself, the Queen, several servants, and a few men-at-arms. The household sprang to life when she whirled about and began issuing the appropriate orders. Her eyes sparkled with excitement as she spoke to one of the ladies-in-waiting.

"Catherine, fetch my hunting dress—the brown one with the blue cloak. 'Tis quite brisk and we like not the sting of morning frost. Bring it to my apartments. We shall be there shortly." She turned to the Earl. "We would be pleased if the stalwart knight who is your nephew be among the company."

The nephew, Sir William Marshal by name, was a favorite of the old Earl. He had shown enormous talent as a fighter in the tournaments, and the Earl was personally engaged in his training. The young knight had been the talk of the scullery that very morning. The youngest winner at Sorel they said. He had won in such convincing style the cook claimed he was bound to become a great champion. It led to an argument between the cook and the baker. The kitchen master said he was the second son of a minor English noble and that would probably limit his prospects. I recalled it vividly when I heard the Queen's remarks.

Earl Patrick raised one graying eyebrow and replied somewhat askance, "Yea, Majesty, but pray be careful what ears may hear, lest tongues soon be wagging at court. The King might be ill tempered from such talk." The old Earl knew her answer would be curt. He winced as she barked a rebuke of his advice.

"The King! Henry's eye is constantly spying soft cheeks and healthy smiles when he travels. The fool's cap sits not upon my brow. The King cares not a wit for my feelings. Besides we inquired only because 'tis rare a young man so skilled in knightly combat possesses the level of intelligence found in this knight. We find him interesting. 'Tis not thoughtful conversation the King seeks when his eye roves. If there be difficulty, a knight of his skill could prove useful," she said tossing her head back with a regal air.

"Exactly and why I beg you to reconsider this outing, Majesty. There are many in the area objecting to our presence." Again the Earl knew the response and shrugged as the Queen ignored the warning and continued to issue commands.

"You boy, Lewellyn, find the falconer and tell him to be sure he brings my favorite bird. Alain tell cook to prepare sweet meats for our noon meal in the field." She was now exiting the great hall toward her apartments. Several of the ladies-in-waiting trailed the Queen at an appropriate distance. They passed by several banners that added color to the dreary gray walls. It was part of the Queen's attempt to add an air of gaiety to the recently occupied Lusignan castle.

Castles often reflect the personalities of their owners. It was clear that the previous owner, the Baron de Lusignan, was more concerned with the military necessities of his home than fanciful court life. It had not proved effective since King Henry had dispossessed the Baron in a short siege last year. Dower surroundings would never do for Eleanor of Aquitaine. Poitiers, her favorite residence, showed that she was a lady used to the finest accouterments. She had spent the winter months planning and large sums of the King's gold would bring this castle up to her standards now that the warmer weather was at hand.

I raced down the corridor to carry out my mission. One in service to a Queen does not dally if he values his skin. I completed my mission and came back through the yard, hoping to see this young knight of whom the Queen had spoken. Like all who have the opportunity to observe the famous, I was intensely curious about someone who could evoke an intemperate remark by so great a lady. To my distress I saw nothing.

Why is it those of us whose lives are insignificant wish to know so much about the rich and powerful? They are oblivious to our existence. Why should we concern ourselves with the trivialities of their lives? Perhaps, we imagine ourselves somehow more important if we are privy to the details. I was just as guilty of this brand of curiosity as any in my class.

I proceeded to the kitchen where the cook, a fat and ugly man, tossed a leather sack to me and ordered me to accompany the party to fetch downed birds. He cuffed my head and said, "See to it they are properly dress when you return knave." The lowest of the low in the household I accepted the blow without a thought. Secretly, I was happy to be freed from the drudgery of the scullery if only for a day. I took my sack and headed to the armory where the party would assemble. Again hopes rose for a meeting with the mysterious Sir William. My life was soon to become far more involved with this knight than just a young boy's curiosity.

I reached the place where the men-at-arms designated by the Earl were preparing for their role as bodyguards for the hunting party. It was lightly awash in smoke drifting from the smithy's forge. The dust of the courtyard mingled with the smoke as several war horses pranced nervously awaiting their riders. The knights were donning their hauberks with the assistance of their pages. The links of the chain mail rattled softly as each man prepared. It contrasted with the rhythmic sound of the smith's hammer ringing on the anvil and reverberating off the stone walls behind the courtyard. I spied the Earl sporting a blue and white tabard with his coat-of-arms emblazoned on the front. The Earl chose not to wear armor since a hauberk would make hunting with a hawk most uncomfortable. I surveyed the gathering of men-at-arms. Four of the seven men were clearly older than twenty-six. Two of the younger ones were already known to me. It left one to be the object of my inspection.

He was taller than the rest. His arms and shoulders rippled with muscles developed from hours of practice with a broad sword. His countenance was far more appealing than his companions. The light brown locks which rested with a slight curl on his large shoulder were soon covered with the chain mail hood of the hauberk. A small mustache and neatly trimmed beard framed his lips and covered an angular chin. In sum I can say he appeared as all young boys hoped they would look when they reached the age of majority. I suspect there would be many a happy lass if all young men were so blessed. It was easy to see Queen Eleanor had noticed far more than a nimble brain. It appeared to my young mind that a woman was inclined to deny a handsome countenance captures her interest and claim a more noble reason for an admiring look. On the other hand, the men of the castle tended to boast of their base desires. Even at my tender age I had heard many a bawdy tale told in the scullery.

He did not bear any noticeable scars. It was unusual for one whose reputation as a tournament champion was growing. Most champion knights were older and bore the marks of their brutal contests. It was immediately clear he was comfortable with a sword when he practiced a few brief moves before sheathing his weapon. He cut the air with a few flicks of a powerful wrist and then made the blade disappear into the scabbard with a motion so smooth that the arm and the sword appeared to be one and the same. He jested with some of his fellows that he would catch a rabbit for the stew pot on the point of his lance.

Guy, the oldest, said, "A large boast for so young a pup. I would fain see such feat, William. You possess good skills, but by God's eyes I will see if they match your words."

"How do we improve if we set not lofty goals, my friend?" was the retort of the handsome Sir William.

"Lofty, methinks yours surpass the keep! The hawks should fly so high today. I, for one, consider modesty most important of knightly virtues," Guy responded in a mocking tone. They all laughed.

With this last jest, the men returned to their preparations. Suddenly, the handsome, young knight looked straight at me with eyes that made me look down as though a strong invisible force would hit me if I continued to hold their gaze.

"You, boy. What be your name?" he asked in a rich powerful voice.

"Lewellyn, Sir Knight," I said meekly as I lowered my eyes.

"Well, Lewellyn, a fine Welsh lad should know a gage."

"'Tis an armored glove, Sir Knight," I said proudly.

"Good lad. Make haste to the shop and ask the smith for one he just repaired for Sir William Marshal," said he while pointing to the armory.

I darted into the armory and quickly retrieved the appropriate item and again received the customary cuff by the smith's heavy hand because I had interrupted his work. I was too flushed with excitement to feel pain since I had been given a task usually reserved for the pages. When I returned, the young knight was already astride his horse. He reached down grasping the gage with a huge hand and thanked me for the speed and success of my quest. I was surprised by the warmth he showed for one as lowly as me. Knights rarely acknowledged the existence of the serving class. His bright blue eyes kept me transfixed as he continued his thought.

"Lewellyn, you have been of great service. Dost thou sing as well as the rest of your countrymen?" He grinned at the last comment.

"Some say, kind sir." My face turned quickly the color of an evening sunset.

"Then perhaps you shall be a troubadour." It was strange how prophetic the words, casually mentioned in friendly banter, became with time.

I returned to the great hall. The hunting party was assembled. The ladies-in-waiting fussed about the Queen to make certain every fold of cloth enhanced the loveliness of her figure. Although she had borne many children, the Queen's shape could still turn the head of most men. Queen Eleanor took the heavy leather glove for the hunt and folded it neatly in the sash of her hunting dress. She turned and addressed the assembled group of ladies and servants.

"Catherine, be sure Giselle feeds my John at two. Marion, be sure Henry and Richard are at their lessons. Now let us be off. The birds await and we desire a fat fowl for supper."

With that command, all bowed gracefully and followed her to the courtyard. The horses, each attended by a groom, were gathered in the front of the great hall. The Earl mounted first, followed by the queen, and the rest followed in order of their rank. The seven armored knights waited by the main gate with their horses pawing the ground impatiently.

Lusignan castle was not an impressive fortress when compared to some in France, but it was strong enough to withstand any attack until the forces of Henry could be summoned to relieve those within its walls. It was sturdy protection for the Queen and the young offspring of King Henry. It was well garrisoned with fifty men-at-arms. If attacked their numbers would be swelled by several hundred farm folk. Thirty-foot walls of stone and four towers gave witness to the wealth of its former owner, the Baron Lusignan. The royal apartments surrounded the great hall. At one end they connected to the massive stone keep. Vertical slits were the only openings in the structure. A banner proclaiming the Queen's presence fluttered atop this last line of defense. Quarters for the serving class were small wood structures that seemed to cling to the stone walls of the central apartments. Their closeness to the main building was an ugly compromise to assure prompt service to the occupants of the royal apartments. The Queen had made plans to change this. I had come to this place with my mother last spring when Earl Patrick had been ordered by King Henry to strengthen this new acquisition. He was making those improvements when the Queen and court arrived in the fall. Sadly my mother died of the fever shortly after the arrival of the Queen. As an orphan, I no longer deserved living in these buildings. My mother's passing had the effect of moving me to a straw mat in the loft of the horse barn. I was truly the lowest of the low.

Only seven knights would be needed to accompany the hunting party across the field to the edge of the woods in the distance. The party would not venture too far from the safety of the walls. As the Earl had earlier suggested to the Queen, these were dangerous times. All the remaining men-at-arms would continue their practice at the post and some would be posted on the ramparts to watch the progress of the hunting party for as long as possible. The Earl barked a command and the dark oak gate was opened and the portcullis raised. The loud rattle of large chains signaled the lowering of the bridge.

The procession passed under the portcullis and clattered across the drawbridge. Several guards peered down through the murder-holes at the riders and those of us following on foot. Once on the road, the royal party rode about a quarter of a league before turning left into a broad field just losing its brown coat as green shoots of new growth emerged from a winter sleep. They stopped at the edge of a woods made up of brush and pines. Behind the forested area several small green hills dotted with outcroppings of chalky-colored rock contrasted with a clear blue sky. It was several minutes before those of us on foot, trotting, caught up with the mounted group.

The Earl was engaged in conversation with the Queen as I approached with my leather sack, but she seemed to be preoccupied watching the knights gathered to the left of the hunting party. She returned to the Earl's conversation when he announced the arrival of the hawks. The Queen removed the heavy leather glove from her sash and thrust her right hand into its protective embrace. She extended her arm, and a servant dressed in a red velvet vest and green breeches carefully placed the hooded hawk on her glove-covered wrist. She firmly grasped the tresses attached to the bird's leg.

Soon all attention was focused on the woods as several pages carrying long sticks marched into a promising cluster of shrubs. No one cared about the lone figure on a distant hill I saw observing the hunting party. To be sure it was a villein who would inform his neighbors of the activity. In the spring the royal sport often entertained villeins before the needs of the fields called them to all day toil. I was sure we would soon have several freemen perched on the rock outcroppings cheering the hawks. When I looked again, he was gone.

My attention shifted as the pages were now approaching a cluster of shrubs with their long poles. The Queen, seated on a fine-looking black palfrey, was the first to raise her gloved arm. With her left hand, she quickly removed the hood and urged the bird into the air by swinging her arm with an upward motion. At the same time, she released the long leather straps tied to the hawk's leg. With several beats of its powerful wings, the bird accelerated into the sky. It floated above the field like a leaf caught in a spinning wind.

The signal was given and the pages began flailing the shrubs with their poles. The thicket exploded as the game birds took flight to escape the danger of the poles, not knowing they were fleeing into a more deadly trap. In a move, almost too fast to be seen, the circling hawk fell like a shooting star into the middle of the flock, crashing into one of the birds with a loud shriek. The wings instantly opened to support the weight of its newfound burden, and the hawk began its descent.

A cheer went up from all those present. The falcon master began to swing a leather pouch tied to a long strap above his head in a long, sweeping motion. The hawk dropped its catch and immediately flew to the swinging pouch. I raced over to the dead prey and ran back to the Queen who was clearly pleased with her performance. I held it over my head and displayed it to her.

"A fine bird! If any best my count we shall have a good repast this evening," she shouted. I knew she did not intend to be bested in anything and the others knew it as well. A little exaggeration of their feats and a discreet omission of their faults can increase royal generosity. Those who live off the crumbs from the royal table are skilled in the art of flattery.

"In sooth, I must not be slow lest your majesty embarrass me in front of my own men," Earl Patrick exclaimed and the company clapped in unison.

"A wonderful start to a beautiful day," the Queen replied.

Three hours passed quickly in the excitement of the hunt. Several fine birds were in my game sack. I was dreaming of the leftovers that were sure to be available after the dinner when I heard Sir William shout to Earl Patrick, "Riders, my lord, a sizable number cresting the hill. They bear arms!"

"Stay here with the Queen. I shall see what they are about. If it is mischief, we court trouble. It is too late to run. Perhaps I can negotiate since I am unarmed." The old warrior was clearly nervous, but he knew that the code of chivalry required knights not to attack an unarmed man. Sir William leaned forward in the saddle and spoke to the Queen.

"Majesty, be on guard and be ready to fly if the chance arises. They are many times our strength," he said glancing back at the empty road to the castle.

The Earl marched his horse forward in the direction of the oncoming knights. I glanced about and saw that the servants with the poles had melted into the underbrush. The Earl's men quietly walked their horses to form a line in front of Queen Eleanor. Their lances were tilted slightly forward. I knew the odds were impossible if a fight was necessary. I stood holding my sack of game and watched events play out. Why did I not join those in the woods? Certainly, the force of men in front of us would not react to a small boy's flight. Was it a brave commitment to my mistress? Nay. Bravery is not in my nature. I was simply too frightened to move.

The large company of knights, some thirty or so, parted as the Earl reached them about fifty paces from our party. It revealed a large man with a red tabard and a black griffin emblazoned on the front. Earl Patrick only had time to utter the single word, "You!" The blade of an ax flashed, and he slumped forward in his saddle. In what seemed like the same instant the ax blow fell, Sir William's horse charged the mass of men around the Earl. Sir William's lance lowered into the attack position. The cluster of opposing knights seemed frozen in disbelief because the action was so sudden and surprising.

"KERWHANG!!!" The collision was like that of a storm-driven wave smashing into a rocky shore. The impact of the lance striking the unlucky knight in the front was so violent it drove him clear off his horse and into the knight directly behind him. Both men landed on the ground, and the riderless horses bolted. The first was surely dead from so fierce a blow. The lance shattered, and the splinters showered on those adjacent to the two unhorsed knights. In the middle of the pack, he wheeled his horse, and using the remaining part of the broken lance, unseated a third knight. Sir William dropped the broken lance and, as if by magic, a sword was in his hands. His blows rained down on all in arm's length as they tried to recover their wits and respond to this onslaught. Later, the Queen would say the moment liken to that of a wild boar when attacked by a pack of hounds kills any within its reach.

All present seemed bewitched by the moment. Most remained motionless as though some invisible hands were holding all, forcing them to witness the amazing spectacle. Alas, the spell lost its power after a few moments, though it seemed like a longer time. So terrible had been the attack of this warrior none of the attacking party saw the Queen swing her horse around and begin to race in the direction of the castle. They were far too intent on surviving the whirlwind in their midst. One of the unhorsed knights recovered his feet. He raced over and plunged a dagger into the heroic knight's leg. Sir William groaned as he pulled it out, cursed as he killed the man with a single stroke and continued his fierce assault on the large group surrounding him.

Clubbed from behind by a knight with a mace, Sir William fell to the ground senseless. It saved his life because the much larger force, freed from the initial shock of the hopeless attack, unleashed the full fury of their superior numbers on all those left in our party. Sir Guy was first, struck from the left side with a lance. It penetrated his hauberk just below the armpit and hurled him violently to the ground with the end of the lance breaking from his weight. He lay there with the shaft protruding up from his body. I knew it was a lethal hit. Walter de Brais and one other knight I did not know were unhorsed by numerous sword hits from all sides. They lay on the ground mortally wounded. Two more were wounded, but not seriously. The one remaining knight of our band realized the hopelessness of the situation and yielded. Though it seemed a long fight, it was only minutes.

I had been transfixed by the action in front of me. The screams! The shouts! The crashing clang of metal on metal was like a potion that dulls the senses to the pain and agony being endured by those involved in the struggle. 'Tis strange I felt nothing but excitement as I witnessed the carnage. I was so overwhelmed I did not comprehend the danger of my own circumstance. I was seized from behind by a rider, lifted off the ground and my rapture instantly became fear. A warm trickle of liquid ran down my leg and soaked my clothing.

It was then the attackers became aware of the Queen's flight. The one who had struck the Earl shouted a command, "The Queen is escaping. Make haste, you churls."

Six knights put spurs to horse, but too late to recover the distance between them and Queen Eleanor. An excellent horsewoman, the Queen would reach the safety of the castle and her garrison. The knights soon returned without their quarry to report to their master.

One of the knights rode to the leader and exclaimed, "My Lord Lusignan, we could not catch the bitch."

Now, the purpose of the attack was plain. He was none other than the displaced lord of the castle now occupied by the Queen. It was his demesne King Henry had seized last year. The ambush was to gain a royal hostage for a ransom. Deprived of his land this noble was reduced to seeking succor with other wealthy nobility. The condition would last until he could find a way to regain his land by performing a service for the French King who might reward him with the fiefdom of some other luckless lord.

Baron Lusignan considered the problem for a few moments and then ordered, "Kill them all. No, a moment, bring the one who fights like a badger. Perhaps he is worth something. I would buy a soldier like that myself. Perhaps I can gain something from this failure." The large man glanced at me. My face turned pale and my limbs were shaking violently. I knew my short life was surely over when he added, "Bring that boy. He will be useful as a messenger. We shall send him to the castle with our demands. If they kill him as an answer, no matter. It is better than losing one of our own. Kill the rest. Quickly!" He turned his horse and headed down the road in the opposite direction.

"This one has wet himself," snarled the rider I was placed behind. "Why am I always the one to get the dirty job? If you shit your pants, boy, I will make you eat it." Fortunately I had not eaten all day or I might have had a most unpleasant meal. My thoughts began to wander when I was sure my bowels were empty. I thought to myself, *Lewellyn, you ass, why did you not run like the others? Your mother bore an idiot for a son.*

When you realize that stupidity is your finest trait there is little to recommend God's mercy. None would mourn the passing of another fool. Life held little for the lowly. Desperation and the desire to survive caused my head to spin with thoughts about the Baron's orders and what lay ahead. Escape could be possible! Once I was released with the ransom note I would pretend to make for the castle. Once my minder left, not wanting to be captured, I would throw away the note and slip away unnoticed. Those in the castle would assume that I had perished with the others and would not come looking for me. It would be hard making my way in the world, but death was certainly harder still. It was a sage observation. Perhaps my mother had done better than I first thought.

We stopped briefly and I was forced to use one of my sleeves to bind the wounded leg of the unconscious William Marshal; the men tied him across the horse of the knight he had killed in the first charge. I looked back hoping to see a rescue party from the castle, but none came. It was clear that the Queen's safety was the only thing that mattered. The death of the Earl would be avenged at some other time. The other knights who lay with their throats cut were unimportant and would be replaced by others.

We rode for several hours and stopped again to bind the hands of the recovering Sir William. I listened to several of the men-at-arms discuss the objective of this daring raid, a raid which had failed because of the insane attack of a single man.

"There would have been rich rewards for all had we succeeded. I believe King Louis wanted to see the Baron make Eleanor hostage. It would create resentment in Aquitaine if King Henry refused to ransom his wife. The price our lord would charge was bound to be exorbitant. King Henry could be expected to balk at spending a large sum to save a wife he has little use for. Louis would then encourage the nobility of Aquitaine to rebel and thereby regain what he had lost to an ill-considered divorce. The plan has failed. Louis will deny any knowledge of the plan. We will never see so much as a copper. It is our fate to remain poor," the knight holding me grumbled.

I knew it was a world built on intrigue and treachery designed to enrich some lord so he could enrich a greater lord, but it was ridiculous that someone as insignificant as I was caught up in this madness. The color of the banner that flew over any castle made little difference in my food ration. Clearly God saw some strange plan in placing me in this position.

Now the plot had shrunken to a feeble attempt to rescue some kind of profit from a failed venture. I was sure the great Queen would not waste any of her treasures to save this knight. She would send the Baron my headless body as a defiant gesture of contempt for his actions. Why would she worry about the lives of two unimportant members of her household? Royalty never hesitated to send entire armies to their deaths. Two more deaths would be no more important than the lost birds of the morning hunt. The life of this knight was surely as over as those of his comrades. It was a grim fact he faced every day. He was rewarded to take such risks. He had some kind of code to live up to. I on the other hand was merely a serving boy. He could die heroically if it fit his code. I had a different code to live up to. I reasoned that if he died of his wounds, they would kill me as a useless messenger. Therefore I would have to make sure he lived long enough for me to be sent with the ransom note when I could make good on my escape.

My brilliant assessment of the situation was, as always, wrong. I had little understanding of the female mind. To Queen Eleanor, Sir William Marshal was not just another of her many guards. Fear had caused me to forget the words the Queen had used that morning to describe this particular chevalier. I was only ten at the time and can be forgiven my naive nature. Queen Eleanor was no ordinary woman. Those surrounding Eleanor of Aquitaine found life full of strange twists and turns. My plan to flee would become one of these strange twists and my life would forever be changed. I saw the walls of a town in the distance and wondered how odious our captivity would be in the days ahead. As the walls came closer, my mind continued to envision the moment of my escape. I would show the powerful that the powerless could be just as indifferent to their situations as they were to ours. That which transpired next would change my feelings for the man tied to the horse ahead of me and groaning from his poorly attended wound.

Chapter 2
A Friend for Life

My thoughts filled with fear as we approached the dank and bad-smelling entrance to the dungeon. Though I was used to poor quarters as a serving boy, I was not one who would bear up well under such adversity. My scrawny body was shaking all over as Sir William and I were marched down the stone steps deep into the bowels of the chateau's foundation. The light faded as we descended. Torches were used to light the way even though it was late afternoon and quite bright above this passage. It was as if we were being ushered into Hell itself and it did little to help my already tearful state.

A large wooden door was opened. I glanced around my new home and saw only four damp walls with small bits of black moss clinging to the cracks between the courses of stone. Three guards stood with their pikes menacingly pointed at Sir William still in a half swoon from the blow he received in the fight. In the dim torch light I was certain he was unaware of my presence. One burly guard took a dagger and cut his bonds. Sir William was bending over from the pain I was sure he felt from the injured leg. The wounded knight and I were shoved and we fell to the floor, each landing in different parts of the room. The armed guards and torches withdrew quickly. The solid oak door banged shut. I could hear the iron bar dropping into its slot.

At first it was pitch black. I could not see the walls or even my companion. The floor was a damp, cold uneven surface of hard packed earth. I crawled on my knees with my right hand stretched out. I resembled a blind man seeking the nearest wall. It did not take long to make contact. Standing up, I worked my way around the wall constantly feeling for the next wall. That, too, did not take long. In this manner, I went all the way, around the box-shaped room and soon realized it was not much larger than a stable for three horses. On the floor in one corner was some straw. It had a bad smell. This surely would be used as our area for depositing bodily waste. I felt the tears run down my cheeks. For a moment, I appreciated the darkness because I was too ashamed to let this brave knight see what fate had given him as fellow prisoner.

My eyes got used to the darkness and I could see that it was not totally black. A dim crack of light shone under the large door. Slowly, I could make out a shadowy figure in the middle of the room. He sat in the center of our prison with his legs straight out and holding his injured thigh. I coughed from the dust in the room.

"Who goes?" came a startled voice in the blackness of the dungeon.

"'Tis I, Lewellyn, Sir Knight," I replied meekly.

"By Hell's fire what be the reason for your presence?" he queried, clearly perplexed by the presence of one so lowly as myself.

I explained, stammering out the story, "I failed realize the danger and failed to run away and then the Baron decided to make me the carrier of a ransom note and Earl Patrick and all the others are dead and the Queen has escaped and..."

"Slow your speech, boy," he commanded. "I fear we have time aplenty to discuss all the details. Presently my first concern is one of your help. 'Tis needed to deal with my leg. I cannot stand. Pray help me slide to the wall so I can put my back against it," he said extending an arm somewhat blindly. "Can you see well enough?"

"Yea, Sir Knight." I stumbled over to him and reached under his armpit and pulled with all my strength. He did not move.

"'Tis not possible with the weight of my armor," he said reacting to my failure. There was a pause and then he spoke again. "It must be removed. I will roll to my stomach and you can untie the laces on my hauberk. Once it is removed we will try again. By God's legs this will hurt, but if I swoon you must continue your task. My language may be unseemly, but 'tis not directed at you. It helps with the pain." The evenness in his voice had a calming effect on my trembling hands.

"I understand, Sir Knight," I said trying not to let my voice betray my fear.

He lay on his back and then rolled to his left side. The injured leg came in contact with the floor and he shouted, "Son of a whore!" He groaned and then said, "Continue, boy." I worked at each knot as quickly as my little fingers could respond in the absence of good light. I had to use my teeth occasionally to loosen a recalcitrant lace. Fortunately, Sir William did not swoon, and after another roll and a few more curses, new to my youthful ears, he was stripped of his armor. Once freed from the extra weight, I was able to move him to the desired position against the wall. In the gloom he began to deal with his wound. I was not prepared for the unusual way he repaired his injury.

"Lewellyn, you must do one more task and then you will be done. A small piece of my chain mail has lodged in the wound in my leg. I can feel it. My fingers are too large for such a task. Yours are not. Can you do it?" he asked expecting a positive response. I shuddered at the thought. For one of my low station failure had always brought punishment.

"I know not, Sir Knight," I said meekly.

"Yea, you can lad." There was authority in the statement.

I was afraid to say what I really thought, so I blurted out, "Yea, Sir Knight." He removed the cloth that was covering the hole in his leg and placed it in his lap. In the dim light I could make out the blood-caked hole still oozing the precious life-sustaining liquid. In the dark it appeared black.

I moved closer to begin the task. I was sure I would not succeed in the darkness of our prison, but I had spent my life following the orders of my betters. It was normal for me to do as I was told. My servile nature came to the fore, and I started probing for the missing links of metal while Sir William spread the gash with his hands to make the entry of my small fingers more accessible. I could not make out the expression on his face in the dim light, but I could hear the grunts and grinding of his teeth. The pain must have been excruciating. I could feel the soft flesh getting wetter with blood. If he died from my incompetence I would soon join him in death's embrace. I was beginning to feel the dizziness that precedes a swoon. Cold sweat dripped on the edge of my eyes. Just as my worst fears were about to be realized, my fingertips touched something. I pushed two fingers even deeper into the wound and made contact with the offending metal rings. I pinched my fingers together and pulled out three metal rings linked together and held them like someone who had found a piece of gold in a pot of stew. "Success, my lord!" I shouted with pride. I had done it!

"Aggh, those French bastards shall not bury me this day," he groaned. "Shit." Sir William swore from the pain and a new problem. The blood was beginning to pour profusely from the wound.

"We must stem the blood. Boy, press the cloth against the wound," he ordered. I took the cloth and pressed it gently against the wet leg. "Press harder! Give me the rings!"

Taking the metal rings I had just removed, he used his powerful fingers to pull each ring so that it opened slightly. He placed each one on his lap while I sat dumbstruck. Once again, I saw my life as forfeit. He would bleed to death, and they would kill me as a useless captive. My second headlong rush to oblivion was short lived. Again, I had underestimated the fortitude of my fellow prisoner.

"Remove the cloth quickly, lad," he said in a hoarse whisper. I did as commanded. Taking each ring he proceeded to squeeze the wound with one hand and pinch the rings shut to hold the flesh together like a blacksmith uses tongs to hold hot metal. I was aghast at the willpower this man exhibited.

The flow of blood subsided. He wrapped the wound with a new cloth ripped from his sleeve. "That should suffice. Now I must sleep," he said with calm satisfaction. He acted as though the scene I had just observed was no different from watching a tailor sew a ripped garment. I sat shaking all over and wiped my bloody fingers on my tunic. It would not be the only time I witnessed this man do something extraordinary and behave as if it were something that everyone could do. I trembled thinking about how close I had come to failure.

Whether I fell asleep or fainted, I am still not sure, but the eventful day was over and I was still alive. I also had come to know that I was with a remarkable individual. Perhaps in the morning he would rip the door off the hinges, slay all the inhabitants of the chateau with his bare hands and carry me on his shoulders triumphantly back to the Queen. Such were the dreams of a very frightened ten-year-old boy. I was sure Sir William would find a way in the morning. The small light under the door faded, and the dungeon became totally black as I drifted into a dream.

There was no way to know what hour of day it was when I awoke, but I knew it was day because the slit of light had reappeared under the door. I was now so accustomed to the dark that I could see the entire room in the way one makes out shadows by the light of a waning moon. It was a while before Sir William stirred. I heard him sigh and I asked, "Does your leg give you much discomfort, Sir?"

"It does indeed, lad," he said emphatically.

I was surprised to hear this after witnessing the previous evening's events. I was sure this champion's wounds would heal overnight, more than likely without a scar. My education was about to begin.

"Have I been asleep for long, Lewellyn?" he asked as he adjusted his position against the cobbled wall.

"Nay, Sir Knight. I think it has been but one night; I am not sure."

"Have they brought us any food?"

"Nay."

"No matter. T'would be no more than kitchen waste anyway, but that will be welcomed with time," he grunted as he surveyed our bleak prison in the dim light.

"My lord, can we escape?" I asked hopefully and remembering the miracle escape my youthful imagination had conjured up.

"Nay, Lewellyn, we cannot." He sounded certain.

My fanciful dream was shattered and I began to sob. The knight I thought invincible looked at me and realizing my need for some consoling began to explain. "Lewellyn, all is not lost. I shall stay alive a while longer, and you, my lad, will be sent on your errand. The Queen, of course, will not be willing to pay for one as lowly as I. You will be back where you are no longer under the Baron's control. Fortune has not seen fit to smile on me, but that is the course I chose as a knight errant. If necessary, boy, you must run away at the first opportunity. You should not be penalized for my sake. My fate is sealed, and there is little anyone can do."

Without a warning, the bolt on the door clattered, the door opened briefly but the sudden rush of light left me stunned and blinded. Something was tossed in and landed a few feet away from me. Just as suddenly, the door banged shut and the bolt slammed again. My eyes welcomed the return of darkness. Again I could make out the shadow of a bundle in the middle of the floor.

"Our victuals are served," Sir William announced in a sarcastic tone.

I crawled over and retrieved the bundle. I untied the knot and spread the small cloth and revealed a stale hunk of bread, some foul-smelling cheese and a leather water skin. I briefly recalled my former thoughts of leftover game birds and smiled at the way my hopes for a feast had come down so far. It was not surprising to me. After all, one of my station in life was used to such disappointments. I was sure the disappointment was far greater for the knight. He was used to much finer fare. Appropriately, I gave the bundle to him with a silly bow considering our present condition, but a lifetime of training is not overcome in a single day. He tossed it back.

"Lewellyn, eat your fill. 'Tis probably all we get for a while," he said while I stood holding the bundle with an unseen look of surprise. I continued to misread my companion and I looked at him confused as to what he wanted.

"I am not allowed to eat before my betters, sir," I said humbly. My speech was followed by laughter. What had I said that was taken as a jest? My quandary was soon solved as the knight stopped laughing and explained.

"Boy, look around. We are in a dungeon. Just you and I, fellow prisoners. There are no betters here. A young boy needs food more than a man soon to meet the Maker. So eat! It will not be very good, but it will keep us alive and surely one as small as you cannot eat it all. There will be enough for me." His voice was soft and kind.

Again, I was confused about my companion. It did not make any sense. I was a serving boy. He was a knight. My mind fixed on a solution. It was because he knew he was going to die and a kind deed might help his soul to Heaven. As always, I followed orders and gnawed at the bread and choked down some of the cheese. I did secretly disobey for I did not eat my fill. I was doing it to make sure he stayed alive long enough to have me sent with the ransom note. A coward is not capable of self-sacrifice. I was afraid to trust this chevalier. My life had been one of accepting kicks from his kind when I reacted too slowly to a demand. Yet, he seemed different. A swallow from the leather water skin helped to wash down the bitter aftertaste of the cheese. Again, something in me made me leave more than I might have in other circumstances. Was it fear of punishment or the desire to reward the unusual kindness from an unlikely source?

After finishing what I had left, Sir William said, "Lewellyn, help me to the straw. I need to relieve myself. I do not think I can stand without help." Using me as a crutch he hobbled over to the corner and made water. We hobbled back. He sat with his back against the wall again. He broke wind.

"Bad cheese," he chuckled.

He smiled at me. He was mortal after all. I was beginning to feel like a fellow prisoner and not chattel. Still I resisted the strange offer of friendship from one whom my life's training said was clearly superior. It was all too strange. Had I risen in standing by being a prisoner or had he, by virtue of his capture, gone down in the world?

"Well, boy, shall we amuse ourselves by recounting the story of our lives? I do not expect they will give us musicians to pass the hours. Tell me the story of your life; owing to your tender years 'tis likely a short one. Then I shall tell you mine." He spoke as though we were sitting under a tree in some sunny meadow instead of a foul-smelling dungeon. I was no longer thinking about the dire straits we were in and my thoughts turned to my mother.

"Well, Sir Knight, 'tis little to tell. My mother was a seamstress in the service of the King and Queen. I know not my father, like many of my kind. My mother never spoke of him. It vexes me but 'tis a mystery I likely will never solve. Shortly after I was born we left the King's service. I was told by one of the kitchen maids it was at Queen Eleanor's request. I suspect it was some minor offense such as failing to have a gown ready on time. Such things happen often to people like us. We were sent to Earl Patrick's household where we remained. My mother died of the fever last winter, and I was kept on as a serving boy. When the King sent the Queen and their children to live with the Earl I found life more difficult. A royal court makes hard demands. I try to please, but that is often not enough for a Queen. The Earl is more forgiving. So I remain in the service of the Earl or did until yesterday. I am afraid if I return they will not be so kind without the Earl to take my part. I shall miss him. He was kind." As I stopped I was suddenly taken with a terrible thought. I had said more than was prudent. I had forgotten the knight was one of them. What a fool I had been!

"Lewellyn, it is another reason for you to run when you are released from here." He leaned forward and patted me on the head. "Thou are the same age as Prince Richard?" he inquired.

"Aye, sir. I have locks like his brother Prince Henry, but Prince Henry is better looking by far."

"Do not sell yourself so cheaply. Your mother must have been a fine-looking woman for you are a rather comely lad."

"Oh, she was, my lord. All who knew her said so," I explained with great pride. It caused me to reflect on the face I remembered with a warm glow. It had been three months, but in that darkened place the vision of my mother's face was easy to imagine. For a few moments I was transported out of that dungeon and was back sitting at my mother's feet while she sewed one of the fine ladies' gowns. 'Tis funny when we think upon a simple task that our mothers performed we are somehow comforted by the quiet, calm image it brings to our minds. Mothers have that effect. My momentary escape was ended when my companion began to speak.

"You and I are not so different, Lewellyn. Your father is unknown to you. Mine sent me away because I was not first born." His words came out with a tinge of bitterness. "The rules of our class say the first-born son inherits all titles and lands. Those who come after are largely dependent on the good will of the first born. Good will that is not always in abundant supply. It is a hard system, but it keeps ancestral fiefdoms from confusion and shrinkage as each generation succeeds another." He coughed and then continued to relate his story.

"I was not willing to wait on crumbs that might fall from my brother's table. Our estate in England is but a trifle. Many men in similar circumstance waste their strength bemoaning fate and do nothing. I believe being a victim is a poor profession. It takes little skill, and there are too many practitioners. Worse yet, some plot wicked deeds against their kin. Fortunately I said nay to such evil thoughts. I choose to seek an honorable solution, no matter how limited it might seem. I vowed to make my fortune as knight errant. It is a hard life that leaves little time for self-pity. If you fail the suffering is over quickly. I asked my father to find someone to train me to be a fighting man. I was given over to an uncle in Normandy. I began my knightly training at fifteen. His instruction was true and my ardor for the craft bore fruit. I received my spurs at seventeen to the surprise of many who thought me young for the honor," he said with a discernable degree of pride in his voice.

"I entered the lists. I have labored hard at my trade. I won my first tournament and also the second. After some additional successes I came to the attention of King Henry. At his request I was bound over to the Earl two years ago, to continue my training and to continue to compete in the tournaments. I, too, shall miss the old gentleman. He was a man of great honor." Again he coughed several times and winced from the pain the cough must be causing.

"I felt in time I would earn the favor of the royal family and thus be granted a small estate of my own. The Queen shows a passing interest in my career. She has looked at me and smiles whenever I am in her presence. On several occasions she has even entertained brief conversation with this lowly knight. Now this! Perhaps the crumbs of a brother's table were better fare. No, never that. With all my heart I honor my knightly vows and therefore will not curse my luck. The Lord's will is always done. I cannot change that. I was destined to be in the hunting party," he said with conviction.

"God owes me little. I ask for naught so he is not bothered with me. Now my hour seems at hand and I shall meet the Almighty as I truly am. It matters not what the outcome of such a meeting may bring." I cringed that one should speak so plain about the Father of us all. I looked to the ceiling fully expecting bolts of lightning which would turn us to cinders.

"Are you not fearful of being so plain spoken in your words, Sir Knight?" I asked nervously. The knight's blunt talk could be easily heard by God. Even in this dungeon, we were surely under His watchful eye. The priests had always made that point clear.

"Lewellyn, God knows my heart or He would not be God. Why wouldst I be so foolish as to disguise my meaning with false words? Too many of my colleagues suffer under such a delusion. I do not. Be straightforward with God and men and you will find little need for excuses later when your true meaning is understood." He spoke with sincerity.

Those words would come back to me again and again as our lives unfolded. It was the first rule this man lived by. He was about to explain several others. There was a code that governed his every action. In the darkness there were no distractions so I listened to every word attentively. The world of this paladin was so very different from my own. I was ignorant of the tenets since I had no need to know. After all, the people of my station only needed to know how to serve. There was no more a connection between our lives than the connection between a farmer and his ox. Yet I listened with much wonder.

"Loyalty is the most important thing a man shares with his fellows. Treachery destroys the foundations upon which a successful life sits. Nothing lasting can be accomplished if we trust not each other. From the highest born king to the humblest villeins, we must at some point rely on each other's trust," he said holding up a single finger to show how this rule was of primary importance to him.

"Yesterday a man promised in fealty to Queen Eleanor was ready to commit murder to enhance his purse. It might have worked but for the loyalty of the Earl and my fellows. The Queen escaped, and the Baron Lusignan will never be able to mend the tear. He must now fear her retribution for the rest of his life. His oath to all is now forfeit and blows away as dust before wind. Even the King of France, whom he sought to please with this act, must harbor suspicion he might do the same to him if conditions change. They almost always do," he said nodding in agreement with his own thoughts.

I cringed a little at this rule. I was always ready to save my skin. My first thought upon being captured was to find a way to save myself at the expense of this knight. His first thought was how to save me at the expense of his own life. Embarrassed at these thoughts, I looked for an excuse for my behavior and asked, "My lord, how does one find the courage to do what I saw you do against a force as large as the one you faced?" I was hoping he would understand there were many of us who could not muster the courage it took to live by such a code.

"You do what you know to be right, Lewellyn. One must do it straightaway. Fear is a slow-growing vine. The longer in the deciding the more the tendrils of fear grow round you and grip you until you are unable to move. If you think upon each stroke of your sword, your fight will end badly. One trains to act quicker than your foe. Confidence be on a par with skill. Courage is nothing more than acting before fear has time to bind you. We must accept we all die at the time of God's choosing. When that is, who can know? Waste not time over that which you cannot change! That be one of the hardest rules of life to accept. Those in my calling have come to terms with this rule since we see so much death. Trying to avoid death and one's fate is a foolish wish. We are all mortal. Fear grows best in the fields of doubt. I have faith in my skills. I will continue to do what I must do. When I cannot, it matters not."

"Is it easier when a rich reward can be obtained by brave deeds? Those of us unskilled in the art of fighting have little hope of acquiring the skills which lead to bravery. You have great skill. I beheld that in the fight. Then, the way you repaired your leg, I could never do that." I was most bold in my speech but I felt strongly not everyone could be brave.

He laughed and said, "Oh, you tried to repair yours and failed? How will you know 'til your time to act comes? I am a prisoner; therefore my skills be not as great as you say. You did not swoon when probing my wound and you displayed your own courage. My life was forfeit without that act. There is more in each of us than we know. Your time to hold at bay the tendrils of fear will come again and again. Each time you succeed your confidence and courage will grow."

I had not swooned. I had surprised myself, but I did not believe it was an act of bravery. It was merely an act to provide the chance to escape. There we were—the man destined to become the greatest knight of all time and the greatest coward of all time—together. God must have been amused at the drama he was creating.

"Surely the Queen will know you saved her and will pay the ransom," I said trying to reassure myself and give this knight a reason to remain alive.

"Lewellyn, I serve the Queen like you. My service is of a different kind, but it is service nonetheless. I did no more than the service she was due. Another will take up my duties, and I will be nothing more than a line in a story she tells her ladies-in-waiting on a rainy afternoon when they are bored," he said amused at the thought.

"If the powerful care so little for us, why is honor so important?" I asked trying to understand these lofty ideas.

"Because it is the only thing I control completely. No king can take it or borrow it or destroy it. 'Tis my fiefdom and on its ground I am sovereign. From this comes another truth. If you know me to be honorable, you will trust me. If my honor cannot be compromised then your trust in me will not waver. From that foundation, we can build a relationship that makes both stronger. As you succeed, I also succeed." He spoke these words and I listened unsure of their meaning.

We spoke for several hours telling stories of our lives. We laughed and talked. Occasionally, Sir William would grunt as the pain in his leg manifested itself when he shifted his position. The sliver of light around the door faded again. I was having a more difficult time making out the shape of the large man seated across from me. As it grew darker, we stopped talking. I had not thought about the pitiful condition of our captivity all day. Having someone to talk with had made the captivity more bearable. Solitude is the worst form of torture. It gives fear time to grow. I was beginning to understand. Being able to share even the simplest moments with someone usurps time fear would use to engulf you. I was at peace as the day drew to a close. Much of what had been said was difficult for me to grasp. When and if I returned to my world, our conversations would have little meaning. Codes of conduct, mortality, courage—these were things I knew I could never comprehend, but somehow I felt better about my chances for survival.

I looked one last time at this man in the growing darkness of our prison. I would have the entire night to ponder the ideals he had expressed. I have continued to ponder them to this day. I know not if I understand them even now, but I do know he lived by them for his entire life. A door between our different lives had been briefly opened, servant and master sharing their stories as though both mattered. I knew if I successfully passed through the oak one on our prison the other would be closed again. I would be Lewellyn the serving boy and he would be Sir Knight. I drifted into a satisfying sleep no longer concerned with such foolish thoughts.

I awoke suddenly when the door of the dungeon slammed against the wall. Three men with pikes dashed into the room and immediately positioned the points an inch away from the knight's chest. The flood of torch light again made me squint and cover my eyes for a moment. Sir William did not move. He tilted his head up and looked at men with seeming indifference.

"A rude entrance. I could have been relieving myself," Sir William said in a calm voice.

"You are a feisty bastard," boomed a deep voice from the corridor. Through the doorway came a very large man in fine clothes. It was obvious Geoffrey of Lusignan had decided to pay us a visit. He had black curly hair and mustache. His face was pockmarked and several scars indicated that the man was no stranger to battle. A red tabard covered a barrel chest and a large belly. The black griffin with two small fleur-de-lis embroidered neatly on the tabard demonstrated that our captor was more powerful than I first believed. The heraldic symbols said this man had powerful connections to the King of France. There was arrogance in his manner and no sign of fear like that of his retainers holding their pikes on Sir William.

"We shall soon see if Eleanor is willing to part with some of her gold to get an impertinent varlet like you back. My host tells me that he saw you win the tournament at Eu last year. That should add a few marks to the going price. You are William Marshal?" He spoke the elegant French of the royal court and not the more common variety I was used to hearing.

"I am he, but hold fast your expectations, my lord. I doubt her Majesty will part with as much as a sou," replied Sir William with surprising equally elegant French.

"You had best hope otherwise, my aggressive friend. You cost me far more than the pitiful sum I am asking. Were it not for my need to recoup something from this failure, you and your little friend here would be feed for the crows. Eleanor desires her troubadours to sing of handsome knights saving ladies. Methinks she would fancy the tables turned. She might see your rescue as material for a future ballad with her the hero. How she saved the daring chevalier from the lair of the evil lord. 'Tis enough to move a tear to my eye," Baron Lusignan said mockingly.

"Step closer, bend over and I will see if I can remove it most gently," Sir William said with wicked grin.

"Perhaps I should kill you as my host suggests." The Baron's tone seemed to suggest he was reconsidering his options. "Keeping such a dangerous man alive might have future consequences." Fearing my fellow prisoner was asking for his own death soon to be followed by mine, I interjected myself into the conversation with careless regard for my lowly status.

"My lord, the Queen is quite taken with the career of this knight. I heard her say so to the Earl." It was true. The boldness of the remark from one so young caused a sudden silence. Sir William was stunned by my remark, but he quickly recovered himself and perhaps realized my life was also in the balance. If he were dispatched I would quickly follow. He curbed his anger and sat silently.

"The urchin has just upped the value of your skin, churl. I am in no position to throw away a financial opportunity, even a small one. That bastard Henry has left me sorely charged. I think a hundred marks will be the price. Boy, come with me," he ordered as he turned to the doorway.

"Lewellyn, I trust you will take the opportunity." The knight was reminding me to run at my first chance. He smiled knowing full well he was assuring his own death. I stumbled up the stairs in front of the Baron. I saw the three spear men retreat from the room, quickly slamming the door and bolting it in great haste. They acted as if they were retreating from a dragon's lair and were relieved they had escaped with their lives. I surmised the story of Sir William's fight against the Baron's men had been shared over brew. As I mounted the stairs, many emotions surged through my body. On one hand, I was elated my captivity was at an end. On the other hand, in that short stay, I had grown fond of the handsome knight. I would probably never see kindness from his type again. His end would be brutal and without honor, much in the way the Earl had perished. I wondered why God would spare so miserable a creature as myself and destroy such an honorable man. When we reached the top of the stairs my arm was grabbed by one of the three men who had accompanied the Baron. We followed him into the great hall. He sat on a large chair at the end of the wide planked table, stabbed an apple with his dagger. Removing the apple from the blade he jabbed the knife into the table. He proceeded to talk to me while chewing the fruit.

"Well, boy, you will deliver the letter I am about to prepare to the drab you know as Queen Eleanor." He replaced the apple with a quill and began to write as he spoke. "My man Philip will accompany you until you are in sight of the castle. There you will make your way to the castle on your own. He has no desire to be captured by the Aquitaine bitch and her men. If you flee, your kind always does, I shall have to kill that insolent knight as my friends have suggested and Philip will then more likely kill you too. Either way, I will be no worse off than I am now. If by some miracle the Queen receives the note and is interested in buying back this knight, you claim she is fond of, she can send the money with a priest. Once the money is exchanged, I will allow the priest to return with the prisoner," he said condescendingly. It was irritating him to entrust his words to a lowly sirrah.

I took umbrage that he thought me incapable of honor, even though this had been my plan from the beginning. Somehow, things were different now. What had William Marshal said? Honor was mine alone to possess or squander. Did I foolishly believe my position in the scheme of things had changed because I had been a prisoner with a knight? Insults by my betters were common fare for me. Why did this one burn so deeply? For a fleeting moment, I considered grabbing the dagger and killing him in the same type of unexpected attack as I had witnessed several days ago, but the more I thought the less I felt like acting on the impulse.

He finished the note and folded it twice. He handed the letter to Philip, a thin and sinister-looking yeoman. A jerk on my arm and I was removed from his unpleasant presence. As Philip and I walked across the yard, I took a last glance at the staircase that disappeared below the ground and led to the man who had said so much about trust. Was he right: honor leads to trust? The words repeated themselves over and over in my mind. Was it possible for me to have honor or was such a thing above a boy from the serving class with so little hope of rising in life? Knights could have expectations. I could not.

The soldier who was my keeper for the journey back to Queen Eleanor mounted his horse and pulled me up behind him. We rode out of the town and traveled for several hours without a word being spoken. The fields occasionally became brief patches of woodland. We passed no travelers on our way. At noon, guessing by the sun, we crossed the stream where the Marshal had regained his senses and had to be bound by his captors. I knew we did not have much farther to go. We reached the crest of the hill where I first saw the man watching the hunting party. I surveyed the field where the fighting had occurred two days ago. As the horse trotted by the scene of the attack, I could see the dark stains on the trampled grass. The bodies were gone, but the evidence of a brutal encounter was still very clear. Chunks of earth and sod were scattered on the ground indicating the sudden and violent movements of the horses. The patches of blood were now dried and rust color with the passing of time. It marked where each blow had struck with the expected result. Darker spots bore witness to the places where the kindly Earl and each of his men had met their end. Philip stopped his horse and surveyed the field briefly. He coughed and then urged the steed to go on. We left this place of death and villainy at a slow trot.

My keeper turned and spoke slowly to be sure I did not misinterpret his speech, "We will reach the castle of Lusignan soon, serving boy. If you value your throat you will give no alarm when I drop you. Once you dismount, begin walking slowly in the direction of the castle. Do not turn around. Where you go after I leave, I care not. As the Baron said, you will probably run away. That would be a wise move on your part. Queens do not take kindly to messengers with ransom notes." Philip had made it clear my best choice was to flee. He would not stop such an act. There was no knightly code for this one. He was more concerned with his own skin than the Baron's ransom note. I knew my freedom was at hand.

In the next few minutes, I could see the towers of the castle in the distance. When we reached the point where we could see the walls, my captor turned to me and growled, "Here is the letter, urchin. Get off and do as I instructed." He thrust the parchment into my hand, grabbed my arm and swung me off his steed. I walked slowly toward the castle. I could hear the hoof beats as he galloped in the opposite direction. The sounds quickly became faint and then could be heard no more. I was still too afraid to turn around to see if he had really gone.

My moment had come. I was free. Since my masters in the castle believed me dead, I was, for the first time in my life, truly free. I could run cross the field and off to anywhere I wanted to go. I began to run. Then, the most curious thing happened, a moment that put my feet on a longer path than the one to Castle Lusignan and one from which there would be no turning back. I looked at the note still in my hand. Without another thought, my feet accelerated their pace straight for the castle gate. I was not running across the field but up the road, right where I had convinced myself for the last two days was the one place I would not go. Was it because I feared life on my own and sought the certainty of the life I knew, no matter how odious? Was it anger at the arrogant Baron Luisgnan and a silly chance to prove him wrong? Was it the foolish dream planted by a knight in a young boy's brain? I did not know. The Baron was wrong. I was running but not in the way he predicted. In the moment when I was free to choose, I chose the honorable path. I could be trusted, and I was proud. It did not matter what happened to me because I was, at that moment, the freest anyone could ever be, and it was exhilarating.

I raced through the gate and straight for the great hall. As I crossed the compound, I heard one of the guards exclaim, "By God's legs, Lewellyn! We thought you dead."

"Get the Queen." I shouted waving my message. "I bear important news."

I was escorted into the great room and told to stand and wait. I remained motionless with the important paper grasped tightly in my hand. I heard a commotion as Queen Eleanor came down the hallway and into the room. I bowed instinctively and held the precious letter out in front of me. It was then that all the terrible thoughts of the previous days flooded my brain. What had I done? I was surely going to die. The tendrils of fear were growing very quickly, and I was beginning to shake.

"Give me the note, boy," the Queen commanded. I did as ordered and looked up at the great lady. When she saw my face her hand froze on the parchment. For a moment we both stood motionless. She recovered herself and looked at the note. She turned to one of her handmaidens and shouted. "He's alive! They seek one hundred silver marks. A thousand would not have been too many." Her face was flushed with excitement. She turned to one of the nobles and said, "See to the payment." Then she returned to looking at me and laughed a wry sort of way. She said, "'Tis strangely grateful I am that I did not get my way." She shook her head and a smile came across her beautiful face. The green of her eyes flashed and I knew I had done right. My entire body relaxed. The Queen addressed me again, "Tell me, Lewellyn, and how is the knight? Have you seen him?"

"Sir William is injured, Majesty. I have assisted him for the last two days. He is the bravest man in the world. We have been in a dungeon under the control of the Baron Lusignan. He is lucky to be alive because of a severe wound to his leg. Majesty, he repaired it with the rings of his chain mail! I was able to be of some assistance in the task," I said with pride. I wanted to be sure she knew of my action and proceeded to explain the operation. I spoke of his bravery and the events with the Baron. I left out the personal conversations I had enjoyed so much. They were mine and not to be shared. I feared she might lose respect for the knight who had shown friendship to someone so far below his station.

"The rest of the company was foully murdered," I continued. I wanted to continue my brief run of importance I was so caught up in the excitement of this moment.

"Sadly we know. The Earl is dead also," she added with a wince.

"Majesty, the Baron said I would run away, but I have not. I promised Sir William I would faithfully deliver the note." It was a lie. It was time to gain some benefit from a Queen that was obviously delighted. I then added something that brought a surprised look from the Queen. "If it please your Majesty, I would return with the priest and help bring him back."

"Well, it seems Sir William inspires the best in each of us, even you, sirrah. When all is ready you shall return with the priest. Bring him back to us with haste. We will treat his wounds properly, and I assure you he will want for nothing. You have our thanks. You depart at first light." She turned and walked away. Laughing and hugging her attendants, she vanished down the hallway into her private chambers.

I was brought to the kitchen. It was a place I knew well. This time the experience was very different. Instead of being asked to take the tray of food to the banquet hall as I had done a hundred times before, I was seated and told to eat. I did not have to be coaxed. I attacked the meal like a starving wolf. The cook laughed instead of hitting me and told me to slow down or I would choke. Perhaps honor was rewarded. I thought about my captive friend and hoped tonight's meal of stale bread and bad cheese would soon be replaced with a repast even finer than the one in front of me.

I went to my usual place above the stable to spend the night, but I found it difficult to sleep. I kept thinking about what I had done and how it all turned out so well. I was so pleased with myself that I smiled from time to time as I recalled the events of the day. I would be going back to the dungeon, and this time I would be the rescuer. Lewellyn the hero! How fine it sounded. I conveniently forgot it was not I who paid the ransom that would free Sir William. A ten-year-old boy is allowed to conjure up his own victories, even if he has to ignore a few details. I wondered. Will they write a song about me? That night, my dreams were about heroic deeds that only I could do: jumping a hundred feet into the air to slay a dragon and leaping over a dozen horsemen trying to catch me. Were dreams like these God's reward for a good deed? Again I forgave myself the small lie I had told the Queen. After all it was the result that mattered. I did deliver the message.

I rose early and joined Father Renee in the courtyard. He was watching the grooms prepare the horse and cart for the journey. The sun was just coming over the horizon casting an orange glow which seemed to match my feelings. I sat next to the old priest grinning at my own thoughts as we passed out of the gate. Most of the residents of the castle were still in slumber. A few of the grooms who had readied the cart called out to us as we left. They wished us speedy return. We headed down the road and by the field I remembered all too clearly. The priest shook his head as he gazed at the bloodstains on the grass. He crossed himself and muttered a few words in the language of the Church. It was another pleasant spring day and we made good time for a horse and cart.

As we entered the town, two men stepped in front of the cart and stopped our progress. I could see the chateau clearly. It rose above the walls of the town. It was of the standard French design. Multiple layers of defense made attacking such a fortress a major undertaking. It explained why there was no attempt to attack the Baron in retribution for his brazen plot. It was far better to ignore such an insult and save the cost of a major campaign. The Queen saw the trivial sum of one hundred marks as a minor annoyance to achieve her goal. The Baron had lost far more when King Henry had dispossessed him.

The larger of the two men asked, "Where are you bound for, Father?"

"Take us to Baron Lusignan. I have important business with him, my son," Father replied in the dialect of the common men in this region.

"You come to ransom the knight in the Baron's keeping. We heard the Queen was willing to pay," the shorter man said smiling and displaying a mouth of jagged and rotten teeth. It was surely the same man I saw on the hill several days ago. His doublet was the same color. I knew why the Baron and his men appeared so well prepared to take the Queen hostage the day of the hunt. It was not a chance meeting. He probably watched every day for just such an opportunity. I suspected his teeth were rotted by a long history of sweet wine rewards for his spying and other nefarious activities. After this short exchange, the large man ran ahead to the chateau to announce our arrival.

"Your escort seems a little young for a knight. Is he armed?" The short man laughed. I returned his comment with my best sneer. It had no effect.

"God is my escort," the priest said calmly.

We continued on, gathering a small crowd of townspeople as we reached the outer gates of the chateau. Two men stood in the yard with a large number of knights. It was a show of strength for the priest to carry back to the Queen in case she had thoughts of revenge after the return of her knight. It was a needless worry. She would not be able to convince her husband that such an effort was worth the time or money. I recognized the Baron as one, and I guessed the other was his host and owner of the chateau. We stopped the cart, and the good father stepped down and approached the Baron. He reached inside his cloak and retrieved a leather pouch. Holding it by the strings, he held it out to the approaching noble.

"Here is the agreed to sum," he said in the same calm tone he had used with the two men who met us earlier, but this time using formal French. The Baron glanced over to the cart where I sat silently.

"Well, boy, you surprised me. Perhaps, you are his bastard. Why else would you return?" he said demeaning my efforts.

"Nay, my lord." I tried to be as calm as Father Renee, but I know my voice quivered slightly.

"I should keep the money and send you both on your way," the Baron conjectured. Father Renee spoke in soft tones, "God expects you to be a man of honor, my lord."

"I shall honor my word, although something tells me this knight is dangerous. He has already beguiled some of my guards. You will find him over there." He pointed to the steps that led underneath the chateau.

As we approached the steps, we heard a roar of laughter. When we reached the bottom of the steps, to my surprise, the large door was open. On the floor seated in the same position as when I left the day before was Sir

William. Four guards were squatting in a circle around him. One was picking up a set of dice. He looked at Sir William and spoke. "'Tis well they have arrived. If you had more time you could have paid your own ransom, Sir William. You are the luckiest man I have ever met. Take him, father, before we are all paupers." I was perplexed at how Sir William could gamble when he possessed no coin when we were captured. It involved honor in some manner. I would learn later this was not uncommon in the knightly class. Stories of chevaliers going to extreme lengths to repay debts were quite true.

"Lewellyn, you did not take my advice. I am in your debt as well as the Queen. I shall not forget. We knew you were coming, so we decided to pass the time with a game of chance." He laughed and reached out for me to give him a hand up. His leg was still bandaged with the same piece of cloth. It was more stained than it was when I left. He groaned a little as we helped him to his feet, but he did not swear in the presence of the priest. "Well, my friends, I take my leave and hope that we shall never meet again except in the lists of a friendly tournament," he said gesturing grandly with his free arm.

"I have seen your skill and would prefer to meet only for a drink and a game of chance," one of the four said in a very serious but friendly way.

Father Renee helped me assist the wounded knight up the steps. Sir William blinked several times as his eyes adjusted to the daylight again. As we crossed the yard there was a far larger crowd gathered, but the two nobles had already left. We helped our companion into the cart. He assumed the same seated posture with both legs stretched out straight. He draped one arm over the side of the cart, and with the other, he waved at the crowd. Father Renee climbed up and took the reins. I scrambled up beside him and turned back to look at our passenger.

"Give us a good Welsh song, Lewellyn. We shall sing our way out of this town."

I suggested a tune. "Do you know it, my lord?" Sir William smiled.

"Perfect." We began to sing. We sang at the top of our lungs all the way out of the village. We would sing together many more times. William Marshal loved music. Once we were on the road and no longer in sight of the town, he stopped singing. He groaned, slumped down in the cart and appeared to fall asleep. The singing was only a ruse to hide his true condition. I too had been fooled. Again I was puzzled by his behavior. It would be evening before we reached Lusignan castle. I was happy everything had gone so well. I was too excited to think about what lay ahead for me. I had rescued a knight! My mind continued to build elaborate fantasies about my role in the affair.

We arrived at Castle Lusignan as a reddish twilight settled on the land. We were met in the courtyard by the Queen and most of her court. Queen Eleanor's ladies rushed forward and immediately looked after our reclining passenger. He momentarily disappeared in a mass of colored gowns. Sir William attempted to rise for the Queen and in a very weak voice said, "Majesty, I am in your debt for my release. I can never thank…." With that he swooned.

"Do not speak of debts. Mine is the greater debt," she said softly to the unconscious man and turned to her retinue. "Take this knight to my chambers where we will see to his wounds. Take care in placing him on the litter. Send for my physician. Have my seamstress prepare new clothes for him when he is well enough to be fitted. Tell the master at arms to see to it that all of his armor is replaced with the best available." She gave orders, and each of the appropriate people rushed off to execute them with all possible speed. She accompanied the litter bearers down the hall and disappeared into her private chambers.

Father Renee and I remained for a few moments in the now empty hall looking at each other. We had been overlooked in the excitement. The good priest turned to me and smilingly said, "We are no longer needed." It ended my fantasy as the brave rescuer. Crestfallen, I went to my quarters above the stable. I stared at the oak beams trying to assess what had happened.

"Well, Lewellyn, you are nothing but a serving boy again. Maybe you should have run away," I said out loud to myself. Things had not turned out as wonderfully as I thought they would. "What did you expect, the Queen to thank you and reward your good deed with a knighthood?" I had been shocked back to reality. There were the privileged few and those who were expected to serve them. It was not going to change. I would soon be forgotten by all including the knight I thought was so special. "Honor, ha!" The stable smells which had been mysteriously absent the previous night assaulted my nostrils. My thoughts bitterly turned to the moment when I had forsaken my chance for a different life.

My life returned to its tedious and insignificant chores. I did receive a new jacket from the Queen, but rather than be grateful for the gift I was angry that I had been bought so cheaply. I was doomed to be a fool easily seduced by fine words.

It was three days before I was summoned to the great hall. I put on the new green jacket with yellow sleeves. To appear to be ungrateful before the Queen would surely bring a severe beating at the least. Upon entering, I saw it was a formal occasion because all the ladies and gentlemen were dressed in their finest clothes and the room blazed with bright colors. I stood meekly in the back beside the man who brought me to the assembly. I did not know him, but I was sure he was part of the court. Prince Henry and Prince Richard were present seated on the right with their hands folded and looking very bored. I rarely saw them, so this had to be a special event. The Queen sat in the ceremonial chair. It was on occasions like this you could see what a beautiful woman she was. Seated to her left, attired in a fine dressing gown, was Sir William. He looked better. Color had returned to his cheeks and his good looks were again evident. The hall buzzed with soft voices of the many courtiers assembled.

The Queen rose and a hush grew over the assemblage. She spoke in a clear and commanding voice. "We owe much to this knight. But for his bravery, I would be a hostage. Our thanks cannot be measured in gifts alone, but we shall try. To William Marshal, we give five of our finest horses, two new hauberks, one hundred silver marks and the responsibility for the training of Princes Henry and Richard. May they learn to be as skillful and brave as their mentor. We shall keep Sir William close to our person, as none is more loyal or steadfast to the crown." She paused and looked at the knight being honored with eyes that expressed more than gratitude for service. I had heard the troubadours singing songs of courtly love and suspected that such was the present situation. She turned to the gathering again and her tone changed to a more formal one. "Lewellyn, the serving boy, step forward."

The words struck me like a thunderbolt. I was pushed forward by my companion. As I approached the great lady, I automatically began bowing as I had been trained. What was this all about? Had I not been forgotten? The Queen spoke slowly. Her eyes seemed to look right through me, and I was not sure I was going to survive the moment.

"Lewellyn, at the request of this knight you are no longer in service to our household, but are henceforth personal body servant to him. Serve him loyally."

I glanced over at Sir William and saw him grinning broadly. We now began a long journey together. He was the driver of the cart of fate that would carry me to many new places—some wonderful and some that I would have gladly missed. I would learn that like a cart on a bumpy road bounces up and down, so too life seems to rise and fall. My life and Sir William's would be no exception to this rule.

Chapter 3
A Teacher of Kings

Two years had passed since the day Queen Eleanor transferred my service to the man the world would soon call "the Marshal." He was now mentor to the two sons of King Henry II and Queen Eleanor. Knightly training was the most important thing in his life and he was obligated to pass on those lessons to the two princes. Henry was fifteen and Richard had just turned thirteen. Geoffrey, the third son, was twelve and considered too young to actively train with the heavy weapons. He would begin his training next year or the year after that. Richard was also considered young, but his size gave him an early start.

Young Henry was of a stocky build, reasonably good looking and had the Plantagenet temper. He had his father's dark blue eyes and reddish curly hair. His brain was not as nimble as his illustrious sire. He was clearly his father's favorite. Favoring the eldest son was common among the nobility. As I had already learned from Sir William the eldest son would eventually inherit all. I did learn that with kings it was slightly different. With so many holdings a king could, and usually did, give lesser titles and land to their younger offspring in the hope of preventing family squabbles. This often failed since sibling rivalry and greed were also common among the royalty.

Prince Richard, the Queen's favorite, was tall and very good looking. His eyes were the same blue, but the hair was long, wavy and auburn color like his mother. His arms and legs already showed promise of great strength. Even at this early age the ladies of the court would stop and cast admiring glances whenever the young prince passed by. He did not seem to have inherited the temper, but he too could not match the King's wit.

The Queen had specifically stated that I was to keep my distance during their training. I was relegated to watching from the window of the Marshal's quarters when not engaged in my personal chores. I did have a clear view of the practice grounds, and I could hear the Marshal bark out his instructions. He always demonstrated the proper technique first and then told the boys to try it. He observed their actions and corrected mistakes. After he was satisfied they were executing the movements correctly, he ordered them to practice the new technique over and over. While they practiced he practiced alongside of them. The boys rested more than the Marshal, but he did not allow them to rest for long. They marveled that their teacher did not appear to need any rest.

Henry seemed to enjoy the sessions. He joked about his growing prowess with the sword as he laid on each stroke. The dull thud of the blade against the practice post was interspersed with his comments to an imaginary opponent.

"Take that, churl! You dreamed you could challenge your King!" Henry snarled at the post. When he tired, he concluded with, "We spare you this time, but by God's eyes thou shan't be forgiven twice." The Marshal smiled and urged the young Prince to try and push himself with a few more strokes by saying, "Sire, a knight who tires too quickly will soon to have a permanent rest." Henry responded with a few more feeble swings and then dropped to his knees exhausted.

Richard was different. He was taller than his brother, even though he was two years younger. He never uttered a word. He listened intently to every word his tutor said. He attacked the post with a commitment that bordered on vengeance. It was as if the post had done him personal injury and he needed to inflict pain on it. After several minutes, the sweat would bead up on his forehead, but the attack continued as forcefully as it had in the beginning. There was no need to encourage a few more blows. When Richard stopped, it was because he was no longer able to deliver another stroke. He was totally spent. His favorite weapon was the ax. The day would come when all would fear facing Richard. All save one man. Ironically, that one man stood a few feet away and gave approving smiles to his young charge. As they practiced I heard voices. I leaned back concealing myself better while I could still observe the action below. It was the Queen and a few ladies of the court come to see the young princes.

"Sir William, a demonstration if you please," the Queen commanded.

"Majesty, the lads are weary. We have reached the end of today's session."

"Henry, a small token for your mother," the Queen cajoled.

The lad smiled and raised the sword with tired arms and weakly struck the post. The blade barely creased the target. "As Sir William said I am tired. Had you arrived sooner you would have seen much more." The excuse was followed by polite clapping from the ladies.

"Richard, are you also tired?" the Queen asked knowing full well the response she expected.

"Nay!" snapped the irritated prince, annoyed that his session had been disturbed. He seized the handle of his weapon and launched a mighty swing. It bit deeply into the post with a loud thud. He sneered at the gathering.

"Bravo, my son," responded the Queen as her ladies applauded enthusiastically, while discussing the skill and good looks of young Richard. Richard's arm was beginning to show the muscular features that would give his ax its lethal reputation.

"The ax has less heft than the sword. His arms are still too weak to handle a man's weapon," Henry said mockingly. He tried to make light of Richard's growing skill, but the jibes were merely a poor cover for the jealousy he felt. Henry did not like to be bested in anything especially by his younger brother. The Marshal was keenly aware of this and made sure not to be too rich with his praise with either boy.

"The sword is heavier, Majesty. Both are progressing nicely," he said with a kind smile to Henry and a "well done" pat on the shoulder of Richard.

Nevertheless, it was clear from the beginning who would be the better fighter. Even the Queen did a poor job of concealing her preference for Richard's accomplishments on the practice grounds when she visited their sessions, something she did often.

The morning sessions were always followed by discussion of defense and attack strategies. The Marshal explained the ways to defend certain types of attack and how one should counterattack. He included the rules a chivalrous knight should live up to at all times. The two boys asked questions about his experiences in the tournaments and in battle. He responded with accounts of some of his experiences, but always underplayed his accomplishments. It was a change from the brash young knight I had first met in the castle yard two years earlier. He smiled whenever Henry pretended to be him during one of his imaginary adventures at the post. Richard was always Richard.

The afternoon session of horsemanship was preceded by several hours of formal lessons by scholarly tutors. The Queen would not have sons who were unschooled in the classics. Music was included with language and philosophy. On Saturday, the priests would instruct the two Princes in religion and the catechism.

The Marshal made arrangements with one of the court musicians to give me an old lute and a few lessons. I learned to feebly play the lute with some effort and even tried to compose a ballad. This pleased my master since he loved music. I was on my way in developing the skills that would be my life's work. One day, I was just finished with my music tutor when I heard a familiar voice call, "Henry, hold!" I continued down the hall when again the cry of, "Henry, I said hold fast for me!" I turned and saw Prince Richard running after me. Realizing that he had mistaken me for his brother, I stopped.

As he approached, he realized he had made a mistake. I bowed respectfully and said, "Your pardon, Sire, I fear I made you mistake me for the Prince. We have the same hair and a similar build." It was always wise to blame yourself whenever royalty made errors. They were not to be corrected by the serving class. I kept looking at the floor, not wanting to make eye contact.

"You are the servant of Master William, my weapons instructor, are you not?" He spoke with a commanding tone, as one accustomed to giving orders. He had a regal air even at this young age. "There is a fair match to my brother. Your features are pleasing, sirrah. We have seen little of you at court. Does Sir William keep you secret?" he asked as he lifted my chin to stare at my face. He paused, waiting for my reply.

"I do serve Sir William, Sire. My duties are most pressing leaving little time anything else, but I have occasionally had a chance to see you on the practice ground and the skill you have shown eclipses any I have seen from those of a similar age." Flattery is also a good choice when conversing with one's betters.

"I intend to become without peer! What be your name?" he demanded.

"Lewellyn, Sire," I said keeping my gaze on the floor.

"Lewellyn, perhaps we meet again." He turned and went down the hallway.

I was troubled by his last comment. I did not tell him that I was not to be around the royal family by order of Queen Eleanor. I returned to the Marshal's quarters and put the lute away. I began straightening up the rooms. I was still engaged in this chore when the Marshal entered. He removed his tunic and slumped down in his chair. He was returning from his own practice sessions. He would use the time when the Princes were being tutored to keep himself in top condition. The muscles bulged as he breathed heavily. His arms and shoulders were covered with sweat. It accentuated the development they had achieved from hours and hours of swinging the heavy weapons of his trade.

"You require something, my lord?" I asked respectfully.

"Some drink and a moist cloth." He closed his eyes as he spoke.

I went to the nearby table and brought back a pitcher of beer and a goblet. From the next room, I fetched a cloth and a basin that already contained some water. I dipped the cloth into the basin and handed it to the Marshall. He began wiping off the sweat and then leaned back. He opened his eyes, looked at me, and said, "There is a release of the soul born from exhaustion."

"Pray something to eat, master?" I asked seeking to serve.

"Nay, lad. How go your lessons?"

"I am improving. I composed my first song." I smiled with pride because the ballad was about the Marshal and the day we met.

"Wonderful. Fetch the lute and play for me. I shall give you fair appraisal of your progress. I need a soft moment." He sat up straight and took a deep breath.

I dashed into the other room and returned with the instrument. I was excited, but also nervous, to see his reaction to my song. I began. The words and the music came out of me with a mixture of nervousness and pride. He smiled and chuckled as I sang of the fight and the bravery he had shown the day we met. I even included myself and the experience with the Queen the day I returned with the ransom note. His brow furrowed and a distant look came over his face. I ended with the audience before the Queen and a rousing shout of praise. There was a brief pause before he spoke.

"That time changed both our lives, Lewellyn. I was an ambitious young knight looking for some recognition, and you were a serving boy. Now things are very different." He spoke seriously and slowly.

"The Queen shows you much favor and admires your tutelage of the young Princes," I said feeling great pride in our rising fortunes. I knew she called him frequently to come to her chambers. I assumed to discuss the progress of Henry and Richard.

"I have tried to be deserving of the trust she has in me." His words had the sound of melancholy in them. "The King comes for the Easter celebrations. He desires to see how his sons have progressed in their training. We shall have to prepare them for the river jousts."

He was referring to the games that involved a young man standing on the bow of a rowed boat while another came at him in the opposite direction. Each had a shield and a lance with a leather bag on the tip. The object was to take the other's blow without losing one's perch. Many of the townsfolk watched from the bank, cheering them on and laughing when one or both received an early spring bath. It was great sport. I knew opponents of the Princes would be selected carefully to be sure they were the wet ones after the joust.

"The Queen appears to favor Prince Richard when she visits the practice yard. Does she not, my lord?" I was curious to see if I alone imagined this fondness for a second son.

"You see that too. Yea. I fear jealousy develops between Henry and his younger brother. Henry will be King, but Richard oft outshines him and that is a dangerous thing. Kings do not tolerate rivals. I have warned her Majesty and she seeks a plan to calm the waters. Prince Henry has been married since he was eight. Princess Marguerite, his wife, will soon be ready to assume her duties in that regard. Richard is to marry King Louis' other daughter Alais, but the negotiations are not yet concluded. Although the Queen rejoices at his lack of response to the offerings of the ladies at court she chides me for filling his head with thoughts of knightly combat to the exclusion of other things." He grinned as he finished my lesson in royal politics. I would soon learn why he did so because I had little need of knowing such.

I then related the chance meeting Prince Richard and I had earlier. I expressed my pleasure of his friendly manner. With that, the Marshal frowned and said, "Lewellyn, take care to avoid the Princes. The Queen will not take kindly if you get too close." The warning was said with conviction.

"My lord, why is the Queen so protective of the Princes? She must know I would do them no harm. I could not. They would each make short work of someone like me. You have trained them well, and they show it," I said with a degree of frustration.

"Someday I will explain, but now is not the time. Now is the time for my thoughts on your ballad. You sing wonderfully. Your lute playing shows promise. The words are well crafted even if somewhat exaggerated, but such is the tendency of the troubadour. I do thank you for the tune. I once joked you would be a troubadour. Now it takes the shape of a prophecy. You have also fulfilled my need for trust. You have become more than my manservant. You share not the thoughts I express in private. You provide me a chance to think aloud and I have no fear that my words will be whispered at court. 'Tis something I need and truly appreciate," he said placing both of his strong hands on my shoulders and staring straight into my eyes.

"I would give my life for you, my lord," I said with all the conviction a twelve-year-old boy could summon.

"As would I for you. Pray that it not be necessary for us to test that level of trust," he said with a smile and a laugh. He patted my head and tousled my hair. We both laughed, and I returned to my chores while he rested.

Later, as evening approached, I brought a fresh tunic for the Marshal. I placed it carefully on the oak bench. He dressed himself and splashed some water on his face from the basin still on the table. He took a razor and trimmed a small part of his short beard. When dressed for supper, he cut a dashing figure. Many of the ladies of the court whispered in secret of his good looks, but none seemed to catch his eye. They were careful not to let Queen Eleanor observe their longing stares. I was beginning to hear that the Marshal was more to the Queen than just a tutor of her beloved sons. His actions were always proper so I chose to ignore such slanders. One thing was certain—King Henry was no longer interested in Queen Eleanor. In truth, I had heard them in a bitter quarrel Christmas season past. The entire castle heard them! They had fiery tempers when aroused, and that seemed to happen often when King Henry was in residence. It was doubtful they had any romantic inclinations toward each other after the birth of John three years ago. Even then, the marriage had evolved into one for political reasons rather than the passion that first brought them together. I was surer of the Queen's feelings for my master than I was about his feelings for her. He rarely showed much emotion. I never shared my thoughts with any of the court because loyalty to the Marshal was the one virtue I considered sacred. His statement about our private conversations showed I was not wrong in my actions. I was trusted.

We proceeded down to the dining hall. As we entered, I quickly took an inconspicuous place against the wall near the kitchen door. The table was set with several platters of fish, boiled meats seasoned with potherbs, and several types of bread. Next to each plate was a goblet that would be filled with wine or beer by a gesture to one of the serving people stationed around the room. No words were necessary since the preference of each of the diners was well known to the servers. Several musicians played constantly during the meal. Eleanor's court was famous for its entertainment and lavish dishes. It was something her husband Henry bemoaned for its extravagance and high cost. Henry cared little for music and food. He cared mightily about the accounts. It was another source of conflict with his Queen. When they discussed the cost, she would quickly remind him Aquitaine provided him with much of his revenue, and the subject was dropped.

The Queen saw the Marshal enter and called to him, "Sir William, come sit beside me and speak of my sons and their progress. Celine, fill his cup with the fine claret we received today."

A dark-haired serving girl with ivory skin brought a silver ewer and filled the Marshal's goblet as he seated himself next to the Queen. As Celine returned across the room in my direction I could see she was very attractive. Her eyes met mine and she flashed a faint smile. Our arms brushed as she proceeded back to her station. I felt blood rush to my face. I saw one of the ladies-in-waiting wave her hand and Celine rushed forward again with the pitcher to fill her cup. On the return trip she brushed against me a second time. This time, the contact seemed to linger a split second longer. It was no accident. Now, the entire hall evaporated from my consciousness. My eyes were on her exclusively. I looked quickly at the hearth, but to my surprise there was no raging fire, only two half-burnt logs that had not seen a flame for days. Each time wine was requested the contact was repeated. I was in a daze. It was not a good state for one who should be watching his master for a request.

My dream state was broken by the Marshal's cough. I looked at him. He was smiling, and he was shaking his head. He motioned to me. Embarrassed by my failure, I stumbled in my haste to reach him. The Queen was talking to one of the other nobles seated on the other side of her and was ignorant of my presence.

He whispered and chuckled, "Lewellyn, a pretty face has caused you to neglect your duties. Fetch my cloak." My face flushed, and I raced out of the banquet hall and up to our quarters. In times past with other masters, that mistake would have meant a beating for my failure, but I knew from his tone he was amused at my foolishness. Still, the feeling of making physical contact with the beautiful serving girl would have been worth several beatings. She was small of stature with eyes that sparkled. My mind was so taken with the vision I almost forgot what I came to retrieve. I grabbed the cloak and rushed back to the dining hall. This time, as I approached the head table, the Queen looked right at me. A cold stare came over her attractive features. I bowed as I approached, holding the garment in front of me. The Marshal reached across the table and pulled it from my outstretched arm. I bowed and began backing away. The Queen continued her thought to my master.

"The King must be pressed on the future of young Henry. What think you?"

The Marshal replied diplomatically, "As your majesty deems necessary. I do not occupy a position to proffer such lofty advice."

"As I suggested earlier let us entertain a quiet walk, William. There are too many ears at court. Perhaps the stars will stir your thoughts. I need your advice. These are important days to come. All must play their part. Much needs changing. Some not of my liking, but I too must play my part." Her voice carried great conviction. They rose and left the hall.

The entertainment continued, and those in the hall continued to eat and drink. I decided to seek a quiet place where I could reflect on the actions of the serving girl. I would go to my old place in the barn loft which was sure to be deserted at this time of night. I took one last glance at the pretty serving girl. I smiled broadly, and she returned the same. I knew we would meet again. I was going to make sure the lovely Celine would see me again. My brain was flooded with the possibilities of the future.

I wandered into the courtyard. I resolved to go to the stable and my now-empty old quarters in the loft. I needed to think upon the young girl causing my blood to race. The moon was full making it easy to see. I entered and climbed the ladder. It was a warm night and I lay back to consider how I would bedazzle the dark-haired wonder. I was gently nudged out of my reverie by two voices below. It was the Queen and Sir William. I peered carefully over the edge of the loft at the two figures, not much more than shadows. The moon's light had diminished as clouds passed overhead. Since I was neglecting my duties a second time this evening I remained still hoping not to be discovered. The Queen was holding Sir William by the arm and speaking softly as they came close enough for me to hear.

"…'tis as good a place as any," she said playfully pulling at his arm.

"Nay, Majesty. If we be discovered we will suffer grievous harm to our reputations at the least."

"All the more exciting. It stirs my blood to passion! I have taken steps to be sure we are alone," she said in a voice dripping with seduction. With that she placed her arms around his waist and began to kiss his neck several times. I was now terrified. This meeting was not meant for any eyes or ears. Should I be discovered I would be killed! I was afraid to move or breathe. The clouds moved on. The scene below was now out of shadow bathed in bright moonlight flooding through the loft door and the many cracks in the walls.

Sir William surrendered to the caresses. They kissed passionately. While still remaining in the embrace they moved toward a pile of straw in the corner. Sir William spoke, "Majesty, a stable is no place for a queen to…"

She placed her hand over his mouth. "Tonight it is a safe time of the month for me and I wish to be no more than a lusty wench." She laughed a wicked little laugh. She began to gently stroke between his powerful legs. He uttered a soft groan. The queen tugged gently on his arm and they both lay back on the straw. She pulled her gown up and exposed her well-formed legs. At this point a strange euphoria took hold of me. I rolled to my side to take pressure of my now hardening manhood. She took his hand and placed it on her thigh pulling it slowly to her most private area. Sir William, now bewitched, became more involved. His hands caressed her breasts and reached to loosen her garments. The top of her gown was pulled down releasing what I had never seen before—two female breasts. Illuminated by the light of the full moon the two bodies appear to be made of silver as they caressed and stroked each other.

The queen sighed and my master began to breathe heavily. I felt terrible guilt at seeing that which I was not intended to witness, but at the same time I refused to avert my eyes. I was experiencing extreme excitement from the scene below and wanted more. Another of life's contradictions had been introduced to me.

Sir William kissed the Queen's exposed breasts. First gently and then aggressively, the pace of their lovemaking quickened as their hands explored the other's body. My arousal continued apace. My master pulled down his undergarments exposing his large buttocks. He mounted the Queen. She seemed to disappear beneath his large form. Only parts of her legs and her arms locked tightly around his back could be seen. To my youthful eyes he seemed to be trying to crush her with heavy thrusts from his hips. This continued for several minutes. The Queen made noises that were in time with the thrusts. Her arms and hands grasped and squeezed the massive shoulders. Suddenly, still wrapped in this position he rose to his feet lifting the Queen and let out a loud groan. The Queen still clinging to him responded with shriek. My manhood released as I stifled a cry.

Happy to be relieved of the bewitching feeling, I suddenly was overcome with a feeling of guilt. As the two below me adjusted their clothes, I lay silently ashamed of what I had seen and done. I felt I had betrayed the sacred trust with my master. I should not have witnessed this passion. I was lower than the lowest creature on the earth. The vision of this evening would repeat itself again and again in my dreams. My body would again react in a similar way. When I would wake I would reproach myself for repeating this wicked sin. I could not control these thoughts no matter how I tried. Part of me was pained by such wickedness and another part of me seemed to like repeating the experience. I was being educated in the nature of man: lust and remorse mixed together in an intoxicating brew—a brew that never seems to quench the thirst for more.

The Queen, now recovered from her ecstasy, adjusted her disheveled garments and spoke solemnly to my master in a complete reversal of her earlier playfulness.

"William, the King returns in a fortnight. Events are moving quickly. Young Henry will be named his father's successor. If he be named future King of England I will demand Richard be designated Duke of Aquitaine. My skills will be challenged. He will not give away any of his power willingly. I shall not stand by and watch whilst he populates the countryside with bastards who may challenge my sons someday. I must control my passions in the days ahead."

Her words had the sound of finality. "Though it sorely vexes one that the King is under no such prescription, my activity with you would only complicate things. Tonight was a wonderful farewell. For a brief time tonight we were only a man and a woman, not who we really are. I chose to end it this way. I will always love you, but now great issues are at stake and I cannot be compromised. You must go with young Henry and Marguerite. He loves you. Serve him as you would me. He is a callow lad and will need a steady hand in the years ahead. Richard shall remain with John and me. Young Henry perceives my feelings for Richard; 'tis best they are separated lest serious trouble erupt between them. If Henry be named successor in England, he will feel less threatened by his younger brother. 'Tis a pity Richard was not first born. Future rewards for your service shall be forthcoming," she added while brushing the straw off her clothes.

"Your majesty has already been most generous. I am grateful," he said as he pulled his tunic over his head and tied the laces.

"'Tis no more than you deserve. William, behold the stars. The astrologers say they control our destiny. Had they been different, you might have been a King, a magnificent one!"

"Majesty, I presume not so high a place. Respect be all I crave."

"Alas, it be why the stars have failed us." She sighed, placed a hand on his arm, and they walked out of the stable.

I waited for several moments and climbed down. I examined the damp state of my clothing. I was about to exit the stable when voices outside stopped me in my tracks. It was two of the Queen's personal guards speaking to each other. I ducked behind the door.

"Her majesty has given us leave to go. Say nothing of our duty tonight if you value your neck." They walked away. I shuddered realizing my own danger and vowed to forget all that had happen. I raced to our quarters to be sure I was there when my master returned. I had no desire to concoct a lie about where I had been. If I appeared to be asleep on my pallet when he arrived the need would not arise.

After a short time the Marshal returned. I feigned waking from slumber and asked if he needed anything. "Nay. I see you are aware of the interest of a certain young serving girl. She will probably stir your loins to life." I lit a candle. It cast a dim light and I hoped it would conceal my guilt-ridden features.

"Forgive me, master!" I felt my face tighten.

"You feel the pains of manhood, all quite natural. You will soon discover women possess powers that weaken the strongest arm. 'Tis God's way of giving them fair chance." He chuckled and patted my head. I winced thinking of what I had just witnessed. "Your experience is beginning and mine is changed," he said with a sigh.

"How so, my lord?" I was puzzled by this last comment.

"The politics, which you are mercifully unaware of, seek to play themselves out. I have been released to return to the life I prefer. No more must I play the courtier, but a knight in service to a young prince. The King and the Queen shall plan the future of their sons. The Queen seeks to wield power through her sons. King Henry's purpose lies in constructing a great empire where only he rules. Such diverse ambitions portend a colossal struggle. I have no wish to choose sides between the King and the Queen. I have taken an oath to serve them both. I have never broken my oath." He paused and looked up acting as if there was some answer written on the ceiling of our small room. He continued, "Law requires me to show first fealty to the household I serve. The Queen has decided it will be the household of Prince Henry. What that will bring only time will tell. The positive lies in the fact Prince Henry loves the tournaments, and will be our patron. I shall make money by winning tournaments and selling the spoils I win. I will continue to instruct him and prepare him for knighthood. I shall seek to keep his thoughts focused on those knightly pursuits. Prince Richard will follow a different path."

"I would think that a good thing. Jealousy keeps them from being close." I added my thought on this new change.

"Perhaps. The King's design is to use his sons by giving them fiefdoms to rule in his name. Richard will be the next part of the plan. He will be married to the French Princess Alais when she comes of age in two years. Then Geoffrey will be married off, and then John, and so it will go on until King Henry is ruler of all Europe. 'Tis the way of Kings, fighting wars or marrying off sons and daughters to expand their realm. It is not however the Queen's design. She sees a kingdom ruled by her and her sons without their father. Prince Henry harbors little affection for the King. Queen Eleanor has had many years to shape the sons to her designs. She has not shown inclination to endear them to their father. To make matters worse the sons have inherited their parents' ambitious nature, but little of their cunning—a dangerous mixture."

"What will we do if this unfolds, as you suggest?" I could feel the pangs of fear creep back into my life. The idyllic life I had thought was ours was fading fast. This was the dark side of life with the powerful.

"We watch and listen quietly from the shadows, saying nothing and hearing everything. You, Lewellyn, must be a second set of ears and eyes for me. I shall have great need of you. The mouse is often ignored in the corner of a large room if he takes care not to make noise. Watch and learn as the powerful let slip a word here or there, but take care not to squeak. Reveal what you see to no one, but me." The Marshal looked at me with that serious gaze I knew was both advice and a warning. "Now to bed. The king will arrive in several days."

The day King Henry arrived dawned in splendid fashion. The fields of rapeseed were in full bloom and the warm air was exceedingly pleasant. It appeared that the land was paying homage to the arrival of the King by spreading carpets of yellow beside the roads. The streams were still running full from the recent rains and would serve the upcoming events well.

I had few opportunities to observe King Henry, but I did know some from the past years of serving meals in the great hall. He was stout of build with reddish hair and blue eyes. He was a man who was always in motion. He rarely sat for more than a few moments. Eating was accomplished between moving around the room and stopping to whisper in this one or that one's ear. He paced incessantly. His mind was constantly leaping from one conversation to another. In spite of this, there always seemed to be a carefully considered purpose to his meandering whether it was mental or physical.

He made a grand entrance with his retainers. He was dusty from his days in the saddle and made little effort to have his garments changed. Fashion was never a concern of this king. His greeting to the Queen was proper but not warm. The greeting to his sons was just the opposite. He immediately asked the Marshal about their progress. My master indicated he would be pleased with what they had learned and the King would soon be able to judge for himself in the upcoming river jousts.

The King roared his approval. "Wonderful! I am eager for the contests. I will be the most interested spectator on the bank." He glanced at the Queen and said, "Richard is inclined to your height, my dear. He grows like a willow. Henry is of my build, sturdy and can take a serious blow with such a good foundation. We shall see anon. I am pleased."

"Richard will likewise stand the impact," she quickly added. The meaning was clear.

It was as the Marshal had foretold. The contest would match the King and the Queen as well as the boys on the boats. I looked at my master, but discerned nothing from his face. He was expressionless. As he said, he would not take sides. He had taught both, and he expected good results from both. King Henry was for his namesake, and Queen Eleanor with the handsome Prince Richard.

Both of the Princes sided with their mother. Kings pay a price for neglecting their sons while they chase after land and power. In a strange way they think the sons will somehow forgive their absence in return for the right to inherit the empire, but the inheritance, no matter how grand, cannot buy the bonds that develop in the early years of childhood. It is reserved for those who do the nurturing. As one without a father or mother I developed that bond with the Marshal. It was one beyond price. When the day came and I discovered the identity of my real father, it was still the Marshal who held my heart.

The next few days passed without Sir William being summoned into the presence of the royal family. He spent the extra hours at the post practicing his craft. Then, word came that the Queen wanted to see my master. After he returned he told me the Queen had made the selection of the two young nobles who would face her sons. Thomas of Salisbury would be Prince Henry's opponent. Thomas was a nice youth, who would give a good account of himself. He was about the same size and age as her Henry, fifteen. I had seen him on the practice field, and he was just the ordinary sort of talent Prince Henry could confidently best. The same could be said of Prince Richard's foe. Raimund de Braise was also unexceptional and the perfect match. I knew the Prince would easily win this contest. The Queen had chosen well. The opponents would not cause any surprises to embarrass the royal family.

The day of the river jousts finally arrived. The excitement at court was greater than usual since the two Princes would be engaged. The royal pavilion was grand affair placed on the river bank where the two boats would meet in each of the contests. Grand banners hung from canopy covering the viewing stand. Heralds in red jackets with yellow sleeves would signal the beginning of each contest with sennets. The first hour was taken up with the appropriate pomp as the King and Queen and their court took their places. My master was seated to the left of the Queen. To her right was King Henry and to his right was Sir Bertran de Born, an entertaining young knight rapidly becoming famous for his poetic skills. He was most popular at Queen Eleanor's court. The others on the stand were knights of the King's entourage.

Spectators crowded the banks up and down the river. Their titles determined how close to the royal pavilion they were stationed. The farther up the hill, the lower your rank in society. On the opposite bank and down to the bridge were the townspeople. They cheered lustily when a young noble was dumped into the cold water, especially if he were the son of an unpopular landlord. It was one of the few times in the year they could indulge themselves in this type of behavior without fear of retribution.

The first few contests were rather typical, and the royal couple paid little attention. King Henry rose from his seat often to converse with the assortment of dignitaries seated near him. As the contests progressed, the crowd seemed to become one loud voice as each spectator uttered the same sounds in response to the action. One drew a huge laugh when both lads were dumped into the current. Another contest saw the crowd gasp as one of the boys was knocked senseless and required quick action by one of the boatmen who dived into the water and grabbed the unconscious lad before he drowned. The throng cheered the rescue. The next few matches were draws as both contestants broke their lances and remained standing on the prow of their respective craft. The better talent was always saved for last.

The Heralds trumpeted and the final contests were readied. The moment all had waited for was at hand. Prince Henry would go first. He stood on the boat deck with a lance in one hand and the red shield with three gold lions proudly proclaiming the status of the bearer. The King stood up and stared intently at his son. Without averting his gaze from his son he spoke to the Marshal, "I wager a fine horse he wins, Sir William."

"'Tis not a wager I will take, Majesty. The boy is an excellent student. I have every confidence he will be victorious." The Marshal was clearly sure of his pupil.

"He must!" King Henry snapped.

The signal was given, and the crews began rowing feverishly. Prince Henry had been given the superior position by virtue of being in the boat coming downstream. The two boys lowered their lances into the proper position and braced for the upcoming collision. At the last second Prince Henry adjusted the angle of the shield to the position I had seen the Marshal council him was the best way to deflect a blow and lean slightly forward. The result was as expected; Thomas was hurled backward into the stream and a mighty cheer split the air. The reaction from the Royal couple was one of relief and pride. Smiles and handshakes were passed around the nobility.

"You did your job well, Sir William. My son shows promise. We thank you."

"He is the scion of his father." The Marshal knew his sovereign enjoyed the moment.

Now, it was Richard's turn. The boats were returned to their starting points. Once again the racing lions on the field of red indicated which boat held the younger son. Looking down, the Queen smiled at the tall boy readying himself in the small craft. Her smile suddenly disappeared when she looked at the other boat. It was not the shield of de Braise handed to the boy in the other boat but that of William FitzHugh. This was not the match the Queen had arranged the day before. FitzHugh was by two years Prince Richard's senior and one of the best young squires in training at Chinon. The Queen's face went white. She looked at my master and then at King Henry. The King had a wry smile on his face. He spoke in an offhanded manner. He knew exactly what his Queen was thinking.

"We were told the proposed match was not equal to Prince Richard's standards, so we of course demanded a better contest. Surely his teacher and his mother would not want others to think we lacked confidence in his skills," he casually remarked. The King was going to teach Queen Eleanor a lesson in how the game of power was played. After her favorite son was properly chastened by a dip in the water, his first born would be the hero of the day's events. Again, the Marshal had foretold with accuracy the gamesmanship that would take place in the royal family. The Queen knew what was happening and was powerless to protest. If she insisted the contest be canceled Prince Richard would be humiliated. She looked pleadingly at the Marshal for some excuse to stop the event. He surprised her by looking at the smiling King and saying in a perfectly calm voice, "'Tis best, Majesty. The Prince will not disappoint."

The King's face showed surprise from this response. He rose to ponder the cleverness of his plan. Had he made a mistake? He stood still for a moment and recovered his composure quickly. He looked at Sir William with an inquisitive stare, smiled weakly and spoke in a respectful tone, "Well said, teacher." Henry always respected courage. He turned to watch the contest he had so cunningly planned and no longer sure his plan would succeed.

Again, the two boats raced toward each other. The young Prince did exactly like his elder brother with one small difference. Just before impact he dropped the point of the lance several inches. It hit the older boy's shield slightly below center. Prince Richard's shield took a high hit. His knees buckled from the impact but the angle of the shield deflected most of the force of the hit. His own lance bent and then lifted FitzHugh, tossing the older boy into the river to another rousing cheer. The King smiled and again turned to the Marshal. "You have delivered again, Sir William. We are fortunate you serve our cause," he said. Any trace of disappointment from the failed plan vanished as if it never existed. Such is the way of powerful men.

"In fulfillment of my oath, my liege," was my master's reply. The Marshal had a huge grin, as did Queen Eleanor. She beamed as the boat containing her second son reached the shore. The victorious Prince Richard jumped on the river bank to boisterous cheers and was warmly greeted by his brother. The two princes were running toward the pavilion laughing and slapping each other on the back. It was a special moment for King Henry. His sons had performed with skill in front of his subjects. It was good for a monarch to show the world he was going to leave the reins of power in good hands. To be sure, Henry did not want that day to be too soon, but even if his plan to humble the Queen did not succeed, he could not help feeling the pride of a father when his sons accomplished more than even he expected. Happy moments shared with these sons were never many. This day would be one of the few.

When the two boys reached the pavilion their joy was obvious. King Henry greeted them with words of praise. The Queen used the momentary distraction to give the hand of the Marshal a quick and appreciative squeeze. Her beautiful eyes spoke volumes, and my master knew he had her eternal gratitude. I saw the King suddenly look at the two of them with a very knowing stare. In an instant it was clear the King knew of their feelings for each other. My skin convulsed with a shudder of fear. Had those guards revealed to the King that which I had witnessed? Was my master's life forfeit?

The King's stare gave way to a wry grin and an almost imperceptible shake of his large head. A new revelation occurred to me. He knew, but he cared not! Like a man who has had his fill at a feast ignores those who sample the leavings, so too the King's many affairs had sated his needs and left him amused with his Queen's infidelity. As long as there were no offspring to muddy the political waters and the liaison was a well guarded secret, the Queen was welcome to a dalliance with this knight. All knew the King flouted the Church's rules against adultery, but the rules of the Church were no more to King Henry and Queen Eleanor than that of shadows on a wall. In that brief moment of observing obscure gestures and looks my education of court life took a large step forward. I vowed to be ever vigilant at such events as my master had advised. I wondered how many others present were engaged in the same game. Observing the powerful can be useful but also dangerous.

"You have done your father and mother most proud," the King said with real emotion. "Henry, you are a man. Richard, you will be, sooner than even I expected." He shot a glance at the Queen.

Queen Eleanor, never one to miss a chance, added, "We will be discussing what it means for your future." King Henry knew she would press for more titles for both sons, and he would have to agree. He also knew he would need to find a new way to fit his sons into his design for the future. King Henry was a master at adjusting to unexpected events, making them fit neatly in his long-term plans.

The sky was turning pink as the approach of evening turned the river banks to light purple. The river danced with the many colors of twilight as the sun retreated over the hills. The day's festivities were over, and the crowds began to melt away back to the dull humdrum of daily life. The King and Queen headed for the castle where the fate of great provinces would be discussed. Those on the other side of the river had no idea their fates were also being decided. The Marshal and I marched in the long procession behind their majesties and retired to our quarters.

When we arrived at our rooms the Marshal dropped down in the big chair, threw one leg over the arm and started to laugh. I was consumed with curiosity and could not resist speaking.

"My lord, what find you so amusing?" I asked.

"Tonight, Lewellyn, the high king will be hounded into doing that which he is loath to do. All because of simple vanity he will capitulate to the wife he detests and make young Henry a king in England sooner than he planned," he laughed clearly amused at some vision that I failed to see.

"Can this be? Can there be two kings?" I was flummoxed by the contradictions.

"Yes, anything, if the King wills it so. The father holds the real power until he dies, but his son will be a king in name. King Henry has more than enough titles to surfeit even his appetite for lands. He will be young Henry's liege lord. We shall witness interesting times, a young king and an old one—both named Henry. By God's legs the King trapped himself when his plan for Prince Richard went awry. If he fails to make young Henry a king now, people will begin to consider the handsome and very tough Prince Richard a better choice. He must end the rivalry before it begins. His desire to humble Queen Eleanor's favorite has caused much consternation. Had he asked me to choose an opponent capable of defeating Prince Richard. Perhaps it was possible, but he could not. It had to be a complete surprise." He spoke not only to me, but also to himself. He was thinking out loud again.

"Queen Eleanor plots. King Louis, her former husband, plots. The Church will seek a role and Princes Henry and Richard act in ways yet to be discovered. Who knows who else will join in? Lewellyn, we must be careful where we step!" His tone had changed from amused to serious. His eyes narrowed and he stroked his chin slowly.

I was unsure of what all this meant so I asked, "What part do we play, my lord?"

"The one my oath demands. We will be on the side of England and true to our promises. Life in battle depends on your skill and your strength. Life at court requires other skills. The powerful seek those with talents they can use, but they kill those who try to use them. We will use the power God has seen fit to place in my sword arm and stay clear of the plotting. We have been called to serve young Henry. We must avoid the quarrels that are sure to transpire between the Queen and King Henry. Their visions of the future differ greatly. Many will seek to use these differences to further their own ambitions. We are on good terms with both sovereigns. We must stay so by remaining silent and fulfilling the task of training the young King. If he remains consumed by his passion for the tournaments we may yet avoid being sucked into the maelstrom. We steer a narrow course. Now, I shall sup. Fetch a leg of mutton."

I rushed to the kitchen to get the victuals my master requested. Truth be known I was more excited about the prospect of seeing a certain serving girl than I was about the tides of political fortune which I neither understood or cared. The profound thoughts of the Marshal temporarily deserted my brain. My heart was now in control.

The following month was a continuation of my education in observing the gestures and subtle clues of the powerful. I also received an unpleasant lesson in the art of wooing a pretty girl. The ways of the opposite sex proved beyond my talents. Celine soon tired of a boy who was ignorant in the ways of making a young girl happy. She soon found a handsome herald more interesting. When I discovered them together one evening I was left with the thoughts of why I had failed and the usual sulking of a boy with a broken heart. The Marshal saw my misery and offered that he too had been rejected by a maid in his youth. It seemed to make things better.

Before he left, the King announced young Henry would be crowned in England in the summer and his brother Richard would become the Duke of Aquitaine. It was just as I had overheard the Queen discussing with the Marshal a month ago. The year of 1170 still held major surprises and was far from over. We prepared to move to England with Young Henry and his wife Marguerite. The maelstrom Sir William feared would soon ensnare the Plantagenet family and mother Church. The on-again, off-again struggle between the King and his former friend Thomas a' Becket, Archbishop of Canterbury, was on again. It would have great consequences for the King, young Henry and his wife. All would be drawn into the conflict.

Chapter 4
Two Kings in England

We began the summer with a move to Rouen and preparations for a trip to England to attend the coronation ceremony of young Henry. We were packing when I asked the Marshal to explain to me why the King wanted to give his son a title with no power.

"The King is most fond of Henry and seeks to squelch the rivalry between his two eldest sons. By so doing he prevents King Louis of France and others, who believe confusion creates opportunities for their ambitions. Prince Richard is content to be Duke of Aquitaine. He cares little for England. The King is most desirous they be properly controlled until he is too old to care. He just enjoyed his thirty-seventh birthday and needs to keep his sons from becoming impatient for power." I could see he had some doubt in this plan.

"I am happy we are not involved, my lord," I said in my ignorance.

"But we are. It is my charge from the King is to see this is done." He frowned after this last pronouncement. "'Tis all very complicated and made worse by King Henry's feud with his former friend, the Archbishop of Canterbury."

"How so, my lord?" Again I was puzzled.

"Seven years ago, when you were too young to know much of anything, King Henry had a bitter quarrel with Becket, the man he made Archbishop of Canterbury. As seasons came and went, Becket lived abroad, fugitive from King Henry's anger. Many have tried to reconcile the two, even the Pope, but to no avail. Both men are staunch in their positions and neither is willing to bend. Henry feels the Church interferes with his ability to run the state and Becket insists that he defends the prerogatives of Mother church." He selected a tunic from the chest in the corner.

"This has play on young Henry's crowning?"

"Sadly, a great deal. By tradition the coronation of the King of England must be done by the Archbishop of Canterbury. Henry orders the Archbishop of York to perform the deed. Becket implored the Pope to declare the ceremony illegal, saying Church functions are being usurped. Some say the Holy Father's acquiescence in the matter has already been purchased by funds from King Henry. To further spoil the stew, Young Henry and his wife, Marguerite, were most attached to the fugitive Archbishop. It was his hand that arranged their marriage when they were children. Archbishop Becket was Princess Marguerite's tutor while she came of age. She loves him like a father and declares she will not take part if Becket is ignored. Young Henry covets the crown and is not desirous of waiting while his father and the Archbishop continue their feud." He tossed me his new tabard.

"'Tis a pity. I desire not to be a king, master," I said while admiring the new garment.

"Nor I. Pack my finest clothes for the coronation. We must let the maelstrom spin. 'Twill be good to be in England. Too long I have been absent." There was gleam in his eye as he spoke of the home long denied this knight errant. Although seeking his destiny kept him in King Henry's French holdings, he always longed for England. In the evenings he would often ask me to sing an English tune. "We leave at first light," he declared with a broad smile.

At dawn we packed the horses and began the journey. I was excited by the thought of seeing a new land and my first sea voyage. After a day's ride we reached the Normandy coast and the port of Calais. There we took ship for England. When I beheld the small bark that would ferry us to Portsmouth I became quite concerned. We would cross open water in this tiny craft. A crew of ten handled the single sail and oars of this floating coffin. My master seemed unconcerned so I decided to put a brave face on the situation. It did not last for long.

The Channel crossing was the worst day of my life. The rocking of the ship seemed inconspicuous at first, but then I started to have an ache in my head. Next, I began to feel sweaty. I had to move my bowels. Then continuous waves caused me to empty the contents of my stomach over the side of the ship. It was accompanied by the laughter of the crew, who seemed to find my eminent demise as something very humorous. I continued retching and vomiting the entire trip. I was unable to perform even the simplest of my duties. My master did not seem to mind. In fact, he did offer some kind words, but they did little to ease my suffering. I was sure the contents of my feet would soon be coming out of my mouth. Contrary to a most earnest belief that my death would soon occur, I reached England alive. Barely! Even when I reached the security of land, the rolling motion in my brain continued until nightfall. We took lodgings for the night. The next day we began our journey to Winchester. My head was still pounding, but finally sleep mercifully ended my agony.

The journey north to Winchester was less eventful and my spirits were steadily rising. I did not ask Sir William any more questions. There were too many strange ears for safe conversation. I did think about what he had told me and I tried my best to understand the ways of the powerful. Perhaps life is always about getting a little more. The contest has different starting points for different people. For the pauper it means steady meals. For the farmer a bigger field and a little better yield each season. The merchant wants more business or a bigger shop. The lesser noble seeks a higher title and more recognition at court. The greater nobles crave more castles, greater wealth, and a son or daughter married to the very powerful. Kings want larger kingdoms and a place in history. All think they are worthy, and those above them are not. People cling to reasons why they should be the winners and others should not. I thought about these things and then decided I was too ignorant to understand it.

We arrived in Winchester at dusk. There was much activity involving preparations for the coming event. We were taken immediately to see Prince Henry. Although Winchester was not as large as some of the castles I had seen in France the great hall was impressive with huge oak beams spanning a very large space. Colorful banners hung from the walls and a large fireplace dominated an entire wall. We were greeted by Prince Henry and his wife. He bubbled with excitement, as he informed the Marshal of the preparations. His wife seemed more distant and quiet. Small of stature and youthful in appearance, Marguerite was not unattractive. Her dark hair and dark eyes spoke clearly of her Capetian lineage. There was a small birth mark on her neck and her skin was quite fair. She had been raised by the Plantagenet household since she was eight. For this reason she knew every want of her young husband and she endeavored to accede to his every wish. It made them close friends, but they showed no sign of passion in their lives together. It almost seemed as thought they were brother and sister, not man and wife. They were only a year older than me and I had just reached my fifteenth year. Beside Sir William they appeared to be children, yet they were over him in all things. I stood silently by one of the doors observing while being easily ignored by the principals in the room.

Marguerite's face showed displeasure and a lack of interest in the event soon to be held. She said in a dainty voice she had preparations to see to and returned to her chambers through a side door. Her hasty retreat left little doubt of her concern over the absence of her beloved Archbishop. Henry continued to speak to my master and walked close enough for me to overhear.

"William, you are more than tutor. Yours shall be a place of honor in the festivities. 'Tis the beginning of great things," the Prince said with sincerity as a smile creased his youthful cheeks.

"You are too kind, my liege. My sword and my knowledge are always at your disposal," Sir William said softly. He bowed gracefully.

"William, mother said always trust and listen to Sir William. I know she is right. We keep you near for counsel and support. These be troubled times. With father and the Archbishop at odds...well...it has presented us with difficult choices." The Prince shook his head and looked at the door his dispirited wife had just exited.

"Where does the matter sit with the Holy Father, Pope Alexander?" Sir William inquired.

"Father succeeds in getting the appropriate dispensations, but Becket demands the approval be rescinded. I have great regard for Thomas, but it vexes me that he stands in the way of my coronation. We could be helpful to him, once crowned. He fails to see the opportunity. He is not the same man I knew before this happened." His downcast eyes expressed his disappointment. I was now a careful observer of facial clues and studied them intensely.

"I heartily agree with that, my Prince." My master's face wore a concerned look.

"I wish the thing be done soon so life can return to some semblance of calm. Marguerite protests the absence of the Archbishop. She insists she will not take part, unless he officiates. I care not. I must be crowned. Then, perhaps, I can set things aright." He stood straighter and showed his determination to be taken seriously as a future monarch.

"I am sworn to serve you, my Prince, but take care not to insert yourself between the King and the Archbishop. No good will come from your best efforts. Only they can heal this breech. Any who try becomes an enemy of one or the other or both," Sir William counseled.

"'Tis sad those good friends now harbor such bitterness. Ah, well, we discuss this no further. Your loyalty begs a reward. You shall carry my scepter in the procession at Westminster," he said changing the mood of the conversation as the young can so often do. The Prince reached out and grabbed his tutor by both arms, oblivious to the forebodings just exchanged. The naive optimism of a parvenu was now firmly in control.

"You honor me too much, my Prince," Sir William said also changing the subject and seeing that further warnings were a waste of time.

"You are most deserving and mother agrees. It brings to mind. I have received a shipment of excellent wine from mother's Aquitaine. We shall drink a toast, or two, to the future and the tournament season ahead." The Prince placed his arm around the broad waist of my master. They turned and walked toward the great hall. I followed behind, carrying the Marshal's cloak. From this position, I could observe the two friends in a strange relationship. Prince Henry appeared very small next to the much larger Sir William, but Prince Henry was about to become a king in the eyes of the world. Size mattered little.

After several days of feasting and making the proper arrangements the royal company journeyed to London for the investiture. The Marshal wore robes of silk. His colors of green, yellow and red were striking. He had been granted his own coat of arms, a red lion rampant on the field of yellow and green. The granting of the symbolic lion showed how far my lord had risen in the esteem of the royal family. The honor was not granted to many knights. I was dressed up with new clothes. I thought how proud my mother would have been to see her son in such finery. A jacket of green velvet with yellow sleeves and a beautiful cap of similar make made me feel like royalty too. I thought I would burst with pride as my master marched behind the young king with the scepter of the realm. It was a glorious day.

I stood in the back of the church holding Sir William's banner, straining to see the proceedings, but unfortunately I could not see much. It did not matter. For the first time in my young life I was inside the church for such a special occasion. I would be able to boast of this honor for months, even years afterward.

I could hear Archbishop Roger of York saying the solemn words, but I did not understand them. It was the language of the priests. Lewellyn, the former serving boy, present at the crowning of a King! All the most important people in the kingdom were there and I was inside the cathedral. I had to pinch myself to be sure it was real. The King, the Queen, Prince Richard, Prince Geoffrey and every nobleman of note attended. Everyone except for Princess Marguerite, who, true to her word, refused to be crowned with her young husband. No matter, I was there! I was very pleased by my lot in life. How far

I had come in just a few years and all because of a knight I failed to leave in a dungeon. The wheel of my life was on the ascent. Little did I know I would be present at the crowning of three more kings.

After several hours, we left the church to the ringing of bells and the cheering of the crowd. From that day forward Henry would be known to all as the young King. I was convinced life for the Marshal would now be perfect. I told him so as we returned to our rooms.

"My lord, it was wonderful. Prospects could not be better. Could they?" I said confidently.

He smiled and shook his head. "Nay, my young friend, the clouds will soon gather. Today is but a sunny break in the storms that are sure to follow."

I was surprised. After a few seconds I asked, "How so, my lord? The young King adores you. He is positioned to make your life most easy. You have the Queen's trust, and the King's admiration. I have heard this from others in the court. How pray tell could life be better?"

"You are too naive to see the danger surrounding us. King Henry enters the prime of life. He has wrongly deduced his eldest son will be content to play at being king. The 'young King' will, for a time, and then the desire for real power will pull at him. Gently at first, but like the tide at Mont St. Michel, ambition will rise higher and higher until all else is submerged." He used his hands to simulate the rising waters. He continued his thought, as much for his own understanding as mine.

"The Queen sees in her sons, a chance revenge herself on her less than faithful husband. I have sworn loyalty to the King, but now I serve the son. If it comes to blows, my first duty is to his son and that portends evil. I shall do my best to thwart these evil stars from aligning. Perhaps, the young King will heed my council, but I fear he is his father's son and ambition follows its own council. Others will feed the jealous beast. There will be other problems in being a king's favorite. 'Tis where your eyes and ears will be useful. There are many at court that seek to replace a favorite and will do all manner of mischief to see him brought down in the sovereign's esteem. I need know from whence these threats come, as surely they will. Be alert, my inconspicuous friend, and apprise me of any slanders you hear around the scullery. Plots will grow like weeds. No, life will not be easy, but we will be well fed. Now, enough of intrigues and plots. Fetch me a brew!" His mind satisfied with his assessment of our future trials turned to the more immediate needs of the body.

I quickly did as asked, and we spent the rest of the evening discussing how fine we looked in the new clothes. As the beer took effect, the Marshal related a story of how he almost died at the tender age of five. His father had given him as a hostage to King Steven. It was during the wars between Steven and Matilda. When his father went back on his word, Steven laid siege to his father's small castle. King Steven announced he would kill William by launching him from a catapult into the walls. They placed the youthful William in the bucket and shouted the dire threat to John Marshal, who stood watching from the battlements. His father shouted back, "Proceed. I be young enough and have the tool to make another like him." Fortunately for William, King Steven felt sorry for the lad and did not follow through on his threat. At the conclusion of the story the Marshal laughed.

"Master, I should love to know my father. Alas, 'tis doubtful," I said dejectedly.

"Perhaps I could make inquiries. I expect it will come to naught, but as a favor I shall try," he slurred. Drunk, he slumped down in the chair and fell asleep.

I shook my head in disbelief, and wondered if my unknown father would have done the same. The world of the nobility had many advantages, and yet the price they had to pay in not knowing who to trust, even family, seemed a terrible one. No wonder the Marshal put such a great store in trust and honoring one's promises. Perhaps those who enjoy power and wealth are always suspicious of those nearest to them. Whether real or imagined, the threat of betrayal is ever present. I see no motivation on the part of others to take what I have, since I have little. As a result, I can take all acts of kindness and compliments as sincere. I do not have to spend hours trying to divine intentions. Since I am not very smart and would find it hard to discern such devious motives, it prevents needless worry and helps me to sleep easily.

A fortnight after the coronation we returned to Rouen. The Marshal said we needed to prepare for the tournament season. The crossing was no different from my first. It was made worse by the foreknowledge I possessed of the wicked ways of the sea.

The first tournament of the season at Gourni was a small affair. The young King was our sponsor and King Henry supplied funds. The King was happy to keep his son distracted with the excitement of the tournaments. I would not be directly involved. It was the role of the squires in training to arm and assist him, but as his personal servant, I would be on the field next to his standard.

The day was overcast and a little foggy. There were about forty participants. Knights of all different skill levels would compete, each hoping that he would make a name for himself and gain the favor of some lord with a large purse. The contest saw the forty men split into several groups. They faced each other across the open field. It was a mock battle. The knight with the most "captures" at the end of the contest was declared the winner. The two sides charged each other with blunt lances. Each knight tried to unhorse a foe in the first charge. After several charges the weapons were changed for close combat. Maces and swords were used to disable one's opponent and achieve a "capture." In time I would learn it could even result in the fatal wounding of an opponent. It was a very dangerous game that tested courage as well as skill. My master said it gave knights a chance to show their talents to rich lords who might purchase their services. Tournaments were officially frowned upon in England. It was the reason we had come to France.

I had lifted the Marshal's broadsword on several occasions. I cannot imagine swinging it for more than a moment or two. He could do it all day. I understood why he spent hours every day at the post, and why his arms were like tree trunks. He told me he had already participated in many of these contests. He had won them all! It made him a marked man. To unseat Sir William Marshal would make a knight's star rise quickly. I asked my master why men were so willing to risk injury or death for so little.

"It may appear to be little, but for those of us who have little hope of gaining land it offers much. In addition to the glory, there are material advantages to the victor as well. A knight receives the armor and horse of any knight he bested. Since a knight without equipment is useless, the losers will have to buy it back from the victor. Money is supplied by a patron like the young King. Several losses and a knight is sure to be released from service. These knights disappear from public tournaments until they can raise enough to rearm. Many will rob or kidnap travelers to gain these funds," he remarked casually.

"I do not understand. How this can be justified by the code of honor you hold in high regard?" I asked in all innocence. The Marshal only smiled, shrugged his shoulders and rubbed my head.

As the Marshal was helped to his horse, it was clear to me he was about to engage in the activity he loved. He was laughing and joking with his attendants about who would be his first foe. He mounted his horse, turned to me, and said, "Lewellyn, be sure to have a flagon of beer ready for me. This is thirsty business."

"It shall be done, my lord," I shouted overjoyed to be a part of this grand spectacle.

They placed the heavy helm on his head and lowered the visor. The joking stopped, and a serious attitude overtook the very large man whose stature was made even more imposing by the armor. He wheeled his steed and took his place in line. On the opposite side you could see the more experienced knights move to a position not opposite the shield of green and yellow. They were not eager to face Sir William in the first charge. The flag was dropped and a roar went up from the crowd lining the field. The two sides charged headlong toward each other. Shields up and lances lowered into the attack position, the inevitable collision occurred, with a loud clang and crack of wood smashing into metal. At the same time, adding to the noise, cheering came from all sides of the field. It caused a sensation on my skin, making it feel like all my hair was on fire.

Four riders burst out of their saddles backwards and my mind raced back to the day the Marshal and I first met. My whole body shuddered. The knight with a blue and gold shield had the misfortune to be opposite my master. He landed on the ground with a loud thud. Groggy he was escorted from the field by the squires. Several lances had shattered and were dropped by their owners. The two sides returned to their respective positions. Those with broken lances had them replaced in preparation for the next round. The same procedure was followed and the two sides charged again. This time I watched the Marshal very carefully. Just before impact I saw his long legs bend to push against the stirrups. His toes pointed down sharply. Again, his opponent was ejected from his saddle and landed heavily on the ground. The riderless horse was led away while its master sat dazed on the ground. He, too, was helped to his feet and he stumbled toward the tents.

The next phase of the contest involved the more experienced knights. The din of swords striking shields was continuously amplified by the screams of the spectators. Groans and shrieks went up when a particular favorite was unhorsed. If any other knight was planning to make a name for himself this day, he would be disappointed because my knight in green and yellow was clearly master of the field.

I was grinning widely as I held out a large flagon of beer for the hero who approached our standard. I saw the young King waving and cheering from the reviewing stand. He knew his champion was the winner and was eager to have him come over. The Marshal wasted no time in galloping his horse to the stand, and bowing his head to his young patron. The young monarch was delighted his mentor and champion had demonstrated his dominance.

He spoke to the sweating paladin, "Sir William, you have again shown you are without peer on the field of battle. We salute you and hope you will instruct us to become as skilled in the months ahead. We long for the day when we shall fight side by side in the larger contests."

"I am your humble servant, sire. I hope to train others to serve your majesty."

"And so you shall! So you shall."

I was still holding the flagon as the Marshal rode back from the reviewing stand. Once again, I held it up for the victor. I saw a large smile on the handsome face as the powerful charger approached with my master.

"A greeting most worthy, my friend," the Marshal shouted as he reached for my gift of refreshment. He gulped down the libation and tossed the empty container to me. I was thrilled. In a strange way, I felt part of the success achieved. My role was insignificant, and yet each time the Marshal won a tournament I felt partly responsible for the victory. It is hard to explain, but even those who did no more than cheer his name felt the same way.

He turned his horse and said to his attendants, "I need make arrangement for the spoils." He rode off in the direction of the other knight's tents.

Later he returned to our chambers. He had a sack of coins and a very fine lute in his hands. He tossed the purse on the table and it landed with a rather large thud!

"Well, fortunes smile this day. We have two more horses, coins, and this!" He held out the lute. "'Tis yours, Lewellyn! It comes with lessons from the court's best musician, Sir Bertran de Born. He was among those I bested. I let him off lightly since he is a favorite of the young King and Queen Eleanor. He will also teach you how to read and write. I have not had time to develop such fine skills and I need a scribe. I said you would be my eyes and ears, and by God's grace you surely will."

I was dumbstruck by such a wondrous gift. For a moment I just stared. This was too much. I stuttered, "I, I, I…I deserve this not, my lord." Tears rolled down my cheeks. I reached to accept the treasure held in front of me.

"Lewellyn, you saved my life and that be more than I can ever repay. I shall always be in your debt," he said. I knew he meant every word. "Now, make plans for your lessons."

"I shall work as hard at my lessons as you at the post!" I said with all the sincerity I could muster.

"I believe you will," he answered with equal sincerity.

The following day, I met with Sir Bertran de Born for my first lesson. He was a favorite of the Queen because of his talent in making verses and his clever conversational skill. He was a very bright, engaging man and was very popular with all the members of the court. He was devoted to the young King and his Queen. I was lucky to have such a fine tutor. His skill with the lute was the envy of many. He was exceptionally handsome. I had to concede that he surpassed my master in fine features. His skin was untouched by the summer sun and his eyes had a blue color that seemed to sparkle. He was nicely muscled with little bulk. He appeared to be too delicate to be a fighting man but I was told his skill with weapons belied that impression. He spoke with almost a musical voice and it was plain why his reputation as a troubadour was well known. His clothes were of the finest quality.

"So, you are Lewellyn. Well, young man, show me what you know of this instrument." He smiled warmly and immediately set me at ease. My nervousness dissipated and I played a few chords. He listened and smiled again.

"Fair. I think we will make good progress. You must attend to me. Hear what I say and practice often. I trust you will give this lute the same care as I. It has been a friend to me, and now it has saved me from losing horse and armor. I expect you to do well. Your master is fond of my music. I want it said Bertran de Born honors his debts. Tell me, how came you to be worthy of this gift from the magnificent fighting machine called Sir William Marshal?" he asked with a twist of his head showing his befuddlement.

I explained how we had come to be prisoners of the Baron Luisgnan, and the events which occurred that fateful day. I left out the more personal parts, but spent the better part of an hour explaining how brave the Marshal had been and how he trained the Queen's sons. I included my brave actions which seemed to become more important each time I told the story.

"I see why he holds you in such high regard. Well, Lewellyn, we all hold your master in the highest regard. His loyalty to the royal family is well known. No man is more trusted by the young King than is your master. 'Twas my dubious honor to experience his prowess on the field of gentle combat yesterday. I am still sore." He rubbed his backside and laughed. "We shall see that you become what he hopes for you—musician and scribe."

"I shall practice 'til my fingers bleed. I fear, however, the reading and writing will be more difficult. I am a dunce."

"'Tis not what Sir William told me. You will be able to master the finer arts."

I began to like this knight of letters. He was not like many of the others at court who treated serving people as fools, useful only to fetch and carry for them. I felt we could become good friends. We spent the remaining time discussing how to clean the lute and keep it in good condition.

As the months passed my skills began to grow steadily. I learned the formal language of the court and proper manners. Sir Bertran was more than a teacher. He not only instructed me, but would talk to me like the Marshal and would listen to my troubles. Only the Marshal held a higher place in my esteem. He admired my master. We talked about his incredible strength and his loyalty to young Henry. We wrote several songs together about his exploits. Sir Bertran's were far better than mine. He said the same thing the Marshal told me when we first entered the service of the young King.

"Lewellyn, we must be vigilant. There are many who would do your master harm if they could. Since they dare not face him in combat, they will use other methods. The attacks will be subtle and hidden. It will be in the whispers at court. Those of us, who are friends, must always be alert to the danger. They will be as disguised as the grouse on the moor, so we must find them for him," he said in a soft voice as thought unseen others might be able to hear.

"I know of what you speak. The Marshal himself gave just such a warning." I too whispered in the empty chambers where we sat as though I also saw invisible eavesdroppers.

"Your master knows well the treachery lurking in a royal court. Then we are agreed. As his good friends, we shall remain alert. Wouldst I hear or see anything I will inform you and you will inform the Marshal." He placed his hand on my shoulder and smiled.

"I surely will, Sir Bertran," I said proudly.

"I feel we will be good friends." He laughed and tousled my hair. I was thrilled that one so far above me would think to call me friend.

We finished the day's lessons and I returned to my normal duties. I knew the Marshal would be finishing his instruction of the young King soon.

Henry was avid in his training with the Marshal. He gave full measure, and was beginning to show promise as a pupil. Knightly training was all he talked about and it was clear he sought to be like his instructor. His conversations at court were always about the next tournament and how the Marshal would vanquish any warrior put against him. He talked excitedly about the day he would compete beside his champion. There was never talk about his father or the day he would be the true King. Knights and tournaments were his passion.

Next in consideration was his Queen, Marguerite. The daughter of Louis of France, she was very smart. She seemed to know everything going on at court. She, too, was fascinated by the glamour surrounding the tournaments and the prowess of her husband's teacher. She frequently watched the practice sessions and applauded the good moves. She loved the stories of knightly valor. She encouraged Bertran to make up songs about knights and courtly love. She clearly followed the pattern of the ladies of the court. The interest she showed to Henry's passion brought them closer together. That she had refused to be crowned because of the Becket situation was almost forgotten. She did not care for her father-in-law, but was careful not to show too much animosity toward the real King. She played her role at court with a skill. It belied her youthful age. I was sure that she would welcome the day when her husband was no longer overshadowed by his illustrious father.

We were all enjoying the summer season when exciting news arrived. King Henry and Becket had reconciled in Normandy. The Archbishop, so beloved by the young King and his wife, would be going home to England and a new investiture would take place in the spring. Marguerite was thrilled that she would now be able to be crowned with her husband. It made for great merrymaking and heavy heads the following day.

The rest of the summer and fall were filled with more tournaments and parties. The results were always the same. The Marshal was victorious. Henry watched his hero and tried to learn his techniques. Marguerite hosted the banquets. The young King's father sent constant notes complaining he was spending too much. Bertran and I wrote songs about the Marshal's victories. It seemed to be a perfect world. The Marshal did what he loved the most and was as happy as man could be.

The tournament season ended as winter approached. This Christmas holiday was going to be special and we had made preparations for several days of feasting. The Marshal's winnings during the past season had made us quite comfortable and we were looking forward to a festive Yuletide with a largess of treats. We drank and sang happy songs of the season. We prepared for the religious rites the holy day would bring.

It was Christmas day when the Marshal stormed into the room late in the evening.

"By God's holy son we are in for it now. I knew it was too good to last." He threw his cloak against the wall, kicked a chair and slumped down on the bed.

"Are we at war with King Louis?" I asked trying to guess what had caused the outburst.

"Nay. Becket has just excommunicated Roger of York and all those who assisted in the young King's coronation. War with France would be an annoyance. This is a war with God and there will be no winner. I must counsel young Henry to stay clear of the quarrel," he said frustrated that he would need to give such unwelcome advice.

He had barely finished the sentence when the door to our chambers flew open and in burst the young King.

"Have you heard?" His face was white and he was breathing heavily. "What does this mean, William? What will Father do?" I retrieved the kicked over chair and pushed it to the panting young King. He sat and stared at the Marshal who was already on his feet pacing.

"We must remain calm and see what the diplomats work out, Sire. I have told you on many occasions, when the situation seems most dire, the knight with a cool head will strike the telling blow. Your Father and the Archbishop have quarreled before and eventually accommodations have been found. I hope this will be no different," he said trying to masking his own doubts which I could sense.

"Does this mean I am not King?" he asked with the pleading voice of a sixteen-year-old.

"Nay, Sire. You are a King," Sir William answered quickly. It was a reassuring reply.

As if this scene was not enough, the young Marguerite now appeared in the open doorway. She had a glum look on her face as she surveyed the room for another chair. I ran into my quarters and brought forth a bench. She winced, but was seated and said, "I warned naught but bitterness could come from such a poor arrangement."

"Is it God's judgment upon us?" Henry asked. Once again my presence in the gathering was ignored.

I frantically looked for something more suitable for such regal persons to be seated on, but there was nothing. These were the quarters of a knight and his servant, not the royal chambers. How strange it was to see a Queen seated on a plain oak bench. I backed into the corner to be as inconspicuous as I could in such a small room. Bertran appeared. He bowed and stood in the doorway. He scanned the room and said nothing. The Marshal broke the silence.

"We must all be abed. On the morrow with clear heads and more comfortable furniture we will discuss the import of the news." The benediction worked and they all exited the room. The Queen was more than happy to abandon the wooden bench and Henry was trying to show the Marshal he could be calm in a crisis. Bertran followed the pair down the hall. I bowed respectfully and closed the door behind them. I turned and saw the Marshal pacing back and forth. I picked up the discarded cloak and looked at him and asked the same question as the young King, "What does this mean, master?" The reply I received was quite different and much shorter.

"I do not know. We will see!"

It was a restless night. I tried to sleep, but the Marshal kept lighting fresh candles and staring at the flame. Eventually the candles were exhausted and he sat there in the dark room. It was like the first days we had spent together. Only this time there was not a feeling of the Marshal being in control. It was a very uncomfortable feeling. The Marshal said things can change quickly in the house of the powerful. I was getting a taste. The powerful may shape events, but they are also shaped by them. The greater the power a person has, the greater the number of events that can threaten to shape them.

Several days passed. The usual Christmas celebrating was abandoned. All in the household debated what would happen. Then word reached us with the worst news possible. We were at supper when a messenger rushed into the great hall. He was breathing heavy and the lack of court etiquette in his bold entrance made all eyes turn to him.

"The Archbishop has been murdered!" he shouted.

There was a moment of stunned silence and then Marguerite broke into tears and screamed, "He has killed my beloved Becket." She threw her goblet, full of wine to the floor and raced from the room. We all knew the "he" she was accusing of this terrible deed.

"Who did this thing?" cried the young King not wanting to believe the accusation by his wife could be true.

"It is not known, sire. Only that he was killed by knights as he went to vespers," the breathless knight said as he tried to regain his composure.

"Do you know the names of the knights?" the Marshal demanded.

"It is not clear, Sir William, but rumors have it they were the King's men." The messenger seemed to be confirming the worst fears. The goodwill which had flowered so gaily that fall was now dead, frozen by the frigid news which had arrived as suddenly as a winter storm.

I saw the young King shudder at this pronouncement. The Marshal saw it as well and said, "Hold, sire. First news is often erroneous news. We must not judge until all the facts are clear." The meal was now forgotten and all left the hall to ponder the import of the dastardly deed.

As the details became known in later days, it was clear to us, men loyal to the King had done the killing. A pall settled over the castle. The young King said he was glad none of his men were involved. He and the Queen did not speak to each other for two days. She finally realized her husband was just as outraged by his father's guilt. It seemed to mollify her anger. Just what role young Henry's father had played was still unclear. Some said King Henry was devastated by the death of Becket and claimed that his men acted without his approval, but this did little to satisfy Marguerite. As far as she was concerned, he was responsible for her beloved mentor's death. King Henry II was guilty in her eyes. Nothing would change that.

The following spring there were reports of miracles at Canterbury. Public anger at King Henry was running high. He had gone to secure lands in Ireland and was not seen in England.

The King eventually made a pilgrimage to Canterbury and did penance for the words he had uttered in anger. He said his men had misunderstood. At least, that is what he said. It was to no avail. God would find many ways to punish him for defiling Holy Mother Church. The first would be the loss of the love of his son. The young King began more and more to look to Sir William as a father. Even though he was appreciative Sir William did not want this role and would try to keep the father and son together. I believe he remembered his unhappy childhood and was affected by those memories. He did not want his young charge to suffer the same remorse such an estrangement can bring about. It was in this vein that he spoke to me one evening as we retired for the night.

"Lewellyn, the sweet fruit of the Plantagenet tree is beginning to wither. My counsel more and more falls on deaf ears. The young King's interest in the new tournament season is beginning to wane. We must try to revive it by assembling a strong team. Victories might salve the wounds created by this sordid affair of Christmas past. I pray 'twill get his mind off political matters. If it does not there is sure to be a break with the King. I have sent Bertran to see where things stand with Queen Eleanor. The evil stars are aligning and there is little I can do," he said staring into his flagon of brew. His head kept shaking from side to side after each sip and I knew his worst fears were sitting heavy on his shoulders. My skin began to prickle as I envisioned the horrors of family warfare and the headless bodies of a trusted advisor and his servant. Was there any way out of this nightmare or was it the inevitable result of being tied to the fortunes of the mighty?

Chapter 5
Tournaments and Traitors

The death of the Archbishop cast a major pall over Winchester castle. Young Henry and his wife were most distressed by the events. A cold and dreary spring rain closely mirrored the feelings of the household. My master tried his best to steer a middle course. Keeping King Henry and the young King on civil terms was becoming almost impossible. Young Henry spoke less frequently to the Marshal and when the subject of his father was broached you could see the tension mount. There was a line which even Sir William was forbidden to cross. Eventually the Marshal decided not to discuss the subject and instead chose to speak of the new tournament season. The young King's youthful nature caused him to relegate the death of the Archbishop to a corner of his mind, but the same was not true for Marguerite. I was hopeful that some of the rancor in the mesne would disappear when the tournaments commenced.

The Marshal set about assembling a team of knights. Discussions of the tournament season began to drown out all other conversations. Young Henry truly loved the tournament scene. Ever since he was first tutored, it was part of the fanciful image he had of himself. Although he was still too inexperienced to participate, he did everything he could to be part of the process.

The training regimen under the Marshal was vigorous to say the least. No one dared to complain because the Marshal trained harder than anyone. Quality horses and weapons were provided by the largess of King Henry's allowance to the young King. My master said it was given grudgingly by the high king, but the Marshal convinced him it was best to keep his son occupied under the circumstances.

The circle of young knights grew to include: Adam d'Iqueboeuf, Thomas de Coulonces, Bernard de Seville, Baldwin de Bethune and Bertran de Born.

Adam was a hot-tempered Norman knight. His left arm bore several scars from his violent encounters. He was ambitious and overly sure of his abilities. He was very skilled, but was not as formidable as Sir Bertran and the Marshal. It made him surly when anyone suggested such was the case. Thomas was the youngest of the group and had a good sense of humor. He was short with a large chest and arms. He took direction well and showed promise. Bernard was a dark, curly-hair Spaniard and was the opposite of Thomas in disposition. He spoke infrequently and loved to fight. He was powerfully built, but he made mistakes often which caused Sir William to correct him more than the others. Baldwin was gregarious and the knight with the most important lineage. He came from a rich family in Normandy. He too was a second son and because of this he had a close relationship with my master. Adam became close with Bernard and Thomas. Because of their breeding, Bertran and Baldwin became friends. The Marshal enforced discipline on all.

Each day the young King escorted his knights to training area. The mesne would practice and train for hours knowing they would have to perform against some of the finest knights money could buy. The grueling sessions were followed by discussions of strategy. The young King would listen to the Marshal describe what other teams would do during the melee. As the weeks went on, I noticed that Henry was no longer leaving the field with his arm around the Marshal as he had done so often. He would leave by himself and return to his chambers alone. One day I remarked on the change to my master.

"Master, is there something amiss with the young King?" The Marshal resting in his chair and wiping his sweaty arms nodded and looked to see if the door was closed. I continued, "I have heard rumors in the kitchen that he becomes more difficult to please."

"Someone poisons my counsel to the young King. There is a serpent in the haystack and we must find it less serious damage be done. Speak to no one, but see and hear all you can." He put his finger to his lips and said no more. I knew his charge to me was of the utmost importance.

After that I did my best to see who could be trusted and who could not. I was ever mindful of the Marshal's warning about intrigues which swirled around royal households. Marguerite was my greatest concern. Even though she had been raised in the Plantagenet household since she was eight, I considered her a risk. She was Louis VII's daughter and potentially dangerous. After all, she was the one most upset by the death of Archbishop Becket. She was beginning to weary of young Henry's infatuation of knightly pursuits. Her husband's growing desire to be with the bachelor knights led to coolness in the marriage. In spite of it all, she seemed to really like the Marshal. She appeared pleased whenever he was with her. It was hard to believe she would do anything to harm him. Yet, she was certainly clever enough to deceive a dolt like me.

As far as I could tell, Baldwin had become as good a friend as Bertran. The three youngest knights appeared as possible problems, but their influence with Henry seemed small. I was perplexed. I was convinced that whoever it was would not succeed, because with each day and each training session the young King grew more excited about the approaching tournament. With my fears receding I spoke to my master.

"My lord, perhaps, you could share who you suspect causes trouble between the young King and his father? I cannot see anyone in our company capable of such treachery."

"I do no better than you, Lewellyn. 'Tis a subtle hand at work. I pray they reveal themselves before they succeed in their plotting and create a gap between father and son I cannot bridge." The Marshal shook his head and scowled.

"You say 'they.' Are there more than one?" I said knowing who now led my list of suspects

"Perhaps. There can be many hidden motives in a royal court. Conspirators must work in secret; therefore they are unaware that others are involved, and they may not be working together for the same purpose. The threads of their plots intertwine until they trap the unwary. Power and wealth attract plotters as honey attracts bees. For now, I believe Henry is content to seek glory in the tournaments. As long as that occupies his thoughts, our serpent has little bite. So, we are off to Rouen on the morrow," he declared with happy anticipation. He was no longer thinking of intrigues.

I began preparing the chest of clothes that would be needed for our trip. I groaned because I knew another sea voyage was upon me. I was never able to abide the trip across the Channel. No matter how many times we made the journey, the result was the same, my stomach rebelled and my head ached. God made me a singer, not a sailor.

When we arrived in Normandy, we were immediately entered in the great tournament to be held at Eu. The Marshal and the young King set about preparing the team. An additional twenty knights were added to the core of five regulars. Henry spent money freely and my master made sure it was well spent.

In the larger tournaments, like Eu, the fighting lasted all day. I asked my master how this was possible as we journeyed to Eu. Surely even one like the Marshal would weary after wielding heavy weapons all day.

"Master, will you be able to fight so many for so long?" I asked in my ignorance.

"Nay, lad. Some chose to attack the inexperienced teams first and thereby pick up some easy spoils, but the best armor belong to the best knights," he said with a smile. "Lewellyn, I learned in my first tournament there is more than just attacking the nearest opponent. The experienced knights will allow the novices to fight and weaken each other while the experienced ones save themselves for the tougher struggles later in the day. Strategy is important. In my first tournament I was all about unhorsing as many as I could. I rushed about hoping to gain great honor. I thought I had been very successful until a veteran of the lists approached me after the contest and said he had broken a stirrup and would I lend him one from my large pile of spoils. At that moment I realized I had never secured any of the horses of my fallen foes. While I was riding to the next encounter they simply remounted and rode off the field. I had no spoils. He laughed until tears ran down his face. The lesson was not lost on me. Ransom money makes life for the knight errant more comfortable. Setting traps and ambushes are vital to a successful team and securing your spoils just as vital."

He went on to explain more. "The most embarrassing loss is to be knocked senseless and be carried off by your opponent to his team's staging area. It is the way to get the most points and the greatest honor, but money to buy better horses, better armor and better clothes is the real goal here at Eu. The winners tend to spend it quickly and soon find themselves in need of more. The young knights see the contest as an opportunity to showcase their skills. If they succeeded, they can attach themselves to a more powerful lord with a larger purse." Finished with my lesson he rode up to talk to Bertran.

The roads leading to Eu were busy, filled with wagons and all kinds of people. Each was desirous of a place and a purpose at the event. The best tournaments drew large crowds and where there were large crowds, the merchants were also found. Money and goods changed hands rapidly. The Marshal said a knight was expected to be generous if he was successful. It would add to the honor of being victorious. It was a part of chivalrous behavior. The merchants knew this and were always on hand to relieve a champion of his coins in exchange for gifts the champion was expected to distribute after the contest.

We arrived in Eu and I marveled at the seemingly endless clusters of brightly colored tents surrounding the site. From the hill above the town it looked as if nature had produced the most marvelous colored mushrooms sprouting from the sides of the brown and green hills. Our tent had already been erected and banners with heraldry declaring to all who resided within were being placed at the entrance. There was activity everywhere you looked. Common spectators watched from behind fences and the nobles watched from boxes on raised platforms. Knights and squires busied themselves checking horses, armor and weapons. Greetings and jibs filled the air with good-natured banter. It was hard to think that these men would soon be attempting to knock each other senseless. The knights assembled by the Marshal and the young King were not considered to pose a serious threat to the more experienced French knights.

"Master, I have heard men speak poorly of our chances. Are you considered not the equal of any assembled? You have won so many." I was upset that so little respect was given to my hero.

"Lewellyn, here you will see the finest warriors. Great honor can be won by a champion. I am no stranger to the likes of these, but they are not convinced as to the prowess of our company of new knights. 'Tis somewhat of an advantage. 'Twill be their scheme to take me out first. I can use this thinking to set a trap. If my fellows perform well and according to my instructions, there will be some surprises. We will do nothing to discourage them from believing we are buffoons, not worthy of being on the field." He grinned confidently.

The rest of the day was spent in practice and discussion of the strategy. The young King looked on, wishing he could participate, but that would not happen for two more years. He had to be content with the role of patron. To that end he spent lavishly. His free spending continued to be a source of friction with his parsimonious father, King Henry.

The day of the event dawned with servants scurrying about. It reaffirmed to me the generous nature of my own master. Many were cursed or struck when they failed to please demanding nobles. I saw Sir Bertran enter the tent and in the excitement of the day I forgot myself and called, "Bertran, luck to you, my friend." In that same moment I knew I had made a serious mistake when I saw Adam shoot an angry look at me.

"Sirrah! Know your place!" He began to advance toward me with his heavy gage grasped firmly in his right hand. Those present knew his intent. I was of the serving class and should act accordingly. A beating was called for. I cowered as he raised his arm, but when he attempted to bring it down he found it restrained by the hand of Bertran de Born.

"Hold, my friend. It would not do to start the day thrashing the servant of our champion. Save your strength for the contest. I will see to the punishment of the sirrah," Bertran said chuckling.

"Agh, I suspect Sir William does not want his kept boy scarred," Adam sneered.

"Be careful, my friend. Do you wish to make such an accusation to Sir William?" Bertran's tone changed from one of light banter to a more threatening one. Of course none dared speak to the Marshal about their feelings. Adam thought for a moment, shrugged and turned toward the opening and left grumbling. Bertran smiled and gave me a knowing nod. It was a mistake I would not repeat.

Some five hundred participants had assembled for the contest. Our knights were prepared with new armor and excellent horses. This fact had not escaped the notice of the more experienced teams. The Flemish team from the Count of Thibaut was given the best chance of victory. They were followed by the Count of Clermont's contingent. As the squires prepared them for battle, I heard good-natured banter from the knights nearby. They called out to the Marshal as they rode by, "Sir William, you have been good to us. You offer up such fine weaponry and good steeds. We thank you for making our day a profitable one. We shall be generous when we sell it back to you tonight. Of course it will have to be discounted because of the battered condition." This was followed by a great deal of laughter. The Marshal shrugged and smiled. Baldwin turned and made a derisive gesture at the passing company. This brought on a series of mock cheers from the Flemish knights. Their champion, one Roger of Gaugi, looked at Baldwin and said, "I shall look for you. Mark this shield well; 'twill be the last object you see before you kiss mother earth."

This last comment brought an instant reaction from the Marshal. He said nothing but shot an angry look at the boastful knight. Baldwin had become a good friend of my master. The company rode on to the cheering of the multitude gathered to witness the event. It was clear most of those assembled were convinced Roger's threat was no idle boast.

Baldwin turned and addressed the Marshal, "That strutting peacock. I shall seek his shield and then we will see who kisses mother earth."

"A care, my young friend," the Marshal said in a warning tone. "He is a knight well disposed to back such a boast. The Count of Thibaut pays him well for a reason. Follow my instructions or we will be buying your weapons back at the end of the day." Baldwin grumbled under his breath and mounted his charger. Bertran and Adam were already in the saddle. Our company assembled and followed the path of the confident Flemish team toward the meadow.

Banners marked the staging areas for each group of knights, and the squires stood behind a barricade where each member could go to rest or make a minor repair of equipment. Each team had twenty warriors. They rode into previously chosen positions. The large meadow had several stands of trees and a farm house. High on a hill, overlooking the scene, was a viewing stand where the young King was seated along with the other wealthy sponsors. He was much younger than the others, but his title gave him a privileged position from which he observed the band of knights purchased with his father's money. It was easy for him to spot the green and yellow shield carried by his champion. He showed no signs of nervousness as he joked and wagered small sums with the nobles surrounding him.

I, on the other hand, was terrified. What if the Marshal was killed? It did happen to knights at these gatherings. I would be back in the scullery. Worse than that, what if the Marshal's team was disgraced as the Flemish knights had suggested? Henry would be humiliated and we would be sent packing without as much as a crust of stale bread for compensation. Hundreds of equally grim visions raced through my mind, and all ended with me begging in the streets of some god-forsaken town. My hands were shaking as the crowded hillsides began to grow increasingly quiet. Conversations ended, and all eyes strained to see the heraldry designating their favorites. It was almost silent when a horn split the air with a shrill note and announced the commencing of the combat. Several groups began advancing toward each other. Bright banners stirred by a breeze seemed to join the crowds in saluting the moment. The struggle was about to begin.

Several groups charged forward to engage other clusters of knights. The collision sounded like thunder during a bad summer storm. Lances shattered, shields buckled and several unlucky riders were unhorsed in the first wave of attacks. A few knights dazed from the shock of hitting the ground staggered toward their riderless mounts. A number of the novice knights, judging from the poor quality of their armor, who had succeeded in the initial charge acknowledged the cheers of the crowd by raising their shields. The more experienced ones raced in and seized the reins of the horses of the fallen knights. They galloped to their barricades and deposited the captured animals. The fallen, now horseless, fought a futile action to avoid capture, but in the end they were forced to yield to their attackers.

The Marshal had ordered his men not to participate in the initial attack but Adam, anxious to share in the spoils, raced into the melee. Almost immediately the Flemish troop charged the melee. Adam was unaware of his peril. I saw the shield of Roger of Gaugi leading the charge. He went straight for Adam, who remained unaware of the danger. Adam only had time to turn his head slightly when Roger's lance smashed into his side. He was hurled violently to the turf. Had the lance not been blunted for the tournament, he would have been killed. He did suffer a bruised rib for his acting in defiance of the Marshal's orders. One of Roger's companions marched Adam to the Flemish barricade. Roger scanned the field.

The Marshal shouted and the team was off. They made straight for the melee with lances in the attack position. Roger was too wise in the ways of tournaments. He would not be caught in the same manner as Adam. He wheeled his horse and ordered his men to disengage immediately. When the Marshal and his men struck, Roger's men were already regrouping at some distance from the fray.

The noise coming from the melee could be heard all around the meadow. The tightly bunched knights were fighting with hand weapons. Battle cries were screamed. It seemed as if a real war had broken out rather than a mock battle. Swords struck shields as knights battled each other at close quarters. I saw two knights fall from the heavy blows of the Marshal's broadsword. No one could penetrate the raining blows his sword arm delivered. One of the unhorsed knights attempted to run toward the safety of his barricade when the Marshal did a most amazing thing. He galloped after the fleeing foe. With his free hand, the Marshal reached under the girdle of the hauberk and lifted the running knight as if he were grabbing a mere bundle of sticks. In the same motion he placed the captured knight across the neck of his horse, thumped the flailing captive with the pommel of his sword and galloped toward the barricade. The spectators went wild. Hoots and jeers were hurled at the helpless captive as he was delivered to the English standard. The hapless knight's tournament was abruptly ended in a most embarrassing manner.

"Renaud's treachery will not be repeated this day," my master exclaimed, and returned to the contest.

I learned this most humiliating capture was to settle a grudge from a previous tournament. Renaud had been defeated by the Marshal only to sneak back onto the field to help his losing team. There would be no repeat of his treachery today. I stood shaking my head in disbelief at what I had just seen. Lifting a fully armored man with one arm and swinging him onto his horse required more strength than I could imagine. I knew my master was very powerful, but this was more than I expected. The crowd knew what they had seen was special, because they turned to each other and started to talk about this knight with the green and yellow standard.

The Marshal stopped momentarily and called for something to drink as he surveyed the field. I raced over with some beer. He gulped it down and belched. He spurred his steed, and rejoined the fighting. I saw him motion to his cohorts. They separated from the main group, and began advancing toward the little farmhouse where the Flemish knights were gathering. Most of the inexperienced knights had been swept from the field. Now, the serious combat began. It would be the best against the best. When the English reached the farmhouse Roger had his men fight briefly, then withdrew. The odds were not yet to their liking. A group of French knights from Champagne attempted to take advantage of the English who were distracted by the retreat of the Flemish team. It was a mistake. One of their company suffered a broken arm from the Marshal's mace. The attacking and counterattacking, capture and rescue continued for several hours. The remaining members of each team took more frequent rests behind the barricades as the afternoon wore on.

It was late in the afternoon when the event everyone was waiting for happened. Baldwin and several of the English knights were trapped by the remaining contingent of the Count of Thibaut's team. Roger had timed their attack to coincide with the Marshal's rest trip to the barricade. The Marshal saw the ambush and rode to the rescue of Baldwin who was going down under the furious attack of Roger of Gaugi. Just as he had promised, Roger was besting the young knight. Baldwin, weakened from a long day of fighting, was unhorsed. Four other knights of Roger's group watched the slope for what they were clearly expecting. They ignored Roger and Baldwin and prepared to meet the Marshal.

He exploded into the group of four—a sword in one hand and a mace in the other. He ducked under the flashing sword stroke of one of the sentinels and simultaneously hit him in the helmet with a devastating blow from the mace, knocking the visor off and leaving him stunned and bloody. The other three were quick to surround the Marshal and his horse.

Roger disengaged from the fallen Baldwin unconcerned with the valuable horse and armor he was abandoning. He urged his mount to close on the Marshal. It was a trap. Roger knew the Marshal would react in this manner. He had used Baldwin as bait. Defeating Baldwin would not bring a champion of Roger's stature any glory, but defeating the Marshal, who had never been beaten, was very different. Realizing what was transpiring, the eyes of all the spectators were on this group. In an instant the Marshal must have realized it was a trap and reacted. He reared his horse and charged out of the encirclement between two of the knights before Roger could join the fray. Discipline broke down. The two who had allowed the escape went charging after my master. Seconds later he wheeled his horse and knocked the first knight off his horse with a single stroke of his massive sword. The second faired no better, and was knocked senseless before Roger could reach his comrade. It was now Roger and the Marshal in single combat. Baldwin had regained his senses and remounted. He, Bertran and Bernard were engaging the last of the Flemish knights.

Champion against champion. A throaty shout of approval came from the crowd. It was a magnificent sight as the two titans traded strokes. The Flemish captain put up a valiant struggle. Blow after blow were launched and defended. Finally the power and stamina of the knight in green and yellow prevailed. Knowing it was over; Roger broke off the battle and retreated to the safety of the barricade, leaving the Marshal as the master of the field. The assembled crowd screamed their approval for the bravery and skill of the victor.

Evening was now descending on the meadow and the tournament was declared over by the same single note of the herald's horn. The spoils were counted and a winner was declared. Capturing seven knights and ten horses, the Marshal was declared the winner, to the cheering of the crowd. He acknowledged the cheers by trotting his great chestnut charger along the fences and raising a single hand in salute. The crowds melted away seeking refreshment in the pubs of the town. Uninjured knights returned to their tents on the hillside. The wounded were attended by local healers. There were no fatalities.

It was time to settle up and pay for captured horses and arms. The young King was delighted with the day's events. Most of the spoils would go to him. It was doubtful he would profit from the day because of the expense, but such was not his purpose. It was about honor, and he was going to have a full share, just as if he had been on the field. He joined his tired knights.

"Marshal, the dispatching of Renaud was marvelous," he chortled.

"I thank you, sire."

"Count Thibaut was seated near me. His arrogant attitude faded as the day wore on. He ceased calling me the boy king and showed respect when Roger was defeated. We are pleased. Take these coins and any arms you desire." He tossed a leather bag to the Marshal. "What is next?"

"The first thing is to buy back Adam's possessions." He shot an angry look at the crestfallen knight sitting in the corner of the tent. "Disobey my instructions again, you will be looking to your own devices. Here, buy them back." He tossed the appropriate number of coins at the red-faced knight. It was clear neither was happy.

The young King came to the fallen knight's aid. "Be not so harsh with him. Surely his error will be corrected in the future. We have good regard for this knight. Let us rejoice in our victory." His rebuke of the Marshal stirred my suspicions as to who bore watching in the future.

The Marshal stared for a moment then turned to see Roger of Gaugi entering the tent. It caused a needed change of attention. I could see Baldwin tense up as the Flemish champion approached the Marshal. Roger was smiling. He extended his hand.

"You are all they said, mon ami. Our next meeting, well, I shall entertain with reluctance. The Count has two years more of my services, but when it expires I should like to join you. We could profit from such an arrangement. And you, my young friend," he looked at Baldwin, "I am sorry I used you. You have courage. I paid for my mistake. Your captain is more than I expected. I salute you all." He dropped a bag of coins on the floor and exited.

Baldwin was smiling. The young King was slapping the Marshal on the back. He was again basking in the glory around his champion. The Marshal picked up the purse and shared it with his comrades. Even I received a coin. His generosity did not stop there. He told the squires to take some of the poorer pieces of armor and find the owners.

"Return them without cost. 'Tis doubtful the owners of these can pay anything. I remember how it was to be a young man without means," he said as a grin creased his face.

It was always like that in every tournament he entered. Those who could afford it would pay. Those who could not, were given back their means of living at any cost. The Marshal and the young King walked from tent to tent conversing and recounting the day's events well into the night. Bertran and I were given the task of recording the winnings. Later Bertran joined Henry and the Marshal in drinking and sharing stories with the others, still gathered around the meadow. Two days later we set out for Epernon the site of the next tournament.

Tournament followed tournament: Epernon, St. Brice, Gournai and Anet. The Marshal was becoming a crowd favorite and chants were shouted when he took the field. The green and yellow shield with the red lion was loved and feared. He was respected by his peers for his skill but also his generosity. Other sponsors tried to lure the Marshal to their service with promises of great wealth, but his loyalty to Henry was unwavering. Henry's affection for his champion was also the envy of his friends. In truth, a little jealousy was beginning to develop between some of Henry's younger friends and the Marshal. Henry frequently showed his appreciation to his mentor by offering gifts after each victory.

So it went through the summer months and then into the fall season. Family quarrels were almost forgotten, except when Henry would ask his father for more funds. Then a seemingly insignificant event changed life for everyone. Word reached us Prince Geoffrey would marry the Countess of Brittany.

The Marshal asked Bertran to come to our quarters to discuss the news. It was late in the evening when our friend walked through the doorway and tossed his cape to me.

"I know what you are going to say, my friend. How is it that Geoffrey weds before Richard?" Bertran said acting as a soothsayer.

"Correct. All are happy for Geoffrey, but this comes as a troubling surprise. Alais, Richard's intended, is of age and yet King Henry has delayed setting a wedding date. I need you to seek out some of your friends in the Loire and find out what you can," the Marshal ordered.

"As you wish. I should be back in a fortnight."

It was very early in the morning as he rode away. Few were awake to see the departure save the Marshal and me. I asked the Marshal, "Why are you so troubled, master? Should we not be happy that another of the King's sons marries?"

"For Geoffrey to marry before his older brother is highly unusual. Not only that, but Geoffrey is not the Queen's favorite, and granting him a rich bride before her darling Richard will not set well with her. There is trouble brewing. I must know why. King Louis of France asked all who were near why his daughter, Alais, was still in England under Henry II's care and not wed to his second son as promised," he said surprising me with his knowledge of events in many different places. Once again more was happening than I could understand.

Sir Bertran returned in a fortnight as he promised. He walked into the Marshal's room and plopped into a chair. He looked at the Marshal with a worried look. He signaled for the door to be closed. After checking the empty hall I closed the door and nodded that we were alone.

"My friend, there is much to tell. I went to Queen Eleanor under the guise of discussing what role the young King and his wife were to play in the upcoming nuptials. The Queen is not happy. She does not like Constance of Brittany—Geoffrey's bride to be. In spite of that, she is willing to give her blessing since it would give one of her sons a powerful and rich fiefdom. However, the situation with Princess Alais is becoming an embarrassing scandal. Informants told the Queen her husband's roving eye has settled on his future daughter-in-law and he is now engaged in an illicit affair with Alais. Richard is being cuckold by his own father. All of this is rumor, but Henry's actions seemed to give it weight." His report complete his eyebrows raised as he look to the Marshal for some reaction. The Marshal swore.

"Damn! This will make keeping peace in the family impossible."

"So it shall, my friend. So it shall." Bertran turned up his palms and shook his head in frustration. He tossed his blue velvet cape over his shoulder and rose to leave. The Marshal was very concerned. He looked at me with a very worried look as Bertran left.

I shall not bore you with the details of the wedding, only that it came off without a major quarrel. As with most Plantagenet events, it was splendid. King Henry did not remain for long and soon all the parties went their separate ways. Richard and Eleanor went back to Poitiers. Henry II was off to many of the places under his dominion. The young King went back to training for knighthood with the Marshal in Rouen and Geoffrey was off to Brittany with Constance. All promised to get together as soon as events allowed. Now, when I look back at this time, I laugh at the professed good will of the Plantagenet clan. Intrigues, secret messages and spies were the real actions of the members of the royal family. Most of this happened without the knowledge of Sir William or me. It was only after it was too late we learned who was behind much of the plotting.

The Marshal and I followed the young King and his wife back to Normandy. The wagons and riders stretched into a long line on the road. In the front of the procession was Sir Adam, the young King and several of our knights. They were followed by Queen Marguerite's wagon and several wagons of her ladies and their baggage. In the rear of the train were the Marshal, myself, and a wagon of valuables. Behind that was Sir Bertran, Sir Baldwin and the rest of the men-at-arms. As we traveled along to the steady clip clop of our horses, I asked about the wedding.

"Perhaps Sir Bertran's information was wrong. All seemed to go well at the wedding. The Queen and King Henry did not quarrel," I said naively.

"I fear the Queen is part of our problem, Lewellyn. Her displeasure with her husband grows each day and a woman of her ability will not stay silent for long. In fact, 'twould be better if she were more open about her desires for her sons. The way things are now, all is behind closed doors and that is not good for us. She sends messages to the young King and I cannot for the life of me find from whence they come, and what is being suggested. It is equally certain her ex-husband, the King of France, is trying to ingratiate himself with the sons. He is also communicating with them through someone unknown to me. King Henry had best watch his flank. On the battlefield I am good at spotting an ambush, but not so adept in spotting them at court. Have you seen or heard anything?" he asked looking around to see if any riders were close enough to hear.

"Nay, my lord. I am suspicious of Queen Marguerite. After all she is the daughter of King Louis. I know she does not like King Henry very much," I said withholding my feelings about Sir Adam, assuming it was just a personal dislike.

The Marshal laughed. "We make poor spies, my friend. 'Tis best we learn more lest there be nasty surprises in the months ahead. The only people I trust with surety are you, Baldwin and Bertran. I have asked each to be on the lookout, but their information is not any better than ours. Bertran even went to Paris for me but was unable to discover anything useful. The young King is still very loyal to me, but I can see his affection for his father grows weaker every day. I have kept his ambition focused on knighthood and the tournaments, but 'tis beginning to wane. It is not helpful to have his father carping about the cost. King Henry does not realize his money well spent. When you have made your son a king with no real power you must keep him occupied with other pursuits. If not, there will be those who suggest he pursue the father's throne and take the power being denied. I have tried to convince the King, but he will not believe his favorite son could be turned against him," he said as he reached down and patted his horse's neck.

"You have passed messages with the King?" Again I was surprised.

"Yes, my friend. I have ways of quietly being heard."

"I am a dunce. There is much going on I have not seen."

"'Tis why you are such a good friend. You are without guile. There is far more than you can imagine. Some things, I cannot share with you. I wish it were so, but it could cost you your life and I am not willing to risk it." This last statement added a new mystery. Cost me my life! I was unable to deal with this new revelation so I simply said, "I trust your judgment, my lord."

"I know. I shall do my best to keep us both with skin on our bones," he said with a deep breath. He spurred his horse and rode up to the wagon carrying Queen Marguerite, now trailed by the young King, to converse with them. I dropped back to talk with Bertran and Baldwin. So much was happening that I could not understand so I was left to trusting my master. I was confident he would find a way. Trust! No wonder he placed such great store in this virtue.

A month passed and we prepared Rouen for the Christmas season. The Marshal would remain in Rouen and the young King would journey to Poitiers to spend the holiday with his mother and brother. The Marshal suggested Bertran and Baldwin accompany them for protection. I knew the real reason was to spy out Queen Eleanor's world of Aquitaine and the problems swirling around the great lady.

The arrangements were made and the group departed. I finally had time to practice my playing and my writing. Since Bertran had taught me how to write, I was keeping a record of life with my master. I would also write any correspondence he had and read anything that he received. Since the name Lewellyn did not seem imposing enough, I took to signing official correspondence with the name Wigain. He asked me to write to his brother, Anselm in England. He hoped Anselm would join him for the upcoming tournament season.

The holiday season passed uneventfully. The young King and his entourage returned. I was sent to quietly request Bertran and Baldwin meet my master in his quarters. They arrived separately, looking around as they entered our rooms. Light from the window slit flashed off Bertran's bright red tunic and danced along the far wall.

"Have you observed any change?" They nodded their assent. Bertran informed him the Queen was very unhappy with her husband and for good reason.

"The rumors about his liaison with Alais are certainly true. The people of Aquitaine, normally unhappy with the King, are ready to rebel because of this latest insult to our beloved Queen Eleanor," he said disappointedly.

"You are sure this be true?" the Marshal asked. His eye burned with anger as he stared at Bertran.

"Yea, my friend. 'Tis most certain there will be a break with King Henry. Where will we stand?" Bertran asked as he looked intently at Sir William.

"I am pledged to both, but my first loyalty by the code is young Henry. I fear any attempt to challenge his father will end badly, but I have no choice," he said clearly distressed by the news he was absorbing.

"What about the King of France?" Baldwin interjected. "Could we ally with him?"

"Perhaps, but the fool would run at the first sign of a tough struggle. He is not a worthy ally. Pray be careful of what you say. You suggest treason. We have not been asked to choose sides, yet. I say the young King is not ready to play such a dangerous game," the Marshal said and began to pace around the room. "I must continue to try and keep this illness from spreading."

"That may be a forlorn task. We shall help in any way we can. Baldwin and I agree, now 'tis not the time for a cub to take on the lion," Bertran concluded.

"No more talk of plots! We begin preparations for the spring tournament season and trust to providence," the Marshal said hopefully and dismissed the gathering.

I knew it would be a difficult time for the Marshal. He did not like to split his loyalty. One of his most cherished principles was loyalty. The discussion which just transpired had to be very troubling. If any in the room wanted to do the others harm, the talk just held was a death sentence. Where was all this going? I could do nothing except stare glumly at the gray stone walls of our quarters and hope they would not be exchanged for the blackness of a dungeon or a more permanent blackness from a headsman's ax.

As spring approached two things happened giving me some hope. First, the young King held a second coronation administered by the new Archbishop of Canterbury. Marguerite was crowned with him. Second, the tournament season had begun. The young King was totally engrossed in another successful year in the French tournaments. The Marshal had assembled a powerful team and the young King was sure this would be an even better year. It was all of that and more.

The Marshal continued to win every tournament he entered. Teams tried every trick to defeat him. They tried traps sending four or five knights after him. They tried to get him early in the contest, late in the contest, or somewhere in between, but each time the result was the same. At Eu, Epernon, Lagny, Gournai, St. Brice, Anet, Pleurs, Maintenon, Sorel, and Joigni the name "Guillaume le Marechal" became the chant of the French crowds. Eventually, it was shortened to "Le Marechal, Le Marechal" I recorded each event and the names of the knights bested by my master. As his fame spread, his influence with young Henry increased. Henry was content to bask in the glory his champion garnered. It kept the peace in the Plantagenet clan all through the summer and fall of 1172.

It was with some trepidation I regarded the end of the season and the holiday rest period. Christmas had always been a joyful time for me, but lately it ushered in the season of intrigue, unseen meetings, secret messages and the feeling you could not trust anyone. I realized why the Marshal had need for extra eyes and ears. People were unable to talk about how they really felt or what they were thinking. Ideas withered, and plans were never made. Even the usual scullery gossip ceased. None knew who might inform for a reward: so better to say nothing. Suspicion poisons the water hole of friendship, and all go thirsty.

The young King announced he would journey to Limoges for the Christmas season. The site had been selected to make accommodation for a special friend. The young King insisted the Marshal join the festivities this year. A friend of the Marshal's, Raimund of Toulouse, was going to be an honored guest and King Henry was also joining them. The Marshal sensed things were coming to a boil between the father and his sons. Duke Geoffrey had spent much of the fall complaining and Duke Richard was silent. Worst of all, young Henry was constantly arguing with his father over money matters. He was not as willing to hear the Marshal's counsel. When the subject of King Henry came up, the young King did not want to discuss it. He spent more time with Adam and Bernard. Thomas de Coulonces was sent on several trips to Paris. Each time he returned, he was silent on why he went. We knew the hand of King Louis was somehow involved in stirring the boiling pot of Plantagenet discontent.

The Marshal took things in stride, but knew he had lost control of events in the household. He tried to learn what was happening by talking to Queen Marguerite. They would often be seen walking after the evening meal in the courtyard. I asked if there was any information coming from these walks.

"Only the obvious. She is being ignored and is lonely," he said pensively.

I told him of the coming and goings of Sir Thomas. "He goes at the young King's behest and speaks little of his purpose. Even the serving girl he is involved with is finding her bed empty. She is learning of the folly of liaison with those above your station. She is bitter and would tell me anything to revenge herself, but she knows nothing," I said to show the lengths I was willing to go to be of assistance. The Marshal thanked me for this attempt and concluded the conversation with a hopeful thought.

"To be sure a plot is being hatched with the French King's help. At least we know who is talking to King Louis. I hope Raimund will be able to shed some light on things. He is very active in the French court and is rumored to have the best spy system in Paris. We must wait for him to join us and perhaps give us sorely needed information. "

The trip to Limoges was very quiet. All in the company were occupied with their own thoughts. When we arrived, the greeting was warm. Wreaths and greens were in abundance in the great hall. All wore their finest garments to match the decorations that festooned the halls and rooms of the castle. Queen Eleanor had done much to see that the holidays were spent in the style she was accustomed to. She wanted to impress Raimund. Their association went all the way back to the abortive Crusade where Raimund and a young Queen Eleanor, then married to King Louis, almost perished.

The Queen and her sons spent considerable time together. For the first time the Marshal did not attend their sessions. The Queen took pains to be sure she was never seen with the Marshal. It was not a good sign.

Raimund of Toulouse came through the main gate slightly past noon. King Henry had not yet arrived. Raimund was showing his advanced years. Gray hair which turned white around the temples framed a face, though wrinkled, still spoke of what must have been a very handsome man. The Queen and her party gave him a warm welcome. His provincial accent was thick and pronounced. His impeccable manners showed this was a man comfortable in the courts of the powerful. He was shown his quarters and informed of a banquet that night in his honor.

The evening meal was filled with stories of days gone by and Crusading. Musicians played softly in the background. Sir Bertran sang a song that chronicled the Crusader's exploits in the Holy land. I am sure the heroic tales of the Queen were slightly exaggerated to flatter her Majesty. I learned how Queen Eleanor had almost died and what a failure the entire venture had been. It contributed to the split between the youthful Eleanor and Louis. The split never healed, and eventually led to divorce. Now, life with King Henry was not much better, and she made it plain to Raimund.

"My Lord Raimund, many are the trials I now endure with my husband." He listened to a string of complaints about the King's philandering and his treatment of her sons. I stood next to the wall behind the guests at the banquet table in my usual position to serve the Marshal's needs. I could hear even softly spoken words, but I could not see their faces. I had learned this often revealed more than the words.

Raimund was uncomfortable with the direction of the conversation. It was getting dangerously close to treason. He sought to change the topic.

"I remembered how happy you were as young girl. Your uncle's household was always filled with such merriment," he said cheerily and held his goblet aloft to ask for more wine.

"Always the diplomat," she replied in a sardonic tone. The queen replied realizing his true intent. As they continued he counseled patience. She smiled and said, "'Twill be my sons' task to make life better." To this Raimund said nothing.

The Marshal was an interested spectator, but did not speak. Much of his time was spent talking to the young King. He was seated several persons away from the two principals and never said a word to Queen Eleanor. She never acknowledged his presence. From their actions at the banquet, one would not believe how close they had been during the years at Luisgnan castle. The wine flowed freely through the night. It ended when the topics of conversation waned. The Queen rose and the entire hall emptied after she left smiling and nodding to her guests. The servants were left to scavenge and remove the unfinished food.

Two days later, King Henry arrived. The mood changed immediately. It was though the castle had been invaded and the inhabitants were fearful of the new lord. The young King was just turning nineteen. Richard was seventeen and Geoffrey was sixteen. Queen Eleanor was now fifty-one. The King was a robust forty. My mind cast back to the comment by the Marshal that the high king would not be ready to give real power to any of his sons for years. During the evening meal the table was reshaped into a large U to accommodate the additional guests. My master was seated on the left side extension. It gave me a chance to observe the head table from my position against the wall. I no longer could hear the words passing between the Royal couple unless they were in a raised voice. King Henry requested Raimund sit next to him. The Queen moved several places to accommodate the new arrangement. During the evening, I saw Raimund whisper something to the King. For just a moment, King Henry's face went blank. He recovered quickly. The songs and the food continued to be devoured. King Henry pounded the table with his goblet as he prepared to speak.

"We acknowledge the fine hospitality of my Queen. 'Twould be loathsome indeed were we not to respond in kind. Therefore it be our command that all accompany us to Chinon in the morn. There the feasting and good cheer will continue." King Henry rose and departed with his retainers.

The announcement stunned all present. It could not be debated. When the king speaks, all must obey. Glances raced from person to person. It was not a popular idea, but no one objected. To do so would be treason. The evening ended with long faces and unspoken displeasure. The great hall emptied. I saw Raimund tug at the sleeve of the Marshal. They walked down the hallway toward the Marshal's quarters.

When I entered the two men were seated. Raimund looked up at me and stopped what he was saying. "Who is this sirrah?" he demanded.

"Worry not, he is my personal servant. He is privy to many secrets. I trust him with my life," the Marshal said to put Raimund at his ease. "Lewellyn, fetch some beer."

"I will trust your word, but the years at court have taught me too many ears can lead to trouble." He looked at me with suspicion as I went to get the pitcher sitting on the table. He continued. "I told the King his family could not be trusted. He suspects as much and wants to test them. He loves the young King and does not want to believe he is plotting against him. What do you know?"

"Through Lewellyn here I know Sir Thomas de Coulonces is in contact with King Louis. We hoped you could shed some light on what is happening in the French court." The statement seemed to put our guest at ease as to my trustworthiness.

"It is much bigger than just the French court. Your own English nobility feel Henry is becoming too powerful. It threatens their ability to dominate their fiefdoms. Taxes for Henry's constant warfare and expansion are heavy. Louis sees the opportunity to regain some of the provinces he has lost to Henry over the years. He is encouraging the son to seize more power and thereby weaken his old nemesis. I think the sons plan to kidnap him and force him to abdicate," Raimund said revealing his conclusion.

The Marshal shook his head. "The King is surrounded by those loyal to Eleanor. It explains the sudden move to the friendly walls of Chinon!"

"Precisely. Henry will see who follows tomorrow. I told him you have tried to keep the young King loyal, but your influence to do so is weakening. What will you do?"

The Marshal took a deep swallow of beer. "You know I must support the son as a member of the household. The code leaves me no choice."

"I knew 'twould be your answer. You would not break your oath if a hot poker was shoved up your ass. I admire you, my friend, but you will be on the losing side," he said in a voice that expressed his admiration and disappointment.

"I know. The boy cannot win, but he is like his father and ambition wins all arguments. I accept my fate. King Henry knows I can do nothing else." It was said with finality.

"He loves the boy. He will be spared and forgiven. I cannot say the same for you. Out of friendship I will say nothing of this talk. I must go." He rose and left the room. The Marshal just sat staring at the wall and sipping his beer.

One hour later the young King entered and issued this order, "William, we leave tonight for Poitiers, not Chinon. Richard will join us and Geoffrey will leave for Brittany. Mother travels to Chinon with father so as not to arouse suspicion. Then she will quietly leave in the night. I will explain on the morrow. Make haste and tell anyone who asks we start for Chinon tonight." The door was closed quietly as he left.

The Marshal turned to me and said, "It begins. Make ready to leave, Lewellyn." A cold shiver went up my back. I was now involved in treason to a King. All for a cause the Marshal knew was not winnable.

At midnight, by the light of a full moon, we quietly rode out of the castle with the young King. The Queen made excuses the following morning when we were found to be missing. She said she had sent us to Poitiers to get some extra clothes for the unexpected trip. King Henry continued on to Alencon. He learned the truth when the Queen disappeared during the night. Henry II's sons were in open revolt.

This time, Queen Eleanor was not quick enough and was captured by her husband. She was imprisoned in England under the watchful eye of Ranulf of Glanville, the King's loyal servant. There she remained, under house arrest, for the next sixteen years. King Henry made sure she would not plot against him again. To be sure, Ranulf's prison was a pleasant one, but she could no longer play a role in the affairs of her eldest son. Age eventually robbed her of her beauty, but never her wits. She would again be a force, but not for a very long time. The tide of fortune had reversed again for the Marshal. War with King Henry was on and it was a war we knew we would lose!

Chapter 6
War and Worry

After several days we approached Poitiers. The morning sun was warming us as the young King rode his black charger next to the Marshal attempting to explain the action against his father. He complained his father had denied him any real power to make decisions. He said King Henry's miserly ways made him no more than a street beggar when it came to funds for his daily activities. He talked about the incident with Becket. He explained the treatment of his mother. The Marshal listened dutifully and said nothing.

He continued, "Father beds my brother's future wife. He has disgraced the entire family. 'Tis whispered laughingly in the taverns! Mother has endured the shame long enough and shame upon him who allows such travails to go unchallenged. You have counseled me to restrain my feelings, but this be more than Job could bear. Some doubt your loyalty, but Mother assures me you are true. It is so?" A look of doubt was revealed in the young King's eyes.

"Sire, your mother is correct. My oaths of loyalty accrue to you and your father. Yours takes precedence because I am of your household. I advised you as I did for 'tis my belief we cannot win such a conflict. My sword is yours to command and will follow you to the death if necessary. I wish I could promise victory, but you need clearness on the issue. There are too many who will speak that you wish to hear. It be swears and lies, false in their meaning. Their words will be like the morning tide which swells only to retreat and disappear by the noontime ebb. I offer no such delusions." The Marshal looked straight ahead as they rode together.

"We have not been idle. We have the pledge of King Louis of France and my brothers, Geoffrey and Richard. We have support from William "the Lion," the King of the Scots. Mother rallies additional help." He spoke with pride of his intrigues as though it would all be a surprise to his champion. "We have some of the best-trained knights in our employ. You of all people know, you trained them and led them to victories in the tournaments." He smiled with the confidence of a novice warrior whose perspective was limited by his lack of experience. He was about to receive his first lesson in the reality of war.

The Marshal faced straight ahead as he rode next to the optimistic youth. The steady rhythm of the horses' hoofs striking the hard packed road seemed to blend in time with the Marshal's words. "Sire, King Louis is not interested in your success. His ends are better served by your failure after weakening King Henry. He gains nothing by trading the son for the father. He gains a great kingdom if you destroy each other. Beware of people with his kind of motive," he said raising his eyebrows and turning his head to see the reaction his bluntness produced.

"But I am his son-in-law and have claim on his kingdom along with my father's," the young King protested weakly.

"All changed with the birth of Philip. You are a rival not an ally. He will promise much and deliver little. Sadly the Queen succeeded not in her escape. Your father bids her to England, a prisoner, where she will be of little help to us. Your brothers, as you, lack needed funds to engage in a protracted struggle. King Henry has made sure money clings only to his hands, as you yourself so aptly pointed out." The Marshal's voice was calm as he delivered this list of failures to his young charge.

The color had drained from the young King's face when his mother's capture had been mentioned. It changed suddenly. It was bright red as he screamed, "You have given up!"

The Marshal's head jerked around to face the angry youth. His calm, matter-of-fact attitude changed quickly and he shouted back, "Never! A campaign must be built on truth. Imagined advantages disappear like the morning fog in the first clash of battle. We must look to help that is real or it will be a disaster from the start. Have the tournaments taught you nothing of strategy? Have you forgotten when young Adam acted out of emotion and what happened as a result of his rash action? If we are to have any chance then we must plan with clear heads and an eye to our back. Your father is a formidable foe. His planning is meticulous; his resolve is firm and his execution merciless. If you trust me not, dismiss me now." His point made the Marshal's face went blank as his mind returned to grappling with the many problems that needed to be solved if they were to have the slightest of chances.

"You are right, William," the chastened boy king replied, his chin on his chest and once again respecting his mentor's advice in subdued tones. "How was Mother captured?" he asked trying to show the same coolness the Marshal displayed.

"I have little information. The word just arrived," the Marshal replied.

"Can she be rescued?" asked the young King pleadingly.

"Nay. It would be my first action if it had even a slight chance of success. We could use her help, but the King also knows. They are ready. No doubt a trap awaits those foolish enough to try. We journey to Aquitaine, and prepare there. We can be sure of their support and with Queen Eleanor now a captive their enthusiasm will increase fivefold. You must get your brothers to press King Louis for as much as they can. First in importance are funds. I suspect they will get more excuses than coin, but they must try. In the next few months we must prepare for King Henry's attacks. We must defend. We lack enough force to go on the offensive. Should we withstand Henry's onslaught for a year or more, then, perhaps, our allies will back their words with actions. We will soon see from whence real help comes. Yea, I do have faith in the quality of our knights, but they are but a handful. Henry can hire hundreds of mercenaries of the first quality. He has the funds and there are many ready to fight for he who has the purse to pay them." With that his hand began to stroke his chin and he returned to thinking those thoughts that only he could understand.

"I have seen you fight great odds and prevail," the young King said confidently. Once again his lack of experience provided a false refuge. It stirred the Marshal out of his contemplations and he again offered a sobering thought.

"Yes, in the tournaments. This will be on a much grander scale. Although they are meant to be similar, war and tournaments are not the same. Now, talk to Queen Marguerite and be ready to act on the things I have told you. Sire, I do believe your father does love you, but we will do what we must and may God help us if we fail." His eyes betrayed sadness. His efforts to maintain peace in the family had failed.

With that, the young King spurred his horse and rode to the wagon containing Queen Marguerite. It was not the last time the Marshal would tell his king things he did not wish to hear. It was precisely what made him special. Loyalty required absolute honesty. To do otherwise, in the mind of the Marshal, would be a betrayal of the worst kind. Only the weak or treacherous shy away from the truth, when a friend needs to hear it.

The early promise of a warm day faded as the skies darkened and a light rain began to fall. The remainder of the journey to Aquitaine would be an unpleasant one. I pulled out a cloak to protect myself from the cold sting of the rain, but I knew it would not offer much respite. It was as if God was telling me that there would be no escape from the troubles we would now face.

I rode up to the Marshal to offer my support. "My lord, I have seen men beaten for so blunt a speech to their king. You showed much courage. It does you honor."

He laughed, "Once again, you assume more than is true, Lewellyn. I am a dead man at the time of King Henry's choosing. Such knowledge gives easy to be plain in my speech. Our youthful sovereign has little idea what he has started. We will be more than wet when this affair concludes. I wonder if you made a mistake not running away five years ago. You could be enjoying a peaceful life in the country. Instead, you ride with traitors to a very powerful king," he said almost as an apology.

"I am glad I chose as I did. I, alone, control my honor, and no one can take it from me," I said to cover my fear.

He smiled broadly at hearing his own words. "Well said. You are the brave one. I salute you!" He spurred his horse and rode up to talk to Bertran who was donning his cloak to lessen the irritation from the sky. For a few moments I was alone with my thoughts. I was too filled with pride to realize the predicament before us. Like the young King, I was too inexperienced to really be afraid.

The shower passed quickly and the late afternoon sun was a welcomed change. As evening approached the sky turned red as if to signal the blood that would be spilt in the days ahead. We were traveling into darkness and there was no turning back.

We reached the safety of Poitiers without incident. Word of the Queen's imprisonment had precisely the effect on the barons of Aquitaine the Marshal said it would. Well fortified and provisioned we waited for an attack which was sure to come in the spring. Our defensive position was strengthened by their pledges to fight. As the crisp evenings of winter in the Aquitaine approached our time was spent in preparation and communicating with our "allies." King Louis promised troops and money, but said it would take a little time to assemble them. Richard and Geoffrey spent most of their time looking to their own defenses. We found out Queen Eleanor had tried to escape dressed as a man, but was discovered. The young King was enraged each time his mother's captivity was discussed. He did not fall on the ground and roll around screaming as his father did when angry, but the royal temper was clearly passed from father to son.

For the next few weeks, I only saw the Marshal in the morning when he rose and the evening when he retired. The days were filled with meetings and planning sessions I was not privy to. His afternoons were spent drilling what troops we were able to muster. It was not an encouraging sight. I offered to take training with a pike to be of service. The Marshal thanked me, but said I would be more useful as his clerk, writing and answering his correspondence. It kept me busy. Most of his letters asking for help came back with polite excuses. Some did not respond at all. We were finding out who our true friends were, as he had told the young King. It seems friendship is much stronger when the friend believes you can win.

We heard stories of King Henry massing a strong force. A few skirmishes in the Norman countryside proved nothing. Henry's strategy seemed to be to ignore his wayward sons and focus on the English barons who had turned against him. These nobles were anxious to curb his power and return to the old system where they enjoyed more power. The King saw them as the greater threat. Little by little, he crushed any vassal who had chosen to defy him. Ranulf, Queen Eleanor's keeper, had captured William" the Lion" by Christmas. Young Henry's title of King in England was proving to be as imaginary as it had seemed to me when it was first proposed. The King's strategy was clear. Bring anyone who might help his son to heel before confronting us in the stronghold of Aquitaine. We saw no fighting, but I received frequent reports of the loss of any noble loyal to us in the north.

King Louis' effort was marginal at best. Just as the Marshal had predicted, the King of France was losing interest as the defeats mounted. The Marshal had led the defense of one castle siege successfully, but he admitted it was not really a victory. Even the knights most loyal to us were getting discouraged as spring approached. Fighting for a boy who had never seen battle was beginning to look like a bad idea. Morale was very low. All agreed something needed to be done.

Bertran suggested there might be more enthusiasm for a youthful king with a sword. Young Henry had never been knighted. How could he be respected as a military leader if he had not been presented with his sword symbolically? It was an honor bestowed by a king, according to custom. The problem was his father was certainly not going to do it and King Louis was already backing away from his involvement in the plot. Who had the prestige to knight a king? It was young Henry who decided the issue. It would be the Marshal!

The Marshal entered our rooms and slumped down in his chair. He turned to me with a look of disbelief. "They asked me to knight him. Never has such a thing been done. I have no title, no authority, and no standing for such a task. They claim the men will take heart in the young King's authority, if he is so honored. It is a fool's dream. No more than a pebble cast at an angry bear. Alas, I cannot say this lest I totally destroy their will to fight," he said looking right through me as if there was an answer written on the wall behind me.

"My lord, if this must be done they could not have chosen better. You, of all here, are most worthy to bestow knighthood. Henry knows it, as does Sir Bertran and all the others. Why are you reluctant to accept the honor?" I asked as my pride in my master ignored the danger such an action would cause for him personally.

The Marshal's blue eyes examined the gray stone floor as he replied, "You understand not, my loyal friend. It be the King's place to do the dubbing. He will be sure to kill me for usurping his prerogative, but why does it matter, he will kill me as a traitor anyway." He was thinking aloud. "No, the honor bestowed on me is too great."

"He means to kill all of us, but too great an honor? Nay, my lord, you are the essence of chivalry. The young King has chosen well. You must accept." I could not believe what I had just said. I was telling my master what he had to do. I had clearly crossed the bounds of acceptable behavior. This surely was grounds for a beating, but I meant what I had said. I stood defiantly ready to accept the blow for my insolence.

Instead of the backhand I expected, the Marshal began to laugh. "Now the servants are giving commands. Who next, the stable boys? Would your highness be willing to fetch a beer?"

My face turned crimson as I ran to get the pitcher. My hands were still shaking when I returned with the beverage.

"Spill it not. All has turned to madness so why not accept this last act of insanity. I am less than worthy to knight a squire, no less a king. Never has it been done this way, and so this must also be of a different design. Marshal, you are a dead man strutting like a king in a household of madmen. 'Tis a dream. Perhaps I died yesterday and God is having some fun with me before my judgment." He was talking to himself again. I stood quietly as he continued the conversation with himself, and then drank his brew sloshing it from side to side in his cheeks before swallowing.

"Lewellyn, inform his majesty 'twill be the greatest honor of my life to conduct the ceremony," he said as though mocking himself.

I raced down the hall where I almost bowled over Sir Bertran. I stopped briefly and blurted out. "He will knight the young King." Bertran smiled as I raced away to the King's apartments. After informing the guards of my mission, I was led into the King's presence. I bowed deeply and summoning up my most official voice I announced, "Your Majesty, I am order by my master to inform you it would be the greatest honor of his life to officiate at your knighting ceremony."

Young Henry exploded with joy and shouted to his Queen, "He will do it! Marguerite, I receive my sword at last. I knew he would. This is wonderful." The young Queen entered the room with a slipper in her hand, looked up briefly, and said, "Henry, why are you dressed...?" She paused and then turning quickly she saw the young King by the door and said, "An honor well deserved. I only wish my father was at hand to do the deed, but these are difficult times. You have chosen the most worthy man to stand in his place." I bowed and received another curious glance from the Queen and left the chambers.

I returned to our quarters and found the Marshal deep in thought. I relayed the reaction of the young King and the Queen. His mood did not change. He muttered to himself and shook his head repeatedly. He kept on saying the ceremony must be different. I had no idea what he meant. All the knighting ceremonies I had ever heard about were the same. First, the applicant bathed. Then he donned new clothes and carried his armor to the chapel where he spent the night in prayer. The following day he would swear to follow the code of chivalry and then kneeling before his liege he would be tapped on the head with the flat of the sword and told to rise. He would then be given a blow to the chest and told it was the last blow he could receive without giving combat. What could be done differently?

The following day the preparations were completed. The young King began his bathing. This was followed by his donning a white tunic covered with a red tabard. Three racing gold leopards were emblazoned on the shoulder. He adjourned to the chapel for the evening of prayer followed by Sir Bertran carrying his new hauberk and ivory-handled sword.

That evening I spoke to the Marshal about his plans, but he simply said, "I hope he prays earnestly for our cause. Only God can help us now. King Louis will not."

In the morning the entire court was assembled in the great hall. Each had dressed in their best clothes. The scene was extremely colorful. Each coat of arms declared which noble house was represented. I always liked such occasions. They were pleasing to the eye. The magical animals: unicorns, griffins and dragons danced on their tunics in gold, silver, crimson, green and every color you could imagine. It seemed to make the room into a land of dreams. Once again I had the opportunity to wear my fine jacket of green and yellow. It identified me as belonging to the large man at the end of the room and I beamed with pride. I have always felt these ceremonies of dazzling colors caused the common folk, who lived in the brown and gray world of leather jerkins and woolen cloaks, to be properly impressed and intimidated by our betters.

Everyone took their places on either side of the room. They created an aisle down the center of the hall. At the end of the aisle were the Marshal, Queen Marguerite, and Sir Bertran. The Marshal's size commanded all eyes to focus on him. His tabard was half green and half yellow with the bright red dancing lion embroidered on the chest. His chestnut-colored hair and beard were neatly trimmed. He was a handsome figure. At his side, below the exceptionally muscled arms, was his massive broadsword sheathed in its red velvet ceremonial scabbard. The Queen looked like a child standing next to her husband's champion. She smiled broadly, showing how much she was enjoying the event.

Young Henry entered clad in his hauberk covered with the red tabard sporting the three gold leopards. On either side he was attended by Sir Thomas de Coulonces and Sir Adam d'Iqueboeuf. Behind them was Sir Bernard de Seville. The group moved down the center of the hall and approached the Marshal. All were silent as the oath was taken. The young King knelt and the Marshal stepped forward. In a loud voice he said, "I, who am not worthy of this honor, ask in God's name that you rise, Sir Henry." With that he leaned over and took the young King by the shoulders and kissed him on the forehead. He struck his chest with the flat of his hand.

He had done it differently! He had dubbed the young King with a kiss. The hall erupted with a joyful shout. The young King embraced his mentor and kissed his Queen. He faced his court to accept the cheers and relished the moment. I wondered if he was remembering the daydreams he used to have when he and his brother would practice at the post, under the watchful eye of the Marshal. Did this moment live up to those fantasies? From the expression on his face, it did.

The rest of the day was spent in feasting. After which the Marshal and I returned to our quarters. As we sat down, still glowing from the food and drink, the Marshal began to speak. "Well, my friend, 'tis done. I do not believe it will do a wit to change our circumstances, but we have a happy leader. The pity is he has not a reliable ally in this battle."

"Does he not have his brothers, my lord?" I asked as a reminder that all had not fled.

"His brothers! Only because they see their chances for the crown enhanced. If things do not change they will waver. This whole enterprise has but a few months left. King Henry has completed the destruction of his major foes in the nobility. We are next on the list. Our pitiful force has no chance. Whoever convinced the young King to pursue this action will be looking for someone to blame. It will be me. Our serpent will be spreading a new brand of poison. 'Tis the only way our hidden foe will be able to continue to possess the ear of the young King. I must quietly explore an accommodation with the King soon. Secrecy is paramount. The young King cannot be informed or he will prevent the attempt out of pride. The time is near when he too will see the folly of further struggle. It must be done lest King Henry loses his taste for forgiving his wayward son." Again the Marshal was thinking of the next step.

"Will you send Bertran?" I asked as he seemed the most logical choice.

"Nay. It must be someone whose absence will not be noticed." He looked at me and smiled. I knew what it meant. My face turned ashen.

"I cannot, my lord. It be not from fear, but because I am not worthy of such a mission."

"It seems to me, I remember a sirrah rejecting the very same argument from his master. Nay, I think the bold command was 'You must accept!' Besides, I have knowledge that makes the choice a good one," he said showing a strange confidence.

The point was well taken. How could I refuse? I was terrified at the prospect of a traitor meeting the very moody Henry II with such a vital message. Before the tendrils of fear could get a better grip, I said, "What must I do?" Death was back on the bill of fare.

He explained how I was to introduce myself and then dictated a letter I was to give the King. I struggled to steady my shaking hand for such an important correspondence. When we had finished I read the contents back to the Marshal.

"Majesty, the unpleasantness existing in your household should be concluded without further bloodshed. The time has come to mend the rip with your eldest son and his brothers. I believe an accommodation satisfactory to your Majesty's needs can be arranged. If this be desirable send a response with my servant. He is instructed to carry such with the utmost secrecy."

As I wrote, I wondered if I was writing my own death warrant. The Marshal seemed to know my thoughts because he expressed the confidence that King Henry would not kill me. I asked why?

"Do you trust me, Lewellyn?" he asked looking into my eyes as if he were testing my very soul.

"Of course, master, but why would the high king speak to one so lowly as I?" There was doubt in my voice even though I trusted my master with my life.

"I have made contact with King Henry and we decided you were the best choice." He smiled and gave me a brief nod. Again he had been communicating with the high king without any in the household knowing. Still my thoughts were troubled. I recalled stories of how kings killed messengers. It was not hard for him, because he would be one hundred miles away behind the walls of a strong castle. I thought for a moment, and then realized my indictment of the bravest man I had ever known was unfounded. I had made the same erroneous assessment years ago when we first met. My courage returned and so did my ability to think clearly. He was in far more danger than I! If I was killed, it would be but a short while before the Marshal and all the traitors in the household would be keeping me company wherever God decided we belonged. If King Henry agreed to the letter, the Marshal was still in jeopardy. King Henry might forgive his sons, but not the Marshal. He was the chief planner of the defense against the King. As he had just said he would bear the blame. I was an insignificant servant and might be ignored or at worst bound to another noble.

I asked, "When am I to go?"

"Patience. Let us first see what the spring brings in the way of assistance. Perhaps fortune will smile and you need not go. 'Tis a forlorn hope, but there is always a chance. Now, hide the letter, and tell no one of it. Premature discovery would surely be disaster. Trust no one with this knowledge, Lewellyn—no one! It could cost you your life and mine." His mood changed and he said, "Now, a song. We need forget the troubles of this household." I reached under the table for my lute and began playing tunes to disguise the fear I felt in my heart. Music has oft been a refuge when unpleasant thoughts need to be vanquished.

The spring saw no change in the fortunes of the young King. King Henry's forces continued to gain and grow. Defections on our side grew faster as the funds dried up. It was clear Aquitaine could not stand alone against the King. Duke Richard was ready to fight on, but the young King and Duke Geoffrey were losing heart. It was time for my journey. I always knew the day would come, but I had tried to deny the reality of the situation for as long as possible.

I had a sick feeling in my stomach as I received final instructions from the Marshal. My departure was explained as a trip to see the Marshal's brother, Anselm, for information about troop movements. I hid the letter under my clothes. I was attended only by a priest so as not to draw attention. It would not take long to reach King Henry, since his forces had shrunken the area controlled by the young King to a fairly small region. I did not know if the Marshal had shared the real purpose of my journey with the young King.

It took two days to complete our journey. We arrive at King Henry's location at Gisor without drawing much attention. I followed my instructions, sought out the Earl of Lancaster, King Henry's seneschal and presented him with the Marshal's letter. The following day, I was taken to see King Henry. My knees were shaking and I must have been as pale as a specter, because the Earl asked, "Are you feeling ill?"

"Nay, my lord. I am not used to such important tasks as speaking to kings," I said nervously. He did not react.

King Henry was pacing back and forth as usual when I entered the hall. His red tabard with the running lions was stained with the gravy of the previous night's meal. His red hair was flecked with strands of gray. I wondered if the man ever slept. He looked up at me as I was escorted into his presence. I bowed and waited for him to speak. One does not speak to a King before one is asked to speak.

"Well, see who comes hence. You are called Lewellyn, are you not?" I was surprised the King knew my name. It was not in the letter, but guessed the Earl of Lancaster had told him. "It surprises me not Sir William sent you, with this." He held up the letter. "Know you what it contains?" His eyes looked at me and then down.

"I do, Majesty. 'Tis my charge to write the Marshal's correspondence," I said with a bow.

"Bright lad. So my sons are ready to realize the error of their ways and cease this foolishness costing me money and time. It has revealed who the traitors are in my realm and that is a good thing to know. We will deal with those who remain presently." A cold shudder went up my back at those words. "Tell your master he must arrange a meeting with my sons and that sniveling weasel, the King of France, within a month. We will discuss the terms to end this folly." He turned and walked away.

I was led out of the hall and given a meal. The Earl said I was to leave immediately with my priest, and return to my master. I pinched my skin to be sure it was still there and left, feeling like Daniel leaving the lion's den. The trip back seemed to take less time, although it was really the same. The time went faster because I could talk about the experience with the good father. The journey to Gisor had been silent for fear of revealing that which I was not supposed to reveal. I babbled about how lucky I felt in escaping the King's encampment. The priest listened and said we were all in God's hands.

As soon as I returned, I went straight to the Marshal to give my report. I explained the details. "Master, King Henry says you must arrange a meeting with him and all the parties involved within a month. He included King Louis in the demands. I also saw a very large number of routiers in the King's camp. The tents were numerous and I believe they have at least three times our number." The Marshal just listened and nodded. He rose without saying a word and went to talk to the young King. I was hurt by the lack of appreciation for my risky mission. Then I remembered what the King had said about traitors and knew the Marshal had more to worry about than a young servant's vanity.

It took several weeks to arrange the meeting at Gisor. The principals were finally assembled. Bertran argued it was surrender and King Henry would use the occasion to kill us. He said it would be better to die fighting than to be slaughtered as prisoners. He was very upset at the whole arrangement. When he found out I had been the messenger, he stopped meeting with me for my lessons. Baldwin shrugged his shoulders, and said whatever happened he would stand by the Marshal. Thomas suggested we might seek sanctuary with the King of France when he arrived. Adam and Bernard said nothing, but I heard from the grooms they had much of their armor packed on the extra horses, just in case a quick escape was needed. The Marshal organized the final arrangements for the meeting. It was difficult to know what he was thinking because he said nothing about what he thought would happen.

We arrived as a small company at Gisor. The King's table was under a large oak which I was told had special significance. Chairs had been placed carefully according to the rank of each of those present. I noticed that King Henry's chair was conspicuously larger than the rest. The shade was a welcome respite for the hot summer sun. There we were joined by a very sullen Duke Richard and an angry Duke Geoffrey. I was surprised to see how much the two brothers had grown. Although they still looked young, they were obviously becoming men. Duke Richard was almost as tall as the Marshal. He had fulfilled his early promise and was a very handsome man. In the discussions which followed it became clear why the struggle was over. King Louis who had just arrived with his son had discovered King Henry was about to turn his forces on Paris. The never-too-brave Louis wished to avoid that eventuality and was ready to sue for peace separately. Duke Richard already knew of the intended defection of King Louis and knew it was over. I wondered how Duke Richard had learned of the intentions of the French monarch. I had not seen any messenger from Paris arrive at court in the past three weeks. It had to be the spy. Most of the household had traveled with messages to different parts of the countryside when the Marshal informed everyone of the summons by King Henry to meet at Gisor, but which one was the spy?

The discussions were really no more than King Henry dictating his terms. He rose and standing behind the table said, "We forgive the errors of my sons. Owing to their youth and bad council they strayed as the young are wont to do, but we are magnanimous and grant them pardon. We shall deal with others differently. King Louis, you will be required to cede certain fiefs to me as compensation for supporting this abortive rebellion."

King Louis scowled but said, "This will be done." King Henry grinned pleased that once again he had cowed the French monarch. Philip, son of the French king, a mere youth, looked King Henry directly in the eye, and said, "This shall not stand! The sun will rise on a day when I will take back all the land you have so grievously taken from my father."

King Henry grunted at the threat and considered it the fanciful imagination of a boy. I was not so sure it was a boast. He was clearly not cut from the same cloth as his weak-willed father.

As the meeting ended, King Henry asked the Marshal to remain as the others departed. My blood began to run cold. This was it. The King stopped his pacing and looked directly at the knight who had helped his son defy him. He spoke in clear tones about the serious nature of the situation. The Marshal returned the gaze without showing any expression.

"You knighted my son. You know it was not your place to do that?" he said glancing up at the much taller Marshal.

"I did, sire." The Marshal showed no expression on his seemingly calm face.

"You left with him, in the middle of the night to begin this foolish adventure." The indictment continued with the King watching for any reaction. There was none.

"It was my duty, sire," he said without any emotion.

"You helped to organize his defenses." The accusation was damning.

"It was also my duty." I was now ready to hear a sentence of death delivered to the man I adored. A tear began to trickle down my face.

"Out of loyalty to him, you arranged this truce even though you knew it would mean your death." The King continued, "According to my cousin Raimund, you did everything in your power to prevent this from happening. You stand here ready to die, rather than to plead the case which might help you avoid responsibility." The King's menacing tone changed. "My son could not have a better friend or a more loyal man than you. We not only forgive you and your comrades, but we hereby order you continue as his mentor and head of his household. We love our son. We know there are those who would turn him against me, but you are not one of them. Thank you for returning my son to me, alive. Let all this unpleasantness be forgotten. You are a remarkable man, Sir William Marshal. Go and see this is never repeated." He signified the meeting was over with a wave of his hand.

"Thank you, your Majesty, for the lives of my companions. I shall do my best to guide him wisely." He bowed and walked away. My heart raced as I followed him. I again heard the birds chirping a happy tune. Once we were out of sight of the tents I came up to him and unbidden I embraced him. The air which filled my lungs seemed sweeter and I heard birds chirping cheerily. Life was once again gay and worth enjoying.

"We are becoming rather familiar with our 'betters,' are we not?" He laughed. I quickly regained myself and apologized for the impertinent act.

"Forgive the boldness, my lord," I blabbered as my face flushed.

"I was not serious, Lewellyn. I feel like Lazarus. Now, let us go for there is much to be done. There is still the matter of a traitor in our midst. I fear it is closer to us than I hoped. The French king will be starting trouble again if he sees weakness. What think you of the speech by Prince Philip?" he said thoughtfully and somewhat impressed by the lad's daring.

"It was said in deadly earnest, my lord. He has pluck."

"My thoughts be the same. 'Tis hard to believe he is the spawn of King Louis. That young man will prove far more dangerous than his father. Let us hope King Louis has a very long life. When I was summoned before the King, and was convinced I would be executed, I had great remorse that I had no children to mourn my death. Children be the only immortality give by God to man. I have never thought about it, but today I did." His eyes narrowed as if he was trying to see into the future.

"I would mourn you like a son, my lord."

"In sooth you would, Lewellyn. I am grateful for the thought, but the day is coming when I must think of things other than the next war or the next tournament. I have no land and no title. You would be just as much of an orphan as if you were my son. I cannot go on forever winning tournaments for bread and beer," he sighed.

"You need not worry about me. The young King will reward you when he comes into his own. I have no doubt about that. Then, I shall be your troubadour and clerk. We will live on a fine estate and you will marry a Princess," I said cheerfully.

The Marshal laughed and said, "Now you add great seer to your many talents? Well, first of all, kings marry their daughters to other kings' sons. I need not remind you, I am not a prince. Secondly, I did not succeed in winning the young King's war and there are those who will be sure to remind him of this failing. My star is surely sinking." I was stunned by this assessment. My mind wanted to believe that all had finally been set right.

"My lord, surely you do not think there will be trouble with the King's sons again? He forgave them when he could have killed us all. You saved us all," I said with pride.

"I wish it was that simple. The young King chafes at the treatment of his mother. You forget Queen Eleanor is still a prisoner in England. It will also be a burr under Richard's saddle for as long as it continues and there was no mention of clemency for her. Princess Alais will be a problem unless the King abandons his madness. Duke Geoffrey's wife will continue to agitate him and we still do not know who gives our lord messages from the French throne. No one was satisfied with today's events save King Henry and us. The storm has temporarily subsided, but this adventure is far from ended. Queen Marguerite is not very happy. She wants children and she has none. The young King has not been an attentive husband."

He again had successfully destroyed my idyllic dream by making me aware of the many forces at work in the royal camp. I admit it was beginning to vex me so I countered with my own version of the future.

"I have every confidence you will be able to work all this out, my lord. King Henry believes it too," I said sure of my logic. My belief in the Marshal's talents had not been shaken by his list of worries. We reached our tent and I began making preparations for our dried beef and bread supper. As we supped I played a song or two as the Marshal continued to explain to me the difficulties he felt sure were ahead. The sun set and darkness caused the crickets to compete with my songs. Finally, tired of thinking about the problems which troubled his mind, the Marshal ended his discourse.

"It is late and we will not solve the problems of the Plantagenet family tonight. To bed with us; it has been a remarkable day." He breathed deeply enjoying the air—a simple act of life that just a few hours ago seemed destined to be of limited duration.

In the morning there was a great sigh of relief in the ranks of the fellows when the Marshal announced all had been pardoned. We made plans to return to Rouen and the young King's estates in Normandy. Horses that had been prepared for flight now would carry the company back to the old life of practicing and tournaments.

Life had seemed to return to normal when the Marshal made preparations for the tournament season that spring. It would be good to be playing at war, instead of the real thing. His brother Anselm joined the group and the young King took the field, instead of watching. King Henry had learned his lesson about keeping his eldest occupied and was pleased to provide the money. The next bit of news was also very good. Roger of Gaugi joined the company. The young King was delighted to add such a talent to the team and the Marshal was glad he would not have to face one more difficult opponent. Adam and Thomas were not pleased. They complained there would be fewer spoils for them. Baldwin, as usual, was unconcerned. Nothing bothered him. Bertran was happy because the young King was happy. Bertran no longer took the field. He spent more and more time as a courtier with the young King and entertaining the household with songs he composed.

Happily a year after Gisor, Bertran and I mended our differences. Six more years of successful tournaments refreshed the friendship. The seasons passed quickly and as Gisor became a distant memory new troubles began to arise. Roger retired and the disgruntled trio of Adam, Thomas and Bernard were still unhappy with their prospects. I sat one evening with Bertran and we discussed events and how the Marshal was contending with the problem. Bertran was convinced there was nothing to worry about and all would right itself by Christmas tide.

Queen Marguerite became more frustrated with her inattentive husband. I wrote a song about summer love and sang it one evening for the assembled guests. Sir Bertran dressed in a very fine new tabard (he spent more time and money on clothes now that he was no longer competing in the lists), rose and with goblet in hand offered a compliment. "A fine effort, Lewellyn. Your skills grow. Perhaps I should be more fearful that my place as a ballad writer for the court will be overshadowed." He tapped his goblet on the table several times.

"Not so, my lord. My poor efforts are but a burgeoning leaf on the muse's tree. Your songs represent an entire branch," I said with all the poetic skill I could muster.

"Again well done," he said and tapped his goblet several more times.

When Queen Marguerite heard it, she said, "I am glad someone is thinking about love. My lords, I feel somewhat distressed. If it pleases you, my husband, I will retire."

"Of course, my dear," Henry replied in an offhanded manner. Marguerite rose and with a sullen look, nodded briefly and left the hall with two of her ladies. I watched as Henry reached over to Bertran, gently squeezed his hand and shrugged. The rest of the evening was spent talking about the upcoming season.

I was anxious for the first tournament to begin. It was at Pleurs. There were to be over two hundred knights in the competition. It was glorious. There were several attempts to trap the Marshal. He was attacked by six knights at one time. Before Thomas and Baldwin could arrive to help, the Marshal's helmet was knocked sideways by a mace blow from behind. Only able to see through one eye slit he unhorsed his assailant with a mighty blow from the butt of his broadsword. Rearing his horse he disarmed one of the knights in front and one at his left side with a single stroke. Whirling around, his sword cleaved the shield of still another knight who immediately took flight. With his free hand he jerked the bridle of the sixth attacker's horse causing him to rear up suddenly and unseat the final threat. It would become a feat of legendary proportions. I have sung about Pleurs many times. I am sure those who heard did not believe me unless they were there. It was the day the Marshal became the greatest knight of all time. From that time on, traps were set for the young King and not the Marshal. All the knights present at Pleurs said it was the single greatest feat they had ever witnessed.

The Marshal continued to win every tournament he entered. He was setting a standard no other knight has ever matched. Some spectators hoped to see him defeated. It was too boring watching him win all the time. They wanted a change, but what they wanted did not happen. He won and kept on winning. Slowly the crowds changed again. As the wins mounted, they began to realize they were witnesses to something special. It gave them a unique status to be able to say to their friends, "I saw him fight." It was a boast only a few could make and it was said with pride. The chants began again. All those present felt a part of the unbelievable record.

The rest of the year saw the English team victorious in every event. The Marshal accounted for thirty-five individual captures. The money and the wine flowed. It was a happy time and events of the preceding year were forgotten. I believed all would be right with the world and this would continue forever. I was wrong.

Showered with gifts and praise, some of his young companions grew increasingly jealous. Envy is another hidden serpent. It hides in the shadows and finds secret ways to destroy. Rumor and innuendo are the fangs which carry the venom. It can strike when you least expect it. The jealousy which destroyed the company had disastrous results for all involved. It would end the Marshal's appearances in tournaments forever and make a new road for us to follow.

The number of men in the tavern has grown. Money for ale is flowing freely. The old one realizes the patrons are excited to know the answer to the puzzle he has carefully crafted. He sees a chance to gain from their curiosity.

"My friends, my throat grows parched and hunger makes me weak. Perhaps among you there is one or two who would help remedy an old man's needs by placing a coin or two for a drink and a crust of bread." With that speech he places his weather-worn hat on the table beside him. Several small coins are tossed and the troubadour places each in the cap. The request is not a surprise to the men and the tavern keeper brings another mug of ale announcing it is his contribution to the evening. The old man smiles, takes a brief swig of the refreshed mug and begins again.

Chapter 7
Mistakes and Mourning

Those six years after the reconciliation at Gisor were the happiest years for the Marshal and me. His victories in the tournaments reached legendary numbers. Teamed with Roger, the Marshal accounted for 103 captured knights. When Roger retired his place was taken by one Hugh de Hamelcourt. Hugh was a broad jolly fellow with flaming red hair, large nose and a foul mouth. Above all he was a very fine knight, who quickly became a close friend. Another was Raoul de Hamars who had decided it was better to fight beside the Marshal than against him. He had replaced Bertran who was now happy to be the young King's companion and troubadour. This bearded veteran had more scars on his body than one could count in a day. He was absolutely fearless. He could drink more ale than any man I have ever met.

By 1181 the young King had become an active participant. He became a target for other knights. After all, he represented the richest prize in every tournament he entered. To capture a king's son would lead to a rich payoff and all knew it. The Marshal used this to set traps for the other teams. It was a strategy with problems.

One afternoon, following the tournament at Sorel, I was napping behind the tent and I heard Thomas and Adam speaking to the young King inside the tent. They were whispering and unaware that anyone was close enough to hear. "Sire, you are being used as bait to enrich the Marshal's purse. For one as high as you to be so shamefully treated is more than we can stand," Thomas whined.

"'Tis not the worst of it, but there are too many hidden ears in camp for me to reveal my information. We shall talk later when we are certain to be alone," Adam added mysteriously.

I heard the Marshal enter the tent and all conversation ceased. The Marshal distributed the day's rewards and each went their separate way. Although I had not heard everything I knew it was not the kind of talk helpful to the troop. I immediately told the Marshal. He nodded and thanked me for the information, but said nothing further. Later that evening the young King and the Marshal were discussing the tournament.

"William, why does thou make me the prize all seek? We find it unseemly to be rescued all the time. Should I not be left to save myself? After all, we have seen you do it," he said as his mouth twisted into a frown. The young King was clearly vexed that his was a demeaning role. Most hearing the conversation knew the real answer. He was not the Marshal. For the young King to be comparing his skills to the Marshal's was the same as comparing a candle to a bonfire. We all yearn to have the same abilities as those we admire, but God has seen fit not to grant such a wish. To me life is a song and a song needs different notes to be complete. If all the notes were the same there would be no music. Life, like a song, requires each of us to be different notes. Wisdom and contentment come from realizing each serves a purpose. None are unimportant. Jealousy and resentment come from thinking one note is more critical than another in making the song. I waited to hear how the Marshal would answer.

The Marshal stared at his cup for a moment, looked up at the befuddled Henry and spoke slowly. "Sire, your worth is more than any and to play your role as bravely as you do helps us all. You have not yet had the years of practice or experience. You will learn more. Until then, it would be disgraceful for the rest of us to allow our leader to be captured."

The young King smiled, tossed his head back and said, "I shall be better and then I shall rescue you." He was satisfied with the explanation. The rest of us knew the young King would never be able to realize such a dream. His station in life was given him by virtue of his birth, not his skill in battle. For most there comes a point where more practice simply maintains rather than improves our skills.

I saw Thomas and Adam glance at each other. A scowl twisted Adam's mouth. The conversation had not gone as they had hoped. The circle around the young King was beginning to divide into different groups. Thomas, Adam and Bernard, the youngest of the troop, were one clique. Baldwin, Hugh, Raoul and the Marshal were another. The young King and the gregarious Bertran shared time with both groups. This simple gesture convinced me the serpent the Marshal was seeking had three heads.

Later on I shared my thoughts with the Marshal. "My lord, I fear Adam, Thomas and Bernard are not to be trusted."

"Your instincts are correct. I have suspected as much for a while."

"Will you ask the young King to dismiss them?"

"Nay, Henry would not accept that. He swims in their flattery and I possess no proof of disloyalty. They are merely unhappy about their lack of success. Ambitions oft fail to match abilities. I have the young King's trust. They will be but a slight distraction. They would never dare challenge my leadership openly," the Marshal exclaimed with a confident smile.

"But can they undermine that trust?" I asked, less secure in this confidence.

"Nay, Henry knows their talents are limited to soft words whispered in his ear, but they do bear watching," he said and returned to enjoying his evening brew.

As the fall frosts marked the end of the season, events took a troubling turn. The young King and his father began to quarrel again over the constant requests for funds. Although the tournaments were successful the costs always outran the gains. King Henry had forgotten the value of providing his eldest son with distractions as the constant call for more money pinched his funds. This was not the only difficulty. King Louis had joined the Heavenly choir early in 1181 and was succeeded by his belligerent son. King Philip had spent a year on the throne of France and was surely up to mischief. I had not forgotten his threat at Gisor. It was a very troubling development.

The young King became angrier with his wife and her constant desire for his attention. He complained about everything. By the end of the season he was in bad humor most of the time. His mother's continued captivity caused Bertran to write a song bemoaning a queen so abused. It was soon popular in the courts of Aquitaine. The Marshal said it was a veiled criticism of King Henry and not helpful.

The Yule events were less lavish than in past years, a sure sign of a shrinking allowance for the young King. Several of our serving staff were reassigned to Chinon. It almost seemed that King Henry wanted to be sure his son knew who held the reins of power. He could make the young King a pauper if he wished. We all were painfully aware of that reality.

I was becoming less concerned with the political strife than I was with relieving myself of my virginity. Many of the squires began to whisper about the seeming special treatment I received. How could a twenty-three-year-old be so ignorant of feminine charms? Was I the Marshal's kept boy? This was an outrage I could not endure. So I determined to change the perception of the fellows. I began openly boasting about my conquests of the female gender.

Imaginary to be sure, but well described as only a storyteller could do. The tales became so bawdy that I knew I would have to have some real experience to continue to be convincing. Besides I was stirred by my own tales to see if all this was true. I vowed to remedy the mystery of lust as soon as possible.

The Christmas holiday was sprinkled with several attempts at seducing two kitchen maids. The first, a very attractive wench, rebuffed my crude attempts by informing me that she would sooner bed a goat than me. Her pleasures were reserved for another. I discovered that it was none other than Sir Adam she blessed with her favors. The foolish girl may have believed she would become his lady and escape the serving class. It was a forlorn hope. Sir Adam would choose a woman of property over a pretty smile. It was for this reason he took up the life of a tournament knight. I knew he would satisfy himself and she would be left with a child that would never know his father. I wondered if this was how I was brought into the world. I thought how sad it was she was so willing to be used so badly, but then it is easy to be won by false promises when our circumstances are less than happy. I turned my attention to the second maid.

The second maid, Giselle, was rather plain, but willing. I was no longer interested in beauty only that I satisfy the urges haunting my dreams. We succeeded in finding a place in the keep where few ventured and proceeded to end my virginity. She had no such need since I was certain she had liberally bestowed her pleasures for others. The great event took all of several seconds as my level of excitement caused my manhood to erupt before I could try all the things I had thought would accompany this moment. Giselle was clearly disgusted with my instant reaction and failure to continue. It was not the fulfilling moment I thought it would be. It had done nothing to relieve my desire and I had to lie to my friends about my experience. It did end the whispers and for that I was grateful. Secretly I was convinced I might become a monk rather than suffer another humiliation of this magnitude. The adventure ended my experience with lust. I had much to learn of love.

The Marshal spent time during the winter trying to convince Queen Marguerite of the need for her husband to be patient. King Henry was getting older and the young King's time would soon be at hand. He spent hours walking with her, trying to get her to understand. She became fond of these walks and became closer to the Marshal. He said she was like a daughter who needed some understanding. It was not easy to be the wife of a frustrated king in waiting.

One night, I asked why he felt sorry for Queen Marguerite.

"Lewellyn, God gives men many outlets for their frustrations. An hour at the post and I forget my troubles. A lady has only children to occupy her time. This Queen has no children. She feels the tug of nature. She seeks to achieve the purpose for which the marriage was arranged—an heir to her family's name. In that she will be honored. Without that, her life will be deemed a failure. 'Tis a sad reality she knows she must face."

"You are her friend, my lord," I responded

"Yes, I can but listen to her frustration. Young Henry holds the key to her happiness," he said with his voice rising in a note of hopeful optimism.

"Why does she not talk to her husband?" I said thinking the problem was a simple one.

"He sees not her need. He spends too much of his time with the younger knights and Bertran. Like the father he berates, he thinks giving gifts will suffice for the absences of affection. We see clearly the faults in others we are blind to see in ourselves. She is now a woman and needs him as a man, not as a king." I could see there was more troubling him than he was willing to reveal.

The discussion of love was also reminding me of my own failure. It was so discomforting I sought to change the discussion. I hoped the Marshal would not notice my red face.

"I have always thought she was the one encouraging him to quarrel with his father," I said mouthing the thoughts I had long held about Queen Marguerite.

"So I too once believed. These past weeks convinced me against the thought. She is a good person who will be helpful to Henry when 'young' no longer haunts his title," he said convinced that my suspicions were unfounded.

"How long may that be?" I said thinking of what my master had said about the hearty condition of the young King's father.

"I know not. King Henry is in excellent health. Things would be better if she is with child before long and offers us a pleasing distraction. Our charge shows signs of rebellion again. The high king will not be in such a forgiving mood if we travel the same road again. Methinks I know who gives him these ideas. There are truly troubling problems that will surely complicate my hopes for the future. The secrets are well hidden!" His eyes narrowed and a serious look came across his face as he stroked his short beard.

"Who, my lord?" I felt my heart pounding. Was the traitor finally going to be exposed?

"I will not say until I am sure, but if I be right..." He did not finish the thought. I was sure the snake had three heads. I was not going to be among the startled. I, Lewellyn, was too wise in the ways of the court to be fooled.

Spring came and with it the villeins began to till the soil for the sowing of the crops. Grooms tended the horses that would soon present us with foals. Several sheep gave birth, as did several cows. Unfortunately in the midst of the eruption of new life Queen Marguerite remained barren.

We made preparations for the tournaments. The smithy repaired and made new accouterments for the knights. The season did not seem to interest the young King as it had in the past. His meetings with the Marshal grew shorter and he showed less interest. The excitement was gone. Something else occupied his mind. I was sure it was going to be trouble with his father, again. I was wrong. The disastrous event happened right in front of me.

It was just before the first tournament of the season when I heard a commotion in the hall outside our rooms. The door burst open. The young King stormed into the room. He kicked over a chair and looked directly at my master and screamed, "You bastard, you have been sleeping with my wife!" For the first time since I had known him the Marshal was dumbstruck. "I could have you killed, but I will not. Get out." I cowered in the corner as he whirled around and left the room. I raced to the overturned chair to right it.

"Leave it! Pack my things," ordered an angry Marshal. I did as instructed. There was absolute silence during my completion of the task. I could not believe it. The man I respected as the most trustworthy person in the world had betrayed his liege lord. It was not possible. Was the code I had learned from him a sham? Was the world all ugliness after all? No! There had to be a mistake. Then I thought of the walks and the sympathy the Marshal had for the Queen. I knew men had been tempted by women before. I thought of the story of Sampson the priests told us as children. I remembered his liaison with Queen Eleanor. No, it could not be my Sampson. There had to be another explanation. I was sure the Marshal would go to the young King and all would be set right, but he made no movement to that effect. We finished packing, loaded everything on the five horses belonging to my master and rode out of the castle without speaking to anyone. My heart was aching, but I was too stunned to show emotion. We rode for an hour. I had no idea where we were going. Finally I could hold back no longer. I spoke quickly and resolutely.

"My lord, I know you did not do this thing. Why did you not tell the young King he was wrong?" I said pleading for an explanation that would put the matter to rest.

"Your loyalty never waivers. I did not do this, but Henry will not listen. His heart has been poisoned," he said shaking his head sadly.

"By three feeble excuses for knights, I wager." I spit the words out as though if they remained in my mouth a foul taste would linger.

"Yea. I failed because of pride. You warned me and like a pompous fool I failed to see the danger. I placed too much store in my teaching the young King the code of chivalry. In his heart of hearts, Henry knows the truth. Innocent though it was, my act of befriending the Queen made it easy to cast suspicion and that makes explanations useless. I be in my right to demand trial by combat to clear my name, but then I would have to kill Henry's friends, friends who have betrayed me for their own gain," he said with a look of disgust.

"Why not? They deserve it. They are no better than Judas," I said. Visions of watching the three knights falling under the bloody blows of the Marshal's broad sword raced through my mind.

"Because Henry needs to trust me completely. Their deaths would widen the gap. I have failed in my promise to his father. Perhaps some day he will see his mistake, but until then we are without a sponsor," the Marshal said dispassionately.

"They are many who covet your service, my lord."

"Yea, but I need time to reflect and think. I have enough money from the tournaments to last a while; then perhaps, Flanders." We rode on without further conversation.

The next few months were without note; suffice it to say we followed the tournament trail, but the Marshal never entered any of the contests. We merely observed. What transpired back in Rouen was far more interesting. I learned this information from my friends in the scullery. The young King and the Queen had a screaming match the day after we departed. She denied the Marshal was her lover. She said he was the truest, most loyal friend Henry had and the Marshal's only crime was to show her a little kindness. She demanded to know who had falsely accused him of this act. Henry refused to speak. They did not talk for months.

Baldwin sent a message to us when he learned we were also at Eu. I read it to the Marshal. "My friend, I have faith in your innocence and offer to help in any way I can. I am willing to challenge those who have accused you if that is your desire."

"Get your writing implements. Tell Baldwin not to jeopardize his standing with the young King by defending me too vociferously. I suggest patience. Perhaps, in time, the truth will out. It has a way of haunting liars. Warn him to be alert for treachery," he said as he ordered me to write a reply. I scrambled to my rucksack to execute the command.

I scribbled the note and gave it to Baldwin's page. It would not be good to be seen delivering it in person. It would mean Baldwin was being disloyal to his liege lord. The next day the page delivered another note and did not wait for a reply.

It said, "I will do as you ask, but it bothers me to see you so badly used. I will seek evidence to help the young King to see the light. Stay well, my friend."

I saw it differently. Henry would not realize his mistake. He was too headstrong. The three serpents in his household would continue to spread their venom. Adam now had what he wanted, control over the troop. Henry would shower him with gifts instead of the Marshal. The tournament victories and the rewards would be theirs and we would be forgotten.

It only took two months before the young King's household realized they had been fooled by a vision which often deludes the weak and jealous mind. It was plain, even to a simpleton like me. If a candle and a torch illuminate a room, the candle is not made brighter by the removal of the torch. There is only less light for all. The tournament victories were not forthcoming. Without the Marshal, the English team was very ordinary. As the embarrassing defeats mounted, the young King needed more and more money to pay for the expense of tournament life. There were few victories to defray costs. Instead, they had to purchase lost armor. He became more sullen and more belligerent to his father. All could see the situation was becoming worse. Adam's influence was in sharp decline.

Meanwhile, the Marshal traveled around and attended the tournaments, but he did not join with any other team. He had many offers. Powerful nobles treated him as an equal when we visited their tents even though he was not a title-bearing noble. He had no title other than "the Marshal," but the respect paid him was enormous. The Count of Thibault offered him a great deal of money to join with him, but the Marshal refused much to my chagrin.

Shortly after the offer, the Count had his prize war horse stolen. The Marshal gave the Count one of his so the champion of the Count's troop could compete. It was a great gesture. It added to his standing among the powerful. I was not so impressed. I was becoming concerned because the money was running out and giving away one of our most valuable assets seemed foolish. As I looked over our dwindling resources I felt I had to speak.

"Master, we have so little left. If we do not seek a sponsor soon we will be begging in the streets," I said boldly. Hunger makes the tongue looser. I wondered if we would have to become bandits to sustain ourselves. The Marshal had told me of such things before.

"Honor is more important than coin," he said stoically. The Marshal was unfazed by our lack of funds. "I refuse to fight against my friends and my former sponsor." The statement made it clear that I was not to continue this discussion.

We sold all but two horses. That money was running out and now sponsors for the upcoming season were becoming difficult to find. I learned King Henry had put out the word he was not happy with Sir William Marshal because of his son. Many potential sponsors had no desire to make an enemy of the high king. It made the Marshal angry when he heard King Henry also believed the lies about him. Just when it seemed our darkest hour had arrived, something unbelievable happened. We received a letter from Baldwin. I read it to the Marshal.

"My friend, Hugh and I decided matters could not be allowed to continue. We went to the young King and protested. We were convinced of your innocence. We had a powerful ally with us, who offered combat to prove Adam and his friends had lied. It was none other than the Baron de Luisgnan. Yes, the same man who had imprisoned you years ago. It was impossible for Henry not to consider the claim. A man who had no reason to help was risking his life to clear you. Bertran also asked the young King to reconsider the case. Forgive me for not following your wishes in this matter but conditions in the mesne were deteriorating alarmingly.

"The young King pressured Thomas, weakest of the three, to tell the truth or face the Baron. Thomas broke down and confessed they had concocted the story about the Queen's infidelity. Henry flew into a rage and banished the three. He told me to find you and bring you back. This note should reach you about a week before I arrive. We need you desperately. All is not well."—Baldwin.

We were in Flanders at a rather poor-looking inn when Baldwin reached us. His dark curly hair, long and unkempt, had to be brushed continuously off his cherubic face. The smile and the sparkle in his eyes were a most welcome sight. Well dressed as usual he looked at us with surprise. He began to explain how the plot had unraveled.

"Marshal, you hardheaded bastard, you look wretched." Our clothes had not been replaced as our funds had shrunk and the wear was obvious. Food was more important. He placed both hands on the Marshal and continued, "Can you not repair the rift with young Henry or are you ready to chase rabbits for sustenance? Luisgnan has compelled the truth. I know your grievance with the young King is great, but we need you. Trouble comes a calling. Without your steady hand the young King begins to plot anew and places us all in peril. He journeys to the south to seek funds and allies. He does so under the guise of a pilgrimage to Rocamadour." Baldwin shook his head causing the locks to obscure his face for a moment.

"My friend, I knew the day would come, but I must admit the way it transpired is a surprise. I have learned to place pride in its proper place. Lewellyn knows full well what I say. I shall return, but first there be something important to attend to." He slapped Baldwin on the back and then embraced him. "I shall not miss the wretched conditions of life I now lead," he said smiling broadly and winking at me. Baldwin was overjoyed but puzzled by the mysterious mention of something important.

"What troubles you, my friend?" he asked tossing his head back to relieve his face from the ever-encroaching brown locks.

"Not yet. Tell the young King I will be arriving shortly. Do not mention my delay. Now we need some ale!" He left us all wondering what was going on in his mind, but we knew it would be useless to ask. We had to trust. We ordered several pints and drank the health of the band of friends that had remained loyal to the Marshal. The Marshal even reluctantly raised the cup to the health of the Baron. I did so too, totally confused about the code these men shared. First I try to kill you, then I imprison you and ask ransom with a threat of death and finally I risk my own life to save yours. It made no sense. In the morning Baldwin returned to Rouen, but not before grumbling to the landlord of the lice in his bed.

I was curious about where we were going instead of directly to Rouen with Baldwin. I was told we were going to Chinon. I was puzzled. The Marshal said it was vital. I would soon find out why and another mystery would be solved as well. I packed our few remaining possessions on the two horses we had left and we headed south. The warmer days of spring and the brighter prospects that loomed ahead made for a pleasant journey

Chinon castle was a massive structure at the center of King Henry's power. The fortress was built on a ridge which paralleled the Loire River. There were numerous gray stone towers linked together with high walls forming a continuous line and enclosing the inner buildings much like a huge boat riding the crest of the ridge. The river ran swiftly past this bastion worthy of a king like Henry II. It would take a huge force to threaten such a well-built edifice.

When we arrived at the base of the thirty-foot walls I was nervous. What if the word had not reached the King about the Marshal being found innocent? It was a foolish thought. Nothing escaped the ever-watchful eye of King Henry. After a day to clean and refresh ourselves the Marshal requested an audience with the high king. We were immediately escorted into his presence.

The King paced behind a large oak table with several documents scattered carelessly across the surface. He looked up at the Marshal with a suspicious stare. "Why are you here?" His nostrils flared and it was clear it would not be a friendly reunion.

"Two reasons, Majesty. First, to seek letters declaring my name clear of the outrageous lie to which I have been subjected. Second, to warn you a traitor is again turning your son against you," he said looking directly at the surly monarch.

"Perhaps 'tis you who cannot be trusted?" the high king said. The King's tone was not a friendly one. His eyes darted back and forth from the Marshal and me. "Who is the traitor of whom you speak?" he asked in an offhanded manner while casually stabbing a paper lying on the table with his dagger which he had removed from its scabbard on his hip.

"I will not say 'til I have real proof. I know the hurt of false accusation only too well, but I shall have that proof soon," the Marshal exclaimed with an air of confidence.

"An easy excuse to use. We know not whom to trust, but we cannot deny you have been wronged. We will grant your request for letters. Time will tell if my son becomes a traitor again. By God's eyes this time pardons will be as scarce as faerie dust. Tell him so when you return!" He turned his back and walked out of the room.

A day later we received the promised letters. I read them to Sir William. He was satisfied and said it was time to return to the young King. The young King was staying at a village near the monastery of Rocamadour. As we prepared for the journey the Marshal turned to me and said, "When we reach the young King, tell not Bertran of our visit to King Henry."

I stopped my packing and with a perplexed look asked, "Why say you that, my lord?"

"Because he is the traitor who has made fools of us all!" he said with passion.

I stood as still as if I had just been struck with a battle ax. I stuttered, "He…he, he is my friend and he helped to clear your name. It cannot be," I exclaimed disbelieving what I had just heard.

"Nay, Lewellyn. He was your friend only for information. Information he passed on to his employer the King of France. He helped me because he needs me to help in the fight brewing with King Henry. He is a truly clever man. We have been deceived." There was disappointment mixed with anger in his voice.

"But how know you this, my lord?" I still needed proof my friend and tutor was a traitor.

"I always knew one of the company was giving the French King aid. At first, like you, I suspected Queen Marguerite. Proving it was not her near cost me my life. I knew it was not Baldwin. He did not know many of the details that made their way to the French court. Likewise Hugh was innocent. He came after the trouble that led us to Gisor. The traitor has always been among us. It had to be our three friends or Bertran," he said making perfect sense. Still my mind would not accept the guilt of the man who had done so much to educate me.

"Why was it not the three conspirators who bore false witness against you? Why else would they do what they did?" I said sure that was the logical explanation.

"Their treachery was because of greed and jealousy. They merely sought more spoils from the tournaments and thought my removal would accomplish that. As I told you once before, there are often many plotters at work in a royal court and they do not always work together. They were unaware of Bertran's real purpose. When they were dismissed, the pressure for Henry to take up arms against his father should have stopped. It did not! Queen Eleanor, imprisoned in England, is in no position to organize such an undertaking. It leaves Bertran as the spy," he said with an air of finality.

"But do we know the young King will still rebel? Perhaps Bertran councils against such and it falls on deaf ears?" I said desperately seeking another answer. The evidence to me seemed weak and not conclusive.

"You are right. I am not sure. 'Tis why I did not expose Bertran to the King. We will see when we return to the young King. If he knows of my visit, he will not continue his urging and will wait for a better time to resume his activities. I do not want that to happen. This is why I have instructed you to be silent. I must be sure."

"Yea, my lord, I shall remain silent. Will you ask the young King to confirm your suspicions?" I asked naively.

"Nay. Henry is far closer to Bertran than you realize. He would protect him at all cost. Now you must forget this conversation. I know you are disappointed, and perhaps, I am wrong, but much depends on confirming my suspicions. You must act your part well." He finished the conversation and we resumed packing. I was alone with my thoughts and vowed to reveal nothing when we returned. Deep inside, I continued to hope he was wrong about my friend. The desire to believe in someone we like can oft outweigh the facts.

The journey to the monastery took us through the lovely rolling hills of the southern provinces. As we traveled we combined with the many pilgrims on their way to the place of the holy relics and healing miracles that were said to take place at Rocamadour. The strong faith of the pilgrims made me feel a little uncomfortable since my own was sadly neglected. All were happy a fighting man like the Marshal was with them in case they might encounter brigands. The pilgrims oft became victims since they were known to be in possession of gifts to exchange for the miracles. As we surmounted a small forested hill the monastery came into spectacular view. It was easy to see why it held such a special place in the hearts of the faithful. It was beautiful and serene all at once. The structure appeared to grow out of the face of a shear cliff. The buildings clung to the rock face as if the Almighty had carved them himself. When the sunlight hit the monastery the stone seemed to turn to gold. A small road snaked up the cliff to the buildings. Throngs of pilgrims passed each other in the narrow confines, each asking those coming down about their experience at the holy site. They refused to speak and it was apparent something was amiss.

When we arrived we were greeted by Hugh de Hamelcourt who welcomed the Marshal and gave us the troubling news.

"The young King is committed to another struggle against his father. To that end he has employed a brigand by the name of Sancho to provide mercenaries for the upcoming struggle. In order to finance his move young Henry has removed several valuable altar pieces from the chapel in the monastery," Hugh said. "It is not a good way to begin a campaign by angering God." The Marshal looked at me with a knowing nod. Bertran was the traitor! I had to be careful and not let my emotions show.

The Marshal shook his head in a manner I knew well. It signaled disappointment and frustration. He was in no position to tell the young King what to do after their recent estrangement. I recalled his father's warning about forgiving another rebellion. I wondered how the Marshal would relay this warning without being accused of being disloyal.

It was late in the afternoon when we were reunited with Henry. Seated near him were Bertran and the aforementioned Sancho. It was an awkward moment. Kings do not make apologies for their mistakes. They simply pretend they never happened. He rose to his feet. He looked tired and the flower of youth had deserted his cheeks. He was no longer the boy I remembered at the tournaments. He had a hard and bitter countenance. He coughed and spoke to my master.

"Your arrival is well timed. The final act is about to be played. I am weary of the King's bullying of my brothers, my mother and me. With the help of Sancho and the forces he can muster; we will end the tyranny once and for all. We have made a small loan from the good friars here. They will be repaid when we have won. You counseled me truly, ten years ago, when you said there be plenty of fighting men available for those with the purse. I will not make the same mistake I made then. We will have the money and men to do the thing right this time. I welcome you back to the cause," he said with a voice tinged with apprehension. I was sure that even though welcomed, the Marshal's return was regarded with some distrust.

"Thank you, sire. I have been absent from your household too long. I shall be of whatever service you have in mind for me." He bowed and cast a suspicious glance at Sancho.

"We shall talk again soon. We are not feeling well and shall retire early." Henry looked pale. His statement was truthful—something was wrong.

I looked at Sancho and two of his bodyguards. He was dark skinned and as hard as a smith's anvil. There were scars on his cheek and arms. This was a man who knew combat. He was eyeing the Marshal. He had surely heard of the Marshal's reputation and was looking to see if the man measured up to the legend. He curled his lip and nodded his head several times. I took it as a sign he was satisfied the stories might be true. My master bowed and we left the room.

We were shown to our quarters. The Marshal examined the room carefully feeling the stone walls as if he was seeking a loose block. He looked out the door and the window slit. Then I realized he was checking for unwanted ears. Satisfied we were alone, he turned to me. A worried look came over his faced as he spoke.

"Sancho comes with a steep price. It is costing Henry more than the gold in Rocamadour's chapel just to have him here with a small force."

"You did not tell him of the King's warning," I said softly also looking around as though I knew what I was looking for.

"Nay. You saw who was at his side. I am sure they have promises from Philip. This time the money will be forthcoming. Philip will not shrink from this undertaking like his father. King Henry is getting old and he has made many enemies. I suspect Philip will regain lost lands in exchange for money and men. The old king will be heartbroken when his favorite son betrays him again. This time will be a fight to the death. I fear there is little we can do. My council is unwanted. There be much to consider, with conflicting oaths and all…" he said stroking his chin and leaving the sentence unfinished as his thoughts turned inward. The Marshal had returned to a nest of traitors. What course would he choose?

I mulled over the events which lay before us. I was angry that Bertran could not be trusted and yet we might be on the same side. It was not a prospect that I relished.

I found it difficult to sleep. I thought about the many times Bertran and I had been together and tried to see if I could remember anything which might have shown his treachery. I searched my memory over and over. I could find nothing. I was convinced my dull wits were responsible for missing what the Marshal had seen.

The following morning the young King did not appear. He did not show for supper in the evening. The same was true for the next three days. The Marshal became concerned and sought word from Queen Marguerite as to what was wrong. She came to us with a very worried look on her face.

"Henry is very ill. I have sent for a physician. Come with me." The Queen guided us to their rooms. We followed quickly. I could not help thinking of Hugh's remarks about angering God. When we arrived in the King's quarters we could see he was seriously ill. He was ashen faced and had lost weight in the short time since we had talked with him. By his side was a very worried Bertran. Bertran looked at the Marshal and whispered, "He has the flux." The Marshal reached over and took his hand. He kneeled beside his bed and whispered something into his ear. The young King responded with a feeble, "Yea, I would." The Marshal rose to his feet and looked at Bertran and the Queen. He motioned for them to join him outside the room. They quietly reconvened in the hallway.

"He is dying. I asked if he wanted to see his father. It is not good to leave this life with anger possessing your soul. With your permission I will send Lewellyn to get the King." A white-faced Bertran nodded. Marguerite began to sob and also nodded as she leaned on the Marshal's arm for support. The Marshal turned to me and said, "Take the best horses. Sir Baldwin and Sir

Hugh will accompany you. Go to the King and tell him of this grave situation. This will end quickly so you must make all haste. My lady, I fear you must seek one of the friars. He needs a priest." He dismissed all to accomplish our tasks.

I turned and dashed down the hall and out to the stable. I informed the groom of the urgency of my mission. He ran to make the necessary preparations. In less than an hour, I was on the road with a pouch of bread and water hanging from my side, and racing down the road we had traveled just a few days before. With me were Baldwin, Sir Hugh and two men-at-arms. It was not safe to travel such a distance alone.

We found King Henry in two days holding court at Tours. I was told to wait when I explained my mission and who sent me. It was afternoon before I was shown into the King's presence. He had a strange look on his face. It was more one of anger, rather than one of concern. He spoke.

"Well, William sends you again. This time it is with a message my son is dying. Does he expect me to fall into such an obvious trap? I know what is going on there. The Marshal plans poorly. I expected better of him."

"But Sire, 'tis true. I saw the young King's failing condition myself," I pleaded.

"Be careful, Lewellyn. If you have become part of this treason your life will not be spared because of my feeling for you! Return and tell my son to come to me alone if he seeks my understanding. This audience is at an end." He turned his back. My hands were shaking as I was led away. I was told to get on my horse and with my companions leave Tours before the King decided to imprison us. In utter despair, I did as instructed. It would be hard to face the Marshal having failed so miserably.

It took two and a half days to make the return trip. With my head low, I went in. The Marshal was keeping watch in the young King's rooms. I explained my failure and the shortness of the meeting with the King. I could see young Henry was even worse.

"The King will regret this decision for the rest of his life," the Marshal said somberly.

Five days later, Henry, the young King, was dead, his body a wasted shell of what he had been. God had taken revenge for the violation of his holy sanctuary. The Marshal and I prepared to take the body back to the King. Hugh was sent ahead to inform the King of the death of his son. Bertran, after many tears the previous night, was gone in the morning. Queen Marguerite had left for Rouen to make burial arrangements. As we prepared to take the body to the cart, we were suddenly approached by Sancho and several armed men.

The Marshal was unarmed except for a small dagger. It was going to be a difficult moment.

Sancho began, "My men and I have been promised money not yet paid. We will keep the body until the terms are met. If you wish, you may pay us now. I know you are said to be the finest knight in all Christendom, but armed as you are you are in no position to fight men like us," he declared confidently. "We seek only that which is due us."

The Marshal looked at the men around us. They were a very rough lot, hardened by years of plying a very dangerous trade. I looked to see if there were any weapons within reach. The only ones were in the hands of Sancho's men. The Marshal addressed Sancho in a totally calm voice. "I am not adverse to the odds. I have faced worse, but your claim is a just one. As one who has earned his living in the same manner, I accept your need to be paid. I am presently without the funds you request. I have just returned to this household after a long absence, as you know. I give my oath I will return as your hostage, if you give us leave to go and arrange the burial of my liege lord. The time it will take to raise the funds would leave the body in a wretched state and unsuited for a decent burial. I will guarantee your payment. You have my sacred word of honor."

Sancho paused for a moment, and then said in an equally calm voice, "Most pledges of honor are worthless and a man in my profession would be a fool to listen, but yours is different. Go, bury your king. We will wait here for you and the money." Some of his men began to grumble. "Silence! I have no desire to lose some of you. We are not dealing with some soft, pampered nobleman. It is well known that Sir William Marshal never breaks an oath. I still command here unless one of you would like to challenge me." There was silence. "Do what you must, William Marshal. I shall send five of my men to see you are not accosted by outlaws on your journey. This be not safe country." It was true, but I knew Sancho had found a polite way of watching us without insulting the Marshal.

We finished preparing the cart and I climbed into the driver's seat. The Marshal and Sancho's men were mounted on horseback. I do believe Sancho trusted my master because the Marshal had put on his sword for the trip to Chinon.

It rained before we reached Chinon. Even though the monks had prepared the young King's body, an odor of death was beginning to rise until the gentle rain cleansed the air. We sought the King to finish our task and were met by Sir Hugh. I was nervous returning after being so angrily sent away. We were received by a very different King Henry. He had received the news from Sir Hugh the day before and had been in mourning over his favorite son.

As we entered the room, the King's visage was one of despair and brooding. He mumbled the words in a soft unHenry-like way, "You spoke the truth, Lewellyn. In my anger, I was unable to recognize it. God is not done with me yet. You are not to blame." It was strange to see a king so humble before one as lowly as I. I felt sorry for him. "Sir William, tell me about my son's death," he said looking up as if to see into the heavens for some answer to a father's grief. The Marshal told the king of the illness and how it progressed until all hope of recovery was lost.

"Sire, I have an oath to return with the men outside as a hostage until money owed their master can be paid. Lewellyn shall explain the details. I must go. They have trusted my word as a condition of bringing your son's body here. Sire, he asked your forgiveness. I pledge to you those be his final words," he said earnestly.

"It is I who should be asking forgiveness. Go. Keep your promise." The King spoke the words as he stared at the gray stone floor.

The Marshal turned and left me with the King. He asked about the events after the young King's demise and I related all the details, except the information about Bertran de Born.

"The Marshal needs your help, sire. He has no money and will be a prisoner until the debt is paid." I was nervous because I was asking the King to pay money to men who were going to be used to attack him. It was a bold request the King could easily refuse.

"We shall make good his word. He has sacrificed himself for my son. It would disgrace my son if we did not redeem this good knight's honorable deed. We will not add more suffering to this sad happening. The money shall be raised."

He thanked me and said he would send us back with the money in two days. We were instructed to bring the Marshal back to Chinon. He looked very tired. It was very unusual for Henry II. The constant movement was gone. It was the worst news any man could hear. His son was dead. As promised a bag of coins was produced in two days and we were on our way back to Rocamadour.

Sancho received his payment and thanked the Marshal for arranging the payment so quickly. The Marshal, in return, thanked Sancho for trusting him. They were, as my master had said, men who respected the other's calling. Sancho and his men departed the following morning. The business concluded, we set out for Chinon. I rode slightly behind Hugh and the Marshal and listened to their conversation. Hugh informed the Marshal of King Henry's mood and his appreciation for Sir William's efforts to redeem his son's body.

"I believe you have finally won over his majesty. I know not if it be a good thing or bad, when you consider what has happened to some he has called friend," the old veteran said as he cast a skeptical look at his companion.

"I have sworn an oath of fealty to the King which I will always honor. We have several more things to accomplish before we can consider our duty to the young King completed."

"And what might they be?" Hugh asked.

"First, there is the matter of the traitor who led young Henry to be disloyal to his father."

Hugh responded with an incredulous air, "Traitor? By God's eyes, who was a traitor?"

"Our former friend and songwriter Bertran de Born." Hugh was just as surprised as I had been when the Marshal explained the events of the past ten years and Bertran's duplicity. He explained the role of the King of France in the plot. Once laid out, it was easy to see. Bertran had been as close to young Henry as anyone, perhaps even a lover. Hugh just shook his head as the Marshal listed the litany of events.

"The King must be told. He can decide if any action need be taken. I believe he will seek the troubadour and request he prepare a song for the heavenly choir. After that, I swore to the young King, on his deathbed, I would take his cross to the Holy Land and pray for the repose of his soul. I will add a few prayers for my own," he said with glance at the sky.

A shutter ran through my body. I would have to witness the death of the man who had unlocked the secrets of music and writing for me. It was not something I wanted to do, even though he had used my friendship shamefully. The second promise meant a very long sea journey, and my inclination to experience mal-de-mar on such trips was making me fearful. Trips across the Channel were bad enough; this would be a journey keeping us at sea for weeks. I was sure my lifeless body would be buried in the place I hated most—the sea! Each time I was sure my life was going to be wonderful, something happened to reverse my thinking. My head was hanging low as we rode on toward the castle of Chinon. I was not very happy when we spied the stone towers silhouetted against the evening sky.

I helped the Marshal unpack and carry his belongings to our new quarters. We would see the King in the morning. We asked for some victuals to be delivered to our new rooms. We had not stopped for supper in our haste to reach Chinon. It was then the wheel of my life turned again. The door opened and a serving girl handed me the tray. I almost dropped it. It was Celine! I was frozen for what seemed like days, but it was only a moment. She smiled and said in French, "You are the talk of the scullery. I hope you will find some time to tell me of your adventures."

I stood mute. She was as lovely as ever. She was older, but even more pleasing to the eye. I recovered momentary control of my mouth and stammered, "I...I...shall." She vanished out the door and for a moment I thought I had imagined the event until the Marshal burst into laughter.

"I see you have not been cured. Will there be a song of rejoicing written tonight?" he asked with a wry smile and a wink. I was still holding the tray of cheese, bread and beer and unable to respond to the jest. I felt my face flush as I placed the tray on the table in front of my master. "You fail to hide your emotions, my friend. But hold, I should not tease the one who twice brought money for my release. Perhaps, you shall find what I have not. I have known many women in my life, but none stirred my heart as she does yours. I envy you. I have buried the first of King Henry's sons and I have none of my own. This life of mine has left little time for such." It was the second time I heard him speak in a melancholy way. "Enough jesting, we eat. We must see the King in the morn and discover our fate," he said eyeing the food hungrily.

That night, as I lay on my mat, staring at the ceiling, I felt empty. Like the Marshal, I loved the adventure our lives had provided, but happiness and a feeling of permanence were not part of it. Since we are all mortal, if we hope to leave behind some of what we are it can only be through our children. It was the reason the King was so disconsolate. The loss of a child is so much worse than losing a parent. When we lose a child we lose our hopes and dreams for the future. The death of the young King demonstrated one inescapable fact—we cannot know when the thread of life will be cut. The young King had no sons to carry on in his name. Would it be the same for the Marshal and me?

It was plain I was not alone in pondering these thoughts. The Marshal was now thirty-eight and even though he was stronger than any man half his age, he knew he could not go on forever. Would he ever know happiness rather than duty? The question would not be answered for many more years. My answer would come sooner. The Marshal was now in service to King Henry. We crossed the courtyard to the new life under the man who had been our benefactor, then our enemy and now liege lord again. Into his hands our fate was once more delivered.

Chapter 8
Two Tasks Remain

A bright sun showered us with warmth as we crossed the courtyard to meet with the King. The Marshal strode confidently toward the great hall, the red lion rearing proudly in the center of his powerful chest. His large broadsword, half as tall as me, hung from his hip. I waited by the doorway as the Marshal approached the brooding monarch.

"Sir William, welcome back. We owe you thanks for your efforts to ease our grief. What can you tell us about the events? We have heard, but perhaps you can add more." It was clear his spy network was providing more information than we had recently shared. It was though he was testing us to see if we would reveal all.

"Majesty, there be much to add." He spoke at length of the suffering of the young King and his final days. He explained the dealings with the mercenaries and why they were present with King Henry's son. The King's face began to show anger as talk of rebellion was mentioned. It was then, the secret was revealed. Looking straight at the King, the Marshal began.

"Majesty, the last I was here I had suspicions about who encouraged your son to act against you. I now name the culprit. The name is Bertran de Born," he said raising one eyebrow and looking to see the King's reaction.

The lethargy which had gripped King Henry vanished. He rose from his seat and began pacing. "We are not surprised to hear this name. How come you by this information?"

The Marshal told the story I had already heard twice before. King Henry walked around the table. His fists were clenched. The King stopped when the story ended, and paused momentarily. There was complete silence in the room. Suddenly, his fist struck the table, and a cup perched there crashed to the floor.

"This treachery will be dealt with!" Henry snarled. "Summon my councilors. Sir William, stay. The rest leave." The old King Henry was back. Mourning was replaced by revenge. I thought about the gregarious Bertran and knew his life was going to end badly. There was still a part of me hoping he could find a place to hide from the wrath of Henry Plantagenet. The plans to hunt down Bertran would be delayed while we journeyed to Rouen for the funeral of the young King and to say our farewell to Marguerite. It was a sad end to a life that had held promise only to be snuffed out by ambition and intrigue.

The following week the Marshal and I returned to Chinon. Our new quarters had been prepared by the chamberlain. I had already unpacked his few belongings. He smiled at my efficiency and announced I would be packing them again. I asked why and he explained. We would be going with the King to seek Bertran.

"Doest thou know where he is, my lord?" I asked.

"Nay. He cannot go to Philip. He would not implicate his master in the plot. Philip cannot protect him unless he is prepared to war with Henry. Although a war may be in Philip's future plans, 'tis doubtful he believes now is the time for such a confrontation. Nay, I suspect he will seek help in the Loire Valley. He has friends there who might try to hide him. The King has a very efficient spy network. If he is there, they will find him. The future bodes ill for Sir Bertran de Born." The Marshal's demeanor showed little feeling for Bertran's fate. He had betrayed trust and for the Marshal that was unforgivable.

The next day a messenger was sent to King Henry's new heir, Duke Richard, to send men to deal with the traitor. Since fealty was due his liege lord, Duke Richard complied, but said he would need to keep most of his forces in Aquitaine to deal with rebellions there. King Henry agreed, but suspected Richard was not anxious to participate. While Aquitaine brought the King great wealth, keeping the rebellious barons in check was an ongoing task. It was not surprising that Duke Richard was gaining a reputation as a formidable warrior in these continual struggles and now as next in line I surmised he would not cry too hard if his father met an untimely death in such a campaign. Sending only a small force would meet his obligation and maybe advance the day when he no longer owed fealty. When preparations were complete, we waited for King Henry's spies to discover the missing Bertran.

Finally after six months, news of Bertran's hiding place reached the King. His quarry had been given refuge by a baron in his castle at Amboise. A war council was held to discuss how to proceed. The men and equipment were assembled. Two weeks later a large force headed for the very-well-constructed fortress of Amboise.

Bertran had chosen well. It would require a substantial effort to lay siege to such a place. He hoped King Henry would not feel inclined to undertake such an expensive effort. He badly underestimated the fury of the bereaved King.

It was raining heavily when we reached Amboise. Our force had slowed to a crawl as we approached the village. Conditions were awful and the villeins had advanced warning of our movements. The village at the base of the fortress was already abandoned. The residents of the town had either fled or sought refuge in the castle. The mud made moving the trebuchet we brought with us very difficult. Men cursed and yelled as the animals struggled to pull the device until they finally stopped in frustration and announced that we needed to wait for the ground to dry before setting it in the firing position. A trebuchet was an impressive siege machine and I had a morbid fascination to see it in action. This would be my first real battle. There would be no honorable "captures" in this contest. Dealing death with destruction was the aim of this event. We occupied the abandoned cottages and waited for the weather to clear.

The castle was an imposing structure perched atop a high hill. The high walls were thick stone. The entry road was a narrow ramp rising between two massive walls. It switched back after going through a gate with a large portcullis. Murder-holes above the portcullis promised a deadly bath of boiling oil to any who stormed the gate. The switchback design would give archers on the walls deadly access to those who successfully passed the first gate's defense. The side of the castle facing the river had a large cliff which needed to be scaled before one reached the walls. There was no moat.

I asked the Marshal how they would overcome the fortification. He explained, "Lewellyn, the normal course would be to starve the residences in a siege, but King Henry is not willing to waste the time it will take. He is not desirous of giving his many enemies the time to plan mischief in some other part of his sprawling empire. Therefore we will need several malvoisiers. I shall have the honor of leading the attack from the first one," he said with a mocking tone. These huge wooden towers got their name from a French word meaning "bad neighbor." It meant I would also see another of the great siege devices in action. My first real battle promised to be a complete education in warfare. When they attacked the Marshal would be inside the covered tower with a group of experienced fighters.

The towers represented a mortal threat to the defenders. A supreme effort would be made to destroy them, and the men they contained. Those inside the castle knew if the walls were successfully breached by this device the end would come quickly. Leading such an attack was considered a great honor. I considered it a good way to die! I was suspicious that King Henry had devised a subtle way to rid himself of William Marshal.

I was beginning to understand why honor and death were so closely linked in the Marshal's precious code of chivalry. The only way to get a person to do something which could cause their death was to promise great honor, since any other reward was useless to a dead man. When I asked the Marshal he said, "Your reasoning strays little from the truth. Yet any man, who succeeds in a dangerous task, by skill or luck, also enjoys material rewards if he survives. We all die sometime. I and my fellows think now will not be the time. Such is the nature of our training," he explained with no more concern than someone speaking as though he was going to hunt wild boar.

"I agreed we will all die, but I prefer not to hurry the process," I said raising my eyebrows as if I had uttered some profound wisdom.

He simply laughed and grinned.

The sky in the morning had cleared. The Marshal and a crew of workers assembled the malvoisiers by using the beams and planks from two nearby barns and several huts. First a large platform was constructed with two axles and oversized wooden wheels turning it into what looked like a giant flat cart. Next a square frame was built on top of the platform. On that another smaller platform was constructed and then the process was repeated a third time until it resembled three unfinished huts stacked upon each other. Planks were attached to the sides. The top level was even with the top of the walls of the fortress. Large poles extended from the sides of the first level so men could push the behemoth to the fortress walls.

Meanwhile, the King's men took whatever they needed from the town. Years of hard work were wiped out as they stripped farms of any supplies not moved inside the walls of the castle. The villagers had not had time to take more than themselves when we approached. Regardless of who was victorious, it would be a hard winter for the farmers and their families. The baron would suffer only when the castle was taken. His supplies were stored safely inside the walls. He could agree to yield the offending Bertran and save his possessions. The townspeople had already lost, regardless of the outcome.

By sev'nnight, the towers were completed. The ground had dried sufficiently to move them. They were pulled closer to the walls. The trebuchet was also moved into position. We saw the inhabitants of the castle watching from the battlements. Movements on top of the walls indicated defensive measures were being prepared. At a distance of two hundred yards the siege towers were halted. Several arrows were launched from the tops of the walls, but they fell short. Once the malvoisiers were closer, those arrows would be flaming ones. For now they were beyond the archers' range. Just before the attack the sides of the towers would be soaked with water to deter the flaming arrows from igniting them into fiery coffins.

As evening approached, I went with the Marshal to inspect the tower he would use the next day, if the weather held. He took a torch to light his way in the dark interior. We entered through a doorway cut into the rear. I saw, by torch light, the first level had a floor with a ladder on the left side going up to a hole in the floor of the second level. Several narrow slits were cut in the front wall. We climbed the ladder and saw the same arrangement on the second level. Climbing a second ladder to the third level, we reached a room with the same narrow slits as the floors below, but the front wall contained a large trap door which could be dropped like a drawbridge. There was enough room for about ten armored men. The Marshal explained he would be here. They would drop the ramp onto the wall and then he would rush with his force onto the battlements. Others, on the second level and ground floor, would scramble up the ladders and join them on the walls.

The plan was to position the towers to attack the defenders on either side of the entrance road and fight their way down the ramps, to the portcullis, then open it for the main force. The trebuchet would be used to clear the defenders from the section of the wall where the towers attempted the assault. The trick was to place the machine at just the proper angle, so as not to hit the moving tower and still launch giant rocks at the defenders on the walls. It would have to stop firing the rocks for several moments before the tower reached its final position. The timing was critical. Stop too soon and the defenders would have time to mass at the spot on the wall where the ramp would be dropped. Stop too late and you could destroy the tower and kill your own force. While this was going on, the second tower would be pushed into place and force the defenders to keep some troops guarding the other side of the entrance. Archers would launch waves of arrows at the walls to help keep the defenders from shooting too many flaming arrows at the "bad neighbor."

We completed the inspection and went back down. The Marshal went to see the King and discuss final plans for the attack in the morning. I went back to the cottage we had taken and prepared the Marshal's supper. When he arrived, he said little. I knew the attack would commence early in the morning so the sun would be in the eyes of the defenders as it rose above the horizon. He had his squire prepare his hauberk and helmet. He would wear the light one. He needed to see in all directions when exiting the tower. He personally sharpened his pole ax. I spoke only briefly. This was no a time for idle chatter.

"Master, you chose the ax?" His skill with the sword was superior to any man so I was surprised by his choice.

"The weapon is better suited for close-in fighting in a cramped space. Both ends are deadly when used properly. I want to be sure the blade has the edge I require, and for that, I trust no one." He slowly rubbed the stone against the blade in short curved strokes. It made an eerie screeching sound as the stone was drawn again and again in a most deliberate fashion. I think it gave him time to consider if his preparations were as complete as they could be. War was deadly serious. It was not like the lighthearted moments before a tournament. He finished his task by testing the point of the butt, holding the weapon in front of him for several moments as though he was offering some type of prayer. He chose a short mace and placed it next to the ax on a small table. Satisfied he retired.

I found it impossible to sleep. I rolled over on my pallet many times. I glanced again and again at the window to see if the darkness of night was changing into the dim light of dawn. I must have been on my thirtieth rollover when I saw the Marshal rise. He called quietly to me.

"Lewellyn, make ready. Summon my squire. 'Tis time." I jumped to perform the requested tasks. While his squire was helping him dress, I prepared some bread and cheese for the breakfast. The Marshal ate quickly. He gathered his weapons and went out the door. As he was leaving in the dimness of the room he turned and said, " If I do not return, see to it my belongings are sent to my brother Anselm." He walked across the street and headed for the two dark objects stabbing the pre-dawn sky. I saw him disappear into the bowels of the monster followed by about thirty men.

Activity was all about me. Buckets of water were being carried from the river and poured on the front of the two towers from the opened trapdoor. The trapdoor was closed. Men carrying shields offered some protection for the large number of men who would push the towers. A line of archers stood behind the towers.

My attention was drawn to the crew of the trebuchet. On one end of the trebuchet's arm was a basket full of rocks. It was cranked until it was ten feet off the ground and locked into position. The heavy rope sling attached to the other end was positioned long wooden chute below the arm. When the weapon master was satisfied all was proper it was loaded with a large boulder. They had already tested the range on the previous afternoon. The basket was at the proper height according to the captain in charge and release was pulled. The massive basket dropped and the boulder in the sling lurched forward, gathering speed. The arm swung skyward and the mighty stone was launched. It made a squeaking noise as the arm recoiled. The stone, about the size of a small chair, moved in a slow arc through the early morning sky. Men on the wall scattered as it hurtled toward the battlement. It struck about three feet from the top shattering on impact. Small shards of rock flew in all directions. At the same time the men began to push the towers forward. The procedure was repeated again and again. When the tower containing the Marshal was about thirty-five paces from the wall, the archers behind the moving tower grabbed their arrows and nocked their bows. They waited for the command to loose their shafts at the spot where the stones were striking. The order to fire was given, and dozens of arrows made a whistling sound as they showered the battlements. A large group of mounted knights gathered in front of the gates of the castle just beyond the range of the archers scrambling atop the walls. I could see many had ignited their arrows and I waited for the attack. When they judged the towers to be close enough they began.

I could almost hear my heart pounding as the malvoisier containing the Marshal continued to advance into the storm of fire. Flaming arrows hit the structure but none seemed to be able to ignite the water-soaked walls. Many missed. I was surprised a skilled archer could miss such a large target, but then I never tried to shoot an arrow while running and ducking boulders and waves of arrows. You could occasionally hear a scream as a defender was unable to avoid the numerous slender shafts which filled the air. Several archers fired at the men pushing the beast. These men received some protection from shield bearers walking beside them. It had the look of travelers sheltering themselves from the rain. This rain was deadly and occasionally you could hear a scream as some arrows leaked through the protection. When the malvoisier was twenty paces from the wall, the trebuchet stopped. At ten paces the archers launched one last furious salvo.

I imagined what would happen next. The trapdoor would drop and form a bridge from the tower to the walkway on top of the wall. The defenders, no longer cowering from the storm of arrows and rocks, would rush the ramp trying to prevent the men inside from crossing successfully. The Marshal would be in the lead with his death-dealing ax. Everyone with him would scream a battle cry and all hell would break loose on the bridge. It would be the most danger-filled seconds for my master. If he could reach the walkway before he could be attacked from all sides; he would be able to put the parapet to his back and have one less angle of attack. The men in the tower with him were the best. The fighting would be hand to hand.

As the tower reached its final position there was an unexpected silence. The rain of arrows from the walls ceased. I heard the trapdoor drop with a thud but there was silence. No blood curdling cries or crashes of axes against shields. What had happen? Had the defenders been struck dead by a spell from some sorcerer?

Later, the Marshal told me exactly what happened. He saw the wall from one of the slits in the malvoisier. When the arrows stopped, he expected to see the defenders rush back to the place where they knew the bridge would drop. There was no one! Suspecting a trap, he strained to see along the wall, but the narrow slit had a limited view. The door dropped and there walking toward the bridge was a lone figure, unarmed. It was Bertran!

"Marshal, let no one else die because of me. I am your prisoner. Leave the good people of this demesne in peace. Do with me as you will."

The door was closed and the two men climbed down the ladders to the first floor. The Marshal turned to one of his men and said, "Tell the King I have Sir Bertran de Born as prisoner. The rest of you leave, in case this is a trap."

"I assure you, William, it is no trap. As a gesture of good faith the gates of the castle will be opened. King Henry has what he has come after. Tell the King I beg him to forgive my friend, the Baron of Amboise, whose only offense was to grant me shelter."

"Always the grand gesture, Bertran. You never could resist playing to a big audience. I will send a message to the King explaining the surrender."

"I suspect this will be my last performance, William." They sat on the floor in the dimly lighted interior and talked about the happier days of the young King, until the door in the back creaked open. Standing in the doorway, surrounded by the bright outside light was King Henry—sword in hand. The Marshal rose and bowed. "Sire, your prisoner," he said holding his hand above the still-seated Bertran.

"Well, Bertran, 'tis said you be the most gifted of men in your ability to craft words. They say you charm anyone with your flowery speech. Choose the words well as they will be your last." King Henry sneered.

"You can only slay the body for I have already died. When your son died, my heart died with him. I loved him better than any man alive, including you.

Strike as you will. This world holds no joy for Bertran de Born." He went down on both knees in front of the stunned monarch. He leaned forward, bearing his neck for the fatal blow. King Henry paused. He spoke in somber tones. The anger in his face was replaced by a look of sadness.

"I was unwilling to go to him when I was told of my son's fatal illness. I feared for my own life. You have not been so timid. I shall not soil his memory further. I loved him more than you know. I give you your life to honor his. Go." He returned his sword to its scabbard. The disconsolate knight rose. He walked out of the malvoisier and was never seen by us again. It was another strange action seemingly dictated by this code I did not understand. How could the King's rage be changed so quickly? I was living in a world whose rules were so alien to me that I constantly made the wrong assumptions.

Later in the day, the encampment was ended and we all began the trek back to Chinon. My thoughts now turned to the second task that the Marshal had set for himself: a trip to the Holy Land! My stomach was beginning to feel out of sorts already.

The journey back to Chinon was a miserable one. I had bad thoughts about what lay ahead and it rained most of the way. Wet, tired and cranky we reached the castle late in the afternoon. I prepared a supper and dry clothes for the Marshal. We talked about the fortunate turn of events at Amboise. It saved us from heavy losses, perhaps even the life of my friend and lord, the Marshal. It was hard to contain my sense of relief.

I did not tell the Marshal I was glad the King had released Bertran. I was not sure he felt the same way as I did. There were many questions I wanted to ask, but I felt they could wait. Again, my feelings about a trip to the Holy Land probably did not match the Marshal's. He did say the King would meet with him in a few days to discuss important matters. Until then, he would use the time to get in some work at the post.

The next two days Chinon experienced a slow drizzling rain. It did not stop the Marshal. He always had time to practice, even in the rain. He stripped to his waist and after an hour or so he returned to the room and wiped his sword with a greasy rag. There was no talk of tournaments. Other things weighted on his mind. I wondered if he would form a new team and return to the lists. Three days passed before we received word the King wanted to see the Marshal.

It was a cool morning as I followed my master across the courtyard. I was glad the weather had turned chilly. It gave me an excuse to go along. Chinon was just the type of place one would expect to be the chief residence of Henry

II. It was powerfully built but rather plain in its furnishings. Henry ruled from his saddle so a lavish dwelling was not part of his need. Money was better spent on his armies than fountains, clothes and soft surroundings. It was no wonder he and Queen Eleanor held such differing views. The hallway to the throne room was lined with several tapestries but little else. Several corridors connected to this main hallway and disappeared into other parts of the castle. I assumed they were connected to the royal apartments and other important rooms. I never saw any of them, but I was sure they too were spare in decoration. I was allowed to wait outside in the hallway holding the Marshal's cloak while he talked to the King. I had gotten very good at hearing and peeking around corners. It was a handy skill for someone of my station. I took up a position near the doorway as the Marshal went in to see his sovereign.

"Ah, Sir William, we were impressed with your siege preparations. You were disappointed you did not get to execute the plan?" he said expecting a yea from this fierce warrior.

"Success is never disappointing, Sire. I do not crave bloody battle when one is not needed," the Marshal responded. It clearly surprised the King who drew his head back when he heard the remark.

"Well said. We have reflected your request to be off to the Holy Land, but first pray hear my plans and perhaps change your mind about taking your leave of us. Henry is gone, and Richard is the rightful heir. This will please his mother—unfortunately! We are less than happy, but so it must be. You know some of my remaining sons have not pleased me. Richard is rebellious. Geoffrey is not much better. John is too young, but we have been more attentive in training him. Unlike his older brothers he has been protected from slanders his mother utters about me. He shows promise as a worthy administrator. Richard and Geoffrey have no use for day-to-day governing and we blame ourselves for neglecting their training. Of necessity we will do the same with Richard as we did with his elder brother now departed to God's care. We will make him King in England. We will then make John Duke of Aquitaine. Geoffrey will still be Duke of Brittany. We have need of you, my friend, to keep an eye on all of them. It is sad a father cannot trust his sons, but alas, that is my lot in life. There is a fiefdom for you in this plan. What say you?" he said eagerly awaiting a positive response at such a generous offer.

"Majesty, you have right to compel me, but..."

"Wait, my friend, before you speak of your oath to my dead son I ask you think upon the possibilities of that which we offer. We can be generous in titles and land but we will not compel your choice. To do so would give us a man different from the one we seek. Reflect a fortnight before you speak. Perhaps another could be designated to perform your task and allow you to remain with us," he said quickly seeing the offer was going to be rejected.

I was excited my master was being offered the thing he always wanted—land and a title. It was something a knight of his station was rarely given. I was so engrossed in eavesdropping on the events in the great hall I did not hear the approaching footsteps.

"You there. By God's eyes, what are you doing?!" I was about to make the acquaintance of Prince John. He was my size only heavier. He had dark malevolent eyes and narrow lips surrounded by a black mustache and the hint of a beard. He was ten years younger than I, making him seventeen. He grabbed me by the arm and pulled me into the great hall. I could have pulled away easily, but my years of training made me know it would not be wise. When confronted by one's betters, it was prudent to be as meek as possible. I had the Marshal's cloak folded over my arm as I stumbled into the King's presence.

"Father, I caught this man spying by the door," he said as proud as a cat that had just presented its master a captured mouse.

"Be at ease, my boy. He is the Marshal's servant and I suspect he was waiting with his master's cloak. That seems to be it, draped over his arm," he said smiling and pointing at the aforementioned item. The Marshal nodded. The King continued, "We have personally talked with him on several occasions. We assure you, he is not dangerous." The Prince released his hold, but was clearly not as amused as the King.

"Know your place, sirrah!" he said with as much disrespect as he could muster.

"I shall, sire," I said with a bow as I backed out of the room. I walked some distance from the entranceway. Another meeting of the same kind would have serious consequences and the King might not be so amused. More importantly, it would embarrass the Marshal and that was unthinkable at a time when he was close to achieving his dream. I was no longer able to hear anything. Ten minutes later he appeared in the hall and I rushed to hand him his garment. We walked out into the courtyard.

"Well, Lewellyn, you have now met the youngest of King Henry's sons. What do you think of him?"

"He is very different than the others, my lord, and not as good looking," I said trying to express my dislike in the most polite terms should there be other ears to hear my words.

"True. 'Tis said he is very spoiled, but we must hold our tongues. There are many hidden ears here and too much discussion of royal sons can be unwise," he whispered. We walked into the courtyard and headed for our quarters. I was bursting to ask about the King's offer, but I did not. It would have confirmed Prince John's accusation. The Marshal saved me from a death by curiosity when he raised the subject.

"The King has offered me a title if I change my plans. 'Tis something I must consider. The offer may never come again." He pursed his lips and gazed at the ceiling as he did so often when seeking difficult answers.

"Oh, my lord, this be wonderful. Where would your lands be?" I asked excitedly.

"'Tis not yet decided. To be sure it would be small, but at least be mine. However, there is a mouse in the grain sack. I will have to keep King Henry's sons in line, a worrisome task to say the least. I failed before and know not if I could succeed in the future." His brow furrowed as he thought about this last statement.

"You can do anything, my lord. I know you can," I added confidently.

"Were that only true, my loyal friend. Were that only true." He smiled and we spoke no further.

For the next few days the Marshal was back to his regimen. He had no duties to perform as he had in the household of the young King. He was just another knight in King Henry's employ. No, that is not accurate. He was "the" knight in the King's employ. It still placed him below the many nobles who peopled the court at Chinon, but this was tempered by the respect his reputation brought. I was freed from my former clerking duties because of the Marshal's lack of responsibilities. It gave me the opportunity to reacquaint myself with a certain attractive serving girl. I found numerous excuses to visit the scullery.

Celine had changed. She was still beautiful, but the years of hard work had put a worn look on the youthful features that I had thought about so many times. Still, her figure was good and her smile radiant. She possessed the strength a woman has when she leaves the silliness of youth behind and adds experience to physical beauty. Above all it was her eyes that spoke to me. They seemed to say, "Be at ease for I know you and I am pleased by what I see." My natural response to women, especially attractive ones, was to be all fumbles. It was no longer so with her. I was who I was and that seemed to be enough. My nervousness subsided and I found myself strangely comfortable with her.

We began to take walks in the evening after she had completed her work. The Marshal would say he had nothing for me, but I know he was letting me go out of kindness and understanding. I neglected my chores shamefully, but he said nothing. I vowed to work harder to repay the kindness.

It was three days into our nightly walks when a special evening occurred. It was unusually mild. The night was clear and well lit by a three-quarter moon. We strolled across the small field where in the summer vegetables for the larder had grown but now were lying fallow. We reached a small stand of apple trees. Soon the ripe fruit would be picked and the best ones would grace the King's table. We picked a spot under a tree and sat. I took a blade of grass and ran my fingers along the edges as we talked.

We talked about many things: what she had done since we had seen each other last, how I learned to read and write, how I enjoyed playing music, why the Marshal and I were so close. I shared my thoughts on what a great man my master was, and how he treated me with kindness, rarely seen in a master. I explained how I expected to go to the Holy Land with him if he went. She smiled and gently touched my hand as I explained the affliction I suffered when I traveled on the sea.

She said she had never seen the sea. When I made a joke about my sea sickness, she lifted my hand to her cheek and kissed it tenderly. She told me, "Lewellyn, you are truly brave. Most men try to hide a weakness. You are honest. I believe it is why the Marshal trusts you as he does."

"He declares honesty the basis of trust. I have learned much from him," I said proudly.

"We shall share the same trust. I shall be honest with you. I have a special duty I perform for the King which few know," she said preparing to share her secrets with me. I recoiled slightly at this revelation, since I knew of the King's reputation with young and pretty women. She must have read my thoughts because she laughed and said, " Nay, 'tis not what you think. It is this! Several times a week I open the postern gate and accompany the Princess Alais to the King's chambers by a back corridor. The guards are sent away when I perform this duty so no one can see who I am escorting. I have come to know her rather well and she is very sweet. She cares for the King and is very willing to live with this arrangement even though she is promised to Duke Richard," she said glancing down at our intertwined hands.

"'Tis not as great a secret as the King thinks," I replied looking into eyes now wide open with the surprising revelation. I explained I had heard for years of the liaison between the King and the Princess. I said it was a source of tension between Richard and his father.

"I am not surprised; very little is secret in a King's household. I am surprised Richard cares. 'Tis well known he is little interested in women—not like his detestable little brother, John." She seemed to shudder at the mention of his name.

"I met the Prince the other day. He was in a foul mood." I explained the events of the encounter.

"Be careful of him, Lewellyn. The servants fear him and many in the nobility do too. His father has spoiled him because he is interested in many of the things the King does. I fear King Henry would like to make him king, but the law says Richard and Geoffrey come first. I must tell you one other thing about the Prince and it may change your opinion of me." She took my hand and hers was trembling as she prepared to reveal one more secret. Again my body tensed fearful of what was to come. "This time it is what you think. I was returning from my chore for the King when I encountered the Prince in the secret corridor. He knew of my daily ritual and was waiting for me. The vile creature seized me and..."

"No more, 'tis not needed for you to share this sordid tale," I said squeezing her hand.

"Nay, I must. We must have no secrets between us." She continued with a soft sigh. "The Prince pushed me to the floor and proceeded to force himself upon my person. I wanted to scream but I knew it would do little good and only enflame the wretched man's desire further. It was then his animal groans must have alerted the King and Alais. He came down the corridor half dressed and when he saw the scene he yelled, "Cease!" The Prince, startled, jumped to his feet and covered his manhood with his hands..." She began to sob. I could not allow the pain to continue.

"Celine, torture yourself no further. I cannot endure to see you so pained by this most unnecessary confession. Those of us in the serving class have had many such experiences at the hands of our betters." I explained my thoughts of my own mother's life and that perhaps I was the product of such an event. I place my arms around the sobbing lass and gently rock her back and forth. In a few moments she regained herself and said, "There has been no repeat since the King forbade him to abuse me because of the warm regard the Princess Alais has for my person."

I now had another reason to detest the youngest Plantagenet son, a rage that would go unsatisfied for years. I looked into her eyes and knew the bond was made. We moved closer and kissed.

"I must share my secret." I explained my futile attempts to seduce the two serving maids. She smiled, caressed my cheek with a soft hand. Her other hand found mine and gently placed it on her breast and said with loving eyes and a soft voice, "Wouldst thou try me."

The blood coursed through my body as we kissed more passionately. As she guided my hand to explore her I discovered that this time was different. I did not rush. My excitement was excruciating but somehow under control. I was discovering love not lust. I knew she would satisfy me again and again and therefore I had no need to hurry. I wanted so for her to savor our lovemaking as did I. As our bodies joined, all thoughts of kings and knights melted into oblivion.

I had found the happiness still denied the Marshal. I, Lewellyn, had what my great hero did not—the trusting love of a woman. It did not seem fair. What had I done in my life to deserve this most precious prize? Even in old age I cherish the thoughts of that first night. As a writer of songs, I should be better able to describe these things, but for me, it is not possible. I can write about heroes and battles, but my knowledge of love is sadly limited to a brief span of time.

When I returned to my quarters, I began to think of how much I would miss if we went to Jerusalem. This time, would I lose her forever? I was very depressed when I entered the dark room. As I went to lie down, a voice came out of the dark.

"My minstrel has found his true love. Is that not so?"

"Yes, my lord. I am inexperienced in such things, but I believe you are right," I said slowly.

"Experience in these matters is not required. Enjoy the moment. I envy you, my friend."

I went to sleep with mixed emotions. On one hand I had just experienced the most wonderful evening of my life. On the other, I was about to lose all I had just found. The wheel continued to roll on the path of life. I hoped we could stay and the Marshal might ask for Celine's transfer to his household. Then we could be married. I was too afraid to ask.

The fortnight past and the Marshal had not returned to give the King his answer and my hopes were rising it meant we would remain. Another month passed as the Marshal struggled with his decision. Celine and I continued to see each other as often as we could. In these days with her I would learn much. She gently showed me how to pleasure her during our lovemaking as much as she pleasured me. I discovered ways of touching and tasting the parts she said men too often ignore in their haste to find release. It broadened our desires and brought fulfillment that I could share with no other. When the days began to show winter's chill, she told me the summer of 1185 would hold a present for me. She was with child. I told no one because I did not want to jeopardize her position in the King's household. Two days later, the Marshal went to the King with his answer.

I waited in my usual spot with the Marshal's winter cloak as he when to the King with his decision. I could feel my knees shaking and I listened nervously to the words.

"Your Majesty, I must sadly decline your generous offer. Honor allows no other course. I pledged to take the young King's cross to the Holy Land and cannot be appointed to another." He had made a promise and he would keep it.

The King replied, "I feared such would be your response, but we are not surprised. Go, honor your pledge and we shall see that you are provisioned properly for the journey. It is with much regret we see you take leave of us."

I was devastated by the news. My child would be born without me. The Marshal came to me and retrieved his green cloak. As he donned the garment we exited the building. Returning to our quarters the Marshal saw my dejected look and asked if something was wrong.

"Nay, my lord. You must do what your honor demands and I must do the same."

"That be a strange answer. Lewellyn, I demand you tell me that which has caused you to have the visage of a mourner." His voice was stern and he spoke with a commanding tone. I stood silently for a moment and then confessed all.

When I had finished I stood straight and said, "I am yours to command. I would not be here but for you, my lord. I will follow you wherever it may take us. I, too, have honor to uphold."

"I believe there be a solution to fit all. You did not promise the young King and so are not bound by the honor you now express. I believe there be one more boon the King will grant."

"What might that be, my lord?" I was puzzled.

"You shall see. Let not your heart be troubled," he said with a confident air.

The next day, the Marshal went to the King. When he returned there was a big smile on his face. Baldwin was with him.

"Lewellyn, pack my things, but not yours. I have news that should lighten your heart. I have transferred your service to the household of Baldwin de Bethune. The King gave his permission for the transfer. He has also granted permission for the marriage of a certain serving girl. I will be going to Marseilles to take ship for Amalfi and from there to Jaffa," he announced with a big smile. Once again, I forgot myself and threw my arms around the Marshal. I was unable to restrain my joy. Baldwin laughed and said he hoped I would be a little more formal with him. I recovered my senses and apologized for the impertinence of my actions.

"The things you will do to escape a sea voyage," the Marshal quipped. We all laughed. We sang a few of the Marshal's favorite songs and drank until supper. We were all quite drunk when we fell into bed. The following morning I shared the good news with my future wife. We made arrangements with a priest for a small ceremony. The Marshal and Baldwin attended our vows in the chapel. Afterward, I moved to the section of the castle Baldwin occupied. They were smaller than those of the Marshal, but I experienced more cramped places in my life, so this would do fine. Despite our marriage Celine would still be required to live in her quarters to serve the needs of the Princess Alais, who I was soon to meet. I went back and helped the Marshal pack for his journey. The King had given him two horses and enough money to finance the trip. When we finished, I started to think, this would be the first time we had been separated in sixteen years. We spoke about his plans and I thanked him over and over for all he had done. This time, it was the Marshal who grabbed me and we embraced.

"My friend, know not what God has in store for me, but I shall miss you. You have been the ear for my thoughts and I have needed that more than you know. If I return, I hope your family will be large and happy. Perhaps, I will be lucky enough to find the same kind of joy. If you have a son, I hope you would consider calling him John. My father and I were never on good terms and since I shall probably never have a son, such an act might atone for some of the bitter words we had before he died. Stay well and take care of Baldwin. God knows he needs help," he said as he gave me the customary rub on the head.

He had finished his speech and said no more as I walked him to the courtyard where his squire held the horses. I resolved to show no emotion as he mounted the dark chestnut charger and rode across the drawbridge and on to the south road. As usual I failed and a series of small tears had to be quickly wiped away. My benefactor, friend and teacher was gone and I might never see him again. The many adventures we had shared raced through my mind as I returned to do my chores to begin a new life without the Marshal. Celine and the child she carried were now the focus of my existence, but the road of life seldom travels in a straight line and it would not be long before the great man would re-enter my life in a most surprising fashion. Tragedy and rebellion would shape events in ways that I could not imagine. My life with the Marshal had only reached the halfway point. The adventures which were yet to be experienced would prove to be even more exciting and far more dangerous than those we had already shared. I was blissfully ignorant of this, but my happy world would soon be shaken to its core and I would be forever changed.

Chapter 9
No End to Suffering

Five months after the Marshal had departed my life at Chinon was taking a new shape. So was Celine's belly. Baldwin was proving to be a good master, but different. Baldwin was not one to share his thoughts or stories of the conflicts swirling around the Plantagenet family. I missed my talks with the Marshal. I could not expect him to trust me the way the Marshal had. I learned of events by the usual method of the common staff—loose talk. Court gossip continually fed excitement into the otherwise dull lives of the serving class. I had to weigh the truthfulness of the information, based on the motives of the informant, but it was always interesting. The nobility were so obsessed with themselves they rarely took notice of us. Our ears heard things we were not supposed to hear and sometimes we saw things we were not meant to see. I had already experienced that one moonlit night in a barn years ago. I would now have a similar experience. It would be both a danger and a blessing for me personally.

We were expecting a visit from one of King Philip's advisors. The resentment the new and youthful King of France held toward King Henry was well known. The stated reason for the visit was to collect a small tribute owed Philip, as liege lord, for some of Henry's fiefdoms, fiefdoms Philip believed to be stolen from his father by the Plantagenets. Failure to pay would be justification for Philip to seize the aforementioned demesnes. Henry would not be so foolish. The small sum was already prepared. We suspected the real reason for the visit was to ask why the contract to marry the Princess Alais to Duke Richard had not been honored. I knew and many suspected the reason, but Philip needed proof of the illicit affair between Henry and Alais. Once obtained, Philip could demand the fiefdoms forfeit to him as compensation for breech of the agreement. Little did I know that I would play a part in this important issue.

The event occurred when the Baron de Clermont arrived unexpectedly a day and a half early and demanded to be taken to her rooms immediately. It was no accident. The King had unwisely went to her rooms the night before and failed to rise early, tired from his amorous evening. It was surely the work of a well-placed spy that had the Baron marching briskly down the corridor to Princess Alais' apartments. The King was trapped! I was visiting my wife in her room next to the Princess' chamber to show her the new tune I had composed. A frantic Alais came bursting through the adjoining door and exclaimed, "Celine, we must hide the King!"

It was the first time I had met the lady and there was no time for an introduction. The Princess was petite and thin with a pleasing face that was somewhat spoiled by a rather large nose as is often found on the French. She was fully dressed, but that would matter little if the King was discovered in her chamber. At that moment the King entered clad only in a shirt. He looked around and saw me holding my instrument. His eyes darted around Celine's room sparsely furnished with a chair, a small table and her bed. The large green bed cover draped to the floor. It could possibly conceal him but not for long. The Baron was sure to look everywhere. His surprise visit had purpose. Henry looked at me again. I could see from his smile that his nimble brain was inventing a plan. He spoke quickly.

"Lewellyn, take your instrument and take the Princess into her chamber. You are giving her a lesson in how to play the lute. My dear, look at the sirrah; his height and build are similar. The hair is the same. At a quick glance he could be taken for me. You understand? Celine, busy yourself with that broom," he commanded. With that he ducked under the bed. The lady and I went to the other room. We sat on her bed, she took the lute and I turned my back to the door the Baron was soon to enter. Seconds later the door opened without a knock. I could see the Princess' surprised look as the Baron exclaimed, "Aha! Henry, I..." I turned my head and faced the Baron de Clermont. He stopped in mid sentence with a shocked look. The Princess was quick with her reply.

"Clemont, we know you held us as a child, but that does not excuse so rude an entrance!" she barked. "Who is this Henry you seek? This is my music instructor, Lewellyn," she announced calmly.

"A thousand pardons, my lady. A scurrilous knave claimed King Henry was in your chambers taking advantage," he said somewhat apologetically, but the tone lacked conviction. He began to walk slowly around the room looking for places of concealment. Satisfied there were none his eyes turned to the open door to my wife's small room. He could see her sweeping the apparently empty room. She bowed as his eyes met hers. The Princess spoke quickly and sharply.

"We demand to know who spread this wretched calumny, although we understand the error when one looks quickly at my musician. His resemblance to the King is apparent and perhaps has given rise to false rumors, but this in no way excuses such vile thoughts. I demand to know the culprit. The King shall hear of this!" Her eyes flashed with anger and even I was convinced she was outraged.

The Baron stopped his movement to my wife's room and returned to take a closer look at me. I bowed and spoke softly, "I have been mistaken for both the King and his recently deceased son, my lord," I said hoping to continue the deception before the Baron could examine the adjoining room more closely. The Baron took his hand, placed it on my chin and turning it from side to side examined my features.

"The man does bear some likeness to the King," he said, slowly releasing my face then turning to the Princess. "Again I beg forgiveness, my lady. I only seek to protect you as I have done all my life. The knave will be severely punished for spreading so malicious a rumor. I remain your servant," he said with a more humble air tinged with disappointment. His mission had failed and someone would have to bear the blame.

"We trust there will be no more of this. I shall not inform King Henry, lest there be further repercussions. And now we would like resumption of our lesson," Alais said in a dismissive voice.

The Baron turned on his heel and exited the chamber with a rather red face. I knew someone would pay with his life for the failed intrusion. The lady and I continued the mock lesson for several minutes until the King's personal sirrah came with some new garments and informed us that the Baron was being shown his quarters. Moments later the King appeared. He smiled and while he dressed he turned to me.

"Lewellyn, you played your part well. We shall not forget." He cinched his girdle and smiled as he left quickly. I was left with the Princess Alais and my wife. They were smiling and embracing each other. The Princess brushed a lock of hair from her forehead and looked at me.

"So this is the man who has given my Celine her large belly."

"I am her husband, my lady," I said with a bow.

"And now a friend of mine. The secret is safe," she said with confidence.

"Were it so, my lady. I fear there are many rumors." I bowed my head.

"We are aware, but they remain only that. We have been less than discreet in recent months. I fear my beloved Henry begins to fail in health. We choose to make the most of our time." There was sadness in the remark. I too had noticed the decline in the vigor of the King.

"I am most sorry to hear that, my lady. The difference in age makes such inevitable," I said hoping to show some understanding of their problem. I was a little blunter than I had intended, but under the circumstances it was overlooked.

"We know many question why we would engage in such a liaison but it all happened innocently enough. The King, despite that which is said about him, is a very lonely man. He treated me with great kindness as I came of age. As the days passed he discovered my company was soothing relief to his constant troubles. My feelings grew apace. I know my appearance is rather plain, but it is no matter to him. Were I to go, as required, to the very handsome Duke Richard I would be no more than a convenience in a sham marriage. Here I am truly loved by an aging man in his declining years. I am willing to risk all for whatever days are left!" Alais declared defiantly.

She was living proof of my belief that even the mighty are shaped by events that neither wealth nor power make bearable. Were they members of my class there would be no problem and they could live their lives out as they chose. Now they must steal moments like common thieves ever wary of exposure. A love as beautiful and undemanding as this was forced to be hidden in dark corners and visited only briefly through secret passageways.

"But we must not burden you with our trials. What reward will you have for your timely service? Be it in my power it shall be granted." She took my hand and held it firmly.

"I would not presume on your generosity, my lady," I said trying to be gracious.

"Pooh! You have saved the King important lands. You must take something."

"There be one small thing. My lovely wife, your loyal servant, is too oft absent from me while she tends to your needs. If it could be arranged to visit me in the quarters of my knight, Baldwin de Bethune, more often I would consider it the greatest boon."

"We shall do better. I prize my Celine highly, but know too well the pain of an absent love. She shall be transferred into this knight's service. It must be done discreetly, lest we make many aware of our little deception today. In a fortnight we shall say owing to the condition of Celine she is no longer capable of serving our needs and must be replaced. So it shall be done. We wish you well on the birth of your child. Lewellyn, you and I must continue to play at music lessons until the Baron returns to King Philip," she said with a gracious smile which lit her face with a kind and gentle glow.

My heart was so full that I grabbed my wife and momentarily forgot her condition and hugged her a little too hard. "Husband, do not force our child to be born now!" she scolded. I quickly released her and held her by both hands still beaming at our good fortune. After an appropriate time I left with my lute, humming happily as I went down the hall. Four days later the Baron left with his money. One of the King's grooms was found in the forest with his throat cut. It was attributed to bandits who must have mistaken him for a rich noble. A month after that the Princess Alais announced that she had abandoned her attempts to learn the lute. She also complained to the King that her pregnant serving girl was unable to meet her needs and she was replaced by a younger maid.

Life returned to normal and again I satisfied myself by following the gossip of the court. I knew King Henry had planned to make Richard the new "young king," and make John the duke of Aquitaine because I had overheard the plan on the day I met Prince John. I also knew the Marshal had shown reluctance to be the King's watchdog. Events were now showing how wise his reluctance had been.

When Duke Richard was informed by his father of the plan, he flatly refused to relinquish his title. He said he was not interested in "an empty crown of a cold little island." He had spent too much time and effort pacifying the rich Aquitaine province to relinquish it. He was not going to surrender any title to his little brother. As the eldest son, he would inherit all of the King's lands and then he would decide who received the choicest fiefdoms. The apple was ripening nicely. King Henry was entering the twilight of his years and a date with God had to be near. The heir to the throne was more than happy to shake the tree and make the apple fall. He was becoming bolder with each military triumph in Aquitaine. The promise he had shown as a boy under the tutelage of the Marshal was now realized in the man. Richard was a true warrior prince and a force to be taken very seriously. Ten years ago at Gisor, Duke Richard had succumbed to his father. He never reconciled. He simply recognized the need to hold his tongue. His love was reserved for the mother his philandering father had locked away in Winchester castle. He also had the irritation of his father's continuing affair with his promised bride. This was a minor concern and only useful as an excuse to gather allies. Except for the tiny stain the arrangement was placing on Richard's honor, King Henry was welcome to her.

The King's attempts to change Richard's mind were fruitless. Bringing the wayward son to heel, the way he had done in the past, was impossible. King Henry's health was in decline. He no longer was the fearsome warrior of old. A fully grown Duke Richard had become a formidable fighting machine. The nobility of Aquitaine could attest to the skills he had learned under the watchful eye of the Marshal. In addition, he had become closer to King Philip. The French king could help thwart any action King Henry might undertake to force his will on his most handsome son. Philip was living up to the Marshal's assessment.

The realistic King Henry finally decided if he wanted to give his favorite, John, a title, another course would have to be followed. The King concocted a plan. He would make John king of the Irish.

Arrangements were made and a force was assembled to accomplish King Henry's goal. The eighteen-year-old Prince John, accompanied by some of Henry's best men, went to Ireland where the investiture was to take place. It would not be easy. The Irish chieftains would not accept John enthusiastically. Making them fall into line required force and diplomacy—attributes sadly missing in the young prince. It was on this campaign Prince John first demonstrated his unique talent of insulting those assigned to help him. It was a talent he expanded throughout his life. My new master, Baldwin de Bethune, was included in the force and went with the Prince. I remained behind and helped take care of his household while he was absent.

By the end of July the reports coming back from Ireland were not good. I paid little attention to them. My concern was with the impending birth of my child. Celine had not had an easy pregnancy and I spent much of my time trying to help by doing some of her work. Late one night, she began the last step in bringing new life into this world. It made me glad to be a man. I began to understand the closeness a woman has for her child when I saw the effort involved. It was midnight on the 17th when the midwife told me to leave. I had seen enough and left willingly. It was my duty to wait nervously for the call to return. It was still dark, on the morning of the 18th, when I was summoned by Elaine, my wife's friend. Her demeanor caused me to fear what I was about to see. Instead of a smiling, happy announcement she spoke in serious, slow tones.

"Lewellyn, come and see your son. Celine needs you." Her head slumped to her chest and I knew all was not right. I rushed up the stairs and entered a room of solemn-faced women. One was holding a crying baby wrapped in a cloth. The child was a reddish color with some purple stains on his face. Immediately, I thought the child was not right, but I soon learned he was very normal. The one in distress was my wife. The midwife addressed me quietly.

"She has the fever. Your son is fine." She looked at the floor rather than face my panicked eyes which desperately sought hopeful information.

"What does this mean?" I demanded. I knew nothing about such things.

"Speak to her. There is nothing more I can do," she said with a series of tears welling in her eyes. With that horrible statement I knew what was about to transpire.

My emotions switched from great joy at the birth of my son to disbelief and fear. This could not be happening. My life, when it had finally reached a pinnacle of happiness, was being destroyed in the same night. With tears flowing down my cheeks I kneeled over the mat and spoke with all the love a bursting heart could summon.

"My love, we have a beautiful son," I said trying to act joyful, but the tears flowing down my cheeks exposed the pain of a bursting heart.

"Husband, call him Jean. I shall not be able to watch him grow, but I know God has given him the best of fathers, to see him develop into a fine man," she whispered weakly. Perspiration beaded on her forehead and soaked the pillow. I placed my head on the mat and held her hands. It was the most devastating two hours of my life. Why had God left such a wretched person as myself on this earth and taken the kindest soul to his keeping?

As dawn broke and I lay sleepless on the floor next to my wife's lifeless body staring dumbly at the grey stone walls. They finally made me leave the room saying there were things to be done. I had lost the one person who brought gentleness into my life. We had too short a time with each other. There would never be another woman to touch my soul so deeply. As a result of the loss I became less willing to show compassion to others. After all, how could anyone suffer more than me? It was an erroneous and selfish conclusion, but it would be many years before I would awaken to that fact. Grief builds a very hard shell which prevents us from absorbing understanding.

Exhaustion forced me to sleep. When I awoke I prepared to seek the priest for the burial of my beloved. The bitter grief I felt was also mixed liberally with anger, anger for what God had stolen from me. Why was I to be punished in this horrible way? I had waited beyond the age most men find a mate and then had happiness snatched from my grasp. I had done nothing to deserve this. Surely our attempt to save the King and his lover from discovery was not worthy of such retribution. The priest sensed my anger and warned me not to dispute god's wisdom. It only angered me further.

The rites of the Church were given a day later. As she was laid to rest my brain was numb and I hardly remember the service. Only Elaine, my newborn son and I were present. Members of our class leave this world as unnoticed as we had been in life. I do believe if the Marshal or Baldwin would have been there that might have helped, but one was in Ireland and the other was somewhere in the Holy Land.

Arrangements were made for Elaine and her husband to care for my son. Baldwin was unmarried, and had no women in his small quarters. I was in no position to care for an infant. Elaine was still nursing her daughter and assured me she could care for my son as well. I expressed my gratitude and watched as the only connection with my beautiful wife was taken away. I sat alone that day in utter despair. I went to the churchyard and found the fresh mounded dirt at Celine's grave cool to the touch. As I sat on the ground next to the grave a kindly friar passed by and seeing my need stopped. He tried to easy my sorrow with the usual comments about God's plan, and how He needs the best of us in heaven. It offered little comfort. We began to talk.

"My son, your grief will ease with time," he said in a well-practiced voice.

"Father, why is God so hard to understand? If He exists as all powerful, why can he not end suffering and evil?" I asked still hoping for some explanation that I could accept. I took some of the loose soil and rubbed it in my hands.

"Because, my son, He chooses to give us some control over our lives. Were He to do as you suggest there would be little need for us to live." He smiled as he replied with the same answer I was sure had been given to many before me. Clearly he expected the same time wore reply. It was not to be.

"I think not, Father. I believe that we created God to give us comfortable answers for the things we fail to understand! God is a collection of contradictions because we are filled with contradictions. Our lives are rife with inconsistency. I know for that has been my life," I said fully expecting a thunderbolt to strike me for such blasphemy. I did not care. The friar's kindly round face changed.

"Take a care, my son, lest ye be consumed along with this newly departed loved one." His rebuke was clear. He rose and left quickly as if he too would be a victim of god's wrath if he remained with me. The fear that my sins would be visited on my precious Celine's soul caused me to change my thoughts. I slept next to the grave all night. I did not fear a visit from the specters known to rise at night in graveyards. Let them carry me away. None came. It added to my doubts.

I rose and returned to my quarters. I thought of the many that had been comforted by the friar's words which had done little for me. Perhaps belief is a good thing. If this be the reason men create God then it does serve a purpose. If the friar was correct then what I thought mattered little for God would still be God and life would continue to offer challenges. If I were right the same would happen. It mattered little. I vowed not to think on such things further. I did not succeed.

Days struggled to become weeks and weeks blurred into months. It was three months before my life began to return to a reasonable degree of sanity. The promise to raise my son slowly caused me to return to the real world and daily life. It was without excitement I worked at my chores. Just when I was convinced nothing would ever again be interesting, I had a visitor. He brought news of the Marshal. The man had just returned from Jerusalem and came with a letter. He had met the Marshal and, like many, took an immediate liking to my former master. I took the parchment and felt some excitement return to my life. I thanked him and returned to my room to devour the news about my dear friend. It was a private moment I did not want to share with anyone. There were two pages, one addressed to me, the other to Baldwin. I began to read mine.

"Lewellyn, I have found a scribe in the market. He gives me the opportunity to send you greetings. I trust by the time this reaches you, your lovely wife has presented you with your child. I envy you." At this time several tear drops dripped onto the page. I continued to read. "I have seen most wondrous things here in the birthplace of our Lord. I have visited and prayed at both the Church of the Holy Sepulcher and the Church of the Nativity.

I have been received by the King of Jerusalem. He has many enemies. A new leader has risen among the Muslims and I fear there will be trouble before long. I have fulfilled my promise to the young King. I am prepared to stay with the knights of the Temple and defend the Holy Land if need be. I have found these knights to be brave and resourceful. If we do not meet again, I wish you and your family happiness. I am in the element God has intended for me. My sword will be his to command. I have heard the Saracen leader is respectful of the code of chivalry. Pray it does not come to all-out war, but King Guy of Jerusalem is not always wise in his dealings with others. It surprises me not, since he is a brother of the Baron Luisgnan! Stay well, my friend, and give the other letter to Baldwin."

Thoughts of our previous adventures flooded my mind and for a moment I was spared the grief of the past few months. His reverence for the holy places made me feel ashamed for my recent thoughts. I was pleased my friend had found something to believe in and I hoped that I would someday be able to do the same. I envied him. For a few seconds I thought about the possibility of joining him, but the thought of being separated from my son precluded any such ideas. The letter for Baldwin would have to wait. He was still in Ireland with Prince John and would not be returning for several months. I folded the two brown parchments and hid them behind a loose stone in the wall. It was my most secret place to hide that I did not wish to share with anyone.

Reports coming from Ireland continued to bring bad news. The campaign turned into a fiasco. The Prince quarreled with his advisors and insulted potential allies. The title his father had bestowed on him was proving to be unreachable and was having the effect of emptying the King's treasury. It caused the parsimonious King Henry to reconsider the whole adventure. By the end of August it was clear the title, King of Ireland, was not in John's future. The only title he would have was the one people whispered laughingly in the taverns—John Lackland.

Another month passed before Baldwin returned home. He was sorry to hear about my loss. I had Elaine show him my son and he delighted in the good looks of the child. I delivered his letter and then showed him my letter. He shared the contents of his communication with me and we discussed our remembrances of the Marshal. Our relationship began to change. Baldwin's letter contained a part where the Marshal mentioned how he used to talk to me and his secrets were safe from the rest of the court. Baldwin found that he too needed this release.

Prince John had been quick to blame everything on his advisors when he returned. The exasperated Baldwin finally unburdened himself to me. He shared the frustration of the last six months. I poured some wine. Baldwin, like most Normans, preferred it to beer. The chill of fall was in the evening air as he prepared to release a flood of repressed feelings.

"Lewellyn, 'twas the most incompetent, blundering campaign any knight has ever endured. Our Prince spent more time worrying about the inventory of wine and food than he did about the disposition of his troops. He cannot be given suggestions. His treatment of friends is appalling. 'Twas doomed from the day we landed," he said as his head slumped upon his chest.

I knew I had gained his trust, because he had said things would be considered treason if they were shared with the King. I reassured him by uttering my own treasonous comments.

"The King is blind to the faults of his unworthy son, my lord."

"Blind be too kind a word. 'Twould be wise to be most wary of him and trust him no more than he trusts his other sons, but alas, he is convinced John loves him best. John loves John best, like most spoiled children." His usually twinkling eyes narrowed in a look of fear as he uttered this assessment. He sighed. "Lewellyn, I miss the Marshal. He had a way of making light of royal failings. I fear we are in for bad times. Duke Richard is showing more resistance to his father's wishes and there are many who would exploit the split." We looked at each other and agreed we should say no more. Politics had to be avoided if we valued our lives.

Things settled down during the Christmas season. Most of the court used the holiday celebrations to erase the memory of the Irish disaster. John gleefully joined his father in the activity they both enjoyed the most—collecting the scutage (tax). King Henry had to recoup the Irish losses. Baldwin and I rejoiced as we saw them and their retainers ride out of the gate followed by the wagon that would be filled with leather bags of coins when they returned in two months. The large company of knights that were needed to assure the safety of the haul made a steady thundering sound as their horses crossed the drawbridge. It was most revealing that those knights who had accompanied Prince John to Ireland were not included in the company. Baldwin knew his star was in decline, but he did not care. We spent the two months by making songs and jokes about the detestable Prince in the evenings when we were sure there were no ears to hear. My favorite was this: "John, John, the King's fat son; seeks a crown to have some fun. Has no friends, has no couth; has no need for the bitter truth." I thought Baldwin would die from laughter when I composed that one.

Once they returned we ceased this dangerous form of entertainment. From time to time we would look at each other and break out in laughter without a word being spoken. We heard rumors the King of France, Philip, and Duke Richard were spending an increasing amount of time in each other's company. A communication from King Henry to him remained unanswered. It did not auger well. The political pot was beginning to boil again.

The tournament season was fast approaching and we hoped for something to end the tension building in the court of King Henry. It came in the form of a letter from our old friend Hugh. It said Duke Geoffrey was eager to follow his older brother's path to glory on the tournament field. Baldwin was invited to join him in the first tournament of the season. Baldwin happily accepted. He wanted to get some distance from the sullen John, who continued to blame those who had accompanied him to Ireland. I was to go along. We were eager for the distraction of the tournaments. It would be a return to the happy times I had shared with the Marshal. I was sick of hearing about Plantagenet intrigues.

In April, I accompanied Baldwin to the tournament at Epernon. There he joined the team of Duke Geoffrey. I had not seen Geoffrey in several years and was amazed to see how much he had changed. He was not as big as his older brother but to my amazement he was even more handsome. The ladies would become speechless when he would make an appearance. It was almost humorous to observe his impact on the women—young and old alike. To be sure, it was not like the old times with the Marshal. It was different. The victories were less dramatic and less often, but it was refreshing to feel the excitement and forget the sorrow of the past year.

At Pleurs we were ready to enjoy the biggest tournament of the year. This would be the most difficult test of the Duke's men. Like most young knights he was excited to be in his first big tournament. The horn sounded and Duke Geoffrey charged across the open field. His lance lowered into position as several of his team followed his lead. What happened next was etched in my memory forever. I had seen the Marshal fight enough to know his point was low, and his shield was at the wrong angle. The opposing knight was in perfect position. When the collision took place the result was the one I expected. Duke Geoffrey was lifted out of the saddle and thrown violently backward. His right foot twisted in the stirrup and he dangled inverted from his horse. The horse began to race across the field to escape the melee. The Duke's helmet was dislodged by the constant banging against the ground. Baldwin, and several other knights, raced after the runaway steed and the unconscious Duke. His skull was taking a vicious beating from the rocky ground. By the time they secured the reins of the horse, his body was bloody and limp, hanging by the trapped leg. The crowd was silent as the Duke was freed from the stirrup and carried from the field.

I saw the look of horror on Baldwin's face and knew fate had delivered another painful blow to King Henry. Another son had been taken at an early age. This time I was fully aware of the pain such a loss caused for life had delivered a similar blow to me. I had always known the tournament scene was violent and deaths could and did occur, but my years with the Marshal and his amazing success had submerged those fears. This was a sobering experience and a reminder of the brutality of the games.

For the second time in three short years a prince of the realm was laid to rest in pomp and pageantry. Again King Henry and Queen Eleanor were briefly reunited in their grief. I believed the family divisions might be forgotten during the service for the handsome Geoffrey, but it was not so. I was bringing clothes from the laundry to the Queen's chamber as a favor to a friend. It would give me a chance to tell the Queen of my correspondence from the Marshal. I was certain she would welcome the news. As I entered the Queen was occupied with two of her ladies. She did not see it was me behind the pile of clothes. She glance at the incoming pile and said, "Catherine, take them and see they are properly stored." Catherine and Yvette relieved me of my burden. Catherine gasped when she recognized me and blurted out, "Lewellyn!" The Queen spun around and a stare turned into a smile.

"By God's eyes, 'tis you. We thought the Marshal in Syria. Is he here?" Her voice rose to an excited crescendo.

"Nay, Majesty, I now serve Baldwin de Bethune." I quickly explained the events which caused me to remain. I could see the years were finally exacting their fee on the beautiful lady. While she still was thin, the face had lost the radiance it once held. Creases and wrinkles now lined the cheeks and forehead. The wimple carefully concealed all but a few of the now gray hairs. We had both changed in many ways, but her mind was still a formidable force.

"I have recently received communication from my former master. I would share it if it pleases your majesty," proudly announcing that I was the privileged possessor of news.

"Of course it would please us. We miss him greatly." She clasped both hands together and prepared to hear what I had to say. I was honored.

"I miss him too, Majesty. He is well. He fears trouble anew with the Saracens. He has joined with the Templars and vows to protect the Holy Land if trouble starts. He feels the King of Jerusalem handles things badly. I suspect we will ne'er see him again," I said with a shake of my head.

"'Tis more the pity. I have only bad memories of the wretched country he now calls home!" she exclaimed. "We could use his council at this time," she said wistfully. I was puzzled by the tone of this remark when the door opened and in strode her magnificent-looking second son. He was a head taller then I, flowing auburn locks, uncommon good looks and muscled in the way I remembered the Marshal. He began to speak in a powerful deep voice.

"Mother, I have little time to..." Duke Richard started, then stopped when he saw me. "We know you."

"Yes, Sire, I am called Lewellyn. We met when you were under the tutelage of my former master, Sir William Marshal," I said with a deep bow.

"He is here?" He asked excitedly.

"Nay, Sire. I am no longer his."

"Then leave us," he commanded while looking around the room. The Queen nodded and I backed out of the chamber bowing several times. There were things to be discussed that were not meant for my ears. The seeds of rebellion were being sown. Again, they fell in fertile soil. The fertile soil was a mature Duke of Aquitaine, Richard Coeur de Lion! I said nothing of the event, but I knew King Henry's excellent spy system was sure to pick up the scent of danger. It was confirmed several days later. The ever-alert King Henry made sure his wife was quickly sent packing back to Winchester under heavy guard. Duke Richard returned to Aquitaine without bidding his father farewell. I knew a storm was brewing.

Sev'nnight after the funeral I was summoned with Baldwin to a meeting with the King. Both Baldwin and I were perplexed. I understood the summoning of Baldwin, but why me? I began to fear our private conversations about Prince John had somehow reached the King's ears. I considered running away, but I knew I would not get far and my son's life would be taken in exchange for mine. If death for treason was to be my fate, then let it fall on me and not my loved ones. I was hopeful I could remind the King of the day I saved him from discovery and therefore obtain clemency for my son.

The following day we were ushered into the King's private quarters. Because we entered from a side entrance, the same one my departed wife had used with the Lady Alais, we both knew this meant the meeting was not to be discussed. A secret meeting with the King was not going to be about disrespectful songs. Something much larger was at stake.

As we entered Lady Alais' chamber, the King was seated alone on the bed. The door to the back room was closed. The guard was dismissed and we were alone as we bowed respectfully. King Henry showed all of his fifty-three years. Grief had taken its toll.

He looked up and began, "You both have received a communication from Sir William. We are interested in the tidings." It seemed little escaped the King's informants. I began to get nervous. Baldwin spoke first, as was fitting our stations.

"He is well, Majesty, and has been of service to the King of Jerusalem and the Temple knights. I know not if we will ever see him again. He speaks of trouble brewing in the Holy Land."

"And you. What did yours say?" He looked at me.

I was far more nervous than Baldwin and stuttered a little. I told him much the same and added the fact he had completed his mission of taking the young King's cross to Jerusalem. I hoped it would please him. I must have appeared to be a fool, because the King snickered at my nervous twitching.

"You have been summoned here in private for several reasons." This was not the melancholic King Henry I had seen after the young King's death. This was an apprehensive monarch who spoke. "The first reason can be shared with anyone aware of your coming here. The King wanted news from the Holy Land. The second and the third are not to be shared. We have need of your friend's services, and we want you to persuade him to return with all haste. We have no right to require him to leave a sacred mission. 'Tis why, you have both have been summoned. Baldwin de Bethune, you know him better than any of my knights and you, Lewellyn, have a special relationship far beyond that of sirrah and master. You both can send a communication that will arouse no suspicions. We will see to it you are given the resources to accomplish this task." I was taken aback by these remarks.

"Lewellyn, you will write the letter. Give him your usual greetings and news. It must seem to be an ordinary letter, should it fall into the hands of someone we do not wish to share our information with. End it with the following line, 'The father and his son miss you and need you.' Baldwin, you will deliver the letter and inform the Marshal that Richard is restless. Be sure only he hears this from your lips. It is information that cannot be written. Together with the letter I think he will understand. Baldwin, you will go as a pilgrim seeking redemption. There will be rewards for all if this task is completed successfully. Go and speak to no one of your task."

We left the chamber and returned to our quarters without talking. Once we were in the room and sure there was no one around we stared at each other. Baldwin broke the silence. "You had better pack my things. It will be a long journey and perhaps a fruitless one. I admit confusion at the King's meanings. What think you?" he said wrinkling his nose and turning his head.

"'Tis a puzzlement, but the King appeared quite concerned and why the reference to my son? He knows more of his subjects than I thought. I had best be busy packing your things and writing the letter the King requested. Unlike the Marshal, we are very much under the King's control," I said reminding him of our obvious situation. I turned and went to prepare Baldwin's things.

Two days later Baldwin departed for the Holy Land. For several months I waited. I wondered who would return—perhaps neither. King Henry's request was just that, a request. It could be ignored by the Marshal if he felt his mission was in Jerusalem and Baldwin might decide to stay with him. I would again be without a master and be assigned to someone of the King's choosing. It was not a prospect I relished since I had been very lucky in my previous masters.

During Baldwin's absence the problems surrounding the King were becoming plainer. Richard was becoming ambitious and more belligerent. King Henry's fondness for Prince John, and a possible successor, made Duke Richard look to his father's enemies for allies. The split between the two widened with each passing day. The Duke, unlike the departed young King, was not willing to play a puppet while King Henry pulled the strings. He would lead on his terms, not his father's. The determined boy I had observed at the training post was now a man, a fearless warrior whose skills matched his ambition. If he rebelled it would mean a struggle far more serious than the feeble attempts of his deceased brother. King Henry had also made more enemies who would be willing to see the end of his rule. A warrior of the Marshal's stature could help to keep wavering barons in line. Even then the task would be daunting. Perhaps the Marshal would also see this and reason it was not worth returning.

It was early November of 1186; I heard a commotion in the courtyard and went to see what was happening. There, to my utter delight, was the handsome Sir William Marshal. His skin darkened by two years in the heat of Syria. He was sitting astride a beautiful black war horse and accepting the welcoming cheers of much of the King's court. With him were Baldwin de Bethune and a younger man I did not recognize. They disappeared briefly as they dismounted into the crowd. I could see the Marshal's head above the rest. He moved through the throng of well wishers and approached my position in the doorway. I saw a smile as he noticed me standing there. I watched in anticipation as the massive shoulders had little trouble pushing through the people.

"It seems destiny wills us together, my friend," he said with the deep voice I had missed so much. "I am most sorry to find you without your lovely wife, but I look forward to seeing your son. There is much to discuss: a song or two to sing and some ale to be consumed. I have someone for you to meet and a King who expects to see me. Baldwin has graciously agreed to vacate his quarters for me. Let us get inside." Baldwin and the stranger went with the horses to make some arrangements, which I assumed included a place for Baldwin to stay until the Marshal could be provided with permanent quarters

"Yes, my lord. I shall see to your needs immediately." I could scarcely contain my joy.

Upon reaching the privacy of Baldwin's apartment I could contain myself no longer. I threw my arms around the Marshal and said, "Welcome back, my lord. I have missed you greatly."

"And I have missed you. Tell me of your gain and your loss." I spoke of the birth of my son and the death of my beloved Celine. I proudly announced my son was called Jean, in honor of the Marshal's request and my wife's French heritage.

"I grieve for your loss, Lewellyn. I am honored by your choice of names and I envy you for the precious gift of a son. I have longed for family and have resolved to change my situation. I suspect the King will be helpful in arranging something. It was one of the reasons for my return. Now, I need know what has happened in my absence. If what Baldwin tells me is correct, things are not good. Henry is having trouble with his son. You are the one person I trust to tell me the truth in its raw and unadorned form. I need to know. Speak freely and spare no one. My ears must hear what others would fear to say," he said reaffirming the absolute trust we shared for so long.

I spoke about the problems between the King and Richard, of Philip's involvement and Queen Eleanor's plots. I talked about the barons who resented the taxes collected under the scutage. I spoke of my dislike for John and his devious nature. I explained Henry's blindness to John's failings and John's reaction to the Irish disaster.

"My lord, Richard is not like his brother. He has become a powerful knight and is gaining support from the King's enemies. You have returned to a nest of vipers."

"I feared as much when I received your letter. Baldwin has confirmed much of what you have said, but said naught about John. I thank you for your candor. I have already asked you be returned to my service. I hope it pleases you," he said as a powerful arm embraced my shoulders.

"As surely as birds fly, my lord," I said with a large grin.

"Then 'tis settled. I have a new squire. His name is John d' Erly. He is a fine fellow and I know you will become friends." I heard voices in the hall and through the door walked Baldwin and the new squire.

"Marshal, I have made arrangements. John will stay here with you and I will take temporary residence with some of the bachelor knights. The King has requested you see him as soon as you are ready; which means now," Baldwin announced cheerfully.

I eyed the new squire who would share our quarters with a certain degree of apprehension. I was not ready to share the Marshal's friendship with this newcomer. He was average in height and rather plain looking. He was blue eyed and sturdy of build. He had a serious nature contrasting him to Baldwin's gregarious demeanor. He was younger than me by ten years, but his status as a future knight made him superior to me. It was not something I liked. Would this fact widen the social gap that never had, but should exist between the Marshal and me? I smiled and continued to contemplate if he was worthy of our trust. Reading my thoughts the Marshal spoke.

"John, this is Lewellyn. You may trust him as you trust me. Now, let us go see the King," the Marshal said as he put his arms around both of us. It made the last two years melt away. The Marshal was back, and life would be exciting again. As we approached the great hall he tossed me the green cloak with the gold border. I folded it carefully over my arm and took up my usual position a few steps behind. I waited in the hall as the three men entered the great room and were greeted by an obviously pleased King Henry.

"William, you are most welcome. We appreciate your haste in responding to our summons." He was pleased but worried by the sound of his voice.

"I serve at your Majesty's pleasure, as always," the Marshal replied.

"You are as faithful as you are skilled, my friend, and that shall be rewarded. We have need of your special talents as never before. My family is restless again. But first, what can you tell me of your experience in the Holy Land?" I could only imagine the scene as I was not able to see into the room. I was sure King Henry was beginning to pace back and forth as he listened.

"Sire, I fear there will be trouble. A leader of Kurdish decent has appeared and his skill as a warrior is substantial. Guy of Luisgnan is now king in Jerusalem and not up to such a challenge."

"You still harbor ill feelings for the Lusignan family, my friend?" the King asked.

"True, sire. I have had little liking for any of the Lusignans for many years, but 'tis more than that. He is overconfident in his ability to control the population, and does not respect his enemies. 'Tis a dangerous mixture. His forces are not properly deployed and he refuses to take suggestions," the Marshal said disgustedly.

"Enough. Protecting Jerusalem is the Holy Father's responsibility. I questioned the choice from the beginning. How was the journey home?"

"Relatively quiet. There was a brief disturbance near Sicily," the Marshal said with that wry smile that often accompanied understatements. I heard Baldwin cough and the King asked him to speak.

"The Marshal underplays the event, Majesty. We were attacked by brigands. Ten of them will never attack a ship again. Those who escaped will tell their fellows to avoid any ship containing a large man dressed in green and yellow." The King laughed and continued his conversation with the Marshal.

"I need my son to think twice before acting foolishly. You know many nobles. They respect you. Find out which we can trust. Review my defenses, and make your suggestions. Unlike the King of Jerusalem, they will be heeded. We promised to reward your loyalty, and so we shall. In return, you will be given the fief of Cartnel and the hand of the Damsel of Lancaster. Go and make it so." With the audience at an end the three men rejoined me in the hallway.

Each took turns congratulating the Marshal. Baldwin was first. He placed both hands on the shoulders of his friend. "Well done! You have land and a bride. 'Tis long overdue." John d' Erly followed with a rousing shout of joy and asked the question the Marshal was surely concerned about.

"Who is the damsel of Lancaster, my lord?" he asked as they walked down the hall. The Marshal could only shrug for he knew no more than the curious squire. Baldwin, knowing well the families of King Henry's court, answered the question.

"She is the twelve-year-old daughter of the Earl of Lancaster. She was given the protection of the King, when her father died without heirs."

The Marshal looked askance. "Twelve? What am I to do with a child for a bride?"

"You have spent too long fighting in the tournaments, my friend. You know nothing of court procedure. She will be entrusted to your care until she is of the proper age to marry. Her dowry, the fief of Cartnel, is a fine piece of land with a hundred or so villeins to work it. It will provide a decent income. 'Tis the way the King rewards service, bestowing his wards on men such as yourself. I will have my quarters back sooner than I thought. You, Lewellyn, will have much work to keep you busy. John, you will have a patron, whose service you will enter when you are granted your spurs," he said proud of the fact he had bested his hero in something—even if it was only court procedure.

I winced at the inclusion of the newcomer in the plans, but assumed that like most squires he would leave after being granted his spurs much like Eustace had done several years ago. Things would return to normal. I was satisfied that my special role was safe.

The Marshal expressed his appreciation for our enthusiasm and then returned us to the matters at hand. "First, I must perform the tasks the King has assigned me. I shall need the help of all of you. Lewellyn and John, you will be in charge of preparing this new home and seeing to the needs of my child bride. Baldwin, you shall join me in examining the political lay of the land. We need the help of Raoul de Hamars. He knows the French court and will know who will side with Henry if the worst happens. The next six months be crucial if we are to be effective. Naught will happen before winter's end," he declared, bringing the discussion to an end.

We reached our chambers and began to consider what would be necessary to carry out the Marshal's orders.

John d'Erly and I went to Cartnel and took possession of the estate for the Marshal. My son was still in the care of Elaine and her family. I contacted them with the news of my new home. I would have Jean rejoin me as soon as he was old enough to be raised by a household of men.

The fief was not impressive. A small manor house and several outbuildings sat on top of a hill. Some nice fields, a village with a mill and forge were located by a stream that meandered through the valley below the hill. It was clear the fief had been neglected after the death of the Earl. There were additional lands that could be developed with work and good stewardship. I thought the Marshal was being bought cheaply by the King. Knowing King Henry's natural tendencies toward parsimony, I was not surprised. Helvis, the second daughter of the Earl of Lancaster, was a plain and uninteresting child. I did not envy the Marshal's future as husband to the dull-witted Helvis, but she was an heiress. A title and land might suffice.

I made an effort to know John d' Erly during our stay at Cartnel. He was very bright and had a good sense of humor. Like the Marshal, he endeavored to treat me with respect. He took the lead in organizing the estate and it seemed unfair that he, because of his noble upbringing, was in charge. I had always handled the household accounts for the Marshal and I possessed more experience than the young squire. After a few weeks he realized this and gave me more of a hand in the daily decisions. Still he retained the final say on all things. I accepted this arrangement to save the Marshal from another problem to trouble his mind. He did like music and we shared the same complete faith in the man who was so important to our lives. He took to calling me troubadour. He asked how a sirrah could be given so much difference by one of the Marshal's standing. At first I was offended but then I realized how strange my relationship would seem to the upper class. I resolved to explain the history.

I shared the story of how I met the Marshal and our adventures over the years. He said I told a story well, which I took as a great compliment. He was surprised I could read and write. Again, I explained by retelling the story of Bertran de Born. He said he would like to learn those skills and I offered to help. My resistance to this man was weakening.

"Lewellyn, we are in the service of a very great man and the wonder of it is he does not know how great he is. I shall make it my business to be as loyal to the Marshal as you. We are very fortunate to be able to serve so fine a lord. There are none so skilled, or as generous as Sir William Marshal," he said.

"Amen, sir. 'Tis by rare fortune I find myself in this most enviable of circumstances. My only fear is our lord is too honest with his betters. His candor is not always welcome. I have learned they do not appreciate the truth as does he." I hoped he would understand the Marshal's need for absolute truthfulness from those closest to him.

"Something I doubt will ever change. His code of honor is more important to him than his life. He is a remarkable combination of courage and the skill to back it up. Many of the nobility lack these qualities even though they are unwilling to admit it; 'tis why men like the Marshal are hired to be by their side. Troubadour, there is work to be done. The Marshal will be joining us in a few days and all must be ready." I returned to the written accounts and he to the saddle to survey the land.

Several days later the Marshal arrived with Baldwin and Raoul de Hamars. Raoul was a grizzled veteran of many campaigns. His craggy face bore several scars that made him a fearsome-looking man. He walked with a limp and his hand rested on the pommel of his sword to balance his irregular gait. His hard-bitten appearance was typical of older knights. I could only guess at how many battles this man had survived.

John D'Erly accompanied a nervous Helvis and formally presented her to the Marshal. The child was trembling as she bowed to her future husband. She had spent an entire morning preparing for this meeting. Unfortunately it had done little to improve her appearance and I felt badly for the both of them. It was an awkward moment as he met his bride to be for the first time. I could see there was disappointment about his future wife. It was sure to be a loveless marriage. I understood why the nobility engaged in frequent affairs to soothe the inevitable heartaches that accompanied such marriages. To my feeble mind it seemed a flawed system. He was polite to the child. He said the right things then dismissed her quickly. I was sent to retrieve some refreshments.

The men were seated on a large bench near the blazing fire. The fresh tankards of ale I brought were welcomed with a hearty cheer and the discussion began. The Marshal paced in front of the fireplace sipping his ale as he spoke.

"I have begun work on behalf of the King. Bitter is the news I must deliver to Henry. I have yet to report to his Majesty, but you, my friends, must hear the truth first. After hearing 'tis possible you may decide to take leave of my service. I tell you plain, I would not reproach any so moved. In sooth the choice to remain might have serious consequences." He paused, looked at each of us, swallowed a gulp of ale and then continued. "Richard is allied with Philip of France. When they decide the time is right they will depose Henry. Do not compare this to the folly of ten years ago. Richard is capable and smart enough to wait until the proper forces are arrayed to his liking. Let not the youth of King Philip mislead you. He has carefully assembled the resources and is ready to supply Richard with sufficient men and equipment. There are enough unhappy barons who will be eager to join such a venture to repay Henry for past offenses. We will be outnumbered unless the King can raise enough funds to pay mercenaries. Our main strength is in England, but they are tired of paying for Henry's wars in France. I fear the best men will find convenient excuses to be tardy. When the tide turns in either side's favor, they will jump to the winning side. It matters little to them who they call King, Richard or Henry. There are some loyal men we can count on, but they do not have sufficient numbers to be decisive. Before you lose all hope, let me say there is one factor which may work to our advantage. I have just learned the Saracens have captured Jerusalem. The old fool Guy of Lusignan has fled to Cyprus. There already is talk of a Crusade. If it ripens to full fruit, the kings will all be asked to send men to rescue the holy places. The Pope will insist on a truce of God among the kings. Fighting among themselves will be suspended. The holy man, William of Tyre, already sounds the cry. It could buy enough time for Henry's age to take a natural course and make the succession a peaceful one."

"I will stand with you, my friend, in any circumstance," Raoul exclaimed.

"As will I," Baldwin said as he placed his hand on the pommel of his sword.

"And I," John added quickly. My response was unnecessary. The Marshal knew I would serve him in any undertaking.

"You are true men. I knew what you would say, but I owed you the truth. Now, Lewellyn, bring more ale and fetch your lute. We shall drink and sing to friendship and foolish knights who have not the sense to be afraid. We shall drink to a Crusade. May it save us from fighting many of our friends. We may yet die martyrs in Syria and that be more to my liking than killing our own," he said laughing and slapping Raoul on the back.

The following day a half-sober Marshal and Raoul rode out to report to King Henry. The rest of us nursed very heavy heads. John went to see about the grain harvest and I set about my household chores. Poor little Helvis struggled with a cross stitch, and complained to one of the servants about the noon meal.

The winter months saw much of the same activity. The Marshal went to many parts of the kingdom gathering information. Each time he returned with less than encouraging news. Fortunately William of Tyre's call for a Crusade was gaining support by the spring of 1188. Many monarchs began to pledge support for war. Those opposing King Henry were among the supporters and Duke Richard was the most enthusiastic of all. He hungered for the glory a Crusade would give. It looked like the Marshal's wish was going to be fulfilled. King Henry joined in the promises of men and financial aid for the undertaking. The Archbishop of Canterbury promised the customary "truce of God."

Most of the year was spent in making preparations. To raise the necessary force was a very large task. King Henry was lukewarm in his support. Beset by jealous rivals at home, he did not want to see his life's work destroyed while he was engaged in a foolish venture in Syria. He knew too well the experience that befell his wife thirty years earlier. How she and her first husband almost perished in the wastes of Syria. He did enjoy the distraction from his troubles the call for a Crusade was providing.

Richard was wholeheartedly engaged in the project. The idea of glory was an absolute aphrodisiac to his warrior spirit. He sensed his father's reluctance to truly commit to the cause. It further widened the gulf between them. To show his disdain, he took an oath of fealty to Philip. He knew this threatened everything Henry had built in the Angevin realm. If something happened to Richard before he married and had sons, Aquitaine could be claimed by Philip.

King Philip, of course, was delighted and was ready to divide the father and son even further. He spent the rest of the year insisting his sister Alais was of age and should be married to Richard as the contract had promised. He was certain King Henry would not give up his paramour.

As expected, King Henry refused. Philip claimed the lands of her dowry should be declared forfeit and returned. Henry said there had been no time limit set and the lands would stay under his protection. Philip cleverly used this as an excuse to take action. A noble crusade was no longer of paramount importance.

The province of Maine was the first to be reclaimed. Philip began to mass the troops he had assembled for the Crusade to back up his demand. King Henry responded to the threat and prepared to defend the province. As 1189 began, the clouds of war were gathering to rain death on Henry II's outnumbered force. Richard would lead Philip's forces against his own father.

The Marshal was at Cartnel preparing to join the King's force with the small band that had rallied to his side. As I served the Marshal a breakfast of eggs, bread and fruit I asked, "My lord, what has happened to the 'truce of God' and the promises made for the Crusade?"

"Lewellyn, greed and ambition oft overrule men's promises to God. Were it not so, we would not need priests to remind us of our responsibilities. The truce will be scrapped. We shall fight our friends and die in the process. Again I see no way to win this contest, but we must try. I will go to the King and inform him of the need for more routiers. They will not come cheap. Good men are not stupid. They will see the odds against us and their fees will rise sharply. It seems I am forever destined to fight in hopeless causes," he said as he shook his head and looked at the ground. "John d'Erly will remain here. He is not yet ready for battle. Baldwin, Raoul and I leave for Chinon at first light. Lewellyn, I need you to come as my scribe."

It was a crisp spring morning as we proceeded down the old Roman road. We rode quietly, knowing the task looming before us would have fatal results. As quickly as it had ascended with the Marshal's return, the wheel of my life was descending again. My thoughts were filled with the questions a man asks himself when he knows his demise is eminent. Have I been worthy? Who will raise my son? What will I say if I am to be judged by God? Will my past thoughts damn me to the horrible eternal punishments the priest promised sinners?

As each of us thought about such weighty issues, we were not inclined to engage in the usual jovial banter. I rode staring at the clouds as they raced across an azure sky. I pondered the same questions that my companions must have been thinking to themselves.

Why is it that men in difficult times seek to know their fate and think of how they might have changed their past mistakes? Both are fool's errands, since one cannot be changed and the other does not yet exist and yet we still waste our precious time agonizing over such thoughts.

I did not know we were headed for a face-to-face confrontation between two of the greatest warriors of our times, a confrontation which would change everything and alter the course of England's future. I would finally learn of my father and the knowledge I had desired for so long would only serve to complicate my life even more.

Chapter 10
Another Lost Cause

It was early spring 1189 when a trio of knights and I entered the cold gray walls of a now familiar Chinon Castle. I knew the Marshal was troubled. He had not joked with his companions during the entire trip. He was far more serious than I had ever known him to be. The conflict between father and son was one he wished to avoid. In fact, as I recalled all the battles of his very long career, he always tried to avoid war. Strange, when one considers the manner in which he earned his position, he constantly preferred the peaceful solution. It was not because of fear. There has never been a more fearless man. I believe he really did not like to kill people. Fighting in tournaments was one thing, but fighting a war was another. His own death was unimportant, but the death of a friend was abhorrent. He knew the impending struggle would mean the death of many of his friends on both sides, yet his code said you honored your word regardless of personal cost.

First with the young King, and now with King Henry, the Marshal was faced with a choice. Which Plantagenet would he serve? He knew in each instance he was on the losing side, and yet there was no parsing of his oath. There was no choice. It was a rare thing to find such loyalty in a world where many men could be expected to switch sides in the middle of a battle. It is true there were others who held to the same standard, often at the cost of their lives, but this man's skill had allowed him to escape a similar fate. This time he would fight for the father rather than support the rebellious offspring. Not even his former relationship with Queen Eleanor, whom he still admired greatly, could get him to break his oath. Each time he was called upon to honor his liege lord, he did so unflinchingly. He would help the King against a son he had trained personally and knew would be a formidable foe. He would not hide the truth from King Henry. Prospects were not good.

Within an hour of our arrival we were called by the King for discussions. The Marshal, Baldwin and Raoul proceeded to enter the great hall to speak with King Henry. I took up my usual position holding the Marshal's cloak. There were several other nobles present. A few minutes later Prince John and several of his friends came down the hallway.

He saw me and said derisively, "'Tis the Marshal's lackey. He spends more time on this wall than a tapestry. He keeps him for his writing skills. One can see from his looks that it is not for other more unseemly uses." His companions immediately erupted in laughter at his witty comment. I forced a smile. If he could have read my mind, I would have been slain on the spot. They entered the room and my ears went to work. The King spoke to the assembled group of supporters.

"It appears Richard has cast his lot with the French King. Philip is marching on some of my lands in Maine. It cannot be tolerated. Marshal, what have you discovered on your travels?" he asked with a very serious tone.

"Majesty, we are not in a strong position. Auvergne has already fallen. Philip has gathered sizable support for his effort. Many nobles are unwilling to commit to their pledges. The men with me have no such reluctance. I believe I can persuade Gilbert FitzRenfrew to join us, but I am suspicious of others. They are likely to turn against us at the moment we need them the most. I wish I could bring better news, but you need know what we face. Can we afford to hire routiers?" the Marshal asked hoping for a positive answer. If not he knew all could be lost.

"You serve us well. Others would have tried to flatter me with false hope. We believe we can raise money, but it will take time. The truce is a farce. Many have given funds for the Crusade and claim they have nothing left to give. Philip chose his time well. It was more to my liking when his father was king. We will take a stand immediately or others will soon be encouraged to defect. We will take our troops to LeMans. With the Marshal's men and ours, we might be able to defeat Philip before his army grows larger. A quick victory might loosen the purse strings of some of those with weak hearts. I will show my son that this old lion still has teeth." It was classic Henry II. At that moment Prince John spoke.

"Father, I suggest I remain here with my small force. Richard is liable to move against Chinon if he knows it is insufficiently protected. We must keep our base safe."

The Marshal spoke up quickly, "Majesty, I do not think we can split the army. We are unsure of how many we face in this fight."

"William, I think John is right. My base must be protected. If we lose, we must have a place to retreat too. Besides, Le Mans is my birthplace. Surely, we will find some additional men of stout heart who remember their King. We still have favors we can grant to those who are loyal. I will demonstrate my appreciation to those who are loyal and therefore offer incentives for others to join us. We shall adjust recent favors to those who serve us best. When the other nobles see the level of my generosity they will be more willing to come to our aid. First, Baldwin de Bethune, I grant you the heiress of Chateaunoux and the lands which accompany her dowry. For Gilbert FitzRenfrew, I will offer the Damsel of Lancaster."

I was surprised the Marshal's future wife was now given to another. The mystery did not last long as the King continued his pronouncements.

"And for you, our most loyal and true friend, William Marshal, I give the hand of Isabel of Striguil." The statement caused an audible gasp from those nobles assembled in the great room for the conference. I anxiously awaited the explanation; I was sure Baldwin would have since he knew every noble family in the Angevin Empire. Who was Isabel of Striguil and what lands did she bring as a dowry? After several more discussions about when the force would depart for the disputed lands, the King called the session to a close. As the nobility left, I waited for the Marshal and his friends. When they appeared in the hallway Baldwin was smiling broadly and slapping the Marshal on the back. I moved quickly to give the Marshal his green cloak hoping to hear the answers to questions about the new arrangement. Baldwin was already speaking.

"My God, for a man who has just be given the richest and most beautiful heiress in all of England you appear less than happy. Doest thou have any idea the riches you now possess? This be Strongbow's daughter! The lands of the de Clares stretch from Normandy to England and even some in Ireland. Outside the King, you are the richest man in England. To sweeten the bargain they say she is a rare beauty," he said as his face erupted with a huge smile at his friend's good fortune.

"What you say may be true, but a dead man has little to enjoy. Without John's forces we are woefully undermanned. I may never live to see this beauty you speak of so glowingly," the Marshal said somberly. The war had to be won or death would be the only reward for my master.

"Well, at least you will have died a rich man, my friend, and that is something for a knight who started life with naught but a horse." The Marshal smiled at this last comment.

"If words were an army you would be invincible, my friend. And you are soon to leave the bachelor life for the manor of Chateaunoux. I pity the poor girl. The King has condemned her to a life of listening to your constant chatter. Come, we have much to do if I am to have any chance of seeing this damsel you claim is such a beauty," the Marshal said as he put his hand on Baldwin's shoulder.

"She is my friend. She is. And I am now a man of property. I care not if she looks like a sow. Chateaunoux is a fine place." I could see what mattered most to my former master. We reached the courtyard and turned left in the direction of the armory.

My questions had been answered without my having to ask. New questions raced through my mind. How rich was the Marshal? More importantly, could we win and make this dream come true? The Marshal did not seem to think there was much chance and he was usually right.

The rest of the day was spent making ready for the march to Maine. It was late in the evening when the Marshal returned to our quarters and requested something to eat and drink. I had anticipated his needs earlier. I had the victuals and his usual beverage already sitting on the table. He was glum as he picked at the piece of mutton and bread. He sighed and shook his head. He looked at me with sorrowful eyes and said in a very morose tone, "Lewellyn, just when I have finally achieved my life's desire, I will fall short of the mark. We cannot win this conflict. By splitting the army we have made a fatal mistake. King Henry has placed his fate in the hands of his youngest son. It was a serious mistake. Unfortunately, you cannot tell a king his favorite son cannot be trusted."

I tried to offer encouragement to the downcast knight, "My lord, you have always found a way in the past. You will find one again."

"I have been lucky. This will be a bitter fight. Philip has the men and the money. Richard has the skill. It is a lethal combination. When we faced this family struggle on the side of the young King, we lost to a forgiving father. Richard's hatred for Henry will not allow him to be forgiving. You must prepare for a new life. I shall try to make arrangements for you and your son with others." He looked directly into my eyes and I could see the frustration he was feeling.

"Do not speak of such things, my lord!" My voice trembled as much from anger as from fear of the fate I was asking to share.

"We have been through too much together to lie to each other now. I will die as I have lived, with honor. I fear only that I drag others to this end with me. 'Tis a bitter thought." He sat staring at the wall tapping his cup on the table.

"My lord, wouldst thou deny them their chance to show loyalty and thereby gain their share of honor?" I asked the sullen warrior. He looked at me, thought for a moment and then his demeanor changed completely.

"Nay, my conscience. You remind me that others share the code. Even some who are not required to do so," he said putting his hand on my shoulder. "Thank you. Now, cheer me up with a good song, while I enjoy this beer and some tasty mutton. We have said enough. 'Tis time to eat." He took a large bite of mutton and began chewing the mouthful with renewed zest.

My songs were not as cheerful as usual. My heart was not in it. The Marshal scolded me and urged me drink with him. As the brew took effect we began to sing more lustily. The tunes turned to bawdy tales of lusty wenches and bold men. We laughed and sang into the evening with little thought of what the rising sun would bring.

That night, I went to sleep wondering again if my life with the Marshal was about to end. As my mind retraced my life with this marvelous warrior, I realized there had been many times when he could have met his end. His was a profession where most did not see the advanced years of forty and fifty. The Marshal was halfway between the two. I had seen the King's son die in the tournaments. The Marshal had been in tenfold as many and each could have resulted in accidental death, but his talent had made the possibility seem unthinkable. Court intrigues had failed to permanently harm him. Battles in foreign lands had not brought down this powerful man. He seemed to lead a charmed life. From the very first day, when our lives together began in a dungeon, he seemed to be invulnerable. Still, in the back of my mind, I knew death was always nearby, and could claim my friend. He had lived with this possibility for so long it did not concern him. It gave him an advantage. The split second fear stole in a critical fight was never lost by the Marshal. Taken with all his other skills and constant practice at his craft, it gave him the edge. But I also knew, he was a man, and as such could be defeated if overwhelmed by greater numbers. Was this to be the time?

As we prepared to move north with our small army, the Archbishop of Rouen informed us he wanted to have a meeting between the King and Philip at Gisors. King Henry agreed to go. We traveled with a small group of men-at-arms to the great oak tree. It was the same site a youthful Philip uttered his fateful prophecy, "I will take back all you have taken from my father."

We rode with a pleasantly warm sun high in a very clear sky. It made me hope that a way to avoid this conflict could be found and the dire predictions of the Marshal would not be realized. We were so tantalizingly close to achieving our dreams: the Marshal a wife, family and land; me a home and reuniting with my son. My small mount had to strain to keep pace with the Marshal's huge war stallion. He was almost trotting and making for a rather uncomfortable ride. I needed to divert my thoughts so I inquired as to why the Archbishop had arranged the meeting.

"My lord, why has the church sought this conference?" I asked while gazing up at the Marshal who looked rather splendid in his hauberk and green tabard. The sun's rays danced on the chain links creating a shimmering glow.

The Marshal explained as the horses' hoofs tapped out a steady rhythm on the hard packed road, "The Church does not want a conflict to interfere with the plans for the Crusade. They seek to make every effort and see the conflict resolved without fighting. Dead soldiers will not go to the Holy Land and fight for the Church. The site was selected as a way to remind the two sides of the futility of the last conflict, but I fear it will do little." We did not speak again until we arrived at the site as the noon sun was giving way to the longer shadows of the waning day. The Marshal said only one thing as he dismounted and went to join the King. "On the morrow we will know!"

The conference at Gisors began badly. It surprised no one, but the Church leaders. Philip had changed greatly since I had last seen him on this very spot ten years ago. Unfortunately the boy, now turned man, had not grown normally in the intervening years. He was shorter than most and a misshapen hunch was poorly disguised by the loose fitting robes he wore. His mind compensated for the physical defects. His verbal arguments were quick and truculent. The youthful King Philip's attitude proved a Truce of God was wishful thinking. He was in no mood for a truce when revenge of his father's rival was now at hand. He and King Henry developed an immediate dislike for each other. It soon developed into a shouting match. The Archbishop suggested another meeting, when tempers had cooled. The meeting site was set for Bonmoulins in two weeks. We rode back to our forces. King Henry showed some signs of physical discomfort. He spoke to the Marshal as they rode side by side.

"William, I know not which vexes me more: the irritation of this saddle on my ass or the arrogance of that French puppy. I was running these lands when he was still having his rear wiped by a nursemaid. Now he thinks he can talk with me as an equal." The King grimaced and leaned forward in his saddle to relieve the rubbing of the saddle on his posterior.

"Majesty, he is not like his father. I fear he will become an even greater threat to Angevin holdings in the years ahead. Your son was not with the party at Gisors," the Marshal said as if he was disappointed and somewhat surprised.

"True. He was probably preparing his troops. I have sent word for Geoffrey, the Bishop of York, to bring help from England. He is my bastard, but it seems my bastards are more loyal than my legitimate sons." The King gave a knowing look to the Marshal.

"It is help sorely needed, Sire. If our forces are not strengthened, the next meeting will prove to be just as useless. Philip knows he is in a strong position." Excusing himself the Marshal dropped back to where Baldwin and I were following. He looked at Baldwin and began to discuss the situation over the noise caused by the large group of mounted men moving in unison.

"I pray the King is right about Geoffrey of York. The force we have now has no chance against the combined forces of Richard and Philip. I know the King will fight even if he has no hope of victory. He does not look well. Neither would I if I had a son trying to kill me. I hoped the Church's desire for a Crusade would calm things, but it was a forlorn hope," the Marshal said as moved his horse to avoid a small rut in the road.

"Marshal, do you think Richard has had a change of heart? He was not at Gisors. Maybe he realizes Philip wants his lands as well." Baldwin asked the question we were all thinking about.

"Nay. Richard sees his father as the problem. Richard is confident in his ability to manipulate the French monarch. The overestimation of his power is his greatest weakness. If it comes to a fight I hope we can use it to some advantage." Just then the Marshal's horse snorted as if he also agreed with the assessment. The Marshal rose up in the stirrups and looked ahead of us. He rode back up to the King since the latter was showing some signs of increasing discomfort. They were out of earshot and I could not hear what was said. The shadows of evening lengthened in the dwindling light and the party sought refuge for the night. In the distance we could see the walls of a monastery perched on a small hill near the road. It was decided to seek lodgings there.

When the abbot heard who was with us the gates were opened immediately and the brothers in their brown robes scrambled to make ready places for the entourage. The friars looked to the needs of the ailing King. We remained for several days while King Henry tried to regain some strength before we resumed our journey to Bonmoulins. The good bread, wine and medicinal talents of the monks did wonders for the King and soon he was ready to continue the journey.

The second meeting between Henry and Philip was a complete disaster. The site was a small chateau on a river with a lovely mill adjacent to the chateau, but the hoped-for truce was about to be crushed just as surely as the wheat under the mill's heavy stone. The two monarchs had already developed a loathing for each other and this second meeting had not improved their dispositions. More quarreling was followed by feeble attempts by the Churchmen to soothe bruised egos.

The meeting was in a second unproductive day when Duke Richard arrived. King Philip made a great show of welcoming the wayward son of his adversary. Richard, for his part, seemed bent on angering his father. In full view of all present he swore another oath of fealty to the French monarch. He said he was his vassal for his entire duchy in Aquitaine. King Henry went white with anger. Here was his son, undoing a lifetime of struggle. He, Henry, had given the ingrate this huge legacy. Richard was acting as if it was Philip who had blessed him with his rich province! I thought King Henry would race across the room and try to strangle his much larger son with his bare hands. The fire in his eyes matched the noontime heat.

I was not the only one thinking such thoughts. Philip's armed escort stepped between the son and his father. I looked at the Marshal to see if there would be trouble. He placed his hand on my shoulder and shook his head. King Henry's expression changed and a look of resignation replaced the one of anger. He spoke slowly and disgustedly, "By God's legs, I have raised a weasel. This meeting is over." Duke Richard sneered at the retort, and in a final gesture of contempt, he placed his arm around Philip. The two left the room laughing. After King Henry left I was left standing alone with the Marshal and the few notes I had scribbled.

The Marshal frowned and said, "Lewellyn, we are at war. You shall witness a real fight and in the heat of summer. I hope Geoffrey arrives at Rouen with help. We have about seven hundred routiers. Richard and Philip can field three times the number. Within a month, five times as many will join their side. I wish I had taught you to use a sword instead of a quill."

"I will fight, my lord!" I exclaimed in an act of silly bravado. The Marshal just smiled and rubbed my head.

We broke camp and rode to Rouen. The truce was over. There was nothing to do now, but prepare for war. Geoffrey of York arrived, but without much in the way of reinforcements. Geoffrey, the King's bastard by an unnamed noble lady, was my height and build but older by five years. He too had red hair that was beginning to thin. As the Marshal had predicted, excuses and empty promises came from the nobility in England. It was also clear the King was becoming sicker with each day. His color grew worse. The Marshal and Geoffrey asked me to stay with his majesty and help him on and off his mount as we traveled with our small force of seven hundred to Le Mans. The King was sure this would be the route of Philip and Richard's army. He was right. It was the route, but wrong in believing the site of his birth would provide needed allies. All the fighting men had abandoned the town when they heard of our coming.

There were some brief skirmishes with the advance guard of the French force on the outskirts of Le Mans. The King stopped on a small knoll that overlooked the town. The road twisted sharply at the bottom and entered the town by a tavern. We were in a good position to see everything that transpired below while being protected from a surprise attack. The King obviously knew the terrain well. Watching them it reminded me of the tournaments I had often attended with my master. The difference was this fight did not see men retire to the sidelines or yield to the knights who unhorsed them. In this contest, the fallen could expect to be hacked to death by their opponent. Even from a distance on the hill, where I sat astride a horse, next to the King, I could hear the moans and see some of the white tabards grow red flowers of blood. It was a sickening sight.

The Marshal had killed two men when the bloody sight in front of me seemed to stop. Most of our routiers turned and raced in our direction. At first, I was surprised. They had easily defeated the small force of men they had engaged. Then I saw it, spilling over the crest of the hills above the town. It looked like a large swarm of colorful ants gathering around a fallen crust of bread. These ants, however, were carrying banners which identified the horde as Richard and Philip's main army. The numbers were overwhelming. The Marshal disengaged and rode up to our position. King Henry's face was ashen. Geoffrey spoke first.

"Sire, we must retreat!" he said pointing to the south.

"Nay, these are my lands. I will not give them up without a struggle." The King was calling for a hopeless stand.

The Marshal heard the exchange and said, "Majesty, this is a poor place to make such a stand. We will be overrun in minutes. We must find another place to fight and soon. Richard's men will stop to sack the town and take some booty. It will give us time. Otherwise, all will be lost. I will try to rally our routiers, who have already abandoned the field."

"Nay, I will fight here. Are you ready to abandon the cause?" the King said defiantly.

The Marshal replied in a firm voice, "I will die here with you, if that be your wish, but if you look around you will see our seven hundred are gone. There are only ten to stand against the entire French army. I doubt it will make a fight. Your son, Geoffrey of York, deserves a chance to die with honor. This will be a capture followed by an execution."

The King surveyed the oncoming army, and then turned his head to see his small force disappearing over the hill behind us. He shook his head sadly, turned his horse and began to ride slowly in the direction of his retreating knights. The Marshal turned to Geoffrey. "Ride with the King. I will stay for a few moments and be sure all the French stop to plunder the town. If they do not, I fear we have waited too long."

From where we were situated halfway up the hill on the knoll I could see the banner of Duke Richard advance into the deserted town. We could hear doors being smashed and saw torches being tossed into barns. Yells of delight went up as stocks of wine and beer were found and broken into. I saw the tavern keeper, who had been tardy in vacating his establishment, running down the road toward our position. Two riders made his escape short lived. He was grabbed and held while a large rider with auburn hair rode up to the captured man. He had no armor, but did carry a lance and shield. I could not see the designation on the shield because he was holding it on the opposite side of his horse. I watched as the knight pointed his lance at the chest of the rotund shopkeeper. We were too far away to hear the distant conversation, but from the gestures you could guess what was being said. I saw the man point in our direction. The knight looked in our direction and saw the Marshal and me. I heard him scream, "Get my guard and follow me." He wheeled his horse, and raced toward us at a full gallop.

The shield was facing directly at us, three running gold lions on red. My suspicions were confirmed. Richard Coeur de Lion was coming to make an end of his retreating father. Once again I had been mistaken for the King. The Marshal calmly said, "Lewellyn, time for you to go." He trotted his steed into the path of the hard-riding Richard and lowered his lance into the attack position and urged his horse to a gallop. He briefly looked over his shoulder at the retreating King Henry. When Richard saw a lone knight coming at him, he prepared his shield and raised his lance. I had not moved, as the Marshal had requested. I was again transfixed, as I had been as a boy. I was about to witness the clash of two of the greatest fighting men of the century.

Both riders braced and prepared for the ultimate collision. Each man, confident he would prevail, showed no fear. Richard was at a full gallop when the Marshal's lance slammed into the center of his shield. The shield went flying into the air from the impact. Richard was lifted from the saddle and landed roughly on the ground. He had managed to retain his sword. His horse stopped and being well trained quickly trotted back to his fallen master. Richard without a cumbersome hauberk was quick to regain his feet. He remounted. The Marshal slowly rode toward his still-armed foe with his lance cradled under his arm. He knew the contest was his.

The Coeur de Lion had been so consumed with dispatching his hated father; he gave little thought to the identity of the knight who blocked the way. After all, he, Richard, could defeat any man in single combat! As the Marshal slowly approached, recognition of his adversary showed in Richard's eyes. For the first, and I wager the only time in his life, the look of fear was written on his handsome face. He knew he was about to die. The Marshal's lance was pointed directly at his chest. He dropped his sword and cried out, "By God's legs, Marshal, do not kill me. I wear no hauberk."

"The Devil shall take you some day, but this day, I will not kill the son of my King! You will follow no further!" He spurred his horse forward, dropped the point of the lance and struck Richard's horse in the shoulder. The horse buckled to his knees. A stunned Richard Coeur de Lion jumped off and stood next to the crippled steed. His plea had been granted and his life spared. The Marshal turned and slowly trotted away. As I rode to join him, I turned and saw the mighty Richard fall to his knees holding his sword by the hilt. In the distance I could see the personal guard of six men riding toward their fallen leader. I urged the Marshal to pick up the pace of our retreat. He laughed and said they would not pursue. They did not.

After half an hour we caught up to the King, and the rest of the force. The scorching summer sun punished the knights wearing full battle gear. Many swooned. I understood why Duke Richard had been without his armor. We rode hard for the rest of the day in spite of the weather. Had Philip's men caught us, they would have shown less mercy than the heat. When we reached Rennes, the King suggested a rest was needed. I could see his condition had worsened from the stifling heat. Geoffrey suggested our best course would be to head for the coast and then to England. Henry would have none of it. He would join up with John at Chinon. He would raise a new army to return and retake Le Mans. The Marshal said Philip and Richard would expect a dash for the coast. He agreed with the King. A retreat to Chinon had the best chance of success. It was many miles to the south, but it would be unexpected. The decision was made and for seven brutally hot days the ever-dwindling army moved south.

When we finally reached the safety of Chinon, the force had shrunk to only several hundred knights. The heat had caused more casualties than the French army. To the King's shock, John was not there. We were informed Prince John had left shortly after our departure, ostensibly to recruit more men. When the Marshal and I retired to our quarters we finally took time to discuss the situation we were now facing.

"Lewellyn, the King is mistaken if he thinks John will return from England. We will be most fortunate if those who remain do not desert. We will be able to hold Chinon against a siege for a while, but we will not prevail. I suggest you make arrangements to take your son back to England before Richard arrives. Once we are surrounded there will be no escape."

"My son is with friends at Baldwin's chateau. Since they are unimportant, I believe they will be safe. I will remain with you. I would have perished in a dungeon many years ago and never enjoyed the birth of my son without you. I shall not leave you now. It is not bravery, but a commitment to one who has proven his concern for me. I do not think you would abandon me if I was in need. We travel this road together," I said earnestly.

"Nay, I would not. You have proven yourself as worthy as any chevalier and more honorable than some of the King's sons. I am proud to call you friend and if we survive this I will share a secret that I have kept for years. The King's days are numbered. Even if he escapes the clutches of Philip's army, I fear his appointment with God cannot be forestalled." He gazed at the setting summer sun through the window slit.

"His Majesty's health is failing. Geoffrey knows and he wants to take him to England. What will happen, my lord?" Again I asked a question that had no answer. I was hoping the Marshal could somehow see in the vanishing red rays of light a glimpse of the future. Although I was curious about his secret this was not the time to ask.

"I know not. The next move is up to Richard and Philip. Philip might be willing to allow the old King a way out. Not because he is chivalrous, but because war is expensive. If you can get your adversary to surrender, you save money and time. Philip has learned this lesson at an early age. Richard has seen death close up. It might cool his lust for revenge. We shall see." He turned from the window and looked directly at me.

I finally got the courage to ask the question which had troubled my thoughts for the past two weeks. "My lord, why did you not kill the Duke?"

"He was defenseless, Lewellyn. The code of honor would not allow it."

"But my lord, if Chinon falls, will he not kill you?"

"Yea."

"I do not understand." I shook my head and gazed at the floor.

"God will decide when I return to him, but when the day comes I will be able to say I always lived the code. To some it is a small thing. To me it be everything. Now, let us speak no more of death. I am thirsty. Fetch the beer and your lute. By God's furnace this heat may be His way of preparing me for my eternal residence." He laughed. I brought the beverage and struck up a tune. We sang songs into the night and waited for the morning to bring news of the enemy.

The news was not good. Provinces in the west and south were rising against Henry. Expecting the inevitable outcome, they were taking advantage of the weakness of the aging Angevin and currying favor with his successors. The King's physical condition seemed to be wedded to his political fortunes, as one suffered setbacks, so did the other. The King, who had always been a bundle of energy, was too weak to rise from his bed. Geoffrey was constantly at his side tending to every need. Unlike his deceased half brother of the same name, this Geoffrey had real affection for his father. I was asked to assist the King and did so. After several days there was some improvement in his condition.

I was helping his Majesty get dressed when word came that a courier had brought a message from Philip and Richard. I was sent to summon the Marshal to a council in the great hall. When we returned, the King, Geoffrey and several advisors were pouring over the contents of the communication. Henry was still in bed clothes and seated in his crescent-shaped chair. The King looked at the Marshal and began to speak.

"They seek to parley at Colombieres to discuss terms," he said bitterly. His color had improved. Anger seemed to be the best elixir for King Henry. "If we had some men, we would meet them in a way the vermin would ne'er forget! Alas, we only have a few who remain loyal. Each day brings news of more defections." He rose to his feet and I expected him to begin his usual pacing back and forth, but he winced from some inner pain and sat down again. He continued, "We have decided not to expose the rest of you to further danger. We will go and treat with my ungrateful son and his hunchbacked boyfriend." The words dripped with sarcasm.

Geoffrey spoke, "Sire, I advise against this action. In your present state of health such a journey could be harmful. If you are committed to seeking terms let the Marshal and I go in your stead." Geoffrey had rightly judged his father's condition and was suggesting the most sensible course of action.

"Nay! I am the King. It is MY son who has brought about this sorry affair. I shall not give him the satisfaction of meekly submitting to this humiliation without showing my contempt for him face to face. We will ride to Colombieres in the morning. The Marshal will stay here and wait to see if John sends the needed help. This council is over." He rose. The pains caused him to hunch over and slowly shuffle out of the hall. I turned to the Marshal.

"Do you think Prince John will come?" I asked knowing full well the answer.

"Nay, Lewellyn, he will not. We are witnessing a sick man's fantasy. It is hard to live without hope. You must continue to help Geoffery nurse the King. I do not see how he can make such a journey. He needs some kindness if he is to have any chance of making it to Colombieres," he said putting a firm hand on my shoulder. We walked slowly down the hall.

In the morning as the towers of Chinon receded in the distance our small band, about two dozen men-at-arms, rode slowly to the fateful conference. Geoffrey suggested the King go in a wagon, but the feisty monarch refused. He would face his enemies in the saddle like a true king. He was in a great deal of pain and we made slow progress. Finally, the combination of heat and pain overcame his iron will; he swooned. I caught him to prevent his falling to the ground. Geoffrey ordered the company to stop at a nearby farmhouse. The King was carried into the house. Geoffrey turned to me and said, "Go to Colombieres and tell them of the King's condition. Tell them he needs time to recover before meeting with Richard and Philip."

I mounted my horse and rode, quickly reaching Tours. My pace was no longer restricted by tending to a sick king. On the other side of Tours, I reached the fields of Colombieres where the French army surrounded the splendid tents of Philip and Richard. I was taken to a white tent covered with gold fleur-de-lis containing the two victorious royals. Duke Richard towered over the young French king. Philip looked as though a strong wind would send him reeling. The soon-to-be "King Richard," on the other hand, looked very impressive. At thirty-two he was in the prime of life. The muscles in his arms made it clear he believed in the training regimen of his mentor. He appeared to be bigger and stronger than the fallen knight I had seen begging for his life a few weeks earlier. I was certain he was unaware I had witnessed his defeat at the hands of the Marshal. Because I had been able to see the powerful Richard begging for mercy, I was not intimidated by his imposing presence. I bowed and addressed King Philip and handed him a note from Archbishop Geoffrey.

"Sire, I have been ordered to tell your Majesties that King Henry is gravely ill and is unable to travel. He requests time to recover before your meeting."

Philip looked at me and then turned to Richard. "What think you? Is he stalling hoping to reconstitute his forces?"

"Aye, trust not the old faker. He is a fox when cornered. Make him come here," he demanded.

I was surprised at the bitterness of his comments. I knew it was useless for me to protest the truthfulness of the King's condition. I was only a messenger. The anger of this son for his father was deep. I began to fear for the Marshal. If Richard hated his father this much, what would he do to the man who almost killed him? Philip spoke next.

"Inform the King we expect him here on the morrow, or we march on Chinon," Philip announced waving his hand in a dismissive gesture while smiling at his powerful companion.

"I shall convey the message, Sire." I bowed respectfully and left the tent. I was apprehensive about how my message would be received when I reached the King and Geoffrey. I watched carefully to see if I was followed. With the King so close and vulnerable I feared murder would offer a quick solution to the succession. Trust was not present on either side. I rode in a false direction until I was satisfied that I was not followed.

I rode back to the unassuming cottage containing the King and arrived by nightfall. I went directly to the King. I was pleased to see him on his feet, but he was still grimacing from his inner pains. I reluctantly shared Philip's demand for the King to appear in person on the morrow. Geoffrey swore. The King responded by putting his hand on Geoffrey's shoulder. He said he would be ready to go in the morning

Shortly after dawn the King rose and ordered his squires to get things ready. Anger flashed in his eyes again. As I helped him mount his horse, he said, "I will win back my land in spite of them."

We rode at a slow pace for several hours. Several times the King appeared ready to swoon, but he kept riding. I wondered at his will to endure pain for the sake of appearances. It was late in the afternoon when the banners and the tents could be seen on the plain ahead. I was very tired myself, but if the King could endure, so would I. As we approached, I saw seats had been prepared in front of Philip's tent. Philip and Richard sat there surrounded by a host of military advisors. Philip was clearly enjoying the moment. King Henry stopped his horse in front of the seated nobles. As a show of contempt they did not rise.

King Henry winced, leaned forward in his saddle and spoke. "I am not feeling well, so say your say and do not waste my time with prattle."

Seeing the mounted monarch's pale color and grimaces, the youthful king realized King Henry's health was in serious jeopardy. It was plain for all to see, even the skeptical Richard. In what I perceived as a compassionate move, Philip asked Henry if he would like to take a more comfortable seat.

"I remain where I am. Now, let us be about this business as I said." Defiance flashed in his eyes as he determined not to let his condition evoke pity.

Philip proceeded to give a long list of terms. Each time, Henry replied with an angry "Granted." As a personal humiliation, the next to last term was the removal of the Princess Alais from his care. She would be placed under the protection of the Archbishop of Rouen. The King hesitated. Anguish replaced the defiance in his eyes and then sorrowfully he said, "Granted." Many of the French nobles laughed. The last term was amnesty for all those who had joined Richard against his father—a list of names would be provided later. The thoroughly defeated King agreed. With the last term affirmed, King Henry turned his horse and our group began riding away from the camp.

Soon, when we were out of sight of the French, the King collapsed. Geoffrey had a litter brought and we helped the once-powerful Angevin ruler into its comfortable embrace. We journeyed back to Chinon, not sure if the King would survive the trip, but the will of the old man was still strong, and despite the ravages of his illness, he kept saying he would get everything back when his condition improved.

We were greeted by the Marshal at the gates and the King rose from the litter and asked if there was any word from John. There was none. The King asked to have his litter placed in the chapel of Chinon. It was a very small room. Only two or three attendants could be with the King as he lay on the litter. The Marshal, Geoffrey and I took turns looking after the sick man. He came in and out of consciousness during the night.

The following day when the Marshal and Geoffrey came to relieve my watch, a messenger arrived with the list of those to be pardoned. Geoffrey took the parchment and turned white as he looked at the list. The King was awake. He saw the look on Geoffrey's face and asked what was wrong. With his hands trembling and his voice cracking, Geoffrey said, "Sire, the first name on the list is that of Prince John."

"John, no, it cannot be! I have endured all this for his sake. He would not betray the father who loved him." His face expressed pain beyond that of the physical.

"My lord, his name is here."

"Ohhh, no. Let death come. I care not anymore," he mumbled with utter despair. The anger, the resolve, the will to live was broken. Henry II, builder of the great Angevin empire, now awaited death. For six days he lingered. Now and again he would turn to Geoffrey and say, "Not all my sons have betrayed me. You have been a true son." Once in his delirium he said the same to me. On the 6th day of July, in the year of our Lord 1189, the great king placed his head on the chest of Geoffrey, Archbishop of York, and after uttering the words "Shame! Shame on a conquered King," breathed his last. His time had come to face God and answer for a lifetime of transgressions. Yet, I grieved for him. He had always been kind to me and I was one of his lowest subjects, not worthy of such treatment. I spoke of this to my master later in our room.

"My lord, I know he earned the enmity of many, yet I grieve for him. He was always kind to me," I said sincerely.

"Your feelings do you credit. I told you once, long ago, I would make inquiries about your father. Lewellyn, he lies on the litter in the Chinon chapel." I froze. My limbs began to shake. My eyes filled with tears.

"My lord, this cannot be!" I said in total disbelief, sinking to my knees. The Marshal took me gently by the shoulders and sat me on the edge of his chair. He stepped back and looking at the ceiling began an unbelievable story.

"The King was never sure until the day you saved him from the surprise visit of the French ambassador. Think back to the many times others saw in you a likeness of the King's family. Queen Eleanor always knew. As a mother she could see the resemblance clearly. When you were placed in my service she said she suspected as much. I said nothing for fear it would place you in danger." I sat listening with my hands trembling.

"Why, my lord, did the King say nothing?" I said still in disbelief.

"Jealous sons who could do you harm and the fact your mother had no standing made acknowledging you impossible. It still presents a danger."

"But Geoffrey of York is in the same danger."

"True, but being of the cloth and having a powerful grandfather protects him more than you. Still he is in danger. I believe that Henry hoped you would be safe if you remained undiscovered. Only the Queen and I know the truth. Recently the King considered a bishopric for you because of your facility to read and write, but that was delayed when the troubles began. Now there is little anyone can do. I will surely be executed by King Richard for treason. 'Tis best that your secret remain undiscovered." With that the Marshal took me by the arms and lifted me off the chair. He hugged my sobbing body and held me for several minutes. I must have swooned for the next thing I remember was waking in the morning on my palette and the Marshal was gone.

That morning I sat and pondered whether or not the revelation was real or just a dream. Many emotions confused my mind: sadness at finding and losing a father in the same day, happiness that the mystery had been finally solved, anger that I had spent all my life as the lowest of the low when royal blood flowed in my veins, fear of the possible consequences that might befall me if the secret was discovered and frustration that I could tell no one. Even if I did, none would believe such a tale. The contradictions were overwhelming. So much so that I finally could think on it no longer or I would go mad. I did skip my chores in protest. When the Marshal returned he said nothing.

Geoffrey made arrangements for our father's burial at Fontevrault Abbey. A messenger was sent to Richard his father was dead and he was King. The Marshal and I waited at Chinon for the arrival of the new King. The Marshal was a marked man. He had been Henry's closest military advisor. It was considered treason to the new ruler. I sent word to Elaine and her husband asking them to care for my son, Jean, in the event of my death.

Richard wasted no time in claiming the throne and rode triumphantly to Chinon. His first orders were to have the Marshal and Maurice de Creon, a mercenary leader, brought before him. Many of the Marshal's friends suggested he flee immediately, but he refused. He said he would face Richard with a clear conscience. He had done what duty required and expected no quarter from his new monarch. With great sadness they all bid him farewell.

Henry's body was lying in state at Fontevrault. It was said King Richard would be going there after he settled affairs here. The Marshal was dressed in his best finery when the guards arrived at our apartments. Five men with long pikes surrounded him. I truly believe had he wanted to escape he would have made short work of the likes of these, but this was not his plan. He smiled and quietly walked with them to the great hall to face his fate.

Chapter 11
What Next?

The Marshal was flanked by guards as he approached the man who was now the King. The oak timbers that buttressed the ceiling were as thick as a man's waist. Tapestries and banners lit the walls with color. The conference table that usually occupied the far end was gone. The king's chair, which had contained a feeble Henry, now held a large powerful warrior king. It was a king who had faced the killing point of the Marshal's lance just a few short weeks ago. There were others in the room that had similar experiences during the career of the great champion who stood alone in the center of the hall. To be sure, many of them were delighted he would now face defeat and death. It was something many had tried to do, but never were able to accomplish on the field of combat. It is human nature to desire to see those greater than ourselves put down because it lessens the feelings of inadequacy. These men proved the rule.

The Marshal was oblivious to their feelings. He walked tall and proud to face his fate. Those who knew him best knew there would be no begging for mercy. His code would not let him debase himself in front of his peers. No, that is not accurate: they were not his peers; they were merely his contemporaries.

As he approached the new King, the Marshal bowed respectfully. Richard stood up, and plainly, the two men were of equal size. They were both physically more imposing than those in the great hall. King Richard spoke.

"Sir William, do you acknowledge me as your liege lord?" The question caused surprised looks on the face of many.

"Yea, your majesty. You are the rightful heir to King Henry as his eldest son," the Marshal acknowledged in a clear and unwavering voice. His eyes looked directly at his former pupil as if he were pleased to see the man who would execute him had lived up to his early expectations. It was a strange sort of pride that seemed to say you are worthy of being my executioner. Richard paused, rubbed his hands together and smiled in a manner that signified he was pleased with what he was about to say.

"Good. It would be a shame to execute my mentor, my mother's friend and a fighting man of your skill. We have need of your services." The shocked silence in the hall was palpable. The Marshal needed? This was supposed to be his sentencing for treason. The King continued.

"You have served my brother, and my father loyally, God rest their souls. Willst thou now serve us in a like manner?" he asked as he casually brushed away a wisp of hair.

"I give you my pledge, Sire," the Marshal said with a bow of his head.

"Enough for us. There be no man in the world whose word I trust more. We have a task we believe you will enjoy. Go hence to England and see my mother freed from her captivity in Winchester. Tell her, act in my stead 'til I arrive. Have her prepare for my coronation at Westminster. She holds you in the highest regard. She will be delighted when 'tis you who unlocks the gates." It was apparent from his broad grin the King was enjoying the moment. The same could not be said for some of the nobles gathered in the hall. Heads turned and many just stared at the scene. To utter even the slightest word of protest would mean a death sentence. The Marshal's face registered no sign of surprise as he gave a simple reply.

"A great honor, Sire. She is a remarkable lady and one whose friendship I have always treasured." Again the Marshal bowed his head.

"There is one more task for you to perform while you are in England. Arrange for your marriage to the damsel of Striguil. Our father saw fit to grant this marriage. Now, he is gone, and we wish to honor his commitment. We regret this recent unpleasantness. It is a small thing we can do to honor his memory." His tone seemed sincere and at odds with the past events.

Once again, the announcement of the hand of the heiress of Striguil was greeted by a massive gasp. The Marshal would not go to the headsman and now he was being rewarded for his defiance of Richard. The perplexed nobles were stunned. Those loyal to Richard assumed one of them would have been given such a prize. The disbelief and consternation were plainly written on their faces. Years of flattery and groveling wasted. What was the King doing? I, however, was bursting with joy. Then something happened sending my hair into a vertical position on my scalp. The King quite pleased with his generosity continued to address the Marshal.

"We are sure many are surprised by these actions, but you will prove your worthiness in the years ahead. Are you now glad I was able to deflect your lance with my hand at Le Mans?" he said with a grin. He surveyed the gathering. The King was changing the events at Le Mans to suit his personal vanity.

The Marshal looked directly at his benefactor and said in a clear voice, "Your majesty is mistaken. You would not be here had I wished it so."

My heart sank. By God's eyes the man has thrown his life away. Was honor so important you could not allow the King to bend the truth? He had rewarded him with everything a knight errant could dream of and the Marshal did not give an inch to the King's vanity—something every noble present would have done without a second thought. Flattering the powerful has always been the way people have sought riches. Was he now throwing away the chance of a lifetime just to speak the truth? Richard scowled and then smiled.

"You amaze us. We are sure your courage matches your fidelity. Go, free my mother." With that pronouncement the Marshal bowed and walked proudly to the doorway.

I resumed my breathing as we left the hall. John was the first to speak in a manner I thought to be offensive, but accurate.

"My lord, were you seized by a moment of madness? You almost threw away everything rather than give the King a fig leaf to cover his pride." The Marshal raised his eyebrows to show the young squire his displeasure at the rude remark, but he answered in a calm voice.

"The King must face the truth, as we all must. I will not begin my relationship with the new king by lying. Richard has many shortcomings, but he does honor the code, as I. I know better than anyone for it was I who taught him." The Marshal's face remained as calm as it had through the entire audience. John shook his head and I remained silent. I was thinking the same thoughts, but fortunately did not embarrass myself with the same questions. His code always came first, no matter the consequences. It was something King Richard understood as well. The other nobles present did not. They would have done anything to survive such a predicament. For that reason, they could never be trusted in the same way as the Marshal. King Richard knew this. It was why he would keep the Marshal close as a trusted advisor. The words of Bertran de Born drifted back to my mind. He had said long ago that wise kings always had need of such men. It gave me hope that the reign of Richard Coeur de Lion would be a good one. It proved to be a false hope.

The Marshal dictated his orders for the preparations that were needed to make our journey and fulfill our appointed tasks. I began to think about the dreaded trip across the water to England. I could feel my stomach begin its rebellion. The Marshal said he would go to Winchester and meet with Queen Eleanor, while John and I journeyed to Pembroke castle to see his future wife. He joked nervously about this ravishing beauty Baldwin had raved about.

"Baldwin thinks beauty is judged by the size of a dowry. The damsel of Lancaster sent to Fitzrenfrew was not much to behold. In truth I was not disappointed to see her bags packed for a new location. This new heiress might be useful to keep the fields safe from crows," he said laughing. "She does come from good stock. Her father Strongbow was a good man. At least, if Baldwin is right, we will have comfortable lives. John, you will act as my overseer. Lewellyn, you can be reunited with your son. When you two have examined my new estates, bring the young woman to Winchester. I should like the opportunity to see my wife-to-be before the wedding," he said as he glumly recalled Helvis his previously promised bride.

I was disappointed that the new knight was coming with us. I had hoped that he would stay in Normandy and be assigned to another liege lord. I waited until John left to tend other matters before I asked the Marshal about John's future. As we were packing I broached the subject.

"My lord, what are the plans for the young d' Erly?" I tried to sound as casual in my query so as not to reveal my jealousy.

"I shall continue his training. As a fighting man he is somewhat lacking. 'Tis my belief he will never be one for the tournaments, but his mind is clear and we can use those talents to help run our holdings, perhaps as sheriff." I could contain my feelings no longer.

"My lord, have I failed in my duties? It has always been I to act as your administrator." My voice cracked from the distress this new plan engendered.

"Lewellyn, you have served me perfectly and will continue to do so, but the vastness of these new lands will require a man with noble standing. The nobles who must now pledge fealty to me would not understand the arrangement between you and me. The one which has worked so well in the past would not be possible in this new life." The explanation only served to enrage my feelings.

I became impertinent and angrily replied, "Noble standing! Royal blood flows in my veins and I am less than a boy whose parents would not even merit an invitation to the coronation." The frustration of years of unfair servitude spilled from my guts. The recent revelation of my father's identity had emboldened me to display such arrogance.

The Marshal did not reply with anger as he replied to my outburst. "The knowledge about your father has released the jackals of jealousy. Lewellyn, I have told you of the danger to you if the truth be known. It is not a desire to keep you in servitude that prompts my actions. If you wish you are free to leave my service at any time of your choosing. I will even try, when my influence is sufficient, to see you take holy orders and achieve the role King Henry once considered. Your loyalty to me deserves no less." The words defeated my anger and I spoke with an earnest desire to understand. I knew my feelings about God would not let me take holy orders. I asked pleadingly, "My lord, I wish to only serve by your side. Why is it so difficult for a man to rise in social standing?"

"Lewellyn, we may change kings before the cock crows, sow and harvest a crop in a single season, but to change the ways of men takes generations. 'Tis not the answer I wish to give, but that be the way it is. You must choose now which path you wish to follow. We must not discuss your heritage again, lest the secret be discovered by unwanted ears."

His eyes stared into mine demanding the most difficult of choices. My head sunk to my chest and I said tearfully, "I choose your service, my lord. Without you I would be but a serving boy carrying trays to tables and being beaten for spilling a drop of wine."

"Then 'tis settled. Seek to know John. He is a good man. There is always room in a good man's heart for another friend. Your friendship has a special place in mine." With that he placed his hands on my shoulders and smiled. We returned to preparing for our trip. I was given time to see Elaine and inform her of the new plans. It was decided that Jean would not join me right away. Once things were settled in England I would make arrangements for my son to join me.

Two days later we crossed over to England. The sea was unusually calm and I was not afflicted with my normal distress. When I mentioned this to one of the sailors he said I was getting my sea legs. I was puzzled. When I looked at my legs, they appeared to be the same. He noticed my quandary and for some reason found it amusing. I later learned what he meant, and was mortified at my stupidity.

The Marshal remarked it was good to be home when we landed in Dover. Even though he spent much of his life in the Normandy region, his heart was always here. I found this attachment understandable when I realized my own excitement at the prospect of going to Wales, my mother's birthplace, and the location of part of my heritage. It is odd how we form attachments to places we have never been. Whenever people heard my name, they always made reference to this place I had never been. Because of this, I developed a bond with this unknown country. Now, I would see if it measured up to my imagination.

John d'Erly and I rode with the Marshal to Winchester. The Marshal was greeted by Ranulf de Glanville. They spoke briefly about the death of King Henry. De Glanville expressed concern King Richard would take revenge on him for being his mother's jailer for the past eighteen years. The Marshal understood his fear, but pointed out his own experience with the new monarch. Had not Ranulf treated the Queen with the utmost respect? She was more a house guest rather than a prisoner. He agreed and said he would await Richard's arrival and trust to luck he would be treated well.

When the Marshal was reunited with the lady who had started his rise to prominence, it was a wonderful moment for the two of them. She embraced him and began to renew an old friendship. I stood by the hearth of the great room with the Marshal's cloak and tried to be as invisible as possible.

"William, I might have known it would be you who freed me. Many years have passed since the day your bravery saved me from capture. Now, you rescue me again. I have grown gray, but the affection I have for you has not dimmed. Tell me all that has happened," she said as she grasped his arm and slowly began to walk beside her old champion. The lady, now in her sixty-seventh year, wore those years surprisingly well and the sparkle in her eye betrayed the feelings she still held for the man walking beside her. The difference in age which was not apparent when they were lovers long ago was now very apparent. The effects of time may be slowed by wealth but they cannot be stopped. They stopped as the Marshal looked into her eyes and spoke.

"Majesty, the color of your hair may have changed, but you have not. All of what I am I owe to you."

"You are kind, but you understate your own abilities. I know my son will be well served." She held out a hand which was tenderly kissed by my lord.

They talked about the death of King Henry, of the struggle leading up to his death, and how Richard had honored his father's promise for the hand of the Damsel of Striguil.

"You are most deserving of such a beautiful prize. I must confess, I am a bit jealous, but at my age I am just happy to be alive to see you rewarded as you deserve. She is the lucky one. She will have the finest knight in the entire world as her future husband," she said as the walked into the hallway festooned with banners and were soon out of earshot.

The Marshal informed the Queen she was to act as regent until King Richard arrived. They went to de Glanville and discussed the needs of the Queen. Word of her release quickly spread and the Lady of Aquitaine, who had been held suspect by the English people, soon won their support by granting amnesties to those held on the minor crimes of poaching and the like. She went to London to prepare for the coronation of her favorite son. He was due to arrive in England the second week of August. Meanwhile, John d'Erly and I continued on to Pembroke.

I now should say more about Sir John d'Erly. In spite of the Marshal's request that I give this newcomer an opportunity to gain my trust I was still holding back. It is easy to find fault with those who stand in the way of our desires, whether the criticism is fair or not. I made sure the Marshal was informed of John's errors regardless of their importance. Envy and jealousy became my unseen companions. When you look only for a man's shortcomings you become blind to his virtues. I fell victim to this human failing and for a time it prevented me from enjoying the friendship of a fine fellow. I still reproach myself for not seeing this sooner, but alas I did not. Understanding is a dish that all too often comes seasoned with the bitter herbs of age and regret. So it was with me and I have no excuse save that of being no better than the next man.

As we rode through the rolling hills, broad fields and stone walls of the Cotswolds on the way to Wales, we engaged in conversation to break the boredom. Thatched cottages and fields of grain surrounded the road. We passed Cirencester, the old roman town, and discussed the desire for John to learn writing skills. He was unaware of my feelings and freely shared his thoughts with me.

"Lewellyn, 'tis a great gift to be able to record one's thoughts. If you would honor me by sharing this knowledge I would be forever in your debt." He stretched and rose up in the saddle to take a large gulp of the fresh country air. Suspicious that his desire was merely to supplant my role in the Marshal's life I ignored the request and tried to change the subject.

"Sir John, do you not wish to follow the tournament trail?"

"Nay, I am painfully aware of my lack of talent. The Marshal is too kind to say so, but I know." He laughed at his own derisive admission.

"There are many at court that also lack talent, though they are loathe to make the same admission. They have gained much by clever words and compliments. You have the talent to rise in this way," I said hoping to encourage such ideas.

"Nay, Lewellyn. To encourage one to live off the generosity of the wealthy is to make a man a slave. Gifts given in this way can be easily withdrawn by the giver. Those who gain skills by their own toil and effort have gifts that can never be withdrawn. Your own ability to read and write is just such a gift. Flatterers and beggars produce nothing; were the kingdom to have only these, all would collapse in a generation," he said surprising me with a wisdom I had not yet seen.

"But we are traveling to examine the wealth the Marshal has been given by King Richard. Does this not gainsay your argument?" I was pleased I had rebutted his eloquent premise.

"You surprise me. Say you the Marshal acquired all this by flattery? Nothing could be more wrong. The King has desperate need of his skills, developed through a lifetime of hard and dangerous work, to say nothing of the need for one who can be relied upon to always speak the truth. Nay, these talents are as needed as much as we need the smith to shoe a horse or the villein to till the fields. You witnessed the moment when the Marshal corrected the King on the events at LeMans. Would not a lesser man have been seduced by the promise of wealth to remain silent? Methinks he would. Nay Lewellyn, the gifts that are earned through toil and effort are the foundations of real wealth."

He looked at me and smiled. I knew he was right. As I reflected on his words I was shamed to think I had dared to question the worthiness of my lord. John had been more loyal than I. The yoke of envy was lifted from my heart and I was ready to move in a new direction.

"Sir John, I would be honored to instruct you in the finer arts."

In that moment our relationship changed and we became friends. Other than me, he came to know the Marshal better than any man alive. His loyalty never wavered. I hope before I die, I will see him again, to share a brew and speak of old times together. We shared many happy evenings with the Marshal.

This fine fellow and I journeyed on to the Welsh country of rolling, treeless hills teeming with sheep. I still remember the day when we reached the top of the highest hill, and gazed down into the valleys dotted with small towns.

We continued traveling until we reached the point of land which overlooks the Irish Sea, and is the location of Pembroke castle. It was an impressive structure. Stoutly built of hard stone, the castle had outer walls that were ten times the height of a man. It commanded a strategic position guarding the outlet of Milford Haven to the sea. I knew Baldwin had not exaggerated his assessment of the Marshal's good fortune. We were met by a small contingent of men-at-arms and, after John had explained the reason for our visit, we were taken to the great hall to wait for the entrance of the lady.

The sheriff of Pembroke, a fine old gentleman, spoke to us about his life of service to the de Clare family and asked questions about the Marshal. He said he had heard many tales of his prowess and wanted to know if they were exaggerations. We assured him they were not and Pembroke would soon be delighted with its new lord. He told us of the proud tradition of its previous master and he hoped many of the customs would be continued under the new lord. He explained the fierce loyalty they had for their mistress. Although she was young, nineteen, he said she was every inch her father's daughter. It was then the damsel of Striguil made her appearance, attended by several ladies-in-waiting.

I was dumbstruck. She was more beautiful than Baldwin could have ever described. She was tall and slender with blue-green eyes. Her hair was like spun gold. It glistened when the sunlight struck it. I was convinced God's angels looked like this. She seemed to float across the floor as she approached John and me. I could see John was just as taken with the beauty of this lady as I was. He did not smile or speak. He just stared at the face of this most delicate of flowers. She broke the spell of silence with her first words.

"Is something amiss?" Her question was directed at the two gawking fools staring at her in awe struck silent. John came to his senses.

"Nay, my lady," he said with a blush. "We come with greetings from our liege lord and your future husband, Sir William Marshal. We are to escort you to London to attend the coronation of the new king at Westminster."

Her reaction was subdued and I could see she was not thrilled with the prospect. She had known for some weeks she had been promised to the Marshal. I gathered her detached air was common for a young girl, whose duty it was to marry at the King's bidding and not of her own choosing. She would have to marry a man twenty-six years her senior, a man she had never seen and, in her mind, past the prime of life. It was not unusual, but I am sure it was never easy. One of the benefits of being in my social class was more freedom to choose your mate, while the nobility had to accept the will of others. It was a strange paradox. I was brought back to the moment when the lady addressed me.

"And you are, Sir?" she said in a sweet almost musical voice.

"Oh no, my Lady. I am but the humble servant of the Marshal. I have no title save the one of friend. I am Lewellyn." I bowed respectfully. She smiled and said something in Welsh. I explained I did not understand the native tongue of my ancestry.

"A lord who calls his servant friend? This intrigues me. We shall talk again, Lewellyn. There are many arrangements to be made for our journey. Sir John, I trust you will understand we must take our leave to begin the process. My ladies and I have much to do."

"Of course, my lady. If we can be of assistance please call on us?" John bowed as the company left the room. There had been no discussion of the Striguil dowry. This would have to be discussed later. John and I looked at each other and we asked to be shown our quarters. Alone in our rooms, John was the first to comment.

"By God's eyes, Lewellyn, have you ever seen such a beauty?" he said slapping his forehead.

"I could not take my eyes from her. The Marshal is in for a shock. If she frightens crows then they are stupid birds." I repeated the Marshal's last words about the Lady of Striguil and how ridiculous they now seemed. Although she was young, she had a great presence and we both remarked at her composure in dealing with a situation determining her future. We briefly mentioned her father's holdings, and said regardless of their size, the Marshal would be well off. We had not yet received a full accounting of the dowry. We had something to eat and rested for a while.

Late that afternoon, I received word the Mistress of Pembroke wished to see me. Her servant said she wanted some help on selecting the appropriate luggage. John looked at me and nodded for me to go with the servant. We walked quickly to her quarters where I found the lady, very much distressed. She was no longer the composed person I had met in the great hall.

"A problem, my lady?" I inquired with a bow.

She looked at the maid who had escorted me and said, "I am about to spend the rest of my life with an old man and he asks if there is a problem? Lewellyn, you did say something this morning to give me some hope my future husband will be tolerable. You said he called you a friend. Will you be my friend and tell me the truth about this man?" Her eyes pleaded for a response.

"My lady, I cannot be objective about a man I have known since I was ten, and for whom I would gladly give my life. You should be aware of that before I speak," I said unable to offer anything but praise for my master. Praise that although true would sound like practiced flattery.

"Then you are the perfect person to tell me what I want to know. You did not try to hide your loyalty and it speaks to the truthfulness of your words. Tell me of the man you so reverently call the Marshal," she said and I knew instantly I would like this new mistress.

I proceeded to give her the full history of my life with the Marshal, starting with the day of our imprisonment and up to the events just transpired in the audience with King Richard. We talked for several hours. She stopped me to ask questions at several points.

"Was he really involved with Queen Marguerite?" she asked with a raise eyebrow. It was clear that I was not the first she had questioned about her future husband. This lady was no fool.

"He was not. It was a plot by jealous knights to discredit him in the eyes of the young King," I replied showing my disgust with the rumors that had circulated in much wider circles than I ever imagined. Now I understood why the Marshal had demanded letters from King Henry denying the event. Calumnies seem to have a very long life! I chose not to reveal the relationship with Queen Eleanor. It was so long ago and was no longer of consequence.

"Have the many tournaments and battles left him disfigured?" she asked looking at her ladies.

"He is considered very handsome by most of the ladies at court. His wounds are limited to a few small scars on his arms and legs.

"Does he have a temper?"

"Nay, my lady. I have only witnessed it on rare occasions and only when someone has gone back on their word." I spoke of his code, "No threat can make him dishonor his principles." I told the story of his response to King Richard's version of the events at Le Mans. She found it particularly amusing.

"I guess so great a warrior has little respect for women, except those with a dowry."

"Not so, my lady. He has great respect for women." I related a story of a certain monk who had attempted to take advantage of a lady on the road, an action the monk had cause to regret when the Marshal, riding down the same road, came upon this sordid scene. "As for your dowry we have no knowledge of your father's holdings except they are said to be considerable. My master has never been concerned with wealth," knowing I was being completely truthful.

"They consist of estates in Wales, Cornwall, the Cotswolds, Brittany, Normandy and Ireland. Some sixty-five castles in all." She said it as if she was giving a list of ingredients for a stew. She laughed when she saw the look on my face. "You really did not know."

I gulped and said, "Nay, my lady. You are betrothed to the finest man in all Christendom. I believe you will be pleased when you know him as I do."

"We shall see, Lewellyn. I have not yet decided if all these things you have told me are true. It will not matter, but it has given me some ease. We shall talk again, and, if all you have said is true, then we will indeed be friends. I ask one additional favor. Please do not discuss our conversation with Sir John or your master. I would like to form my own opinion of the men who control my destiny," she said placing a delicate hand on mine as she made her plea.

"As you wish, my lady. There is naught in your request that asks me to betray my master. I am sure that you will find Sir John and the Marshal to be the best of men," I said reminding her that I would never do anything to damage the bond of trust I had with the Marshal.

"They tell me you play the lute. Perhaps, you shall play for me," she said smiling.

"It would be an honor. The Marshal and I have spent many hours enjoying the benefits of music," I said with a bow and was dismissed.

I was escorted back to our quarters where John was engaged in making arrangements with the household steward for the journey back to London. I told him of the size of the Striguil dowry and he just whistled in disbelief. It explained why the announcement of the Marshal's future bride had such an impact on those present, and why King Richard had surprised everyone with his actions.

"Lewellyn, are you sure we did not die in the recent struggle and we are really in heaven?"

"I have not lived a good enough life for it to be heaven, but it makes one wonder, my lord. I am anticipating a very surprised Sir William Marshal when we return with this lovely maiden. I wager a silver mark, if I had one, his usual cool, detached air will be severely shaken." We both laughed and discussed the details of the upcoming caravan to London over a nice supper of mutton and wine.

It took two days to get all the necessary wagons and provisions for the trip back to Winchester. In that time, I had several more meetings with the Lady Isabel. She took John and me on a brief ride around Milford Haven. We saw the importance of the Striguil holdings. It defended England from the west. I discovered her wits matched her beauty, and I knew fate intended this wonderful match. Her tone still showed apprehension when our talks moved in the direction of her future husband. I tried to reassure her she was not getting a decrepit old man. She found it hard to believe when she looked at her men, of a similar age, in Pembroke Castle. I could understand her doubts, but I was confident it would change when she met the Marshal.

There were several wagons and a dozen men-at-arms as we left the gates early Friday morning, and began the journey to Winchester. There, we would meet the Marshal. From Winchester, we would continue on to London, and the coronation of King Richard. The Lady Isabel kept her wagon curtain open. I saw her looking at the scenery as we traveled over the hills separating Wales from England. Because of the size of the armed force traveling with us, we had no trouble with the brigands who often harassed travelers. As we approached the walls of Winchester, I watched the Lady withdraw into the confines of her wagon. The curtains were closed. It must have been a very nervous time for her.

John waved at the tall figure in green and yellow standing on the battlements as we approached the gate. Once inside, we were greeted by the Marshal and several knights. Queen Eleanor had already departed for London. I could see several of the Queen's ladies watching from the windows of their apartments.

The door of the wagon opened and out stepped the Lady Isabel in a gown of blue silk with white lace on the neck and sleeves. Her hair was pulled back in a long braid, covered with a gold mesh. It flashed when the sunlight reflected off the gold. She modestly had her head down and she bowed before the man soon to be her husband. He reached out a powerful hand and softly grasped the delicate one she offered. He had spent some time and effort to look to his own appearance. He had on his best tabard, and his beard and hair were neatly trimmed. There was complete silence until John turned to me and said, "Your silver mark is safe."

For the first time since I had known him the Marshal flushed. His mouth opened to speak, but when the Lady Isabel looked up with those blue-green eyes and beautiful features, speech was impossible. She was the first to speak. "It seems you are afflicted with the same illness as your emissaries." I could see from the smile on her face she was pleased with looks of the man before her. She looked at me and nodded. My description of the Marshal had not been exaggerated. "My Lord, I have heard much about you. I am pleased to finally see for myself," she said with a polite curtsy.

The Marshal had recovered himself and said, "I hope my emissaries have not filled your head with fanciful tales I will not be able to live up to, my lady." He bowed and finally, but reluctantly released the captive hand. Seeing the two together, I was sure it was a perfect match. Completely ignoring John and me, the Marshal said it would be an honor to show the lady her quarters. It was as if the entire company present did not exist as the two walked into the opened door of Winchester Castle. John and I looked at each other and agreed the Marshal was very impressed with Lady Isabel de Clare.

It was late in the evening when we finally talked to our friend. He entered the room and acted as if the events of the day had never happened.

Unable to contain himself, John asked, "Well, what think you?"

"Think of what?"

"You are among friends. You know very well about what."

"She is the most magnificent creature I have ever met. She is clever, charming and beautiful. I cannot believe one woman could be so blessed. For the first time in my life I am not in control of my emotions. Now, does that answer your foolish question?" The Marshal looked with a sly grin to see our reaction to this uncharacteristic loss of composure.

"By God's legs, our champion is smitten. This is unbelievable. Methinks I am going to swoon." John pretended to pass out and fell to the floor. He struggled to his knees and said weakly, "Lewellyn, I need a beer to revive." I was laughing as I brought the flagon of brew to the half kneeling d'Erly. I was intercepted by the Marshal who took the cup and proceeded to pour it on the surprised knight.

"Perhaps that will revive you," the Marshal said as he emptied the contents and tossed the mug into the corner. We all laughed until tears streamed down our cheeks. The Marshal said, "We have wasted enough good beer on foolishness. 'Tis time to put it to proper use." I brought three flagons and John proposed a toast.

"To the Marshal and his lady, may she find him as great a champion in bed as he is on the battlefield." We drank. As the beers increased in number, I grew bold in my speech and asked if the Marshal had any idea of the size of her dowry.

"Sixty-five castles, my lord!" I said with my voice rising to a crescendo.

"Lewellyn, I would marry the lady if she had only a dress to her name. I hope she will find me acceptable. I would like our match to be more than one of property. I talked to her for several hours and I could have listened to her voice for hours more. John, you are right, I am smitten. I do not believe it, but it is so," he said slurring the words slightly as the large amount of beer was having the usual effect. After several more hours of jokes and drinking, we fell asleep in our chairs and woke the next morning with very heavy heads. I was still in this state when word was sent the Lady Isabel wanted to see me. I cleaned my face with some cold water and headed down the corridor.

I knocked at the large oak door and announced my presence. "'Tis I, Lewellyn. You sent for me, my lady."

"Enter." The Lady Isabel was seated by the window. One of her ladies was brushing her beautiful hair. "Lewellyn, are you busy with chores for your master?"

"Nay, my lady."

"Good, then I would like you to fetch your lute and play for me while I ask you some questions about your master. I want you to know, we will be friends."

I knew from her words she had found the Marshal as pleasing to her as she had been to him. I raced back to our room and grabbed my instrument. The Marshal was preparing for his morning work out.

"What be the rush and why your lute at this hour of the day? I have some correspondence for you to write."

I quickly explained my mission and said, "I think you have won another victory. If what you said last night was true, there are two smitten people in this castle."

"Do not jest about this, Lewellyn!"

"I do not, my lord. Now, if I have your leave, my lord, I shall have more to tell you when I return," I said removing the instrument from the small table next to my sleeping mat.

"Go, go. The letters can wait. We will be leaving Winchester on the morrow to rejoin Queen Eleanor in London for Richard's coronation," he said excitedly pushing me out the door.

I rushed down the hallway to the quarters of the Lady Isabel. I knocked and was bidden enter. The Lady smiled, asked me to be seated. She asked me to play a soft tune for her and her lady friend. As I began to softly strum the lute, she asked me a series of questions.

"Lewellyn, has the Marshal ever been married?"

I replied, "Nay, my lady. He has spent much of his life in tournaments and fighting real battles. He has had little contact with the women of the court."

"I heard he was betrothed to another," she said again surprising me with the amount of knowledge she seemed to have about the Marshal.

"That would be the damsel of Lancaster, my lady. She is a child. King Henry proposed the match two years ago. My master was never pleased with the arrangement and probably was the happiest man in the kingdom when she was given to another. He knew little of you, my lady, when you were mentioned by the King, although he was told you were lovely. He did not know what to expect. If I was not mistaken, you were doubtful as well."

"Lewellyn, you read my mood well. I was very troubled when word reached me I was to be given to a man more than twice my age. I had terrible visions of what he might be."

"And now, my lady?"

"He is magnificent! He is as handsome as you said. For a man as powerful as he is, he is gentle. He makes me feel like I am the only person in the room when we are together. I cannot believe I could be this involved in so short a time. I wanted to know if he had other women, because I was afraid he was skilled at playing with women's emotions. Was it an act or was the affection I sensed in him real? I have always known it would be my duty to marry according to the King's wishes, but like all girls, I dreamed it might be a match of love. Do you think he loves me, Lewellyn? Is it too soon to know?" she pleaded.

"My lady, I am sure he does. God has chosen to reward two wonderful people with the most precious of all gifts—one of love, equally given. I had such a love and I lost her early in my life. For some it takes time, but not all. From the moment she first brushed my arm I knew she was my match. I see, in the two of you, the same kind of love. It can only be known by those who have been lucky enough to share it with another." I explained my life with Celine, and told her of the son I had in Normandy. I told her of the feelings the Marshal had shared last night and how important it was to the Marshal that she like him.

"Lewellyn, this is the most wonderful day of my life. Thank you for your words and your music. You may go, and this time you may tell your master whatever you wish."

"Thank you, my lady. May I say, you are both fine people who truly deserve each other."

When I returned to the Marshal he was pacing around the room nervously. He saw me and his eyes begged me to speak.

"Well, what news?"

"My lord, you have exceeded all expectations. You are a very lucky man." The Marshal threw his arms around me and lifted me off the floor. With my feet dangling in the air he looked at me and with a huge grin he said, "By God's eyes, you bring the best news!"

"Then it will not be necessary to kill the messenger by crushing his ribs," I whispered in some discomfort. I was released immediately and we both laughed so hard tears came to our eyes. Just then, John entered. The Marshal turned to him and said, "Find me a priest. I have waited all my life for someone like this. I shall not wait another day. Lewellyn, tell the lady, if she is willing, we will be married today." The words were barely out of his mouth and I was again racing down the hallway with my message. I was out of breath. Before I could knock, the door opened.

"My lady, the Marshal has sent me to see if it would please you to be married today!"

"Yes, yes of course!" Again I was hugged. Her ladies sprang into action and headed for the trunks containing the clothing. I raced back. I was now so out of breath I could only pant out an exhausted, "Yes, my lord." I fell into a chair as John and the Marshal began to hurriedly discuss what would be appropriate to wear. John left the room to get the priest and have the chapel prepared. Recovered from the running, I helped the Marshal prepare.

With a warm summer breeze caressing the tiny Winchester chapel, Sir William Marshal and Isabel de Clare, heiress of Pembroke and Striguil, were wed in a simple ceremony. The priest performed the rites with only John, several of the ladies-in-waiting and I as witnesses. The vows they took were forged on God's anvil. They were never broken. The love and fidelity they pledged to each other grew and prospered throughout their lives. There was never a time when either was unfaithful during the long periods of separation required by the Marshal's responsibilities. It is why they were blessed with ten children, five boys and five girls. Each year the pattern was the same. We would all be together during the Christmas season. December and January became the months of renewal. Laughter, feasting, song, and the celebration of love were a daily routine. The beginning of February saw me pack his bags for some part of the Angevin empire. The Marshal would resume his function as the King's soldier. When we returned the following Christmas there would be another addition to the Marshal's family to welcome us. The happiness they had was shared with all who knew them. In a life filled with tumult and struggle, her love was always the Marshal's refuge. It is hard to believe when we look at the nobility and their notorious disregard for fidelity, but it was that way with my master and my mistress. It was rare and wonderful.

John and I found different quarters that night. We retired feeling the effects of the wine and celebration. The next day burdened with aching heads we began our journey to Westminster, where a King would be crowned in regal splendor. Unlike the simple ceremony I had just witnessed this would be a bizarre affair. Pomp and pageantry would be punctuated by bad omens and murder. The reign of Richard Coeur de Lion was to begin and end in tragedy. The handsome prince, Queen Eleanor's favorite son, and the Marshal's most talented pupil would not succeed in meeting those high expectations. It is hard for me to be critical of a man who gave so much to my master and yet I must. Even now, as his legend grows, I must tell you much of the trouble caused by his brother was aided by King Richard's neglect. He would see little of the England he ruled. His future wife, Berengaria, would never see it at all.

Chapter 12
No King in England

King Richard's coronation was not a happy time. To be sure, there were the usual ostentatious displays of wealth and pageantry, but there were also evil portends. They signaled a troubled reign. First, there was a bat circling the King during the ceremony. Seeing a creature of the night at such an august moment raised an eyebrow or two. You may know his grandmother was accused of following the black arts. The bat landed on the King's chair. I was convinced it was no accident. I saw a disturbed look on the Marshal's face. Was the Plantagenet family still cursed for past deeds?

The next event proved violence and death often rode at the side of Richard Coeur de Lion. Three days of feasting were marred by bloody riots against the Jews. To begin one's reign with so much blood spilled was another bad omen.

The newly crowned King Richard called a meeting for all the nobles he had recently invested with lands and wives. His mother was seated next to him as each new lord was called before the royal presence. The Marshal and the Lady Isabel were first. They both beamed with the glow that only newly wedded bliss can give. The Marshal with his hand on the hilt of his magnificent ceremonial sword bowed and gave his oath of fealty to his liege. The King smiled and spoke.

"We are pleased marriage has found favor with the both of you. 'Tis obvious to all present the match is more than acceptable. We accept your pledge. You will soon learn we have important work for you, but first my mother had requested to express her feelings." He turned his head to look at the Queen. Queen Eleanor regally dressed with a gold circlet crowning the gray hair rose to speak. She nodded at her son and turned slowly to face the happy couple. A beautiful jeweled necklace caught the glint of light in the hall and flashed with the many colors of the different stones. She smiled broadly as she spoke.

"Sir William, we have held you dear from the day you first saved my life. It is fitting you be rewarded with the love of this fine lady. We are hopeful the love so plain in each of your eyes will soon bring new life to the service of your King. May God bless your union and may you both prosper." They bowed and she nodded as she resumed her seat. The King rose. His gold crown bore the Plantagenesta from which the family name was derived. He was very handsome man and one could see why his mother saw him as the embodiment of the perfect King.

"Sir William, we add a hearty amen to the eloquent words of our mother. Now we have tasks for you to perform. We have decided to prepare a great force to free the Holy Land from the infidels. It has been too long delayed by internal strife." As the King looked around the room at the many nobles gathered in the great hall, I was worried. I would soon be on the sea journey I had avoided in the past. The king continued, "We will lead an army the likes of one never seen before in this holy quest." His voice rose as he spoke the words. The hall erupted in a loud cheer. I saw a look of consternation on the Marshal's face. He was not as enthusiastic as the crowd. When the cheering subsided the King returned to addressing the Marshal.

"Unfortunately, my friend, we must ask you to remain here with our mother, brother, and several others we will appoint to guard the realm. We need know this task will be performed with absolute loyalty to our person and you are the most qualified to assist in this endeavor. What say you?" he asked looking into the eyes of a much happier Marshal.

The Marshal bowed gracefully as he replied, "Majesty, in sooth your request doth please me greatly. I hold great respect for those who take the cross, for I have seen the holy places I know you will rescue. I would follow your wishes as my oath requires, but I confess as a newly married man I am happy not to leave my lovely bride. I am most pleased to accept this charge." Again the hall erupted in a rousing cheer.

I could see the absolute joy in the eyes of the Lady Isabel who just a few moments before thought her new love was going to be taken from her to serve in a holy Crusade. Neither could see the same joy bursting from my countenance. Whispers meant many of the others present in the hall must have been wondering why this talented fighting man with personal knowledge of the Holy Land was being left behind. Did they accept the King's reasons for this action?

I personally believe King Richard, who was taking the cross more for the sake of glory than a desire to serve God, did not want to be overshadowed by the man whose reputation might eclipse his. He wanted troubadours to sing the praises of King Richard in Jerusalem. He would not take the chance there could be competition for the glory. King Richard's later quarrels with the other leaders of the Crusade demonstrated his need to be the center of attention. There could only be one champion to carry the day and he must be Richard Coeur de Lion! As this thought faded from my mind, the King dismissed the Marshal and his lady. There could not have been three happier people in the world as we prepared to return to Pembroke.

As the Tower of London faded in the distance, I turned to the Marshal and asked if he was happy to be going back to Pembroke. He smiled and replied, "Lewellyn, there are no words to describe the joy of leaving all that is soon to come behind me."

"How so, my lord?" I asked unaware of the doubtful future the Marshal seemed to see clearly.

"Before I left, the King appointed the detestable little dwarf, William Longchamp, chancellor. No good will come of that appointment. Longchamp was chosen because of his skill at squeezing money from a stone. His Majesty has one focus now—raising of large sums to pay for his glorious quest. He has already told de Glanville his father's treasury is inadequate for the purpose. I know Saladin, the leader of the Saracen army. He is tough, intelligent and has considerable resources to repel any attack. It will not be an easy fight. The King will require large sums to provide an army appropriate to take on such a capable foe. I informed him of such in private. I am overjoyed King Richard was willing to let me return to Pembroke with my bride. I have had enough of fighting. 'Tis time for me to enjoy the life of a country lord!" he said with gusto while casting a loving look to his bride.

"My lord, you and your lady deserve the tranquility. We shall watch the harvest, and sing songs of the bounty God has provided. I will not miss the scheming which is ever present in the halls of the powerful." My faith was beginning to return with the almost miraculous nature of recent events. Perhaps the hand of God was present in the justice of these happenings.

"We shall send for your son. Sir John will be made sheriff of our holdings. It will be a good life." The Marshal was pleased as he spoke these words. My joy was overwhelming. The many moments where death or imprisonment had stalked our lives seemed a distant memory. As the west road echoed to the hoofs of our horses I had high hopes for peace and quiet among the green fields of Pembroke. My only regret was that my dear wife had not lived to see such happiness. The Marshal, his lady, and my son were now the center of my life.

The next six months were filled with the tasks of establishing the new household. The Marshal planned major improvements to the castle which would be ongoing for many years. I was given the task of clerk. I handled the correspondence, and with the Lady Isabel, saw to the needs of the household stores. The Marshal and John traveled the vast holdings and secured the oaths of fealty from the various vassals. Payments from the recent harvest were collected and entered on the ledger. It was a busy and happy time. When disputes arose, the Marshal was asked to adjudicate. Most were pleased with the wisdom and fairness of his decisions.

I was not surprised when it was announced the Lady Isabel was with child. The coming Christmas season would be a joyous one. My son, Jean, now five, had been brought from Normandy along with Elaine and her husband. They joined the household staff. Their services were a wedding gift from Baldwin who was joining the Crusaders.

John and the Marshal traveled to Ireland to review some of his holdings there. No one was happier than I, when it was decided I should remain to deal with any correspondence which might arrive during the Marshal's absence. I watched from the high bluff overlooking Milford Haven as the cog bounced on the waves as it departed for Ireland. I hoped I would spend the rest of my days on solid ground and my ever-expanding stomach rejoiced. We were happily ignorant of the events at court in London as I waved farewell.

Unfortunately, this state of affairs did not last for long. While the Marshal was still in Ireland, I received a communication from the King's new chancellor. It informed the Marshal, a fee would have to be paid to the King for his appointment. The sum of five hundred marks was due as soon as arrangements could be made for their safe shipment to London. The messenger also brought the news of the court. Two days after the arrival of this unwelcome news the Marshal returned. I was waiting in the courtyard as he dismounted and we walked to the doorway. I proceeded to give the Marshal an account of what had transpired in his absence. He was walking quickly toward his quarters as I spoke, rushing to keep up with his long strides.

"Welcome back, my lord. Your assessment of the King's new chancellor was quite correct. It seems he has concocted a scheme to raise money for the King's venture in the Holy Land by charging all office holders a fee in order to maintain their positions. Your fee is five hundred marks," I said with some emphasis on the hundred.

"I knew that gnarled excuse for a man would be difficult. What other news?" he asked in a disgusted tone of voice.

"Hugh de Puiset is to share the major responsibility of running the affairs of the King with Longchamp while the King is on the Crusade," I replied.

"Good, Hugh should help keep the little troll from creating too much mischief." There was some relief in his voice with this news.

"Geoffrey of York is forbidden to set foot in England for three years," I said raising my eyebrows slightly.

"Richard does not trust half brothers. Too bad, I learned to like him when we were in Normandy." His eyes reminded me of the warning he had given me about the knowledge of my birth. I realized how true this warning had been. I continued my report.

"William the Lion of Scotland has been given his freedom and sent home after paying a very hefty fine." This caused the Marshal to spin around and stare.

"What?! Is Richard gone mad?" He threw both hands in the air.

"Perhaps money mad, my lord. People say everything in England is for sale."

"I smell William Longchamp."

"The King has gone to Rouen to prepare for his Crusade." I continued my chronicle of events.

"I fear we have only begun to see the ways new taxes will be levied to pay for this venture. Richard cares little for our England. The burden will be a heavy one. Enough of this! Make arrangements for paying the money. I am going to see my wife. I refuse to let these events spoil the excitement I feel for the birth of my child. The Lady Isabel believes it will be a son." He turned on his heel and headed for the loving reunion he knew awaited his arrival.

We arranged for the money to be sent under suitable guard to the King's treasury. When they returned, the knights said Sir Hugh had gone to Rouen to join King Richard and help him prepare for the Crusade. Longchamp had not been asked to go and it was rumored he feared Sir Hugh might undermine his authority if Hugh had private access to King Richard. It would not be allowed to happen so Longchamp shamelessly neglected his duty as chancellor with a lame excuse and joined them in Rouen. I hoped it would keep him out of our purse for a while.

The Christmas season was celebrated with merrymaking and no thought of kings, courts or Crusades. It was decided if the child was a boy, he would be named William. The tranquility we hoped for was finally being realized. We were all very excited when the moment arrived in May. It was a boy and the Marshal was bursting with pride as the little one was christened William. My son, Jean, stood beside me in the church as we thanked God for our good fortune and the happiness of my lord and his lady. Our idyllic country life was being enjoyed to the fullest.

Satisfied his position was secure Chancellor Longchamp returned. Longchamp, who spoke only French, set himself up in Windsor Castle and began to appoint his relatives to high positions. He claimed he needed their help because of his difficulty in communication in language of the English. Power which is given to little men often swells their desire for more. Longchamp soon developed a nasty habit of acting as though he was the king. There were reports of excesses by the dwarf in his dealings with the nobility almost the moment he returned.

At Pembroke we had a surprise visit from Queen Eleanor. She wanted to discuss the matter with the Marshal. Seventy years had done nothing to dull her wits even as age bent her body and turned her gray hair to white. She was still an astute observer of political events. Her instincts were far better than her warrior son. She spoke to the Marshal in the great hall. I was working at some correspondences in the corner and heard their conversation.

"William, the King's chancellor, has exceeded his authority on several occasions. The nobles are not happy. I fear my son will return to a kingdom in open revolt. Something has to be done. Chancellor Longchamp threatened to arrest Hugh de Puiset. Longchamp claims he, alone, has the right to rule in the King's absence," she announced indignantly.

"I expect Sir Hugh called him out. The King made it clear they were both to rule. Longchamp was to handle money matters and Sir Hugh the rest." The great lady shook her head.

"The weak-willed Hugh has capitulated and retired to his estates. Comfort has weakened his spine. Richard should have chosen you! The need for money has colored his judgement." She seemed exasperated as she vented her anger by slapping a fist in her upturned palm. "Longchamp is signing decrees using his signet ring rather than the Great Seal. You know 'tis only the King to exercise this kind of power. We must act before King Richard leaves France. I am sure he will not allow this to continue if he is informed by someone he trusts." She looked at the Marshal waiting for his counsel.

"That be you, your Majesty. All others would be held suspect by your son. He will listen to your council. It must be done with haste and quietly. Besides, none would suspect your motives to see the King before his ships sail. Longchamp would be quick to follow me as he once did to Hugh. He would find a way to cast suspicion on my words. I shall remain here and prepare to act once you have received the appropriate papers."

"Again you give me sound advice. I will go at once," she said with a tender squeeze of his arm.

As soon as arrangements could be made the Queen would go to Marseilles where Richard was still waiting for his fleet to be assembled. She would beseech Richard to put an end to Longchamp's power grab. She left Pembroke and returned to Winchester to prepare for her trip. She announced her intention to talk to her son one more time before his Crusade, carefully concealing her real purpose. Two weeks later she sailed for Marseilles. Events moved quickly and I must admit we were surprised by the news that finally reached us at Pembroke—some good, some not.

Queen Eleanor successfully convinced her son to send the Archbishop of Rouen and several barons with letters to rectify the problem. His half brother Geoffrey, Archbishop of York, was released from his ban and was ordered to join the delegation in England.

Queen Eleanor was then asked by her son to go to Navarre to arrange for his marriage to Berengaria, the daughter of King Sancho. The long-arranged marriage to Princess Alais was off. The new marriage was born of a deal for badly needed cattle and grain. Sancho had these stores in abundance. They would be a gift if Richard would consent to marry his daughter. Richard, obsessed with his floundering plans for a great Crusade, quickly agreed.

The new arrangement took King Philip totally by surprise. Richard's new choice for a wife started a feud between Richard and his former ally. Philip, who was also pledged to the Crusade, was outraged. If King Richard had a son with someone other than his sister, Aquitaine and Normandy might be lost forever. It was clear King Richard did not want his father's leftover mistress and had little concern for the French king's plans. It was a bitter blow for Philip, who thought the two great kingdoms would be united someday by his flesh and blood. The breech would never heal. The unity of the Crusade was divided before it ever left the shores of France. We later learned Berengaria and Richard were married in Sicily. Philip was furious and sailed for the Holy Land without waiting for Richard. The friendship of Gisor was permanently ended and the Crusade was doomed.

Here in England many things were happening. It began with the arrival of the delegation and the letters. Longchamp refused to recognize the legitimacy of the barons sent by Richard. Rumors were rampant. It was a quiet summer evening when John d'Erly rode into Pembroke and immediately went to see the Marshal. We were at supper as he entered the great hall.

"William, thou willst not believe what the little troll has done! He has taken Archbishop Geoffrey prisoner and is starving him in a dungeon. He would have killed him when he landed, but his men were afraid. They remember what happened to Becket and had not the stomach for committing a similar act of blasphemy. Longchamp thinks he is safe and can do as he wants because Richard has sailed for the Holy Land and Queen Eleanor is still abroad. As marshal of England you must put an end to this outrage." John was nearly breathless as he finished his statement.

"Lewellyn, have my horse saddled. We cannot wait for morning. We ride to see Prince John and gather a sufficient force to remove this carbuncle from the flesh of England. We need a member of the royal family to give us standing in this action. Has Longchamp much support?" he asked John while stroking his chin, a sure sign that a plan was forming as he spoke.

"Nay. Just his sister Richenda and her husband who are holding the Archbishop at Dover. We will have no trouble in gaining allies in London. Longchamp has offended many," John said smiling and knowing that the Marshal would soon be in the saddle.

"Good, 'tis time to rid England of this French flea," the Marshal declared slapping his thigh. He rose and was calling for his sword and hauberk as I went to gather men and horses in the courtyard. After an hour the appropriate force was assembled and waiting in the main courtyard. Sir John and the Marshal joined us. They mounted quickly and thundered out of the gates. The Lady Isabel and I stood and watched as they disappeared into the night.

"He wastes no time, Lewellyn. I was about to tell him I am with child again. I hope my children will have a father." She was worried and looked at me with sad eyes.

"Have no fear, my lady, the Marshal will prevail," I said confidently. "A bad leader quickly loses support and must become abusive in order to maintain control. Good leaders are followed willingly and do not need harsh measures. Longchamp will not be an exception to the rule. His support will melt like a late spring frost. The Marshal will have no trouble in finding help."

When the word reached Longchamp of the force gathered by the Marshal was moving toward Dover, he ordered his sister and her husband to release Archbishop Geoffrey. He apologized profusely. He said it was all a mistake!

Next, Geoffrey, the Marshal and Prince John rode to London to join with Walter of Coutances, Archbishop of Rouen, to serve Longchamp with the writs from King Richard. Longchamp, thinking he was safe behind the walls of the Tower of London, again turned on the delegation and claimed the papers were forgeries. From the ramparts he called on the people of London to rise up and take his part. His calls for help were met with catcalls and laughter from the citizens of the city. He pleaded with them in French. With good Englishmen, like the Marshal, standing among them, the people of London saw no reason to follow his orders. He screamed the power of the King was being usurped. It was to no avail. He secretly left the Tower under cover of darkness and fled to the coast.

He was captured while trying to escape dressed as a woman. Prince John released him and let him take ship for the continent. Much later on, I discovered the reason for this release was a bribe of several properties given to Prince John. I was not surprised. My opinion of the Prince continued to sink. I had always known the Prince loved money and pretty girls. Land was added to the list, but like most things achieved by treachery it would not last.

The Marshal returned home to learn of his wife's condition. London was forgotten. We settled down again to the peaceful country life. We were too happy to be concerned with court rumors which occasionally reached Pembroke Castle.

By the summer of 1193 we received a letter from Baldwin. I read it to the Marshal.

"My friend, I trust you are all well and enjoying the breeze off the Irish Sea. The heat here is most vexing. The forces of the German King Fredrick never arrived. They returned when the Barberossa was drown in a river crossing. King Richard has succeeded in capturing Acre after it had withstood a long siege under the leadership of King Philip. King Richard assumed the leadership of the forces arrayed against the city and made a successful plan to scale the city walls. It only worsened the relationship between King Richard and King Philip. The capture was followed by a terrible massacre of the inhabitants when the King's demands for the return of the cross on which our Lord was crucified were not met. It must have offended God, for afterward things have not gone well. The Crusaders are quarreling. King Philip has decided to return home. He claimed he is ill. He was really sick of taking orders from King Richard. I am sorry you are not here for God knows we could use a diplomat to still the riled waters."—Baldwin.

"My lord, he is well but not happy."

"It is a difficult climate, Lewellyn," he said knowingly and with that he returned to his task of deciding how to make repairs on a section of Pembroke castle.

Six uneventful months had passed when a rider brought another letter as we were sitting down to the evening meal. Excitedly I took the pouch and hurried into the hall. "My Lord, another letter from the Holy Land," I said excitedly.

"I see Baldwin has not lost his need to converse despite the many miles. We will be receiving regular reports." The Marshal laughed and smiled at Lady Isabel. I opened the pouch and began to read. Immediately saw that it was not Baldwin's distinctive hand.

"My Lord Marshal, it is with a heavy heart that I must inform you of the death of your dear friends Baldwin de Bethune and Raoul de Hamars in the surprise encounter with the enemy at Arsuf." My speech slowed and my voice cracked as I read the horrible news. Tears ran down my face as I remember the last time I had seen the boyish face of my one-time master. I remembered the lock of hair that always needed to be flicked away and the constant chatter that danced merrily whenever he was present. I looked at the Marshal. His head was bowed and his massive arms rested limply on the table. He signaled the servants to remove the food. Lady Isabel gently placed her head on his shoulder. I struggled to continue with the letter.

"Their sacrifice helped King Richard to rally the troops and win an amazing victory over the infidel army. Leopold of Austria has quarreled with the King. He has left and the taking of Jerusalem is no longer possible. King Richard, who had fought brilliantly at Arsuf, has to face reality; he cannot win with the reduced army. He asked me to arrange a truce with Saladin."

It was signed Hubert Walter. We all stayed silent for several moments. The world of fighting men was always punctuated with this type of news, but this was different. We had lost our dearest friend and supper was no longer palatable. We each left to grieve in private. Nothing could be said.

We did not have long to grieve our friends as events do not respect anyone's death. The version of what transpired next depends on who is to be believed. Rumors, suspicions and treachery confuse the known facts. I have my own version and I shall share it with you. Perhaps, someday, the truth will be known, but I doubt it.

Philip declared the Crusade over and the Truce of God ended. He began a campaign to wrest some of the Angevin lands from Richard's control. Prince John seemed indifferent to the action, but the Marshal was not willing to give up Normandy without a struggle. He went to the Prince and said something had to be done. John agreed to send the Marshal to Rouen to take military command of Normandy. We headed for Dover to take ship. On the way we talked about the problem.

"Lewellyn, something is amiss. We have not heard of King Richard since word was sent he was departing the Holy Land. Now the Prince thinks King Philip is not a problem. He is reluctant to act against him. Something smells and I do not mean the cheese!" he said narrowing his eyes and pursing his lips.

"My lord, what will we do when we arrive?"

"I will contact Hugh de Hamelcourt. I have friends who will assist in the defense of Angevin lands. We will also try to discover if treachery has anything to do with the King's disappearance," he declared knowing that the events had to be tied to the missing monarch.

Once again I packed for the journey to Southampton where we would take ship for Normandy. I will spare you the details of the trip for the weather was unkind and the results were not unexpected. The urgency of our trip did not allow me to indulge my personal misery.

We landed at Le Havre and rode quickly to Rouen. The Marshal took charge and strengthened the city's defenses. Two days later Hugh arrived with another man I did not know. We met in the great hall of the Archbishop's residence. The Marshal embraced his old friend and asked him about the situation.

"My friend, what news have you?" asked a worried Marshal.

Hugh spoke after expressing his sorrow on the loss of the Marshal's friends in the Crusade. "Philip has dishonored himself. First, he abandons the Crusade with the lame excuse he is ill. Next, as soon as he returns, his rapacious desire for power and land causes him to break the Truce of God. There are rumors John is involved."

"I see." The Marshal's eyes again narrowed as he mulled this not entirely unexpected news.

"There is no proof, William, but there are those who suspect John and Philip know something about the King's disappearance. I left the Holy Land before Richard's departure. He said he feared to return through France because of problems with Philip. We agreed another route was a wise choice and it was the last time we heard from him. He was traveling in disguise up the Danube.

This be King Leopold's demesnes. I fear some evil has befallen the King. Leopold and Richard were bitter enemies when the Crusade was ending. They almost came to blows. If he is under Leopold's control we may never see King Richard again? The Archbishop of Canterbury died while we were in the Holy Land and Richard named Hubert Walter as his replacement. Walter is a good man and is on his way back to England. The Earl of Leicester has already organized a solid defense here in Normandy." The stranger spoke next.

"I come at Queen Eleanor's request. I am Sir Guy de Noir. The Queen has organized the nobles in Aquitaine against any attempt by Philip to seize the province. There is more iron in that lady's gown than there is in Philip's hauberk. If she asked them, the knights of Aquitaine would follow her to fight demons of the nether worlds. Philip will not dare to attack Aquitaine. They will come here. She has written the Pope to help find Richard. She believes, as I do, he is a prisoner in Austria. She goes to England to watch Prince John and to raise money if a ransom be needed. I am convinced he covets his brother's crown and will prove treacherous. She will try to check any moves in that direction. Amazingly, he is most afraid of the grand dame."

The Marshal thought for a moment and then said, "Our mission is clear. Philip has taken several castles in the Seine Valley. We must stop the advance. We will go to Vaudreuil. Make the appropriate preparations."

Several days later we arrived in Vaudreuil and immediately began preparing the small castle for defense. It was not much to behold. The walls were in disrepair and not that sturdy. I was afraid the Marshal had chosen a bad place to stop the advance of King Philip's army. I spoke to the Marshal.

"My lord, this place does not look like it could withstand a strong wind no less a strong force. Are we wise to make a stand here?" I asked hoping he would say he had reached the same conclusion.

He smiled and laughed, "We have added military strategy to our many talents have we?"

"Nay, my lord, it just appears to the unpracticed eye to be a weak position. Is there something of which I am unaware?" I asked in an apologetic tone.

"There is, Lewellyn. You are correct that this is not a strong fortress. It is precisely why Philip will only send his advance guard to attack the position. It is more important for the location and the opportunity to bloody his nose before he can bring his full force to bear." He smiled at my naïveté and continued to make his plan.

That afternoon we were surprised when John d'Erly arrived unexpectedly. He had left England as soon as he heard of the Marshal's departure and the trouble brewing in Normandy. He brought one hundred knights pledged to the Marshal. Each knight had fifteen or so yeoman under their command.

"Sir John, you are most welcome and your gift comes as a bit of a surprise," the Marshal said as he grasped his friend by the arm.

"My Lord, these men are pledged to you in fealty. I heard there might be trouble from the Lady Isabel when I returned from Ireland. I decided that you should not have all the glory to yourself and so I gathered these men as quickly as I could. As we arrived in Rouen the Archbishop said you could be found here." He grinned at his own saucy remarks.

"How much glory there will be depends on many things, but your quick thinking has given me the edge. I have a plan. The French forces are unaware of the arrival of your men. I will prepare a trap." They walked to the yard discussing strategy.

John was told to take his men into the forests some distance from the castle and hide. He would allow the French to come down the road and prepare their siege weapons. Once they had established their positions he and his men would sneak back within earshot of the castle. The Marshal would act as if he were trapped inside and at the appropriate moment would appear to make some type of desperate attempt to break out. When the French leaders focused their efforts on the Marshal, John would emerge from the forest. The French contingent would be caught between the two forces. It was reminiscent of the way the Marshal used traps in the days of the tournaments.

Before sunrise, John, with his men, went into the woods west of the castle, and waited. The darkness of night began to melt with the approach of dawn. The gradual increase of light was matched by the sound of men and machines moving up the south road. The French vanguard had arrived. They surrounded the castle and set up their siege machines near the front gate. The postern gate was blocked and we were cut off from an escape. I began to worry about what we would do if John did not arrive on time.

The usual demands for surrender were shouted and the usual insults were hurled back. Several mangonels were positioned to hurl stones at the main gate. The French commander was so confident the wall would not last long that he could be seen laughing and eating some bread and cheese. He reasoned the small number of men on the walls would be quickly overwhelmed by his superior numbers. The castle was too small to contain much of a defending force.

The Marshal had given orders for most of the defending force to stay out of sight. The commander gave one last offer for the castle to surrender or be slaughtered once the walls were breached. The Marshal derisively suggested the French commander do unnatural things to barnyard animals. He reacted with a furious string of oaths. The order to commence was given and the large stones began to crash into the walls of the castle. They began to crumble almost immediately. The French commander must have been supremely confident this would be over quickly because he arrogantly sat on a large stone sipping wine from a wineskin.

The Marshal left the wall and went to the courtyard. A contingent of knights stood ready by the main gate. He mounted his charger and gave the signal to lower the drawbridge. A little more than half of the castle defenders stayed concealed as the drawbridge was dropped and the Marshal and his men charged the surprised Frenchmen guarding the siege machines. The initial attack was so unexpected, for a few moments, the superior force surrounding the castle was frozen in place. The mounted knights protecting the machines moved to intercept the surprise attack. The Marshal, at a full gallop, had a sword in one hand and a shield in the other. Steering his horse with his knees, he charged between two knights. The one on the left swung his sword wildly, but the blow missed, cutting only air. With his broadsword the Marshal struck the other knight—shattering the face plate of his helmet. It was a mortal wound.

Directly in front of him was the captain of the group. More experienced than the other two, his blow had to be parried by the shield in the left hand of the Marshal. Before the captain could launch another stroke the Marshal's sword arced down and bit into his leg just above the knee. The stroke was backed with such power the chain mail covering the leg was no more protection than an old piece of parchment. The leg was nearly cut off. A scream of pain split the air and I winced from the violence of the moment. I believe that scream could be heard all the way to Rouen. It broke the spell which held the majority of the siege force watching they thought was a desperate attempt to break out of the encirclement. They all moved in the direction of this small group engaged at the siege machines. They would revenge themselves on the audacious knight and his few men. Then they would sack the castle and enjoy the spoils. The French commander was convinced this desperate move was suicide. He sounded a horn to commit the rest of his force. He would destroy this arrogant little band that had interrupted his lunch.

It was the fatal mistake the Marshal expected. The trap was sprung. John d'Erly and his men poured out of the woods. More men poured out of the castle. Confused, the French army broke and began to scatter. Chaos was followed by slaughter. I stood upon the wall of the castle and finally turned away from the horror of the bloody scene—unable to watch any more suffering. The few French soldiers who had not run, began to surrender. The yelling and clatter of battle was replaced by the guttural moans of the wounded. The Marshal and John returned to the castle yard. Blood dripped from the Marshal's hauberk.

"My lord, you are wounded."

"Nay, Lewellyn, 'tis not my blood. I do not believe there will be any more fighting today. John, see to the wounded. Their losses were heavy. Contact the Earl of Leicester and see if the other regions of Normandy are safe. Philip will lose his taste for Vaudreuil after this," he said with confidence.

In a fortnight we had learned the Earl had also successfully defended his portion of Normandy. King Philip withdrew his force. We returned to Rouen and waited for further instructions. None came, so we continued to wait and fortify our positions in case the French had a sudden attack of courage. They did not.

In England, Hubert Walter began to organize the search for the missing King Richard. Several Palatinate electors, not friendly with Leopold, let it be known to Papal envoys that Richard was a prisoner. He was being held in Durenstein castle. The story spread by my contemporary, Blondel, is complete fiction. He claims he went from town to town seeking the missing monarch by singing a song only King Richard knew. It was a silly story designed to raise his stature in the royal courts and raise a few coins for the clever troubadour. It was the letters of Queen Eleanor, money and the efforts of Hubert that were responsible for finding the King.

Negotiations were soon underway to pay for the King's release. Hubert Walter undertook the task of raising the ransom. Interestingly, Prince John did very little to assist. It is widely believed the Prince even obstructed the effort although none dared say so. The Marshal and I were still in Rouen. There were some rumors Philip and Prince John were ready to pay Leopold not to release King Richard. I am in agreement with this view. Once a large portion of the money had been raised, Walter and Queen Eleanor went to Austria to escort the King back to England. It was said Philip rolled on the ground and foamed at the mouth when he was told his one-time friend and now bitter enemy was free.

Once back in England, King Richard moved quickly, but carelessly, to restore his kingdom. The Marshal said, "Move in haste; repent in leisure!" King Richard replaced the talented Archbishop Walter as chancellor and brought back the despised little weasel, Longchamp, from exile in France. Raising money was again the paramount concern. The King did recognize the good work performed by the stalwart Hubert and made sure his appointment as Archbishop of Canterbury was formalized. King Richard forgave his brother, whose lack of action led to the loss of land in France and then, as quickly as he could, Richard returned to Normandy. He was eager to take back what had been lost by doing what he did best—fighting! Others could deal with the dull routine of administration and Longchamp would raise the money.

The Marshal went to meet the King and together they sailed up the Seine to Rouen. On route they discussed plans to retake the lands Philip had seized. Many castles in Maine had been taken before John had given the Marshal the right to defend Angevin claims. They now had to be retaken. King Richard had to levy additional taxes to support his campaign.

In 1197 the battles began again. I have neither the time or desire to speak of all of them, but there is one in particular that is interesting. It will illustrate that the level of the Marshal's fighting skill had not eroded even though he had passed his fiftieth year. It is one of my favorite stories.

The siege of the fortifications at Milly-sur-Therain started out to be another dreary waiting game. The Marshal's men had surrounded the castle and prepared to starve the garrison into submission. The Count de Milly, defending the position, was a well-known champion of the tournaments. He had fought in the Holy Land and was reputed to be the finest of French knights. His pride matched his skills. When he heard who was in charge of the force outside his gates he was excited. As a boy he had seen the Marshal compete at Pleurs. He could not resist the opportunity to face the great champion. He offered a proposition. He, the Count de Milly, would face the Marshal in single combat. The winner would decide the outcome of the siege. If the Marshal won, the castle would surrender without a fight. If the Count prevailed, the town would be left alone.

John d'Erly and the Marshal discussed the offer. The Marshal was quite willing, but John said the castle could not hold out for long and we would win without risking the Marshal's life. Besides he did not know if the Count could be trusted. John did not want to tell the Marshal taking on a tested champion almost half his age was not a good idea. The Marshal finally decided to accept the challenge and nothing could be done to change his mind. The following morning the Marshal stood in front of the gate and announced his acceptance of the terms. He waited for the gate to open and for the Count to appear. All our men had taken positions to watch the combat. The gate did not open. The

Count appeared atop the wall and announced he was ready. Several of his men produced a siege ladder and lowered it into position next to the gate. The Count called down to the Marshal. "Come up and face your doom!"

John immediately shouted, "Treachery. Do not go, my lord." The Count heard the comment and shouted back.

"You have my sacred word as a Crusader there be no treachery. I am alone on the wall. You may send up two observers to be witnesses," he offered.

I volunteered to go. Again my heart raced ahead of my brain. John also volunteered but said, "Even if what he says is true, he has given himself an advantage. You are to climb the ladder in your armor while he waits. 'Tis not fair."

"It is not a significant advantage. I have climbed many ladders before a fight," the Marshal declared in an offhanded manner as he checked his sword.

"But my lord, we cannot take the chance of losing you for such a small castle."

"Look around you, John. I must lead these men in battle. How they fight when the odds favor the other side is critical. If I am not willing to face difficult odds, will they follow me when faced with a similar situation? I must go. If you wish not to observe I will send another." He had made it clear the matter was settled.

With a look of resignation John said, "Nay, my lord, I will go." We climbed the ladder. I was winded when I reached the top and I had no armor to weigh me down. Just as he had promised, the Count de Milly stood alone, sword in hand. John called down to the Marshal and said all was in order. The Marshal began his climb. The Count, a large and powerful man, stood ready to face the legend. Sure of himself, he anticipated the honor that would be his in the chivalrous contest about to unfold. Honor again was more important than castles or life.

Once the Marshal stepped onto the battlement there was a brief nod of recognition by each warrior. The struggle began immediately. The Marshal had no time to rest from the climb. It was clear the Count had given himself this advantage just in case the old knight was tougher than expected. Underestimating an opponent had been the downfall of many chevaliers.

It was a furious fight. Both men showed enormous skill in their sword play. The blows were struck and parried with great force. I began to fear the Marshal would weaken from the energy he had expended on the climb up the siege ladder. The heavy broadswords began to take a toll on the arms of the two paladins. However, youth would not be served this day. The Count's strokes came slower and slower. A miss! Then suddenly, as if summoning some hidden reserve, the Marshal spun and flashed a stroke and caught the tired Count with his sword down. It crashed into his collar severing the blood vessel in his neck. Blood gushed and death was instantaneous. His large body crashed to the ground.

The Marshal finally allowed his exhaustion to manifest itself. He sank to his knees and then using his mighty sword as a cane tried to get to his feet. He was totally spent. He got halfway up and then sank down sitting on the lifeless body of the Count. All was silent. The Count's men suddenly appeared in large numbers. John and I were afraid the terms of the fight would be forgotten. With the Marshal too exhausted to retreat down the ladder we would be at the mercy of the Frenchmen.

My old habit of chastising myself for reckless bravado took over again. John urged the Marshal to rise and go with us down the ladder, but he waved a tired hand and shook his head signaling he could not move. The captain of the garrison walked over to us and looked at the body of his lord surmounted by the knight with the blood-spattered green and gold tabard. His men surrounded us. The Marshal rose, ready to use his weapon again, but I knew there were only a few strokes left in those powerful arms. The captain looked at the Marshal and then at the body. He signaled his men to put down their weapons. He spoke reverently to the Marshal.

"I saw you fight at Sorel and Eu. It was a long time ago. You have not lost your skill. My lord was also a great champion. He lived his life by the code and insisted I do the same. We will honor his word. The castle is yours. You are the greatest champion ever. There is no shame in being defeated by you. Guillaume le Marechal, we are your prisoners." He bowed. As a gesture of respect the Marshal told the captain his men were free to go if they would pledge fealty to King Richard.

The word of the fight spread through the camp and soon there were stories about the struggle. Each retelling was more dramatic. Just as he had predicted, the men would now follow the Marshal anywhere. It was now a badge of honor if you could say you fought beside William the Marshal. When the story of Milly-sur-Therain reached King Richard, he reacted somewhat surprisingly. He criticized the Marshal for unseemly conduct because he sat on the defeated knight's dead body. Was it the code of chivalry or jealousy that caused such a response? You may judge for yourself.

The fighting ended when Philip and Richard signed another peace treaty. It was not expected to last since the two had developed a sincere hatred for each other. The fighting had cost the life of another of the Marshal's friends. We were sorry to learn Hugh de Hamelcourt was among them. The Marshal's oldest friends continued to be taken from us in the never-ending violence of the King's fighting men. We remained in Rouen, but I know the Marshal hoped to return to his estates in England. We lamented that our sons were growing up without us. We were afraid the bond we had talked about so many times was not being formed. Would our sons be like those of King Henry? We vowed to bring them to Rouen at Christmas to remedy the situation.

After the treaty, King Richard announced a plan to build a fortress on a rock ledge at a critical bend of the Seine. It would protect against future incursions by Philip. The Marshal laughed when he heard the news. He said the treaty was already being violated. Such a fortification was expressly forbidden by the terms of the treaty. He said more taxes would have to be generated in England for its construction. We paid our share.

Chateau Gaillard rose majestically from the rocks. It was magnificent. All the latest defensive inventions of the builder's art were included. No expense was spared. Richard hired every stonemason in France. We paid our share and went to speak with the King as the project neared completion.

As the Marshal walked with the King the clatter of construction was almost deafening. I could barely hear what the two men were saying above the din of hammers pounding scaffolds together and the rhythmic clinking of stonemasons at their craft.

"William, this site controls the river valley to Rouen. We must never let that little monkey take it. All of Normandy would fall into his greedy hands." The King was shouting over the noise. He walked with a proud bearing and an arm on the shoulder of my lord. The age difference was becoming more apparent as wisps of gray hair began to intrude on the Marshal's temples. "Together we will take all of my beloved France from the Capetian clod." As he spoke with his Aquitainian French accent I became aware of how much different I was beginning to feel as I became more comfortable with the language of my new homeland of England. It made me realize that one's feelings for their homeland is strongly influenced by language. It is difficult for anyone to feel an attachment for a country when they speak differently. French was still the common language of the nobility in England, but when caring for the Pembroke holdings I found myself speaking more English with a smattering of Welch. I knew how important England was to my lord and I vowed to become even more proficient. King Richard's heart was held by France and so he had made no effort to learn what he felt was the coarse language of the place he derisively called that cold little island. The Marshal's Norman accent was already undergoing a change as he reverted back to the language of his roots.

"Majesty, it is a most imposing structure. Philip would be foolish to attack if it was defended by brave men. I speak of such men because I have had little faith in walls, no matter how high, that are not backed up by stout hearts." The King gave a somewhat disparaging look at the Marshal for this last remark.

"My child Gaillard could be defended by a fool it is so well built," he boasted. His child? Strangely it would be the only child he would ever father.

"King Philip calls it something else. I know not all the oaths he has found to describe it and my French is extensive. Sire, he has told his advisors he will destroy it even if we make walls of iron." The Marshal saw trouble on the horizon.

King Richard snorted and said, "I could defend it against the likes of Philip even if we built walls of butter." I gazed at the mighty towers piercing the sky above the cliffs and thought the King's boast might be true, but then I harkened back to something the Marshal had said at the beginning of the campaign against King Henry that Richard's overconfidence was his greatest weakness. It was still hard to believe such a fortress could fall.

As they climbed one of the rising scaffolds to gain a view of the river valley below, I was no longer able to hear the rest of their conversation. I spoke to some of the workmen and asked if I would be able to get my first glimpse of Queen Berengaria. They laughed and told me the Queen had not been anywhere near the King since his return from the Crusade. One gritty stonemason told me, "I think the King loves these stones more than his Queen." I never would meet the Lady from Navarre.

Later in the day we rode back to Rouen. The Marshal said, "We will be fighting long before any butter walls melt from the summer's heat."

By Christmas the castle was completed. Back in Rouen we enjoyed the reuniting of our families and the holiday festivities. We waited for the Marshal's prediction to come true.

We did not have to wait long. Fighting resumed when the New Year, 1199, was barely a week old. We were told Queen Berengaria rejoined her husband as the campaign progressed. Everyone hoped it meant the King would produce an heir.

"My lord, I just received a communication. King Richard has gone to Limousin to collect money from the Count of Chaluz," I said holding the letter in an outstretched hand. "Not surprising. He has bled the English countryside as much as he can. Even the devious Longchamp will be unable to squeeze another coin from the people." I laughed.

"The King looks for other sources of funds for his never-ending wars. He heard the Count of Chaluz has found a treasure. A percentage of such a find is due to his king, but the lord of Chaluz claims no such treasure has been found," the Marshal said as he turned up his hands and shrugged, signifying he was unsure of the story.

"The letter says King Richard does not believe this and hurries with a small army to force payment. You are to remain here and protect Normandy," I said finishing the contents of the letter.

"Good. My men need rest."

The Marshal remained in Rouen guarding the quiet borders of Normandy. King Philip had had enough of knocking heads with my master and our days were spent sending messages to our allies to make sure the French armies were not on the move. The Marshal stayed ready by practicing every day. The soldiers could not believe a man of his age had the stamina and strength to do what he did. His brown hair and not just the temples was streaked with strands of grey.

It was raining and I was working late on some correspondence when there was a commotion in the courtyard. The Marshal had retired for the evening so I went down to see what the matter was. It was a messenger from Chaluz. His garments were a testament to the hard rain falling outside. He ran up to me and said, "Where is the Marshal? King Richard is dead!" I raced up the stairs and straight to the Marshal's bedroom. I burst through the door without knocking. The Marshal was sound asleep.

"My lord, wake up!" I shook him. Startled he sat up.

"What is the meaning of this?"

"My lord, there is a messenger downstairs. He says the King is dead."

"Which King?" He was still half asleep.

"King Richard!" That statement cleared the cobwebs and he sat up fully awake. By now, the rider had entered the room.

"King Richard has died from a wound suffered at Chaluz, my Lord Marshal," he said as his clothes dripped steadily on the floor of the Marshal's bedchamber.

"Lewellyn, fetch my clothes and tell my squire to bring my armor. Tell John to gather several men to ride with me. I must confer with the Archbishop immediately. Have the grooms prepare the horses." He was putting on his padded shirt as I left to perform my appointed tasks. By the time I returned he was buckling his sword. His squire was adjusting some of his armor. The rider was explaining how the King had died.

"My lord, the wound began as a minor one, but it corrupted and turned fatal. He was struck by an archer as he rode, sadly without armor, by the wall of the castle. Before he died, the King named Prince John to succeed him." Richard's usual disdain for a hauberk had done him in. I knew Arthur, King Richard's nephew and son of his dead brother Geoffrey, had the proper claim to the title. Naming Prince John heir would surely cause trouble. Arthur was just a boy of thirteen and under the influence of his uncle King Philip! Prince John was, well, I need not tell you what I thought of him. As we rode out of the gates, in the pouring rain, I wondered what decisions awaited us when we reached the palace of the Archbishop of Rouen. William Marshal would now have to swear allegiance to his fourth Plantagenet king. Who would it be this time? Would the choice mean more warfare? It would not be easy. There were dark days ahead as flashes of lightning split the night sky.

Chapter 13
Difficult Choices

The cobbled streets of Rouen echoed to the clatter of our party's horses. The darkness of night could make these streets dangerous to the traveler under normal conditions, but the cold rain and raw wind must have discouraged those who would prey on a lonely traveler because the streets were deserted. If someone did lay in wait they would think again about attacking a party of armed knights.

We arrived at the Archbishop of Rouen's palace. It was still raining hard and our clothes were soaked. I was sure the knights were anxious to shed their cold and wet hauberks. The Marshal had no time for such indulgence. He had to talk to the Archbishop about the death of the King and the problems an uncertain succession presented. A servant handed him a towel. His heavy riding boots squeaked and sloshed as he marched directly toward the churchman's chambers. He wiped his face and hands, tossed the towel to the page and tossed his wet cloak to me. He stopped, sat on a bench in the corridor, and emptied his boots of the accumulated rainwater. The page used his towel to wipe the puddle from the stone floor. We continued down the corridor. A monk, who had raced ahead to inform the Archbishop of unexpected visitors, stood outside the door. Walter of Coutances was ready to receive us. The Archbishop was a tall thin man. His white beard signaled his advancing years. Like many of his position he had been of noble birth, trained in the art of war and a King's favorite before taking the cloth. He was as comfortable in the saddle with a sword in his hand as he was saying mass. He was well respected by the nobility and his influence was considerable. His dressing gown was of the finest white linen and trimmed with gold braid. A purple velvet cowl protected him from the night chill. Churchmen of his stature did not lack for funds to purchase the best of the tailor's art. He had been working late and had not yet retired for the evening when our band arrived. Walter and the Marshal had become close friends during the King's absence. The appropriate greetings were exchanged.

"It must be serious to bring you hence on such a miserable night."

"The King has died in Chaluz. We face a difficult succession problem," the Marshal said pursing his lips and shaking his head.

"I am saddened to hear this and may God have mercy on his soul, but why is there a problem? Arthur, the duke of Brittany, is the next in line," he said with a puzzled look and knowing the law was clear on who followed a childless King Richard.

"Yes, but Richard named Prince John before he died," the Marshal responded.

"John! How could that be? He is unworthy. He betrayed the King on many occasions. He is unfit for the role. Of all of Henry's sons, he is the least deserving of the crown," he said clearly disgusted at the prospect of the duplicitous Prince John gaining what he had so recently tried to steal by allowing Richard to languish in a German prison. Now he was being handed the crown by that same brother's dying breath.

I saw the surprised look on his assistant's face. The young monk was not accustomed to be so bold a speech against one of the royal family. I was not. When I heard the comments all I could think of was a hardy amen. I was not the only one who detested King Henry's youngest son. His reputation for treacherous behavior, womanizing, greed and a host of other weakness certainly made him unfit. I remembered Baldwin's description of the campaign in Ireland and how Prince John upset his father's plans. Why would the Marshal even consider him as a possible choice? The answer was forthcoming.

"What you say, my lord bishop, is true but consider these facts. King Richard properly mistrusted the King of France who covets all these lands. Philip will surely try to retake the southern Angevin holdings now Richard is gone. Arthur is a boy, not ready to fight such a war, and Arthur is very much under Philip's influence because of his mother. Queen Eleanor dislikes her daughter-in-law and will do little to support the choice of Arthur for fear of Constance acting as regent. If we are to defeat Philip's ambitions we must have her support. Lastly, the people of England do not want a French boy as King. They will not spill their blood to save these lands. It is why the choice must be John." The Marshal had made some strong points.

"Yea, but Richard never showed much respect for England either," rebutted the wise cleric.

"Precisely why we must choose John. He has spent his life in England. It is time for an Englishman to be King of England. The people of my home have paid the taxes and died in battle for their kings. I am tired of kings who see England as a fiefdom worthy only as a source of money and manpower. Henry spent his life conquering an empire in France. The young King hardly saw the land he was supposed to rule. Richard loved Aquitaine and foreign adventures. In his ten years he saw England only twice. 'Tis time for my England to come first!" demanded the Marshal.

The two men discussed the politics swirling around Henry II's sprawling empire for an hour. I busied myself with drying the Marshal's cloak in front of the large blazing fireplace and added a log or two as needed. The two principals debated over the possibilities. Who would support the choice? Who would oppose it? What would Philip do? What would Queen Eleanor do? Most important of all, what would John do once he had complete power? As the acolyte and I began to replace some of the spent candles lighting the chamber. The Marshal's point of view was finally accepted. England needed an English king. The unreliable John would be the choice. With an air of resignation the Archbishop uttered an ominous benediction.

"Marshal, I am sure the day will come when you regret this decision more than any you have ever made."

I handed the Marshal his, now partially dried, cloak. We prepared to return to our castle. The Archbishop prevailed on the Marshal to remain overnight. I was happy when he accepted. I did not relish the prospect of returning during the rainstorm.

The following morning we journeyed back to our residence and the Marshal put me to work writing communications to the people who had to be brought into the succession plans. Archbishop Walter prepared to anoint Prince John as duke of Normandy. Queen Eleanor would need to secure the loyalty of Aquitaine for her only remaining son. The Marshal assured me she would do so willingly because of her distrust of Arthur's mother, Constance. The gulf between the two was old and deep. John and his wife, Avisa, were to be crowned at Westminster as soon as it could be arranged. The Archbishop of Canterbury, Hubert Walter, would take care of those arrangements. Preparations had to be made for a war with Philip. It was certain to come as soon as the French king could muster support. The Marshal would hold Normandy safely in John's camp.

King Richard was buried with his father at Fontevrault, April 21, 1199. Almost immediately Walter held the ceremony which made John the duke of Normandy. Constance, the duchess of Brittany, sent her son to Philip for safe keeping while she railed at the men who were preventing her Arthur from being crowned. Before leaving for England, John officially declared the Marshal, Earl of Pembroke, something King Richard had neglected to do. It was a rare achievement for one born as a second son. It would be justified again and again. England was better served by the new Earl than the man who now gained the throne.

By the end of May, John had been crowned king in a ceremony at Westminster. The cheering crowds proved the Marshal was right. Englishmen were happy to have an English king, even if it was John. The joy would be short lived. The fortunes of the Plantagenets changed as frequently as the weather.

King John's first act was a trip to Aquitaine to solidify the support his mother had delivered. It was on this trip King John began to justify the Archbishop's warning. As I have told you before, John always liked two things: money and pretty women. The first, he could get with ever increasing tax levies. His father had trained him in the collection of the scutage. He had learned those lessons well. The oppressive tax was levied more frequently under John than it had been under his warrior brother and his father combined. Unlike King Richard, who sought money for glory, King John sought money for personal pleasures. There never was enough money to satisfy the needs of King John.

It was the other vice which began the undoing of King John. There was not a pretty woman at court who was safe from the lecherous ways of the new King. It was the reason my master's wife rarely traveled to be with him at court. The Lady Isabel was quite content to raise the children at Pembroke a safe distance from King John. One as lovely as Lady Isabel would have surely aroused the worst in the King. We were riding toward Swansea, a small village on the Welch coast not far from Pembroke. The sheep grazed on the rocky hillside that ran down to the sea. The salty air was just losing the foggy clouds to the warm rays of the sun when I spoke to the Marshal about the new King's latest indiscretion—a beautiful woman!

"My lord, I know King John traveled to the southern regions of the Angevin empire to acquaint himself with the riches of his Aquitaine subjects, but how did this trip happen to visit Angouleme? It is little but a hamlet and possesses nothing of value as I recall it," I said knowing full well the discussion would give me more insight into our new king's troubles.

"You are right. It was Isabella of Angouleme that caused the stop. She is reputed to be the most beautiful woman in the world. It is certain King John had heard the stories of her beauty, and came to see for himself. Why else would the high king visit such an insignificant place? Rumors abound that King John has fallen under the spell of this young beauty and is making arrangements to marry her," he said as his eyes glanced up to signal disbelief.

"He already has a wife, Avista, the daughter of the Earl of Gloucester!" I complained.

"Ah, but a trivial obstacle in the way of this match. 'Tis a simple matter for a king as determined as John. He will have the marriage annulled. Silver marks deposited in the right quarters will silence Church criticism. Isabel's promise to marry the baron of Lusignan can be swept away just as easily. Realizing a match with a high king is far more profitable than marriage to a baron; Isabella's parents fell into line with King John's proposal. The new marriage will make John two new enemies—the Earl of Gloucester, who fearing for his life, will say nothing, and Hugh de Lusignan, the man betrothed to the lovely Isabella. Hugh, unlike the Earl of Gloucester, has already had much to say about the new betrothal and none of it friendly. Hugh went to his liege lord, King Philip, seeking relief for his broken heart. King Philip was delighted to help his vassal by demanding compensation from John. John will have to surrender some of the Angevin holdings to Philip. It seems the Lusignan family is always causing me to lose sleep," he muttered.

"I do not understand any of this, my lord," I said with a great degree of consternation. Just how land given to Philip mends Hugh's broken heart was unclear. Then I realized the powerful often find ways to enrich themselves from the suffering of others. "Why should this be of concern to us?" I said seeing no connection with the Marshal's plans.

"King John of course has refused to give up any land and Hugh, a very popular noble, begins to rally support among the nobility of Poitou. There is sure to be trouble unless Queen Eleanor can intervene and prevent King Philip from supporting the cause. Without his help Hugh can only bewail his loss," he said hoping for a solution which might stave off another war.

"Will we never have peace?" I asked dejectedly.

"We will have to wait and see what the great lady can arrange" was the apprehensive reply.

We reached the village and spoke to the magistrate about a matter involving some stolen chickens. In the morning we returned home still wondering what the King's mother could do to save the day. The gentle sea breeze caressing the town belied the political storm rising to the south. We would soon see what the great Queen planned and it would cause future problems, but the mighty often think only of satisfying the moment.

Queen Eleanor attempted to still the riled waters by having her granddaughter, Blanche of Castile, marry Philip's son Louis. It was the way nobility tried to solve many problems. It would please the French monarch by giving him a future claim to several fiefdoms. He had learned the lesson of acquiring land in this way from the departed King Henry II. To accomplish this she traveled over the Pyrenees to fetch the bride to be. It was a difficult task for even a youthful person to make such a journey, and Queen Eleanor was eighty. To say she was remarkable would be an understatement! Her attempts to bring peace succeeded for a brief time as Philip refused to support Hugh enthusiastically. The marriage, unfortunately, gave Louis a distant claim to the throne of England. Years later this marriage would cause a great deal of trouble for England and the Marshal. The unlucky suitor was left to lick his wounds and pine for his lost love. The wily Philip would wait for another misstep by King John and then demand even more land.

The misstep King Philip hoped for was already in the making. It involved the plight of the duke Arthur—the boy who might have been king. Young Arthur and his mother were staying with the King of France when Philip claimed some of the Angevin holdings as compensation for the jilted Hugh. The boy protested to his grandfather. These were his potential lands. If Philip was interested in helping him, why was he taking his territory? Philip ignored his grandson's protests. Arthur and his mother realized King Philip was only interested in securing their land for himself. They left Paris and sought refuge with King John! To use a phrase, he was out of the kettle and into the fire. It was at this time I had a brief encounter with Prince Arthur.

The Marshal went to see King John and I went with him. As usual I was needed if there were messages which had to be written. With a war in the offing there would be many who would need instructions. The Marshal was summoned to an audience with the King. I was not allowed to be anywhere near the meeting. King John trusted no one. It is a common trait among those who cannot be trusted themselves. While I was wandering around the grounds waiting for the Marshal, I met Prince Arthur. I recognized him immediately. He favored his father. He was slight of build. He had reddish blond hair, blue eyes and showed promise of becoming a handsome man. He must have thought I was a member of the court because he came over to me. "Sir, you look familiar. Do we know you?" he asked with boyish curiosity.

"Nay, my lord. I am but the humble servant of the Earl of Pembroke," I said with the appropriate bow.

"The Earl has a considerable reputation. All true?" He obviously did not know that my master had been the one responsible for him not succeeding his uncle, a decision that still bothered me.

"It is, my lord. He is the bravest and most honorable man I know," I said with a smile. I proceeded to tell him some of the adventures I had shared with the Marshal. Like all thirteen-year-old boys he enjoyed stories of daring-do. He listened intently and then frowned.

"It vexes me that others are deciding my rightful claims. I may be young, but I am not afraid. I will press for my rights," he said as a look of determination showed on the cherubic face. The Prince had courage.

"My lord, please be careful. If King John hears such statements..."

"I said, I am not afraid," he interrupted sharply. He stood very straight and held his head erect.

I was convinced he was in for a bad time with the likes of King John. He had too much courage. I decided to switch the topic to his father. If the walls had ears, as they often did, the previous line of conversation could be deadly to the Prince. I explained I had seen his father compete in the tournaments. He was eager to hear the story and when I finished he thanked me and went on his way. Shortly after the prince left, the Marshal arrived from his meeting. He was not happy. I asked what troubled him so as we walk away from the great hall.

"King John does not realize the danger of the situation. He is more interested in making love to his new bride. Half of France is ready to rise against him and he says I am too anxious. There is plenty of time!" he said sarcastically.

"My lord, 'tis though I am having the same conversation I had with Sir Baldwin years ago when he returned from Ireland. He said King John ignored military threats causing the campaign to fail," I added with an uneasy recollection of events the Marshal had never witnessed.

"In sooth then he has not lost the talent. Lewellyn, we made John king for the sake of England. It will be a difficult task to keep it all from falling apart. I need help. Queen Eleanor holds sway over his emotions. Perhaps she can help us before things go too far. We shall try to contact her. I am told she is at Mirabeau," he said looking around for unwanted eavesdroppers as we emerged into the courtyard. Although his reasons for choosing John over Arthur had been based on logic, people and their imperfections can turn logic on its head. I think the Marshal was having second thoughts about his choice for king. I did not tell the Marshal about my encounter with Prince Arthur, since it would serve no purpose.

We returned to Rouen to prepare for the war with Philip. Soon we learned Arthur's mother realized he was less safe with King John than he had been with the King of France. He and his mother had fled south to forces loyal to Hugh de Lusignan. Still smarting for a fight, Hugh was the perfect ally. Both he and Arthur had been denied their hearts' desires by King John. There was great sympathy for the pair and soon they had raised a small army. We sent a communication to Queen Eleanor to warn her of the danger.

Two days later the messenger returned and raced into the great room. He was exhausted as he breathlessly explained, "My Lord Marshal, I was unable to deliver the message. Mirabeau is under siege by forces loyal to Hugh de Lusignan. The force includes Prince Arthur! Queen Eleanor refuses to surrender. She is determined to hold out till help arrives." Constance was going to put an end to her hated mother-in-law and see her son put on the throne.

The messenger had barely finished when the Marshal sprang into action. He spoke quickly. "Lewellyn, send a message to Archbishop Walter. Tell him to prepare for the defense of Normandy if Philip tries to take advantage of the crisis. I will organize a small force to relieve Mirabeau. You must go to Poitiers and tell the King. Ask him to send supporting troops," he called as he left the room. I wrote the letter to the Archbishop, gave it to a messenger and prepared my things for a journey. The Marshal left with an advance guard immediately.

I traveled to Poitiers to inform the King. When I arrived I was told he was in the tower room in the keep and was not to be disturbed. I informed the captain of the guard of my mission.

"My lord, Queen Eleanor's very life is in peril! I must see him now," I pleaded. I explained the situation. He agreed but gave a strange admonition.

"Go if you must, but be sure to make enough noise as you approach the chamber to announce your presence." I raced up the spiral stairs to the aforementioned site. The climb left me winded and as I approached the doorway I paused to catch my breath. I had inadvertently ignored the captain's warning. I could hear grunts and heavy breathing coming from the room. Suddenly I became very aware of why the captain had warned me of a silent approach. I pressed myself against the wall and peeked between the door frame and the slightly opened door just below one of the hinges. King John was standing with his back to the door. Lying on a low table with her legs spread wide was a young girl. She had dark hair cropped at the shoulders. Her skin was tan marking her as Spanish. King John was standing between her dangling legs. He was naked from the waist down. He was thrusting his hips violently back and forth. She gripped the edges of the table with her hands so the violence of the thrusts would not knock her off. In his excitement John pulled her garment and ripped the top revealing a small breast with a dark nipple. The King reached for the exposed prize with an anxious hand and pinched the nipple until it hardened to form a cherry-like lump on the tan mound. She arched her hips to meet his movements and whimpered soft cries in time with the movements. He reached his climax with a groan and withdrew his manhood. The girl released her grip on the table and as she did she stroked the black maiden hair of her female organs. She smiled and kissed the King's hand. This was not a forced entry. As the King adjusted his clothing, I quietly backed away from the door and back down several steps. I waited a few moments to be sure they were properly repaired and began to shout, "Majesty, Majesty Your mother is in danger." I came up the stairs pretending to be out of breath. As I approached, the door closed. I knocked violently. The door opened and an angry King John stood in the doorway.

"What be the meaning of this!" he snarled.

"Majesty, your mother is besieged in Mirabeau by your nephew and forces of King Philip. The Marshal has gone with a small force to rescue her. He needs your help. He says they mean to seize your lands," I said excitedly.

This last statement brought an instant reaction. "I knew Geoffrey's whelp had designs on my throne. We will go at once." Lovemaking was no longer important. Possessions were at stake. As we turn to go I could see out of the corner of my eye the girl he had just enjoyed. She was short and no more than twelve or thirteen. I knew she was not his wife. I pretended not to see her as we retreated down the stairs. I would later learn this excuse for a king had just seduced the young daughter of the Saire de Quincey. His appetite for females knew no bounds.

He organized the force and we set out for Mirabeau. Several days later we arrived and discovered the Marshal in full command of the city. The battle was over. Arthur had been captured and the Queen rescued. Arriving late to battles was another talent of King John. It earned him a new nickname. Instead of John Lackland he was now John Softsword! I rushed to see if my lord was safe and unharmed. I found him in the company of the old Queen. They were walking in the garden, very much like a time many years ago. I bowed. The Queen spoke.

"The faithful, Lewellyn. Your master has saved me a third time. According to legend, it must be the final time. Perhaps, you will play for us tonight at supper," she said in a weak voice that crackled with age.

"An honor, Majesty." I could see the Marshal was unharmed and my presence was not appropriate. I excused myself. King John arrived as I was leaving. We all acknowledged his presence with bows.

"Mother, I have saved you. It gives me great joy." The Queen smiled, nodded and cast a wry look at the Marshal. I slipped away unnoticed. One of the advantages of being considered no more important than furniture is the ease with which you can disappear in full view. The Marshal gave me a discreet signal with his hand to indicate where his quarters were located. I went there and put things in order.

Later, I was privileged to sing at the supper the Queen held for her guests. For the first time, since I had known the great lady, she appeared to be suffering the maladies which come with advancing years. I sang some of her favorite songs. Several had been taught to me by the long-departed Bertran de Born. She was pleased.

King John was quick to punish the twenty-two knights who had been captured with Arthur. Hugh had made good an escape, but the rear guard had not been so lucky. They were sent to Corfe castle. It was one of his majesty's favorite places to imprison enemies. Once again, the Marshal returned to Rouen to oversee Normandy's defense. We learned those twenty-two knights were starved to death in the weeks that followed.

King John had the boy, Arthur, imprisoned also, but Queen Eleanor insisted he be treated with respect. After all, he was her grandson. As usual the King honored his mother's request, but did so grudgingly. I was afraid for the lad. Our one meeting had been a pleasant one and I hoped no harm would come to him.

Arthur was moved to Falaise castle, under the care of William de Braose, a close friend of King John. He would never be seen again. Rumors began to circulate that they had arranged for the boy to be murdered. The mystery remained conveniently unsolved and the King ignored the rumors. Not surprisingly the affair caused major desertions of King John's vassals in Brittany and some additional ones in Normandy.

Seeing an opportunity, King Philip began to prepare to relieve the friendless monarch of all his French fiefdoms. War was imminent and Normandy was first on the list. The Marshal said the thrust into Normandy would proceed down the Seine Valley. Philip's forces grew daily as more defections occurred. Still, the King took no major defensive actions. I saw the Marshal turn red with rage the day word reached us. Vaudrieul had surrendered without a fight and the garrison had switched sides. He had risked his life to recover this land and treachery had given it to the enemy. Undermanned in Normandy, he could do nothing.

King John was oblivious to all the problems swirling around him. Like most inadequate leaders, he surrounded himself with sycophants. The weak and insecure only want to hear how right they are. Any opposing views are deemed to be held by fools, jealous of their brilliant thinking. In this way they delude themselves into more mistakes to be blamed on others. Only the Marshal was willing to tell him things he did not want to hear. When the Marshal did so, he was ignored. It was a frustrating time.

At last, when bad news continued to pour in, King John began to worry. Chateau Gaillard was the final outpost which stood in the way of Philip conquering all of Normandy. The French army began a siege of this impressive structure. Surrounded, the castle would eventually be starved into submission. As King Richard had said the castle was far too strong to be taken by direct assault. A long siege was the only possible strategy. It gave the Marshal a chance against Philip's greater numbers. The enemy was distracted and ripe for a surprise offensive. It was a chance to defeat Philip's plans and the Marshal was excited as he prepared to explain to the King his bold plan to relieve the garrison. I was instructed to bring several large maps to help explain the plan. We entered the great hall of the Rouen palace where the King waited with several advisors. The Marshal bowed. The King sat with one leg casually draped across his chair.

"My chamberlain informs me you have a plan to rid us of the vexing French King. Proceed with the particulars," he declared arrogantly while showing no respect for the only man that could save his French possessions. The Marshal ignored the slight.

"Majesty, the French army has presented us with a rare opportunity. Since they outnumber us three to one they have thrown caution to the wind and split their force. Half of Philip's army has left Gaillard to attack a nearby castle that threatens their rear. If we act now we can make them pay for this mistake," the Marshal said and waved a hand for me to bring the maps.

John sat up and looked at the Marshal. "How so?"

"If your Majesty agrees I will take two thousand men to attack the six thousand men left besieging Chateau Gaillard. As they see us approach by land they will ignore the river." He moved his finger across the unrolled map showing the proposed route. "Your Majesty will take the large force in Le Havre which Philip is convinced is no threat and sail up the Seine on the morning tide which will move you faster than Philip realizes. We will have them trapped before help can be summoned. By the time King Philip returns we will be ready to face him at equal odds. We will hold the high ground with the garrison from Gaillard. I believe Philip will lose his taste for Normandy." He thumped the unrolled map on the precise spot this all would be accomplished.

John looked at the rest of his council and asked, "How say all of you?"

His seneschal nodded as he poured over the map. "'Tis an excellent plan, Majesty." Several others added their voices seeking to be part of the growing approval.

"Then it shall be done. By God's eyes, they will learn to trifle with me!" the King said boastfully. The Marshal finally was able to shake the King John's lethargy. It was typical of the clever traps the Marshal was famous for planning and executing. Naturally, his was the most dangerous and difficult task—distracting and engaging the larger French army. It was the exact moment the Marshal had prayed for. He needed to act quickly to take advantage of the foolish move by his opponent. By the time the other half of the French army returned to Gaillard, the combined force of the Marshal and King John would have the upper hand. It would be perfect. Even though the missing part of the French army was only a half a day's ride away, their return would be too late to change the outcome. The Marshal was pleased.

The plan was put into motion. King John would sail down the Seine just after sunrise. The Marshal and his force would leave Rouen before dawn and should engage the enemy surrounding Chateau Gaillard at mid-morning. By noon King John would arrive and the rout would be on. Philip's blunder had given the Marshal the perfect opportunity to win what he knew would be the decisive battle.

I watched the Marshal prepare in the pre-dawn darkness of September 12, 1203. The ritual was always the same. No one talked. The padded shirt, then the hauberk, next the green tabard with the red rampant lion, last the large broadsword was belted and adjusted. A small hand ax was tucked into the belt on the right side. His squire helped him with the heavy boots. The light steel helmet was placed over the hooded hauberk. The final result was the most feared fighting machine in all of Christendom. Advancing age had not changed that. The chain mail gloves were tucked neatly into the belt on the left side.

They would be put on when fighting was imminent. I was left with instructions of what had to be done if the Marshal did not return. We recited a short prayer and the Marshal proceeded to his horse. There he mounted to ply the trade for which he trained two hours every day. I always wanted to ride with him, but as I was not a fighting man, I would remain in the camp below Rouen. War was for the professionals, not singers of songs.

My son, now seventeen, was living with me. He had learned my trade and was considering striking out on his own. We cleaned the tents and put things in order. It would be a half day or so before we would hear the results of the fight. Chateau Gaillard was a hard morning's ride. So began a nervous time. I would try to fill it by being busy at some foolish task. It was a game I played with my mind—unsuccessfully. I went to the river to see King John's force sail past us. As the morning sun rose steadily, the fleet did not appear. Something was wrong. I returned to our tent. As I was dismounting, a frantic rider charged through the gate. With a look of disgust he shouted, "He's not coming. Softsword missed the tide. The Marshal must be told and my horse is spent."

Without any hesitation I leaped into the saddle. I knew what this meant. The Marshal would be facing the united French army alone with his small force. It would be a slaughter. Trapped between the French besieging Gaillard and Philip's main army they would be wiped out. I shouted, "I am going. Tell my son." I put heels to my horse and raced out of camp.

I could tell from the sun it was near noon when I came upon the battle site. You could hear the sounds before you could see the fighting. It started like a low rumble in the distance and as you got closer there were more distinct sounds. I saw some of the routiers of the Marshal's rear guard.

"Take me to the Marshal. I must see him at once." I did not tell them of the devastating news I was bringing for fear they would flee the scene and leave me with no idea of where to find my lord. I tried to remain calm. As we rode in the direction of the growing sounds, the men suspected my news was not good. They asked the reason for my presence.

"My information is confidential." I tried to sound unafraid. Jacque de Honfleur, a tough Norman knight in the Marshal's employ, spoke up.

"The King should have been here by now. Lewellyn brings us bad news. I will find the Marshal and bring him here. 'Tis a pity, we are doing well in the fight. Many of Philip's men were drunk when we fell upon them. We saw several riders leave to tell King Philip of the attack. It was all going to plan. The Marshal needs to be told." He galloped off. I had underestimated their loyalty to my master. I should have known better. Ten minutes later the Marshal arrived with Jacque.

"By God's legs, Lewellyn, is what Jacque tells me true?" he shouted in disbelief.

"He's not coming, my lord! He missed the tide," I said sadly.

"Are you sure?"

"Yea, my lord."

"Damn! Damn! All is lost. We had them! I suspected trouble when he was late, but the battle was going so well I lost track of time. By mid-afternoon Philip will be here. We must disengage and return to Rouen. The position here is hopeless. If the King does not get to Rouen, it will be lost too! Jacque, tell the captains to begin a retreat. The French will be surprised, but happy to let us go, considering their present state." The Marshal looked down at the ground and slowly shook his head. He mumbled something I could not make out. The garrison at the Chateau Gaillard was now left to their fate.

We remained at the same place as the surprised and disappointed men marched by us in an orderly retreat to Rouen. As he expected, the French did not follow. Within moments the main French army would probably appear over the low hills in the distance. There was no reason to wait to see this. There was every reason not to be here when they arrived. The rear guard approached our position and the Marshal turned his horse and slowly began to ride in the direction of Rouen. He looked at me and said, "Lewellyn, this is a sad day. You have just seen the end of our control in Normandy. A flood of defections will follow. The King will not have enough support to hold on. I have failed."

"Not so, my lord. 'Tis the King who failed you," I protested. I was angry that my lord should take the blame.

"I should not have considered such a daring plan," he said bitterly.

"It was a good plan and the only chance against larger French numbers," I insisted to no avail.

"Not good enough" was the dejected response.

We rode quietly after that. The Marshal was deep in thought and I was seething at a King who was not worthy of the man who blamed himself for this defeat. Had it been King Henry or King Richard this would have been a glorious day. I waited to hear the excuses I knew would be coming. It would be the fault of many, but not the King. Softsword had earned his title!

Walter, the Archbishop of Rouen, was waiting as we entered the gates of the city. There were no recriminations or reminders of the warning he had made on that rainy night. The situation was too grim for any gloating. He respected the Marshal too much to engage in such pettiness. No, they would meet with the King and try to determine what was to be done next.

"Well, my friend, the King will arrive shortly," the Archbishop said with an air of resignation.

"At least Rouen is safe for now. Philip will have to take Gaillard before he can come here. It will take time, but Gaillard will fall. Then we are next," the Marshal said ominously.

"What course of action will you suggest to the King?" the Archbishop asked.

"That depends on the time it takes for the Chateau Gaillard to capitulate, and how many defections occur during the interval. I will take stock of our support. I suspect I will have to recommend seeking terms with Philip," spoke with an air of resignation that was so unlike the man who had to mouth these bitter words.

"Do you think his majesty will understand?" Walter said with his chin on his chest and his eyebrows raised sharply.

"Does it matter? Without reinforcements there is no chance to hold Normandy. With the loss of Gaillard the door is now open. Richard knew it. 'Tis why he constructed the beast. I have a wonderful wife and family in England. I will not be disappointed to see them again. What will you do, my holy friend?" he said forcing a smile.

"As a member of the Church I will be safe enough here. My days as a warrior will be over. I, too, will not be disappointed." The two powerful men walked away together to continue their discussions and wait for their tardy King.

King John arrived with much fanfare early in the evening. He called for a council to convene in the great hall of the Archbishop's palace at once. The Marshal somewhat tired from fighting went dutifully to hear his sovereign explain his failure to arrive on time. I stood in the hallway, holding the Marshal's cloak. I was among several sea captains who were quietly discussing the problem.

"We will get the blame, but I warned his Majesty's men several times, if we did not sail before dawn, we would miss the tide. They kept saying the King will be here presently. When he finally showed up, it was too late." I heard the King shouting numerous oaths as he entered the great hall.

"By God's eyes, you would think these damn sea captains would know the tides. I am not a sailor. Well, so much for their failure, what can we do, Marshal?" he asked as if he had merely tasted some bad wine and simply had to order another bottle!

"We must wait to see what transpires at Chateau Gaillard. Until that is resolved we can do little."

"Why not just take the army there on the morrow?" he said naively.

"My men are not ready to return. They need some rest and the element of surprise is gone. Philip will have scouts to warn him of our movements and he has superior numbers," the Marshal responded, pointing out the obvious to his befuddled liege lord.

"Then we shall wait and prepare. We will take back what is ours!" The King stormed out with his personal guard. The Archbishop and the Marshal walked out together wearing very dismal looks. I knew they did not share the King's enthusiasm for a future triumphal return. Once the Marshal's men were ready the King showed no interest in returning to the besieged castle. More defections ensued as each day passed. The forcc in Rouen was no longer capable of a rescue mission.

The news coming to Rouen was grim. The siege at Chateau Gaillard was horrific. The commander of the garrison had ordered women and children out of the castle in order to preserve food. They left expecting safe passage through the French lines. The French, unwilling to give the garrison's food supply such relief, forced them back to the castle. The commander refused to open the gates. For several days the poor souls suffered at the base of the cliffs, caught between the locked gates and the French army refusing to let them pass. Over three hundred perished. After several months, knowing relief was not forthcoming, the castle finally surrendered.

Philip began to organize for his attack on Rouen. More noblemen turned against John and pledged loyalty to the fleur-de-lis banner. The Marshal asked on several occasions if the King could provide money for mercenaries. The King continued to procrastinate, believing the loss of Gaillard was only a temporary setback. He had no intention of hiring expensive help. He finally called for a meeting of his advisors. I went with my master and this time, because of the numbers, I was able to be in the hall unnoticed.

The council began with the King sitting behind a large table in a large chair. King John's good living made a large chair necessary. He had grown portly. The room was filled with so many fighting men, I stood in a corner of the room, behind several of the King's men. The King had a confident look on his face. I was sure his favorites had filled his head with false hopes. After the usual greetings the discussion commenced. The King stood up and spoke.

"You are all aware of the situation because the cowards at Gaillard have surrendered. We are not ready to give the French pigs our lands without a fight," he said as he thrust his clenched fist into the air. Shouts of "here, here" followed King John's hollow words of defiance.

"We trust you are all ready to serve your liege lord and end this once and for all!" he continued with a broad smile showing how pleased he was with his own words. He nodded to the simple fools who acted as though they believed every word and extended his arms as though he was embracing them all for their blind loyalty.

Again several shouts of support were heard. I looked at the Marshal. He sat with hands folded across his chest saying nothing and displaying no emotion. Several of the King's favorites took turns saying they were ready to fight at the King's side, to the death if necessary. Most had never been in a battle. Then the Marshal stood and all grew quiet. How would the great warrior inspire the crowd? The King anxiously awaited the next speech of support.

"Your Majesty, we must seek terms." The gathering was stunned. He looked directly at the startled King. "You have not enough friends left willing to fight with us. You, who are wise and mighty and of high lineage and whose work it is to rule over us all, have not been careful to avoid irritating people!" he said with bitter invective.

The King looked at his military advisor in disbelief. No one dared to use such terms to a king in private. This was in front of his nobles! Several of King John's close friends recovered their senses and shouted together, "Treason, treason, treason!"

The big man, in the green silk tabard, whirled around and faced the throng. His cheeks a fiery red accented by the graying temples, expressed his rage at the comments. His eyes hurled daggers of contempt and many in the gathering lowered their heads to avoid the withering gaze. The metal glove tucked in his belt was hurled to the floor. It crashed and skidded in the direction of the shouts.

"Let him, who accuses me, pick it up!" he growled. The challenge to combat was met with absolute silence. The King looked around at the gathered multitude of knights and fighting men; his eyes pleaded for a champion to step forward and put this arrogant old man in his place. Seconds passed. No one moved. Then a young man in front of me started to step out of the crowd. His arm was grabbed by the man at his side. He was pulled back. The King stood and waited for a few seconds more. When nothing happened, he shouted, "Cowards!" and stormed out of the room.

For several more seconds there was silence as the Marshal walked over and retrieved the unclaimed glove. Tucking it in his belt he walked defiantly from the room. I turned to go with him when the knight who almost went for the glove spoke to his companion. I paused to listen.

"Why did you stop me? I would have won great favor with the King," he chided his companion.

"You would have died for the King, my friend," he responded in very stern voice.

"I am not afraid of that old man," the young knight retorted boastfully. His friend shook his head.

"You have too few years to know who he is. That old man, as you call him, has killed better knights than you or I will ever meet. His massive sword arm has not yet begun to lose its power. I do not wish to insult you, but you would not last long in a fight with that old man. There were better knights than either of us present. You did not see any of them step forward. That old man, my impetuous friend, is still the greatest knight alive. Come, buy me ale. I just saved your life," he said slapping his doubting friend on the back.

I smiled. I knew his friend spoke words of wisdom. I quietly exited the hall with the rest of the crowd. Returning to our quarters I found a pacing William Marshal.

"Well, I tossed fat into the fire, Lewellyn. I could not stand idly by and watch a court full of flatterers and fools dictate a course of action which would lead to the deaths of many good men in a hopeless cause. The war was lost a month ago. Now we must make the best of things," he said. The anger had been replaced by frustration.

"My lord, you honored your code. You spoke truth when nothing could be gained by it. Those present knew the wisdom of your words. 'Tis why none came forward," I offered as a tribute to true courage.

"Thank you, Lewellyn, but King John sees it not. Bah! I need a beer."

"Yea, my lord." I smiled and happily fetched the desired item.

The following morning a messenger came from King John. It requested my presence in his private chambers. My knees began to shake as we walked down the corridors. I was ushered into the presence of the man who could have me killed with the snap of his fat fingers. Had my actions outside the tower room been discovered? I trembled as I faced the man I was sure intended to have me executed. His lips were curled with hatred as I entered his presence with a bow.

"Lackey. I know your master does not read. Take this message from his King. He will go with the Archbishop of Rouen to ask for these terms from the French King. Those loyal to me will return to England where we will gather sufficient forces to take back that which is mine. We will take his two eldest sons hostage to secure his loyalty. I will not lower myself to talk to the treasonous bastard. He would be dead if it were not for the cowards that surround me." He did not speak the words; he spit them out as if they were spoiled meat. He handed me the document and with his left hand he waved me out of his chamber. I was happy to leave with my life.

I walked slowly down the corridor alone with my thoughts. I was filled with admiration for my master and loathing for the King. I feared for the safety of the Marshal's family. I gave the Marshal the King's orders and explained his threat. He nodded and proceeded to the practice field. As he went out the door he called back.

"Send word to the Archbishop of our task. We will send a messenger to Philip under a flag of truce. The Archbishop and I will need a safe conduct for our meeting. And get me something to eat when I return," he added.

The man had just defied a king and his only reaction was to order some lunch. I spent the rest of the afternoon writing the necessary communications. I arranged for their delivery. I sent Jean to get the food from the scullery. I peered out of the window when I heard the fanfare surrounding the King's departure and watched the Softsword go. There was nothing to do, but wait for the answers to the Marshal's communications. The replies would be slow in coming because King Philip knew more defections would strengthen his bargaining position.

The beginning of 1204 brought more sad news for the Marshal. His dear friend and chief supporter, Queen Eleanor, was dying. We rushed to see her. We were ushered into the great Queen's chamber. She was in bed looking very weak and breathing heavily. She spoke to the Marshal.

"I once said you would not be allowed to rescue me a fourth time, William. It has come to pass. I have lived too long to bury three of my sons. Save John from himself. You are the only man alive with the courage to tell the King to do the right thing," she said weakly as she placed a withered hand on his arm.

"I shall do my best, Majesty." With that promise spoken, the Queen closed her eyes and went to sleep. We left quietly. Soon after our visit, Queen Eleanor surrendered to time. For eighty-two years she had graced the earth with her presence. Sixty-five of those years she was a major force in the affairs of kings. I knew I would miss the great lady who placed me in the service of my lord and friend. My relationship with her started out as one of dislike for each other and ended with warm, respectful affection. Her dislike of me in my youth no longer seemed to matter in our later years. She was buried at Fontevrault with her husband and her beloved son, Richard.

Matters deteriorated quickly after the death of Queen Eleanor. Without her support, many nobles in the French holdings began to switch sides. More vassals began to abandon King John. The leak was becoming a stream. The stream soon became a flood.

Chapter 14
The End of Softsword

Once we had received the safe conduct passes, the Marshal and the Archbishop of Rouen made arrangements to travel to see King Philip. We went with a small contingent of routiers and a flag of truce identifying the group as a diplomatic mission. We were stopped several times. Our papers were examined and on one occasion we had to wait for the captain of a unit to find someone who could read before we were allowed to continue. The Marshal was irritated with the delay, but we were treated with respect because of the presence of the Archbishop. One did not harass an exalted leader of the Church, lest a thunderbolt from heaven would strike you dead.

On the journey, Archbishop Walter and the Marshal discussed what they expected to hear from King Philip. The Marshal was not optimistic. Philip was skilled in negotiations. He had learned not to make the mistakes of his weak-willed father. In many ways he had learned his lessons by observing King Henry. Intimidate your opponent right away. Put him on the defensive. Get a concession and then find excuses to demand more and more until you get everything. Once demoralized, an opponent will concede more before he realizes what he has done. Philip was in a superior position and he knew it. King John's support had melted like a late spring snowfall. The comment by the Marshal, about a lack of friends, was very accurate. In fact, it was probably an understatement.

King Philip's palace was right on the river Seine. The brick walls curved at the base and rose about thirty feet vertically. I asked about the marks on some of the bricks and was told that it was the way workmen had identified their work for the purpose of payment. We were led inside and told the King would see us soon. He was holding his daily session hearing the complaints of his subjects. It was a peculiar practice of the French Kings. We were ushered into a waiting area. The Marshal said the gamesmanship was beginning. We waited about an hour. It seemed longer as such times do when you are nervous. The Marshal talked to the Archbishop and showed little emotion.

We were called to the throne room. As I prepared to accompany the Marshal, I was stopped. The guard said only the Marshal and the Archbishop were to go. The Marshal explained I was his scribe and my presence was necessary. I was allowed to pass.

We entered the room filled with nobles. King Philip meant to demonstrate his overwhelming support, because many of those present were familiar faces. A short time ago they had been King John's vassals. Those I did not recognize stared at the Marshal. I suspected they wanted to see this knight whose exploits had become almost legendary. Was he as big as they said? Was his sword really four feet long? Their facial expressions showed most of them were not disappointed with what they saw.

The Marshal approached King Philip and bowed respectfully. The diminutive King acknowledged the bow with a nod. He stood up and said in a very loud voice, "Where is Arthur?" The intimidation had begun. By demanding to know what had happened to the missing prince, King Philip believed the Marshal would be put on the defensive because he could not answer the question. No one, except King John, knew what had happened to Arthur. It was a clever strategy. Many of those present had joined Philip because of their loyalty to the missing Duke of Brittany.

The Marshal stood tall and rather than the customary downcast eyes most nobles used when they talked to kings, he looked directly at the King. His pale blue eyes failed to show surprise as he spoke in a firm and mocking tone.

"Your majesty, I see there are many present who, in my country, would be put to death or, at the least, lose their eyes for betraying their oaths." He scanned the room with an icy stare. There was a brief moment of silence and then the King spoke.

"They are no more to me than the candle I use to go to the private at night and then toss away when I am done." The King and the Marshal broke into laughter. The tension of the moment was relieved. Philip knew there would be no intimidation of this man.

The real discussions began. For two hours, the two men jousted verbally. It followed the pattern the Marshal had discussed with the Archbishop. Philip kept finding excuses to demand more and the Marshal would refuse. Nothing was being accomplished. The loss of Maine and Anjou were a given, but the Marshal would not hand over Normandy without a fight. The Marshal hoped his earlier successful defense of Normandy would make Philip think twice before invading. It was a bluff.

King Philip knew the fall of Gaillard had left his sword pointed at the throat of Normandy and unless major reinforcements arrived from England, the province would fall like a ripe fruit from the Angevin tree. Before such a force landed on French soil there was no reason to agree to any truce. He would not give King John time to organize. The negotiations ended without results. Our delegation left Paris and returned to Rouen.

As we rode, I spoke to the Marshal, "My lord, what now?"

The Marshal was glum as he spoke. "We pray King John will send reinforcements soon. Without them we lose Normandy."

In one month we had our answer. There would be no help. The Marshal was ordered to return to England. King John said he was needed to plan a future engagement to retake the lost land. It was fortunate because a desperate attempt to hold Normandy would end in failure and the death of the Marshal. I was surprised the King would save him, but King John was unpredictable. Perhaps he feared a French invasion of England and would need the great warrior.

I prepared our baggage and informed my son we would be returning to England. He asked my permission to remain and make his own way in the land of his mother's birth. With a heavy heart, I agreed. I had given him all the skills he would need, and now it was time for him to be a man. The Marshal did not need two scribblers and musicians. I know he would have made room if asked, but I did not want my son to live in my shadow. From time to time I would receive communications from him. He has done well and I have not regretted my decision.

In late September we left Normandy. I know the Marshal felt he would never see France again. He was right. He was glad to be going home, but this land had been the site of many of his greatest triumphs and now he was leaving in defeat. It was a bittersweet moment. He was fifty-eight years old. He felt his fighting days were at an end. From his beginning, as an unknown knight errant, his skill with a sword had brought him great fame and fortune. Now he was a peer of the realm with a beautiful, devoted wife and many children. He had gained these things because of his skill and incredible devotion to a code of honor. He was convinced his quest was complete. He would now rest and live out life quietly at Pembroke if he could persuade King John to release his hostage sons. He could not have been more wrong. Events would shape his destiny in ways he could never imagine. He did not look back as the ship left for Dover.

It is strange how a man's greatest strength can be used against him. So it was with the Marshal. The unquestioning loyalty to his word was the most admired quality he possessed. Other men could not or would not live up to so high a standard. I remembered the time, in the service of the young King, we had sought lodgings at a major tournament. The funds from King Henry had not yet arrived and when we went to pay the bill the young King was short of money. The landlord said he would keep the horses until payment was made. He refused to accept the young King's promise to pay. At that point, the Marshal stepped forward. The innkeeper recognized him immediately. The keeper was a follower of the tournament scene. He said he would accept the Marshal's promise as payment and the horses would be released. The innkeeper said everyone in France knew the champion's word was as reliable as his sword arm. The Marshal agreed and the deal was made. His word was better than a king's. So it was throughout his life. From the day I first met him, he never broke a promise.

Now, his unswerving loyalty was to bind him to another who was unworthy of this trust. He had sworn an oath of fealty to King John and he honored the oath regardless of the consequences. It cost him the love of his eldest son and proved to be the saddest part of his great life. I was angry that he had to allow the King to betray his trust time and again. I was taught to believe that living a virtuous life was the key to gaining God's favor. The experience with the death of my wife had shaken that belief. But then when the man I believed the most virtuous of all men, the Marshal, had been rewarded by escaping death, gaining a beautiful wife, fine family and wealth my faith in God was slowly being restored. Now the wheel had turned again causing more confusion. Was faith in the code of chivalry merely a way to make decisions rather than a way to salvation? Did a person choose the correct path mapped out in the code only to suffer at the hands of the not so virtuous? This seemed to be the fate of the Marshal. The priests would say it was God's way of testing us, but the Marshal had passed that test many times over. I wondered if it was God's test or the capricious nature of men that caused these contradictions. Did it all matter? Future events would confuse me again and again. As the pockmarked chalky cliffs of Dover grew steadily over the ships bow it was the people of England who would benefit from the return of this special man and not the man himself. Perhaps it was part of God's plan.

After three days in the saddle we reached Pembroke and were met by John d' Erly and the Lady Isabel. I could see the lady was visibly upset. She ran to her husband and hugged him. She finally released her arms and stepped back with downcast eyes, filled with tears. She said in a soft and sorrowful voice, "The King has taken two of our sons. Why, my lord?'

"I told him the truth when others would not." The Marshal explained the circumstances under which he and the King had parted. He finished the explanation with a dire prediction, "He continues to believe he will regain his lost lands. It will not happen unless much changes."

"Does this place our sons in danger?" she asked unable to take a breath until this vital question received an answer.

"Nay, wife, they are being kept to assure my support. There be no reason to do them harm. His support wanes with each new moon. He can ill afford to lose me as well. It will not be long before he will have other worries. We shall remain here and give the King no cause to doubt our loyalty. Our sons will be safe," he said unable to disguise the concern in his voice. There was little comfort in these words for the Lady Isabel but she accepted her husband's word. Another child was on the way bringing the total to nine and life had to continue.

It was a dreary Christmas that year. We made the best of it. Still, the two missing sons were like a cloud hanging over the festivities. Our hearts were not in the songs we sang. Eventually we all admitted we were not in the mood for Yuletide cheer. We spoke of the hostage sons and the Lady Isabel began to weep. The Marshal promised to journey to Winchester and London to see the King and check on William and Richard. The Lady Isabel was only slightly comforted by this news and the rest of the Christmas season was gloomy.

It was a month before the weather allowed us to take the trip. The excuse for the Marshal's going to the King was to pay the latest scutage to his majesty. King John's vow to have the Marshal help him plan an attack to retake Normandy had faded and died during the winter months. The visit would involve some risk since it might remind King John of things he had conveniently forgotten. Had the wounds to his vanity sufficiently healed to see the man who defied him in front of his nobles? With no return to France planned, the King did not need the Marshal. It made him unpredictable.

We arrived in Winchester and took lodgings while we waited for an audience to be granted. It was several days before it was approved. I used the time to gather information about what was happening at court. As a servant, I was able to speak to the others in the serving class freely and received a great deal of information. Information I shared with the Marshal.

"My lord, I have learned the King has been up to his old habits. It seems having a beautiful wife has not cooled his blood. There are rumors he has tried to seduce the wife of Eustace de Vesey," I said with disgust but little surprise. I fully expected this debauchery from John having witnessed his actions in Poitiers. I had never shared with the Marshal the sordid details of what he was doing when his mother needed rescue. My news also did not shock the Marshal.

"It surprises me not, but 'tis a bad move by the King. Eustace is a very powerful baron and has many friends. John will regret making him an enemy. His father made similar mistakes and it cost him dearly." The Marshal shook his head. "Lewellyn, I helped make this man king and now I am being punished by God for my actions. I thought I was helping my country. The Archbishop warned me," he confessed.

I was very nervous as we prepared to meet with the man I considered the most evil monarch in the Christian world. He did do some good things in his life, but it was by accident. He often made decisions which benefitted the common people, but in truth he cared little for us. The reason for his generosity was to punish nobles who had angered him.

The Marshal and I went to the great hall to meet with King John. I stayed back as the Marshal walked through the crowded room to the King seated in a large chair at the far end. The Marshal bowed respectfully. He waited to be addressed by the King. I expected King John to make some type of sneering joke or issue a nasty threat. Amazingly, the King gave a warm greeting

"Ah, the good Earl is among us. We have missed you at court," he said in a smarmy voice.

Strange! Something had changed. It was apparent the Marshal was needed after all. He acted as though the Marshal had left France anxious to rejoin his dear friend the King. Was all the rancor forgotten? Why?

"My lord Marshal, we hope you have time to visit your sons who are progressing nicely in their training. They show promise as might be expected, coming from such fine stock." The words dripped like honey from his lips.

"I thank your Majesty for his concern and we shall endeavor to visit them as soon as time allows." The Marshal gave no sign of anger for the unjust treatment he had suffered at the hands of the man who was now after something.

I waited to hear the reason for this unexpected treatment and veiled reminder of the power he exerted over the Marshal's two eldest sons. A thin smile, accented by the King's narrow black mustache, prefaced the answer for this uncharacteristic warmth.

"The Archbishop of Canterbury is ill and not expected to live much longer. We need to be sure his successor is as talented as Archbishop Hubert. The final choice is the Pope's, of course, but a good word from someone as honored as you could help put the right man in the post. We know the Holy Father has great respect for your council," he said in a way that made it clear it was a command not a request.

The real meaning of the speech was that King John wanted someone he could control. He was obviously going to recommend some lackey that would not sit well with the Church. John needed all the support he could muster. Pope Innocent was not someone who could be bribed or intimidated. He was the kind of man King John could not deal with. He was just the kind of man the Marshal understood. They both had codes of honor and wills of iron. A letter from the Marshal could help King John's choice or at least the King believed it would. The audience ended and the Marshal was given permission to see his two boys. As we walked to the stables and our horses the Marshal spoke.

"I told the Lady Isabel it would not be long before King John would have other worries. 'Tis a dicey situation. The King fails to see what little influence I have on the Pope's decision. He is an honorable man who will not listen to the advice of a sinner like me. We will write a diplomatic letter to the Holy Father as requested. I hope the King chooses wisely; it would make things easier, but that is unlikely! Now, we be off to see my sons," he said with zest for the next destination of our journey.

We traveled to London. The two boys were being housed at the White tower, so called for the white coating plastered on the walls. Banners flew from each of the four turrets which also gave the place its name. High walls surrounded the structure built on the banks of the Thames. A dry moat surrounded the walls on three sides. The fourth side abutted the river with a gate under which boats could enter or leave. The last time I had seen this place it contained the nefarious William Longchamp. It was the same river gate he had used to make his escape in the dark of night. We passed through the gates and showed the warders our papers from the King. He had given the Marshal the right to visit, but young William and Richard would not be allowed to leave and return to Pembroke. The usually suspicious monarch was not about to lose his most powerful hold over a man he needed.

We were led up a small hill to the courtyard where the boys were practicing, one with a wooden sword, and the other with a real one. William, now fourteen, was the first to see us. He favored his father, and was already a head taller than me. He dropped his practice weapon and raced to his father.

"Father, you have come to rescue us at last. When do we go home? I hate this place. How is Mother?" he shouted excitedly.

The Marshal embraced his eldest. "She is fine, my son," he responded ignoring the first question. Richard joined the embrace. He was three years younger than his brother and only came up to the chest of his father. He had the features of his mother and was going to be a very handsome man someday. The Marshal rubbed his blond head. I could see all were moved by the reunion.

"You both look fit. Your mother and I have missed you. William, you are becoming a man. You use your weapon effectively. You still have much to learn, but I am pleased," he said still leaving the most important question unanswered.

"When are we going home?" The repeated question brought a look of sadness to the Marshal's face.

"Not for a while, son." The tone of the reunion began to change. An angry look replaced the joy on young William's face. He stepped back from his father and asked again.

"Why not?"

"The King chooses to continue your training," was his unconvincing response.

"Not true. I am not a child. I know why we are kept here. He seeks to control you. He is an evil man." The boy's logic was unassailable. Faced with a son who understood the truth, the Marshal knew he could not deny their status. The Marshal also knew his son's statements about the King would place both boys in danger.

"You must not make such statements about the King," warned the Marshal with a subdued voice.

"Why not? You know I am right. I am not afraid," said the disappointed youth reminding me of the same response of the missing Duke of Brittany. My blood chilled when I thought how that defiance turned out!

"I know you are not, but you also place your brother in danger. I need you to protect him for I cannot. This situation will end soon and you will both be allowed to return. Until then, you are the eldest; it will be your responsibility to see that no harm comes to Richard. Do this for your mother and me," the Marshal requested softly. The older boy thought about the request. He looked at his younger brother hugging his father's waist. He looked up and his answer was tinged with bitterness.

"I will do as you ask." He turned and walked away. The meeting which had begun in joy was now a bitter parting. In young William's mind he had been betrayed by his father. From that day on the two drifted apart. No matter how the Marshal tried, he was never able to completely restore the bond with his eldest son and heir. It is a sad moment when our children finally are old enough to know we are not perfect. The hurt was visible. The Marshal tried to comfort himself by playing briefly with Richard, but it was not enough. It was time to leave before the pain became unbearable. He said good-bye and we rode away. It would be two more years and one more daughter before the King released the Marshal's sons.

We returned to Pembroke. In the following months, I saw the Marshal begin to show the effects of his years. The hours of practice at the post decreased. His hair became increasingly gray with white strands also growing in number. He was now entering his sixties. The captivity of his sons weighed heavily on the household, but the love of the Lady Isabel never wavered as you might expect. She raised the rest of the large family and trusted her husband's word that eventually all would be set right.

In July of 1205, we went to Chepstow Castle to hear complaints from the villeins. I recorded the curious case of a farmer who had a dozen sheep die in a mysterious manner. Upon questioning from the Marshal the facts came out. It seems the wife of the villein was angry because her husband called her a drab for flirting with a neighbor. To revenge herself she had ground up the dry roots of monkshood to make a large bagful of powder. She tested it for potency on the sheep. The husband was sure to be next had not the Marshal discovered the truth. She was flogged, the marriage dissolved and she was banished from the lands of the Marshal under penalty of death if she returned. I took the bag as evidence. After the trial I kept the bag intending to use it to rid Pembroke of vermin when I returned. It proved to be most effective.

It was shortly after the trials the news we were expecting reached us. Hubert Walter, Archbishop of Canterbury, went to his final reward with God. The time had come to choose a successor and the struggle between King John and Pope Innocent III began. King John named a favorite lackey to the post. In fulfillment of his promise the Marshal sent the letter of support to the Holy Father. A copy was sent to King John. The Marshal hoped it would mean the release of his sons.

By fall, the lack of a response from the Pope meant the nomination was in trouble. Visitors to Pembroke kept us informed of the events at court. A kindly monk on his way to Ireland brought us unwanted news. The King's choice did not have the support of the clergy in Canterbury. They appealed to the Pope to choose someone else. My lord and lady knew this would mean their sons would stay in London. We would have to endure another joyless Christmas.

Action by Innocent was not forthcoming until the spring of 1206. The Pope chose an English cardinal from the Vatican to fill the post. His name was Stephen Langton. He was a scholar and just the kind of man King John would not be able to control. The King instantly objected and announced the new man would not be allowed to set foot in England. Like his father before him, King John was in a fight with the Church over issues of control.

By the end of the year the Marshal's sons were returned as the King attempted to gain the support of his barons in his struggle with the Pope. There was much rejoicing in the household. Unfortunately, the breech with young William did not heal. He quarreled frequently and said he was no longer sure of his father's love. To alleviate the tension in the household the Marshal sent his eldest son to his friend, Sir William Mowbray, saying he needed to continue his knightly training in different surroundings. Richard and the other children would remain with the Marshal. Richard would receive his training at the hands of his father.

Life at Pembroke finally settled into a long period of boring bliss isolated from the travails of the King and his court. The Lady Isabel rejoiced at the harmony of her large family and a husband who had been forgotten by a devious King. Visitors were still welcomed, but were rarely asked about the struggles of the King. I on the other hand had to satisfy my inordinate curiosity and so I kept abreast through scraps of information in the Marshal's correspondence and gossip of the servants who came with the more exalted guests.

By 1207 the struggle between the Pope and King John caused the Holy Father to lay an interdict on England. No services or sacraments would be allowed and the bells of the churches fell silent. The King refused to relent. Life at Pembroke proceeded quietly. The Marshal was not about to get involved in another religious struggle. He just wanted to live, what remained of his life, in peace and quiet. From time to time we would hear about the barons and their frustrations with the King. The Marshal would laugh, shake his head and then return to managing his large estates, paying his taxes and trying to stay on good terms with everyone.

In 1209, Pope Innocent, frustrated with the King's continued resistance, took the next step. He excommunicated the defiant King John. It caused King John to wear religious relics around his neck to protect him from demons. John d'Erly said, after returning from a trip to the King's court, he looked like a merchant selling religious favors. It caused the Marshal to lose control of a mouthful of wine.

Not much changed for the next three years. Then two events occurred which changed everything. First, the Pope began to talk to Philip of France about deposing the stubborn English king. He could use the claims of the missing Arthur as a pretext for an invasion. The Pope would provide financial and military support. Rebellious barons, chafing from taxes and the interdict, made support at home questionable. Even the nobles who supported every action of the King said this was serious. They begged the King to make peace with the Pope. A fearful King John sent a delegation to Rome. He agreed to allow Stephen Langton to become Archbishop of Canterbury and agreed to make England a fief of the Holy Father. A sum of one thousand marks was to be paid in tribute to the Vatican each year. It was a trifling sum compared to the revenues King John was exacting in England.

The second event was on the continent. Otto the son of John's sister, Matilda, was elected German Emperor. Queen Eleanor's carefully laid plans were still influencing the continent long after her demise. Otto IV had a great dislike for Philip of France. John saw it as a chance to regain his lost lands. A deal was struck and a plan was made for the two kings to attack Philip: John from Aquitaine in the south and Otto from the north. King John saw no reason to include his old military advisor, Sir William Marshal, in the planning. After all, the Marshal was now an old man and the arrogant John thought he could do better by himself. It was a huge mistake.

Late in the fall of 1213 word reached Pembroke the King was planning to attack Philip. The Marshal's life had been one devoid of politics. It was a situation he did not mind. John d'Erly joined us for dinner and they talked about the King's plans.

"So, you have not been consulted on this plan, my lord?" John asked incredulously.

"Nay, Sir John. Actually, the timing is good for such a venture. The King finally enjoys some good will from the end of the Langton controversy. The people of England are more supportive because of Philip's threat to invade us. Some of the barons are willing to have Philip, but most of the people are not. If they coordinate the attack on Philip carefully, it has a chance of success. The

King always claimed he would recover his lands. Now is a good time to honor the pledge," the Marshal said showing his support for the plan.

"Yea, but the best man to handle the coordination is not going," John added as he stabbed an apple with his knife.

"I have been asked to send men, but I have been instructed to remain here. I am too old."

"Rubbish! Softsword has not the skill to carry it off. He will do something to mess it up. He has a history of such." Sir John waved his hand in a gesture of frustration and almost dropped the apple.

The Marshal raised his flagon of brew, examined it carefully and then said, "I hope you are wrong. If this fails there will be great trouble ahead. One more defeat and the enemies King John has made in England will come a calling. We will be courting a civil war. I understand he recently tried to seduce the daughter of Robert Fitz-Walter." I rolled my eyes at this information. The pig was still at it.

"The man has a beautiful wife and he still tries to bed anyone who catches his eye. Have you seen her?" Sir John asked the Marshal as he sipped his ale. The Lady Isabel injected her observations of the Queen who bore the same name as her own.

"She is one of the most beautiful of women with ebony hair, large eyes and skin as soft as a peach. She does not deserve the disrespect the King shows her. She has given him a fine-looking son. 'Tis a pity that such loyalty goes unrewarded," she said as she gestured for the servants to remove the remains of the dinner. I rolled my eyes at this comment and missed a chord on my lute causing the company to look in my direction. They knew what I was thinking and we all laughed. The Marshal continued.

"It bodes ill for all of us. I regret I must send you, my friend, but it is my obligation." His tone turned somber. He set his flagon down and placed his hand on the shoulder of his friend.

"Unfortunately I still have bad dreams about the prospect. I have heard Lewellyn tell of Baldwin's experience in the Irish fiasco. I hope I will be able to come back alive," John said as he grasped the hand and gave it an appreciative squeeze.

"Stay safe, my friend. Friends like you are hard to find these days," the Marshal implored. The warning caused me to think briefly of those dear friends we had lost over the years: Baldwin de Bethune, Raoul de Hamars, Hugh de Hamelcourt and others. I was afraid another would be added to the list—this man who I once jealously mistrusted and who now was almost as dear to me as my master. The rest of the evening was spent in discussing old times and the Marshal's family. The Marshal shared his thoughts about the estrangement with his son, William. It weighed heavily on him. It would become even worse.

The gradual greening of the fields again spoke of the promise of the spring. The ewes gave birth increasing the flocks and the villeins planted the fields. Once this had been accomplished the Marshal selected the men that would be sent to the French campaign. Families said their good-byes as the young men were armed and prepared to march to the port of Southampton. It was another contradiction that spring, a time of rebirth of the land would see so many young men march off to face death. The next day as John prepared to leave he gave me this advice.

"Troubadour, take care of your master. I know we will need him in the future."

"And you stay well for I know he will need you." I was earnest in my wish for I knew how close he had become with the Marshal. Already saddened by the situation with his son, another loss could have a bad effect on the old warrior.

I climbed the steps of the battlements to the bartizan where the Marshal stood watching his men marching out of Pembroke castle. John d'Erly was in the lead. My lord turned to me and said sadly, "Lewellyn, this is the first time I have sent friends to fight without going with them. This is a bitter day in my life." He stood silently watching until they could be seen no more, as if he was trying to be with them for as long as he could. As the last cart faded from sight, he turned to me and his sad eyes said everything. There was no need for words to pass between us. He turned around and slowly walked to the steps slightly bent over. I followed, thinking of John's statement about King John: "...he will do something to mess it up."

His prediction sadly came true. King John failed to keep in good communication with the forces of Otto. The two pronged attack never happened. Philip did not have to divide his force and on July 27 the full brunt of the French attack occurred at the village of Bouvines. Softsword suffered another humiliating defeat. True to form, he quickly retreated and left Philip in permanent control of the northern part of the Angevin empire. Because of his failure, Otto was replaced as German Emperor and John's hopes of regaining the Angevin lands were gone. The impact of the defeat was tempered at Pembroke castle by the joy we felt when we learned Sir John was not among those who were lost. He returned with tales of more bungling by the King.

The ill will King John had sown for years was fully grown and ripe. Add to this, a king who berates his army for losing, then taxes his subjects heavily to pay for those failures, and you have a recipe for rebellion. King Richard's taxes were just as onerous, but he at least provided victories.

Now all the past grievances came home to roost. When asked to replace the revenues in the royal coffers again, the barons balked. Orders from a poor leader often get ignored. King John had few friends left.

Resistance to the King took many forms. The feelings of the common man were expressed by William Fitz-Osbert. He complained taxes ground down the poor while rich lords did not share the burden. He was hanged for his trouble. Far more serious were the disgruntled barons. The King's disregard for their privileges caused them to organize resistance. Led by men who had been personally abused, Eustace de Vesey, Robert Fitz-Walter, the Saire de Quincey, the barons discussed ways to curb the power of the weakened King John. They were soon joined by the Archbishop of Canterbury and Sir William Mowbray. The presence of the latter meant young William Marshal had joined the opposition to the King.

It was a difficult time for the Marshal. I was asked to send a communication to his son asking him to reconsider his stand. There was no reply. More nobles joined the opposition. Archbishop Langton however still hoped to avoid a civil war. Being a scholar, he suggested a charter be drawn and presented to the King for his signature. It would be a document the Archbishop could write to settle the issues with the King. King John realized his position was a weak one and he prepared to seek a compromise with the barons.

At Pembroke we remained silent. The Marshal could not bring himself to violate his oath. For this reason he was one of the few the King considered loyal. In early June of 1215 we received a letter from the King. I read it to the Marshal.

"My lord, the King requests you proceed to Runnymede on the Thames. You will be his representative in discussions with the forces arrayed against him." I lowered the document and looked to see how the Marshal would respond to this unwanted order.

"Prepare our things. I like not that which I am asked to perform, but I will honor my oath. I must oppose many of my friends, even my own son." I could see the strain of years on his face. His heart was not in this task, but again he would not break faith with his word.

It was a small band who rode to the meeting with the barons. It indicated just how much the King had destroyed the loyalty of his nobles. Even the Marshal had reason to side with the others, considering his treatment at the hands of King John. Tragically, his unwillingness to violate his oath had trapped him into an unwanted position. I would not have been so noble.

The day was warm. It would grow hotter in many ways before the event ended. We reached the collection of tents where the discussions would be held. The barons were led by Fitz-Walter and de Vesey. Archbishop Langton represented the concerns of the church and the lord mayor of London the interests of the commoners. The fact that it was the first time I had seen the Archbishop showed how isolated we had been at Pembroke for the last few years. He was of average height and thin. It meant he was a true man of God, not concerned with the pleasures so many high churchmen with wide bellies enjoyed. His thin face was careworn and stern. This was a serious man. The barons were in full armor as if they expected some treachery, a good precaution when dealing with King John. Many were surprised to see the Marshal instead of the King but were somewhat pleased to deal with a man they respected. It put them at ease. The banners proclaiming which families were in opposition were in full view. As the noon sun grew increasingly intense, some of the formal armor was periodically discarded.

The discussions centered on the traditional rights of the barons to control their estates and the wealth they produced. The complaint was the King's increasing use of the scutage. It was clear the barons wanted to keep their wealth safe from a king who used it in failed wars. Archbishop Langton wished to keep the prerogatives of the Church safe from the encroachment of royal power. There was little concern for the welfare of the common subjects until the Archbishop sided with the lord mayor of London and spoke of common law rights of merchants and townspeople. Not wanting to lose a united front against the unpopular king, the barons went along with the provision. It took two days to finally produce a document for King John's signature. The Marshal agreed to bring the King the next day, June 15, 1215, to the site for the signing.

I spoke to the Marshal that night about the charter which had been drawn up. "My lord, can a mere paper prevent more bloodshed?" I asked with some trepidation.

"Lewellyn, there are some reasonable requests included in the document. The King might not see it the same way as I, but it is a fair compromise. If he fails to agree there will be a war which he will surely lose. Again I must instruct him in ways he does not wish to hear. This time there will be no voices to dispute the facts. The King will agree," he said with certainty.

The following morning the King prepared to go to the signing. He was very aware of the fact he had no choice. King John was stubborn, but not completely stupid. I overheard him speaking to one of his sycophants as we prepared to leave for Runnymede.

"A deplorable situation that we are forced to agree to this rubbish, but it will not stand. These bastards will pay for their insolence. We will bide our time. Then we will see who is master of England." He smiled and prepared to go. The treacherous nature of King John had not changed. As usual, his word meant nothing. I knew, like all the other promises he made, the charter was a promise he would not live up to.

It was a very hot afternoon when the document was signed. A bitter King left the field. A contented Sir William Marshal started for home. He was again hopeful his last years would be ones of peace with his family. He expressed his thoughts to me as we rode home.

"Lewellyn, I hope this will bring some peace to my life and the return of the love of my son. The charter is good for the country and good for the people. I think we have done some good. I hope the King will realize the value of tranquility with his subjects," he said as he looked out over the countryside with hopeful eyes.

I thought of the words I had overheard from the King. They offered little hope the Marshal's wish would come true. I said nothing. The Marshal deserved some peace of mind and I would not be the one to disturb his thoughts, but I knew the King would wait and scheme. The ride back to Pembroke seemed longer than usual, made so because I knew there were more trials ahead, more war and more important roles for the Marshal to play. They would be roles that could cost the dear man his life when all he sought was peace. Sadly, peace is usually determined by the actions of the nefarious not the righteous. I hoped some act of God would remove the festering boil that was King John for the good of the people of England. It would do much to restore my faith. After all, his three older brothers had met untimely deaths.

Within a month of the signing, the King had repented his signature. To gain papal support he offered to finance a crusade. He was able to secure the support of Pope Innocent, who declared the Charter invalid because his vassal, John, had signed it under duress.

For nine months we were blissfully ignorant of these events. We heard very little and the Marshal was content to enjoy his family. Young William had not made any effort to reconcile with his father.

John d'Erly returned from his annual trip to Winchester to pay our tax in late May of 1216. Over a noon meal the Marshal asked if all was quiet in the kingdom. The answer did not come as a surprise to me.

"My lord, King John is hiring mercenaries. His agents have secured the services of some of the vilest routiers on the continent." John then gave a list of names. It was not a group the Marshal wanted to be associated with.

"I pray God will spare us trouble. I am not willing to raise my sword against my eldest son. It may be that I must fail in my oath for the first time." There was great sadness in his eyes as he mouthed the unthinkable. John continued with more news.

"The recent death of his half brother Geoffrey of York has given the King some relief that opposition might rally around the Archbishop. He was with him when he passed. There are those who think King John might have helped advance the demise." It was sad news for me in ways that only the Marshal and I knew. "One more thing, my lord, for some strange reason the King requests the services of your servant Lewellyn. He claims to need a good scribe. I cannot see the need, but he was most insistent that he be sent immediately." My heart almost stopped. I looked with terror at the Marshal. What was the meaning and what could the Marshal do? Failure to obey a royal order could bring a death sentence for the entire family.

"We shall inform the King that our servant was sent to Ireland to deal with some affairs. Then we shall tell the King of his demise on the return trip," the Marshal said casually.

John looked puzzled. I spoke up since it was my fate being decided.

"Nay, my lord. Were this plan to be discovered all at Pembroke would perish. They are all too dear to me. I will not allow you to disobey the King's command. I will go. Many years ago, in a dark cell you told me a man was the master of his honor. Allow me this before the tendrils of fear have time to weaken my resolve," I said trying not to shake. A tear leaked from the corner of my lord's eye as he nodded his assent. I went to my chamber to pack my things. Underneath my mat I removed a small leather bag and placed it in my girdle. If the King's plan for me included torture to make me bare false witness against the Marshal I would rob him of the opportunity.

In the morning I bade farewell to Lady Isabel and the family. I embraced each of the children. Gilbert and Richard shook my hand as men. Two of the older daughters were becoming women. Sibilla the oldest and the most emotional wept when I said I might not return to continue her music lessons. She kissed my cheek and gave me a wonderful hug. The Lady Isabel held both my hands and with tears streaming down her beautiful face said, "We will be together again. This too will pass. God will see you are returned to us," she declared with absolute conviction. I knew then I was making the right choice.

The Marshal helped me mount and said, "Thou art my friend and conscience. I do this reluctantly. I believe it is God's punishment for my many sins that my oath compels us to serve so vile a creature as the King," he said uttering treason on my behalf.

"Nay, my lord, you serve England." I could not bear for my lord to risk anything further or to reproach himself. I turned the horse and rode out of the gate before the tears began to stream down my cheeks. I held my head erect and turned down the path which would lead to Winchester and my fate.

In two days' time I arrived only to find that the King was off gathering his mercenaries. My execution would not come this day. I wondered if John would lock me up and starve me as he did many of those he deemed a threat to his plans. I would have to wait. Softsword was off with his new army. I remained at Winchester contemplating my fate and hoping that divine intervention would make an end of the hated King John.

In late August, King John prepared to let loose his mercenary army. He did not seek the Marshal's active participation, much to my relief. The Marshal would not have to fight his son. I was sure the King considered him to be too old to be of any use. The Pope prepared to support the King by threatening to excommunicate all of the rebel barons.

Archbishop Langton went to Rome to get the Pope to reconsider. The result was not what he hoped for. The Pope refused to see him and suspended him for a period of two years. He was not allowed to return to England. Without his support, the barons forgot the concerns of the townspeople and prepared to defend their personal interests. They sent a delegation to ask Prince Louis of France to come to England and replace King John. Although King John was unpopular, the people of England did not wish to trade him for a French king, a king who would, in all probability, also ignore the new charter. The people as usual were forgotten. The same men who had forced the signing of the Great Charter were now ready to abandon it to save their property. Their word meant nothing also.

In order to discourage Philip's participation, the pope's legate, GualoBianchieri, said anyone who helped the barons would be excommunicated. England was still a fief of Rome. King Philip said openly, he opposed his son going to England. Court gossip said the statements by Philip were a sham. Secretly, he encouraged the boy to seek the title. Louis' marriage to Blanche of Castile, Queen Eleanor's granddaughter, was his claim to the throne. It was a weak claim, but Blanche had her grandmother's ambitious personality. She actively supported her husband's attempt. Engaging the services of the infamous pirate, Eustace the Monk, Louis sailed for England to join the rebel barons. Reinforcements would be sent as soon as Philip could secretly organize them.

The mercenaries were stationed in the castles north of London. They would have to be paid if King John expected them to repel the coming attacks. To accomplish this, the King sent for the royal treasure at Winchester. The wagons that carried the wealth also carried me. We arrived at King's Lynn two days later. I was summoned to King John's chambers late in the evening. As I walked down the corridor with two guards I thought about what I would say. I vowed to face my fate with courage and dignity. I would not grovel and beg for my life.

The King was in a red and gold dressing gown sitting at the edge of his large draped bed. A chamberlain and several other servants were preparing him for his nightly repose. He looked at me and gave that familiar thin smile that was more like a sneer.

"Leave us," he ordered his attendants. He stood by the bed and I could see a jeweled dagger hanging from his hip. Was he going to dispatch me himself? My eyes darted around the chamber to see if a weapon was handy. There were none save the one the King possessed. He read my thoughts.

"There are no weapons, sirrah. Or should I say—brother! Yes, I know. Geoffrey confirmed my suspicions before he died. I always wondered why the Marshal kept you near. Then there were the facial features you shared with our father. I should have seen it earlier, but I could not understand why you would willingly live as one of the serving class. Perhaps to keep you safe so the Marshal could use you to rally support against me someday. His own son takes the field with the traitor Mowbrey," he said as he watched to see if I would make some type of move. His hand was now grasping the hilt of his dagger. I realized running was futile and an attack was just as silly so I decided to play for time.

"Your Majesty is mistaken. The Marshal is your most loyal servant even to the estrangement of his son William. I have served the Marshal since I was a boy. My mother was a seamstress in the service of Queen Eleanor. Is this some game for entertainment? Do you wish me to make up a song?" I remained calm.

"Is it possible you know not the secret?" There was doubt in his voice. "'Tis possible you are ignorant of the facts. We shall see. After we deliver the payment to our mercenaries tomorrow we shall pursue the mystery further. Guards!" Within seconds several burly soldiers appeared in the doorway. "Keep this sirrah near the royal wagons. He will serve my dinner at the Abby after we cross the Wash on the morrow."

I was taken away and ordered to stay in one of the wagons in the courtyard. I slept very little that night. I was to be humiliated by serving my half brother his meal. Rage seethed in my blood as I recalled the Marshal's last words about a vile king. I could not escape; for to do so would mean death for those I loved. Taking my own life with the contents in my girdle would have the same result. I was desperate. Was God punishing me for my lack of faith? I finally prayed, for the first time in years, for God to help me find a way save those at Pembroke who would suffer unfairly for my sins.

The wagons loaded with treasure began to move in the morning. We stopped several times for the fat King John to enjoy several quick meals. We reached the ford around three. The spot was about half a mile wide with water no more than ankle deep. The King was in a hurry and chose to ignore local advice against cross the Wash late in the afternoon. The ford at this spot on the river was heavily influenced by the tides. One had to choose crossing times carefully. The King was sure he could cross quickly, but the shallow marsh mud caused the wagons to move slowly.

It was then the divine intervention I had prayed for happened. God chose to punish the man who had caused a lifetime of pain and anguish. The tide began rising quickly. Water went from ankle deep to knee deep. It rose so fast the wagons with their heavy loads became immovable. Horses and men panicked. What had been muddy marsh became an arm of the sea. Like the biblical story of the pharaoh chasing Moses, the waters closed on the wagons that bore the King's treasure. Those of us on the wagons swam for our lives. Fortunately I was in the vanguard and was close to the far shore. Those who could not swim were helpless. Those in the middle and back of the train had no chance. In the powerful pull of the sea, all wagons and swimmers disappeared never to be seen again. The King could only stand on the bank and scream in disbelief. The money for his mercenaries was gone. Soon the routiers he hired would also be gone. Sadly he was still alive.

Those who survived rode to the nearby monastery. It was October 18. That night as I prepared to serve his supper the King was not visibly shaken by the tragedy of the day's events. Perhaps he believed that he would recover his treasure when the tide retreated in the morning. It was false hope. What the sea had taken it would not give back. The local fishermen told us this when they delivered the fish for the meal. The King gorged himself on several plates of lampreys. It was his last act of gluttony. Even his favorite food had turned against him. In the night he began to have severe stomach pains. The next night, during a howling rainstorm, King John died in horrible pain and deliriously swearing he had been poisoned. It was dismissed as the confused mind of a dying man since all his dishes had been tasted before they were served and the taster showed no ill effects.

Before he died, he mumbled to his servants something about the King's son and the Earl of Pembroke. When the servants told this to the King's chamberlain he decided to ask other members of the court what he meant. The nobles agreed King John in his final moments wisely trusted the fate of nine-year-old Henry, his only son, to the only man everyone knew could be trusted.

Why had the King chosen him to protect his son? Like his father and brothers before him, when times became the most difficult, the Plantagenets had always turned to the same man—William Marshal. Each time they did, it proved to be the correct decision. After all had not the King personally requested the presence of the Marshal's trusted servant? Perhaps he had a vision of the future and that was why he wanted me on this trip. I expressed surprise at this notion, but said I would be glad to return to my master with the dying king's last request. It was agreed. I smiled as I rode back to Pembroke. God had intervened in a strange way. My faith was returning.

Chapter 15
Another King, Another War

Shortly after I returned to Pembroke with the news of the King's demise, the Marshal was summoned to Devizes to meet Queen Isabella and her nine-year-old son. It was a precarious position since a civil war was about to explode. The French prince Louis had landed at Sandwich. He had taken possession of London and the Eastern regions of England with the help of the rebel barons. The outlook for the country was bleak. As we packed our horses for the journey I explained how the King had been called to account by God. I felt little remorse for the loss of this horrible man. The Marshal asked if there was any truth to the rumor the king was poisoned. I turned up my hands and shrugged my shoulders. The Lady Isabel smiled and said, "I would not look very hard for the culprit if the rumors are true. He has done the country a service." She could not forgive the heartache he had visited upon her family.

The Marshal frowned and said, "You should be more charitable to the dead. He was the King. I have lived to see the end of all Queen Eleanor's sons. I owe all that I am to her and I am sad it has come to this. The people will suffer again."

"Husband, you have earned all we have. The great lady knew it. You ignore a lifetime of helping them to see the proper path, help that was ignored to their peril." She kissed his cheek as he mounted his horse. "Now you will be called upon to set things right again. You will answer that call regardless of the cost. Nay, husband, you owe none. 'Tis they who owe you." I mounted my horse, smiled at the Lady Isabel and nodded my approval to her speech. We rode out of the gate with a small company of knights.

I spoke to the Marshal as we rode to the meet with the widowed Queen.

"My lord, what will happen now the King is dead? Will we be ruled by the French prince?" I asked hesitatingly.

"Lewellyn, the people of England will never accept a French king. I have heard William of Kenesham is already leading attacks against the invaders from the forests of the Weald. They are calling him the 'Willikin.' I am hopeful some of the barons will change their position now John is gone. We have the new charter and I believe it has popular support. Although Pope Innocent was against it, we received word of his death while you were gone. It will mean a new Pope. I believe his successor might be more inclined to support it. A message from the papal legate has led me to that conclusion. Louis is not obligated by the charter. I will make sure John's son declares his support for it, and I hope the rebel barons will see no reason to continue to support this French pretender's claim." He snorted his contempt at this last statement and returned to his thinking about the future.

"What will your role be, my lord?" I asked the logical question knowing the high regard in which my master was held by the nobles of England.

"Only one of advice. I am old. I am not the one to set things right. Not withstanding my loving wife's words. Little Henry is the rightful heir. Louis' claim to the throne is not legitimate. I shall pledge my loyalty to the boy when we meet him. He will need guidance and I will suggest the Earl of Chester be appointed Regent," he said with satisfaction that there was another to take the mantle of kingmaker he had born so heavily these past years.

"I would suggest you, my lord!" I offered enthusiastically.

"You jest. Look at me. I am almost eighty. I need to return to Pembroke and live, what is left of my life, in peace. If some of the rebel barons do not see reason there will be a civil war. I do not belong on the battlefield. I will give financial support to whoever is chosen for this difficult task. England must not become a French fiefdom. It has been over one hundred years since the Conqueror. We are a different people and that road need not be traveled again!" he said with firmness. It was the reason why they need a man with his conviction. I knew little of the Earl of Chester, but I trusted the Marshal's endorsement.

I did not say anything else. We were unsure of his real age. There was some confusion about when he was born, but I was sure he was not eighty. Although his fighting skills were nowhere near what they had been, he could still swing a sword as well as many knights, his mind was sharp and no one in the kingdom was more trustworthy. I did agree his long and illustrious career had earned him rest and retirement. He had served four Plantagenets with distinction. Asking him to serve another would be asking a lot. Yet, in my heart, I believed he would be the best man. After all, Queen Eleanor had served the kingdom in her seventies, and served it well. We spoke no more about the subject.

As we approached the plains of Malmesbury, we saw the royal party riding toward us. The colorful banners designating the houses of the various retainers fluttered in the gentle breeze. It added an air of elegance to what otherwise would have looked like a simple gathering of riders. Our small party dismounted to show proper respect. With my head bowed I had a difficult time trying to see the new boy who was going to be named King , but I managed a peek. The Prince was sharing a mount with one of the retainers. He had his mother's good looks, but was small like his father and unlike his uncle Richard. I briefly thought back to the day long ago when a youthful Richard had mistaken me for his brother. I doubted this prince would ever achieve the size or bearing of the Lionhearted. His mother still possessed the beauty which had caused King John to abandon his first wife. She was clothed in the appropriate outfit of mourning. It did little to dim the radiance of the lady. The Marshal knelt. The Prince nodded acknowledging the sign of respect and spoke to him.

"Good sir, we commit ourselves to your safe keeping. May God give you the grace to help us." He looked at the kneeling Marshal and smiled.

The Marshal was moved by the speech from one so young. There were tears in his eyes as he replied, "Sire, I pledge my loyalty to you. Although I am no longer young, as long as God grants me the strength, I will serve you faithfully." The old warrior rose from his knees. The moment moved all to a tear or two, including the young Prince.

The Marshal spoke to quickly remind us of the danger we faced in a country on the brink of war, "Sire, we must make haste for the safety of Gloucester. I would fail in my duty if I allowed us to be caught here in the open. At Gloucester we will organize your support. We must go."

The combined parties now rode swiftly in the direction of the ancient city. The task ahead was a daunting one. Was it possible to organize major opposition to Louis and the rebel barons? We had a nine-year-old boy as the heir to a very unpopular king and the royal treasury was washed out to sea. The other side had everything we lacked: money, control of London, more men under arms and ships to see they were re-supplied. I did not see how we could win. In my stupidity, I forgot the one advantage the Marshal was counting on—the good people of England.

At Gloucester we were joined by the others who supported young Prince Henry. Discussions were held immediately. It was decided the Prince should be crowned at once. The Marshal said if the people had an English king presented to them it would make the task of rallying support much easier. He said we had to rely on the common folk to have any chance of success. The nobles might accept a Frenchman as their king, but the people would not.

The Bishop of Winchester, Peter de Roches, would officiate at the crowning ceremony. He was a man I would learn to dislike. Unlike Archbishop Langton this man looked to worldly power more than spiritual power. He was just the kind of man the dead King John would have appointed when Archbishop Langton had received the blessing from a wise Pope several years earlier. His narrow face and sharp nose gave him a hawk-like appearance. He had a sharp voice with a nasal sounding wheeze. Power was this man's grail quest! Any man who blocked that goal would be considered an enemy. At this time his influence was muted by the presence of the Marshal, and his own inability to inspire men to follow his lead.

The Marshal was charged with the ceremonial responsibility of knighting the boy. It was the second time he knighted a prince of the realm with a war on the horizon. The coronation which followed the next day would be a simple ceremony for many reasons. First, there was a need for haste. Second, the events had occurred with such rapidity, the nobles present did not have time to retrieve their finest garments. Third, the royal crown was lost in the quick sands of the Wash. They only had a plain circlet to use for the coronation.

Several major allies were not able to be present. The Chief justiciar, Hubert de Burgh, was besieged in Dover castle by Prince Louis' army. The Earl of Chester, the man the Marshal preferred to be regent was due to arrive soon, but was still en route to Gloucester. Despite all this, the ceremony proceeded on October 27, nine days after the death of King John.

The reaction of the townspeople to the coronation showed how right the Marshal was in his assessment of the English people. The cries of "long live the King" were heard outside the church after Henry spoke the oath. The handsome boy played his part well. The banquet to celebrate the event was not much more than a Sunday dinner, like the kind we enjoyed regularly at Pembroke. It was a very simple day which belied the significance it held for the kingdom. As I spoke to those gathered outside the church, it was evident they wanted the French chased out of their homeland. When I told the Marshal that night, he smiled and nodded his head approvingly. He said the task was to effectively harness this support.

The following day we rode to Lancaster to begin the work of repelling the French force. Lancaster was a safe place where meetings could be held to decide what actions needed to be taken. Above all was the question of who would act as regent for the just crowned Henry III. There were many possibilities. Peter de Roches, Bishop of Winchester, was anxious for the role. Ranulf, the Earl of Chester, had good qualifications. Perhaps Gualo, the papal legate, would be chosen; after all England was still considered a fief of Rome. There was Hubert de Burgh, if he survived the siege. He had shown great courage in opposing the invaders and last, the one man who did not want the job, the Earl of Pembroke, William Marshal. I was not invited to the meeting, due to my lowly status. I was to learn of the deliberations of this gathering when the Marshal returned with a very troubled look.

"My lord, what troubles you?" I asked fearing bad news.

"They want me to be regent and organize everything," he said as he dropped his chin to his chest and sought refuge in a chair in the corner of the room.

"I knew it! 'Tis the wisest choice. All will follow you! You are the most respected man in the entire kingdom. Even that churl King John knew it before he died," I shouted as my excitement bubbled over.

"Do not speak ill of the dead, Lewellyn," he rebuked me with a tired voice.

"I beg pardon, lord. I heartily agree with those who chose you. You will accept?" I swallowed my loathing for the dead king out of respect for the Marshal and hoping to hear an affirmative response.

"Nay, Lewellyn, I am too old and tired for so difficult a task. There is an army to be raised, a government to be organized and a war to be fought. I am not the one to do all of this. The papal legate was too excited when he urged the others to select me. In the morning he will see reason. I believe the Earl of Chester will be here by then and I will urge the others to support him. I have offered to contribute funds to pay Falkes de Breaute and his mercenaries. He is an able fighter and we need his routiers desperately. The grand master of the Templars has also offered funds. I have counted him among my good friends since the days I spent with him in Syria." With that he tilted his head back and took a deep breath.

"But my lord, who has more experience than you? The people of the towns would follow you in such a cause. They would not trust a strutting courtier like the Bishop of Winchester in this struggle. You, yourself, said we would need the people." I pleaded my case with what I believed to be solid logic.

"You are right about de Roches. He fancies himself as regent. I suspect I was named by Gualo to thwart Winchester's ambitions. Nay, I wish to go home to my loving wife and my family. I do not want to take the field against my own son!" he said reminding me that young William was among those supporting the Prince of France.

I had no answer for this argument. What would I do if my own son had come to fight in England? I could understand the Marshal's reluctance. We spoke no more of the events of the day. I took the Marshal's green silk tabard and hung it by the hearth in our small room. I started a fire in the fireplace as the late fall chill ran through the castle. I knew it would quickly heat a room of this size and make us more comfortable. I was wondering what would happen the next day, when the Earl of Chester made his entrance. Would the Marshal be able to sway the opinions of the others, or would someone like de Roches emerge?

To my great surprise and delight, I was asked by the Marshal to attend the meeting to record the discussions. Once again my skill with the pen allowed me to go where one of my station was rarely allowed. The legate Gualo called the meeting to order. The Earl of Chester was now present. He was a large and distinguished-looking man. I surmised he was fifteen years younger than the Marshal. I could see why the Marshal felt he was a fine choice. Also in the gathering was our good friend Sir John d'Erly who had arrived just before the meeting was called to order. I smiled at him and he nodded.

The first to speak was Sir Alan Basset. I recorded the following discussion.

"My lords, we all agreed yesterday the Marshal is the man we all respect and desire to take up this weighty cause, but he has declined and suggests the Earl of Chester should be named regent. I still believe this room would willingly follow the Earl of Pembroke, but failing in that, will you, my lord Chester, accept the task?" he asked as he reached out his hand. All eyes turned to Ranulf de Blundeville, Earl of Chester. As he rose to his feet the room became very still. Eyes darted back and forth trying to see how each man would receive the answer that was about to be given. He paused for several seconds and then looking at my master he gave this response.

"There is no one in this room, nay the world, that is so loved, so trusted, so feared or so prudent as the Earl of Pembroke. You, sir, are the greatest knight alive. I am ready to serve loyally under you!" he shouted emphatically. A huge cheer rang out. I looked at the Marshal. A tear ran down his cheek. He looked pleadingly at the cheering throng. He held up his hands. The group was silent.

"I beg you reconsider, my lords," he said, again asking that this cup be passed to another.

The room full of men looked at each other and there was a pause while all considered the possibilities of the second refusal. Into the breach of silence, Gualo, the papal representative, injected this comment. "My lords, might I impose a brief rest whilst I confer with the Earl of Pembroke in an adjoining room." He walked over, placed his arm on the Marshal's shoulder and whispered into the reluctant warrior's ear. They exited the room into a small antechamber talking softly. They were soon followed by the Earl of Chester and de Roches.

What was being discussed? We chatted nervously trying to divine the purpose of the legate's private talk. After half an hour the four men entered the hall again. The nobles were hushed and waited for someone to speak. What had been decided? Who would lead them in this difficult but necessary task?

Gualo stood with the Marshal and announced in his most solemn voice, "The Earl of Pembroke will lead us!" The hall erupted with shouts and cheers. I looked at my friend John d'Erly and we both cheered ourselves hoarse. All were excited, all except the man who had been chosen. The Marshal had a very worried look. He did not share the enthusiasm reverberating in the great hall. The meeting was adjourned and we began to file out of the great hall still buzzing with excitement.

We returned to our room with John d'Erly and the Marshal's cousin, also called John. Once again, I prepared a small fire and served some ale. The Marshal looked exceedingly glum.

"My friends, I asked you here to help me. I see myself upon an ocean with no shore in sight. I am asked to save a king that is just a boy and one who does not have a single gold coin to his name. I am old and God has seen fit to give me this responsibility. What am I to do?" he asked. It was the first time I had ever seen indecision wrinkle the aging face. If this man who had spent a lifetime making quick decisions was unsure then things must be dire indeed!

It was the Marshal's old squire and dear friend John d'Erly who spoke.

"My lord, no one deserves a rest more than you, but times like these require more of men than they think they can give. You will save this land and its people to your everlasting credit. You told each of us in this room, at one time or another, of the honor your code demands of each man. You have spent a lifetime upholding that code regardless of the danger it placed on you or your family. I have no doubt you will honor that code again. We have committed our lives to follow you and lead us you shall!" he declared and slapped his fist against his chest.

With John's speech I saw an amazing transformation. The look of determination returned to his eye. His powerful frame stood erect in the way I had seen so many times before. The confidence that inspired men to follow him was back. They would follow because he was what all men hoped they could be. He did not need courtiers and troubadours to sing his praises. Deeds not words were the platform on which he alone could stand. Just to be present at such a moment is a humbling experience. It was as if God wanted to reward his servant by rolling back the years which sat so heavily on the Marshal's shoulders. I felt my skin tingle as he spoke with the look of determination twinkling in his eye.

"By God's glove, we shall do this! If necessary I will carry the king on my back from town to town, and to my lands in Ireland if need be, but we shall prevail! As long as God gives me breath, I will not fail him or you, my friends." His fire had returned and with it the years seemed to melt the years away. The booming heart of the warrior renewed the aging muscles. I knew, at that moment, England was saved. He would find a way no matter what force was arrayed against us.

The men left. The Marshal and I were alone. I was curious as to why the Marshal had changed his mind about accepting the charge of the gathering when until this moment his doubts had lingered. What had transpired in the room that none of us had been privileged to hear? Unable to resist I asked.

"My lord, what did the legate say to change your mind?"

"When we went into the side room, the papal legate said if I took on this challenge I would be doing God's work. He said I would be absolved of my mortal sins. Lewellyn, a man in my profession, as close to being judged by God for his life's work as I am, could use absolution. There are many deaths which rest upon my soul. I have no desire to smell the brimstone when I am laid to my final rest. I also feared the cause might be endangered if the more ambitious were given this responsibility. At my age, ambition is no longer a consideration. I had my doubts, but John has rightly reminded me of the obligations I carry. I am ready to perform this last duty for my country before I die," he said smiling and placing his large hands on my shoulders.

"Do not speak of such things, my lord. I too feel the encroachment of age, but I shall take up the sword and follow you in this hour of need," I said pledging myself to the cause. I placed my hand on his and our eyes expressed that which words could not.

"Thank you, my oldest friend. I fear our numbers will force me to accept your pledge this time. We shall find a way to use your skills, but the use of a sword is not one of them!" he said with a grin.

"I will serve you in any way you desire," I said realizing that my excitement had given rise to a silly promise. Ardor does not replace experience on the field of battle.

"It is settled. In the morning you will travel to the Weald. I should like to communicate with William of Kenesham. I will continue to organize resistance here. We must arouse the populace. I know they will be with us, but it will take some time. Perhaps the activities of the Willikin can buy us that time," he said as the seeds of a plan were already germinating in his mind.

Up to this moment the men in the tavern listening to this amazing and also hard to believe tale have done little to disturb the old troubadour. To be sure there were nudges of elbows and winks as the old one spoke of kings and queens as if he were among them, but since it was entertaining they were silent in their skepticism. His outrageous claim of royal blood could be put down to fanciful storytelling, but as the story reached very recent times the silence is finally broken. One of the men in the back speaks up. His name is Oliver.

"Be careful of what you say, troubadour; I know the Willikin!" He smiles at his fellow patrons and they nod their approval. Oliver's adventures are well known in the tavern, having been shared many times over a brew on cold evenings. Scars on his arms speak of the courage of this local hero. He is confident he will be the one to put this fanciful tale back to its proper place.

Lewellyn just smiles. "I see you still doubt the truth of my story. Fair enough. I shall describe Willikin in such detail you will no longer have any doubts. If I am wrong then you may expose me to your friends as a fraud. I was hopeful when we came to this time there would be a witness to my tale. Now it has happened and I welcome it. Doubt no more.

"Willikin was the bailiff of the courts of the Seven Hundred of the Weald. He was tall and slender. He had brown hair and blue eyes. There was a small scar above his left eye. He said it came from a fall when he was a boy. His favorite weapon was the long bow. He was an excellent marksman and could ride a horse with great skill. He had very large hands and long fingers. I suspect it enhanced his skill with the bow. Is that, or is that not, your man?" he asks with an icy stare.

"Continue, troubadour. You have described him perfectly. I must confess I have doubted much of what you have said, but the fact you know him does not prove all your claims," Oliver says still unconvinced. The old man smiles again and nods his head several times.

"Perhaps, but you must judge for yourself. 'Tis possible I wish you not believe it all. In my excitement I may have revealed more than I should." He smiles again, shrugs his shoulders and begins to strum the lute again. The patrons look at each other and a nagging doubt is written on their faces. Could this man be what he claims or is he just another very clever liar? The troubadour continues.

The Marshal suggested I should travel with my lute. A wandering minstrel would not attract the attention of the rebel forces, whose lands I would have to cross to complete my mission. I was asked to make a mental note of any troops as I passed close to London. I even stopped at several taverns and entertained for my supper, much like I do now. It increased the impression I wished to convey and helped me complete my real mission. Once I entered the woodlands of the Weald, I became increasingly nervous. What if I was attacked by brigands? It was a real possibility. I tried not to think about it, when suddenly out of the brush several bowmen appeared.

"What have we here? A wandering minstrel with a full purse perhaps?" asked the larger of the two in a menacing voice. I decided to take a chance these might be Willikin's men and not highwaymen. After all, if they were bandits what I said would not matter. I would be stripped, and when they found little money, I would be killed.

"You have a poor minstrel who wishes England to remain English," I said hoping that my meaning would be understood.

"A curious answer, troubadour. And what else do you wish?" he asked eyeing me for hidden weapons.

"I wish to see a loyal William with a message from another loyal William."

"Interesting. Hal, bind him and bring him to our leader. We will see if his message is worth his life." My hands were shaking as they were bound. After a short ride into the depths of the forest I came upon a camp of several hundred men. In the middle was a tall man giving instructions to a small group who were mounted. Near him were several men holding horses. It was clear that the entire group could be mounted and gone at a moment's notice. He had a high-pitched voice and looked at me as our small group approached.

"Who be this?" he asked.

"I have a message for a loyal William from a loyal William," I said repeating my previous statement convinced I was in the hands of William of Kenesham.

"My name is William and what is yours?" he asked holding a long bow in his large hands and gently pressing it against my chest.

"I am called Lewellyn, personal servant to William Marshal, Earl of Pembroke, and I have a message for the one they call Willikin. I have a ring to prove my message is true." I produced the proof from under the saddle blanket of my horse when my hands were freed from their bonds. The slender man examined the Marshal's ring.

"You have found him. All have heard of your master. What is the message?" he said returning the ring. This action made it clear that I was not in the hands of outlaws.

"Prince Henry was crowned at Gloucester four days ago. The Marshal has been named regent and is organizing resistance to the French invasion. He needs time to gather men loyal to England and he hopes you can help. He will hold a national council in Bristol in a week. He wants to know if you can send a representative to the meeting," I said excited that I had succeeded in my quest.

"By God's eyes, we are not alone in this struggle. The Marshal you say. Have others joined him?" the Willikin asked.

"Yea, my lord. The Earl of Chester, Falkes de Breaute, the Bishop of Winchester and others have pledged support. My lord Pembroke says he expects more to join. The papal legate, Gualo, persuaded him to accept the post of regent. He believes the charter of Runnymede will be accepted by the new Pope, Honorius III. My master says it will unite the people of England against those supporting Louis. The French prince will not accept such a document. The Marshal feels some of the barons in rebellion will change sides," I said relating the last of my information.

"God be praised. We have a just cause and a legend to lead us. Tell your master I have a thousand men at his disposal," he said enthusiastically. We began walking back to where my horse was being held by a rather rotund man.

"The Marshal said you must continue to harass the French as they land. Slow their journey to London with fresh supplies," I said as I took the reins of my mount from the fat man.

"They already are afraid to come through the forest. I have left many hanging from the trees like pine cones as a warning to new arrivals. They take a long trip around the Weald to reach their destination. It will buy your master some of the time he needs, but first have something to eat before you return. I will make arrangements to see you return safely for you carry important news." He took the reins and returned it to the man. We walked over to a small fire where a pot of stew was cooking. I was given a bowl and spoon. As I ate the humble fare I continued my conversation with the one called Willikin. He listened while given orders continuously to several men around the fire.

"Have you heard anything about the fate of the Justiciar, Hubert de Burgh? We heard he was under siege at Dover," I asked, knowing we were not very far from the site of the struggle.

"He was. The stupid French agreed to a temporary truce giving him and his small force safe passage rather than continue a long siege. They expect it will allow them to quickly land more men. We shall make it a false hope. The Justiciar is on his way here. We shall inform him of what you have said. I suspect he will want to attend the meeting at Bristol. I will send you back with little Tom. He is a juggler and a natural companion to a minstrel. Neither of you will draw attention. Tell your master we now believe we will triumph. My archers will continue to do what we do best. You have brought great news for true Englishmen," he said smiling and rubbing his scar as if it were some kind of lucky talisman. We walked to where my horse was being held and there I saw a small dwarfish man perched atop a grey horse. He was grinning and joking with the man holding my horse. I assumed this was my traveling companion.

I felt proud. I had contributed. The Marshal had promised he would find a way for me to contribute, and like all his promises, it was kept. I had a great feeling of accomplishment as I returned to Bristol with the very funny Tom. We laughed most of the way.

The meeting at Bristol took place on November 11. Bristol was chosen because of the strong position it guarded as the Severn River emptied into the Bristol Channel. To the west were the lands of the Marshal in Wales and a stronghold of support. Cornwall lay to the south and was also a place of support. To the north were the lands of the Earl of Chester. The rebel barons in the east would find taking these strongholds difficult. The meeting place was a monastery atop a very steep hill overlooking the harbor.

I reported to the Marshal about the conditions in the Weald. He was pleased by the report. His confidence continued to grow. He said it was now up to him to justify Willikin's trust by gathering opposition forces. He was also delighted when Hubert, the justiciar, arrived from Dover. Discussions were held to decide what strategies to employ. I saw the Marshal's face light up as he explained his plans. It was as though a youth-restoring elixir had been given to my master. No longer was he a tired old man who resisted responsibility. He was a skilled campaigner, setting traps and clearly in charge of the moment. He spoke to the gathering.

"My lords, 'tis my firm belief we must hit and escape rather than attack the larger French force we face for the present. They will do little during the winter months. As they come west we must harass and retreat till we have sufficient men to launch a counter offensive. They must come to us. Louis is young and inexperienced. I hope it will lead to an error. However we must not forget the Barons Mowbray and de Vesey are seasoned campaigners; if they are heeded we will be in for a protracted struggle. Philip d'Aubigny, as warden of the Channel Islands, you must have ships ready to repel any sea-born invasions led by Eustace the Monk," he said looking in the direction of a burly man standing with his arms folded across his chest. d'Aubigny nodded his agreement. The man had the leathery look of a sea captain and arms that reminded me of the Marshal's in his younger years. He spoke with a confident and gruff voice.

"My Lord Marshal, the captains of the Cinque ports have many scores to settle with the Monk, but he is very feared. There are those who say he possesses the skills of the black arts, but if he be the very devil himself I will not allow him to set foot on my England," he said defiantly. This was not a man to whom fear was a common companion. The storms that often raged in the Channel had the effect of tempering these hardy men.

The Marshal and Hubert were sure d'Aubigny's ships would be critical. The Marshal admired the bold speech. He made a promise to the brave captain.

"Philip, I am aware of how important your work will be. I give you the cog I use to transport goods from my Irish holdings for your use."

"I shall try and see that it be returned in one piece when this adventure is ended." He laughed as did many of the assembly. "I will rally the captains of Sussex and Kent. If my Lord Marshal is successful in turning some of the barons, Louis will need help from France to reinforce his army and that must be prevented at all costs. England's fate could rest with our ships." He bowed as he finished.

With a military strategy developed, discussions turned to the important subject of politics. The Marshal was officially given the title Rector noster et Regni nostri. Hubert was reconfirmed as Chief Justiciar. Peter de Roches was asked by the Marshal to protect the King. The Marshal specifically asked to be relieved temporarily of that responsibility since the planning and execution of military strategy would occupy most of his attention.

The discussion turned to the charter of Runnymede. The Marshal spoke to the issue. "My lords, it is my earnest belief the charter need be affirmed by the leadership at Bristol. It is a reasonable document and the common folk strongly believed in the sections Archbishop Langton had added about their rights. In fact, they now call it 'Magna Carta.' If this body expresses their support for the document it could help rally the countryside. Help that is sorely needed," he said as he scanned the gathering to see if there was agreement in their eyes.

The legate Gualo agreed and said, "My lords, I believe the new Pope could be persuaded to endorse the charter if the Church's rights are protected." The Marshal and the legate suggested a few small changes to be sure there would be a Papal blessing. The assembled nobles approved the new document and several copies were made. As a scribe I helped. They were sent to different parts of the kingdom where they could be read to the people. Mine was sent to Salisbury. One last act was suggested by the Marshal; the loyalists would wear the white cross as a symbol of God's support for the cause. Gualo used his papal authority to sanction the action.

The Bristol meeting adjourned and each member went to execute their responsibility as follows: Falkes de Breaute to the castles in the western counties to prepare for sieges, Philip d'Aubigny to organize the Cinque Ports, Peter de Roches to Gloucester to watch over the boy king, Hubert de Burgh back to Dover and the Marshal to Pembroke to contact as many barons as he thought he could influence.

I spent most of the winter months writing the letters the Marshal dictated. In them, he stressed the need for the barons to return to the royal cause. His efforts were aided by the foolish decisions of the French pretender. Louis angered some of his English allies by refusing to trust them. He refused to accept any English suggestions. He placed less experienced French nobles in positions of command. These arrogant actions gave credence to the warnings the Marshal expressed in his letters. Why should English nobles trust their fate to a French monarch who would be no better than King John? The Marshal emphasized the document they had crafted at Runnymede would be no more than scrap if Louis won. He, on the other hand, would honor the charter. As regent, he spoke for the King. They all knew the word of the Marshal was inviolate. It had enormous weight. In a strange juxtaposition, the man who rode beside King John to Runnymede was now the champion of the charter John opposed to the day he died, and many of the men who demanded the document were now supporting a cause which could bring about its destruction. It is all too easy for some men to find virtue only in that which benefits their purse.

Letter after letter was sent. By spring, things were beginning to change. Much to the utter delight of the Marshal, his own son was one of the first to see the logic of the Marshal's arguments and returned to support the struggle. It removed several more years from the broad shoulders of the white-haired man and was the cause for great rejoicing by the Lady Isabel. The Earl of Salisbury, William Long Espee, came back to the fold. Several other nobles accepted the Marshal's arguments and began to question the wisdom of seeking a Frenchman as King of England. More and more people began to rally to our cause. It helped stiffen resistance. Time was on our side.

Louis' strategy of laying siege to castle after castle in the western lands was not working. It caused his illustrious father to demand he return to France to discuss the progress of the invasion. Our friend Willikin almost captured him when he traveled to the coast to take ship for France. In a hurry, Prince Louis foolishly made an attempted dash through the edge of the Weald. Willikin struck. Only the timely arrival of a relief force from London saved Louis and his men, but the cost of going through the Weald was high. More French "pine cones" hung from the trees as proof of the folly.

The absence of Louis gave the Marshal a chance to invite Willikin to a war council and to personally thank him for his efforts. They discussed future attacks. The two men, one old and wise, the other filled with the daring of youth, enjoyed the fellowship of a united purpose. Each expressed the admiration for the other and they parted best of friends. The same could not be said for Louis and his father. Our spies in Paris reported the two had fallen out over the invasion. Philip was convinced the cause was no longer worth the effort and refused to contribute any more men or money. Louis said he would find the necessary support without him. He succeeded in raising enough money and three hundred knights to continue.

He returned to England in April and prepared for the summer campaign. This time he avoided the Weald as he raced back to London. He was joined by Sir William Mowbray, Sir Robert Fitz-Walter and Saire de Quincey, rebel barons who had stayed loyal to Louis. They informed him of the deteriorating situation. Defections meant mercenaries would be needed. Louis sent a message to his wife, still in France, to hire them. Eustace the Monk should deliver them once they were assembled in Calais. In order to facilitate their landing, Dover would have to be secured. The truce with de Burgh had ended. The resolute Justiciar was back in Dover castle defending the landing site.

Louis would take half of their men to Dover to accomplish that objective. He placed the Count of Perche in charge of the other half of the army and ordered them to deal with the old man who was creating so much trouble in the west. Fitz-Walter protested the choice of the Count. He believed the Count was too young be in charge of leading a force against someone like the Marshal. The Prince and the Count scoffed and said it was not difficult to face a knight whose time had clearly passed. The Count was left in charge. Reports said the Marshal was engaged in a siege of the castle of Mountsorel. The Count promised he would put an end to this irksome old has-been. He assured Louis he would clear the way for major attacks in the west.

At Mountsorel we were told a large French army was on the way. It contained not only three hundred of Louis' best knights, but also Barons Fitz-Walter, Mowbray and de Quincey. Keeping to his plan, the Marshal disengaged and retreated north. When the Count of Perche arrived, he found no one to oppose. He continued to chase us north for several more days, but finally tired of the pursuit. He began the journey back to London in need of a victory. Not wanting to disappoint his sovereign, he decided to stop at Lincoln and subdue the royalist sympathizer, Nicolette de Camville. She was a widow and the attack was expected to be an easy victory. The Count had badly miscalculated his advantage. She retreated to her stout castle and put up a spirited defense. Perche was not going to be denied his victory by a mere woman, so a siege of the ramparts began.

Several local farmers came to the Marshal. They were poor men by looks of their tattered clothes, but loyal Englishmen. The oldest of the group stepped forward. He bared his head revealing only a few wisps of hair and bowed. "My lord Marshal, we have information that could be of use," he said. The words were somewhat slurred since he possessed only three good teeth.

"Speak, my friend," the Marshal said in a kindly voice.

"My lord, the army sent to destroy her is only half of the French force. My cousin was forced to accompany them from London to help drive the cattle they keep for supplies. To assure you I speak the truth, my friends, and I will be your hostages until you can verify my words. We are for England," he said bowing and holding his cap in his hands.

"All in this place are for England. Your information is most valuable. We have received several reports this day to confirm your story. You are not hostages, but soldiers in the cause of England. Lewellyn, see to it that these men are given a good meal." The old man smiled a toothless grin.

Several more reports set the number of knights at three hundred. It was still larger than our one hundred, but when he learned the inexperienced Count of Perche was in command, the Marshal made a fateful decision. We would attack in spite of the difference in numbers. The next day we turned and headed for Lincoln. As we rode to the impending conflict, I talked nervously with the Marshal.

"My lord, I am nervous. This will be my first battle," I said knowing that the numbers would mean all able men would be asked to bear arms.

"Lewellyn, this could be the turning point in this struggle. I shall gamble on the inexperience of the French leader. If I be wrong and he makes no mistakes we could be in serious trouble, but winning battles always carries risk. In all my years of combat, my instincts have served me well. I have learned to trust them. Still we must learn as much as we can about any advantages the site of the battle may give us. For that reason, I ask you to do something very dangerous. You may refuse, if you wish," he said staring at me as if he were seeing into my very soul.

I began to feel a tingling sensation on my skin. I knew if I thought about this for long what little courage I possessed would abandon me. I remembered the vines of fear the Marshal said robbed us of our will to act. Before they could grow I blurted out, "Ask me and I will do as you wish, my lord." There, it was done! Goose flesh replaced the tingle.

"I need you to go ahead of us, in your guise of traveling minstrel, and spy out the French position. When we are a day's ride from Lincoln we will be discovered and you must be back before then or your information will be of no use. I will try to gather more men. I expect to arrive in three days," he explained, patted his horse's neck and looked toward the fields that had turned silver as the afternoon sun retreated toward the horizon.

"I understand, my lord," I said trying to disguise the fear that continued to grow.

"Take your lute and may God go with you, my friend." He reached out his hand in the same manner he had in a dungeon long ago. As our hands met, I felt like I was ten again, and helping the wounded warrior to his feet. I felt a lump in my throat and was unable to speak. I released the still powerful grip and rode off before my emotions betrayed my fear. I galloped southeast in the direction of Lincoln and, as the timid often do, babbled words of false courage to myself.

My thoughts drifted into self-doubt. I was fifty-nine and might not see sixty, but it had been a wonderful life. I had seen what few in my station had ever seen. I would miss the letters from my son in France. He had developed a wonderful writing style and...Nay, I would complete this mission successfully! Had I not gone to the Weald on a similar task and managed it without incident? Who could possibly be suspicious of a harmless old man with a lute?

After a day's ride, I could see the city of Lincoln which sits atop a high limestone plateau and strategically surveys the surrounding countryside. I had passed very few people on the old Roman Way. The villeins' broad fields were deserted. I assumed most of the locals had taken refuge in the castle or fled into the large woods to the northeast of town when the French army approached. As I crested the hill to the north of the city, I was impressed by the size of the large cathedral that occupied the highest point of the plateau. The top of the castle keep could be seen as it rose from a depression below the hill on which the cathedral stood. I decided to skirt the city and approach from the southeast. It would be considered less suspicious if I came from a direction controlled by the French army. As I rode through the woods and brush to the west, I noticed a small path leading into the back of the castle was unguarded. I would inform the Marshal of this when I returned. A low wall of Roman design surrounded the city to the south and east. I continued around until I came to the east gate where two soldiers sat talking in French unconcerned by my approach. My hands began to shake. I told myself I must appear normal, or I would surely give myself away. I took a deep breath and began to whistle one of my favorite tunes. I rehearsed my act to myself. They ignored me and I continued on. The wall was not much of a defense for the town. It was the castle whose ramparts overlooked the high ground that dominated the strategic position.

Once I was inside the town I could hear the distinctive sound of siege machines engaged in their deadly purpose. I began to see more soldiers. The streets of the lower city were narrow and the very broad Roman Road went down a steep hill to the gates of the castle. The half-timbered houses in the lower city had several small chapels belonging to the churchmen of the cathedral. They were occupied by some of the foot soldiers for sleeping. They were mostly new and gave testament to the prosperous nature of the city. It had been so since Roman times when it was called Lindum. There was a tavern at the top of the incline where many soldiers were going in and out. It was the natural place for one like me to seek employment.

As I approached, several knights spoke to me in broken English. I said in French I could entertain in their language. They responded with words of approval. I said I would talk to the tavern keeper about performing for them tonight. I informed them I was only passing through and would be there for only one night. My ruse was working. Encouraged, I asked what was happening at the castle. I was informed it was under attack. They expected to finish the job in a few days and then return to London. I said I was not good enough to ply my trade in London and would probably be going to some of the surrounding towns. They said they would welcome some entertainment since this had been a rather boring expedition. I suggested they bring some friends with the means to toss me a coin or two tonight and bid them adieu.

After arranging my performance with the tavern keeper, I began to survey the area. I tried to be as inconspicuous as possible. The town was surrounded by a crumbling old Roman wall. There were three entrances. The Old Roman Way from the eastern approach was one. It would be difficult to bring an army from this direction owing to the rough terrain surrounding the road. Only a small number of the houses on this side sat on the high ground near the cathedral. The streets dropped down a steep hill to the base of the castle. A relatively flat area in front of the castle was filled with siege machines battering the main entrance. I could see a very small number of archers on the ramparts. The castle overlooked the lower part of the city and was well positioned to give archers a clear shot at the narrow streets below, but it was obvious the defenders did not have the men or arrows to use the position to their advantage.

The second entrance, a small gate facing west, led directly to the rear of the castle. It was unguarded. I reasoned it was left unattended on purpose. It was hoped the defenders of the castle might be encouraged to escape into the forest and end the need for a prolonged siege. It was the position the Count wanted, not the puny force defending it.

To the south, in front of the castle gates, a third entrance was carefully attended by a large body of mounted knights. In the distance the River Witham ran through the wide fields. It was this river that gave the city transportation for their wool products. A large wooden bridge spanned the water allowing the road access to the gate. I recognized the banners flying above the tents of some of the rebel barons in this area. It was the most logical place for invaders to approach the castle and therefore heavily defended. I believed the bridge was the place where most of the difficult fighting would be. I made mental notes of the numbers and positions. I returned to the tavern as the evening of the 18th approached. I knew I must leave in the morning to report to the Marshal before he reached the city. I remembered his warning and a cold shiver traversed my back. I nervously awaited my tavern appearance. I wanted to go, but I knew my sudden disappearance would be a clear signal to the French something was amiss. I would need to act as normal as possible.

The evening began well. I sang a few of the songs that I knew the French troops would like. The drinking was heavy and the keeper was doing well. He smiled at me for helping to increase the crowd. Groups of soldiers and knights came and went as each took turns resting from the boredom of the siege. I was doing well. My cap was filling with coins. I told some ribald stories which I knew would be loved by fighting men. I was feeling confident and relaxed. Then disaster struck!

The door opened and several well-dressed knights walked in. At first, I thought my evening would be rewarded with some larger coins, since these were well-to-do nobles. As I looked closer, my fingers froze on the strings. In the van of the group was Sir William Mowbray, the man who until recently was the tutor of young William Marshal. He looked at me and shouted, "Seize that man! He is the personal servant of the Earl of Pembroke. There is treachery afoot."

I could not run. The tavern was too crowded. My arms were seized by two large soldiers. I was discovered and the impending attack was imperiled. Mowbray said, "I will question him in the morning. See that he is bound securely and watched." I wondered how much torture I could stand before I revealed all I knew. I wagered, not much!

My life had come a full circle, only this time I did not have the Marshal as a companion to bolster my meager reserve of courage. My arms were lashed to an oak staff. My feet were also bound. They would wait until morning to question me. As I sat with my arms tied to the staff, and looking very much like the thieves who were crucified with our Lord. I could think of nothing else so I prayed to God that I could hold my tongue for at least one day. I now understood the need men have for their belief. When I had nowhere else to turn I trusted that the Almighty would overlook my previous doubts and grant me strength. Like the good thief next to the Christ at Golgotha I hoped my return to faith would be accepted. It was not for my soul that I prayed but for those of my friends who would suffer should I fail under torture.

Chapter 16
A Final Service

With the morning light came a kick to my ribs. Two large men grabbed either end of the staff and jerked me to my feet. A third man with an ugly burn scar on the left side of his face led the way. Since my feet were bound, I was dragged along like a fowl on a spit. I prayed the thought would not become a reality. I had heard gruesome stories of the kinds of torture often employed to loosen the tongues of prisoners and I knew I would not do well. As my captors dragged me across the street, my heels banged against the cobblestones. I cried out from the pain. One of the two men dragging me laughed and said, "This one will be easy. He will curse the day of his birth and tell all before we break the fast." I mentally rehearsed the lies I would tell to my interrogators. I knew silence was not possible.

I was brought to a house perched on the edge of the high ground of the city. Broken goods lay scattered on the plank floor. Most of the contents had been looted by the soldiers. I could see the castle ramparts from the doorway. Across the street was the cathedral. My questioning was in the hands of the Saire de Quincey, the very man whose daughter's deflowering I had accidentally witnessed several years before. His hatred of the crown had to be very deep and now I was the object that represented the pain. He stood waiting next to a large wooden table with a smirk on his face.

"Well, well, the Marshal's minstrel has come to entertain us! We shall see what kind of songs you have to sing," he said with a sarcastic tone.

"My lord, I am no longer in the employ of the Marshal. He decided I was too old to entertain properly and sent me away. I am earning a meager living traveling from town to town as you can plainly see," I whimpered. My first lie was greeted by a whack across the face with the baron's leather glove.

"The wrong song, knave. You are too fat to be a struggling troubadour. Besides I know the Marshal does not write and there have been plenty of letters this winter. Your work, perhaps?" he said running his finger across my cheek now red from the blow. "Mowbray says you can write." My lie was not working so I decided to try a different strategy. I would give them true, but old information. Would I be able to last for the twenty-four hours I knew were needed?

"Now sing me a song of where your master is making camp. Save yourself some pain and tell me, where is the Marshal?" he demanded and prepared his glove for another blow.

"He retreated from Mountsorel. Your force was too large to engage. He went north," I said with some hope. It was not a lie. Again, I was hit by the glove.

"You tell me what I already know. You were sent here to spy, why?" My answers only enraged de Quincy and I could see he was tiring of the game.

"I was asked to see if you were returning to London after you captured Lincoln. Nothing more," I responded and winced expecting another strike. I was not disappointed. Again I felt the glove and this time with enough force to cut my lip.

"Not good enough. A little pain will cause the tune to change. My friends here have some methods to improve your voice. I shall return in an hour." He walked out of the house. I had bought only one hour with my lies. It was not enough. The oldest of the three guards swept the large oak table clear with the back of his arm. The cups and a wooden bowl crashed to the floor. The ends of the staff were grabbed and with a jerk I was unceremoniously laid on the table. My leather slippers were removed and my feet were left bare, protruding slightly at the end of the table. My two burly minders held the staff against the table, and the third produced a wooden rod. He took aim at my bare feet and unleashed a savage blow. Pain shot through my body in a way I cannot describe. I screamed and tears filled my eyes. The procedure was repeated. It had the same result. Twice more and the room went black. I must have been unconscious for an hour, because when I revived the Saire de Quincey was standing over me.

"You do not handle pain well, my friend. Most fighting men last much longer," he said thinking it was an insult. The revelation was no surprise to me. "Are you ready to tell me what I wish to know," he demanded, "or do my friends show you the real meaning of pain?" Now, what was I to do? I could not handle the pain much longer. My feet were burning and I knew the next blow would have me blabbering like a fishwife. I resorted to another more believable lie.

"Please, my lord, no more! The Marshal has moved around you to the southeast he expects to attack in two days when he is reinforced," I begged with tears in my eyes.

"Now that's more like the tune I wanted to hear, but on the chance you are a clever liar, I shall keep you here until riders can scout to the southeast and see if you speak accurately. It is just the sort of surprise I would expect from your master." It worked. I had bought some time. I was left on the table until late afternoon. My arms ached mercilessly. It was about four, I think, when de Quincey reappeared.

"The riders have not returned yet. You may be telling the truth, but something tells me there is more. Repeat the treatment," he ordered in a callous voice.

"Nay, my lord. I told you two days. Your riders will not be back until tomorrow."

"Repeat it." Again fire shot through my legs and my back. Thankfully, I returned to blackness. It was night when the doorway slowly came into focus. This time de Quincey was joined by Sir Robert Fitz-Walter. He spoke when he saw I was conscience.

"Your technique is too slow. I will get the answers you seek. Son of a drab, you will tell me what I want to know or…(he removed his dagger from his belt) I shall remove your fingers one at a time!" I knew it was not an idle threat. I also knew I would not survive the treatment. I considered for a moment and looked out the door. It had likely been dark for several hours. By morning they would know the truth anyway. Sadly my courage failed. We spend our lives admiring the courage of great men and dream of the day we too can display bravery in a great cause. Wish not for such an opportunity. The sad reality is that most will fail as I did and the shattering of this dream leaves a lifetime of regret.

"My lord, he comes from the southwest. I can take no more." Tears filled my eyes.

"Send two riders to the south road to warn us if they approach by night and redeploy some of the garrison to the bridge in the morning. You shall come with us and I promise you, knave, this will be your last lie."

"Kill me now. I have betrayed my lord." I cursed my cowardly body and began to weep uncontrollably.

"Nay, you may yet be useful." I was tossed into a corner, still bound. My feet were bleeding. I no longer tried to pray. The strength I asked for had been denied. God had abandoned me. I deserved the torments of Hell which loomed before me. I lay weeping in the corner until I finally slept from exhaustion.

Another kick made me aware it was morning. The bonds on my feet were cut. The oak staff was removed after I was dragged outside. I found it difficult to move my arms. They had been suspended from the staff for so long they were numb. I had no feeling in my hands. I was lifted onto a horse by the same two men and my hands lashed to the saddle. I was led to the south of town by a small group which included barons Fitz-Walter and Mowbray. When we reached the bridge the truth of my confession was clear. Approaching the city from the west was an army. Wagons filled the road, banners and foot soldiers spread across the close-cropped fields. They were far enough away so I could not clearly make out the actual size of the force, but it looked twice the size of the one we had at Mountsorel. The Marshal had been able to double the size of the army. I was excited. Fitz-Walter turned to one of the retainers and instructed him to bring the Count of Perche immediately. He turned to me.

"Well it seems your last story was accurate. You shall be able to watch you master meet his end before you die, but for your help I will make it a quick end." Again the tears flowed down my unshaven cheeks. It was not the fear of death this time, but the bitter knowledge of my failure. I had become a Judas to the man who honored loyalty above all things. My life was a failure. My death would be meaningless.

Several minutes later the Count arrived. Mowbray spoke to him. He gestured to the distant mass of men who had stopped advancing.

"My lord Count. The enemy approaches slowly. I suggest we bring our mounted knights and engage them on the plain. They appear to be mostly on foot with only a handful of knights."

"That is why I am in charge, my lord Baron. They wait because their spy was captured and they need to assess our strength. It is an obvious attempt to draw us away from the bridge and cross the river with ease. The force in front of us is too large for us to take on directly. We will move our foot soldiers from the upper part of the city and make them pay. Leave enough to guard the high ground against a diversionary attack. The three hundred knights will remain guarding the bridge and use the river to good advantage against the attack," Perche ordered in a stern voice.

"My lord, I beg to differ. The force is not that large..."

"Silence! Obey my orders," he shouted. Mowbray shrugged his shoulders and gave the appropriate commands. Soldiers scurried to man the east approaches of the city. The attack on the castle stopped as men were transferred to meet the new threat. I was led back into the city and down the hill to the area guarding the south gate. The men on the walls of the castle could see the approaching army and began to cheer. They were ignored. The undermanned castle posed no real threat. They would merely be spectators to what the Count of Perche hoped would be a major victory. All eyes were focused on the south gate where I was sure the attack would be launched. Soon the noise of battle indicated an attack on the east wall had begun. It seemed the Count was right. The soldiers were scrambling up the hill to defend the east gate. I feared for my master. I was certain the old man would lead the small diversionary force. It was his style.

I was right next to Sir William Mowbray when it happened. Several hundred bowmen appeared on the ramparts of the castle as if by some sorcerer's magic. The banner of Falkes de Breaute was raised and arrows rained down on the upper streets of the city. I could hear the screams. It must have been awful in the narrow streets as death came from the sky. How could this be? Where had the archers come from? Realizing the men racing up the hill would not reach the east gate. The Count ordered fifty of the mounted knights toward the hill with him. Still there was no attack from the army in the south. My minders were part of the group dispatched and I was dragged along as they approached the hill riding slowly. They did not relish the thought of coming in range of the archers in the castle, but as trained soldiers they moved forward with shields at the ready. Still the army in the field across the river did not move. A lone French knight raced down the hill dodging a hail of arrows. He began shouting as he reached us.

"My lord, they come from the east. Hundreds!" No sooner did he utter those words when several arrows knocked the rider from his horse.

Sir William Mowbray swore, "Damn, I warned the French puppy. Now we are in for it. The south gate was the diversion. We are trapped." The Count's fifty knights remained watching the upper city and glancing back at the south gate. Men, many of them wounded, filled the streets as they tried to escape the arrows by retreating down the incline to the lower city. The deadly rain was taking a terrible toll. The soldiers from the upper town ceased to be a fighting force as they scattered and ducked into shops and any covered area to escape the archers' attack. The Count shouted orders for another hundred knights to join him and repel the attackers in the upper city. The upper streets were abandoned by all but the dead. As the last of those able to move reached the bottom of the hill the archers stopped. They repositioned themselves and were now taking aim at us approaching from the south.

The streets at the top of the hill were no longer empty. Every street was filled with pike men and several dozen knights. They massed like a wave ready to break. The Count shouted orders to move forward and meet the attack. An eerie silence fell over what had been a cacophony of shouts and screams. I looked at our men on top of the hill. The foot soldiers parted and in the middle of the road a horse and rider emerged. My eyes filled with tears as a bare-headed knight sat defiantly looking down at the army below. His white locks glistened in the noon sun. I screamed at the top of my lungs, "BEHOLD, THE MARSHAL!"

The Count pointed to me and said, "Kill him." Before his order could be carried out a huge cry came from men at the top of the hill. The Marshal's sword arm signaled the charge. Arrows from the castle filled the air again. Fitz-Walter and Mowbray raised their shield above their heads to ward off the deadly shafts. I was lucky to be close enough to them to benefit from the cover. Killing me was the last thing on their minds. Simultaneously the south gate was charged by the men beyond the bridge.

The Marshal, with his long white hair blowing in the breeze, charged down the hill his broadsword flashing in the air. The foot soldiers charging with him were screaming. The French soldiers panicked. They began dropping their weapons. The Count screamed, "Cowards." He spurred his horse to meet the old knight in green coming down the hill. He would rally his troops by killing this legend. He raised his sword as he closed with the Marshal at a full gallop. My heart stopped. In a move I had seen many times before, the ageless Marshal ducked the wild blow and delivered a single fatal stroke to the Count of Perche. Mowbray turned to Fitz-Walter and said, "This is over." The knights holding the south gate realized they were trapped and began to drop their weapons also. The battle of Lincoln was over and the rider in the green tabard with a white cross emblazoned on his right shoulder turned his horse to us and prepared to accept the surrender.

Sir William Mowbray drew his dagger. I closed my eyes expecting death and heard him say, "You are free, troubadour. Your death would serve no one." My bonds were cut. I sagged in the saddle exhausted and relieved. I leaned forward and placed my head on the horse's neck. Once again it seemed that God had answered my prayer and as usual not in the way I understood.

The rebel English nobles rode over to formally surrender to the victor of Lincoln. Cheers rang out from the archers on the castle walls. Someone in the upper town had made it to the cathedral and the bells began to ring. The battle had been a rout. Hundreds of French soldiers were dead or wounded. I discovered later the Marshal's army had lost no one. I saw Mowbray point in my direction when he finished speaking to the Marshal. The white hair flew in the breeze again as he galloped over to me.

"By God's eyes, Lewellyn, you are alive." He reached over to embrace me. "I feared you dead when you did not return." He saw my battered condition. "Take this man to the castle and summon the physician," he shouted as he cradled my weakened body and prevented me from falling off my mount. The rest was a blur.

I awoke in the chambers of the Lady Nicolette. My feet were bandaged and several servants were watching over me. One left immediately as I awoke. Several minutes later the Marshal and John d'Erly appeared. Sir John spoke first.

"Troubadour, you have done yourself proud," he said grabbing my hand. Ashamed of the wrongful praise I spoke.

"Not so, my lord. I told them of your coming. I could not stand the torture." I rolled my head to the side and looked at the ceiling too ashamed to face these brave men. The Marshal took my other hand and spoke softly.

"Nay, my old friend. The Saire de Quincey told us of your ability to delay them with lies. You withstood much for our cause. As God willed it you helped my plan. While you were a prisoner, a brave knight named Geoffrey de Serland slipped out the postern gate and came to us with vital information about an unguarded path. He said the French had shifted their attention to the south gate. I hoped it would occupy the attention of the French army while Falkes de Breaute slipped into the postern gate with his archers under cover of darkness. It worked. By telling them I was coming from the south you directed their attention to the exact place I wished it to be." His kind words revived my spirit. It gave me to wonder how he had rallied so many fighting men in so short a time.

I asked, "God answered my prayers. But, my lord, how did you amass so large an army in so short a time?" The magnificent old man threw back his head and laughed as he looked at John and nudged him in the ribs.

"See, I told you they would be fooled!" he said with a wink.

"That you did, my lord." John laughed.

"Lewellyn, you and the French Count fell for one of the oldest tricks used in a battle. Older than me! The farmers of the surrounding towns, being loyal Englishmen, assembled with banners and wagons. Seen from a distance, it looked like we had far more fighting men than was really the case. Half the army you saw was a sham. They were only there to buy time for the main fighting force to gain the high ground."

I laughed a little and shook my head when the pain in my feet and arms returned and caused me to wince. Seeing my discomfort the Marshal looked at me and with sorrow in his eyes said, " I asked too much of you, my friend.

With this victory, I hope I will never have to do that again." I looked at him and recalled the eloquent words of the man standing next to him.

"These times ask men to give more than they think they can, my lord." He was moved by the words. He looked at John and nodded.

"Rest, my friend. We have much celebrating to do and I need you to get my beer." With that remark they left the room.

I rested for two days at Lincoln. It gave me time to reflect. I had known tumult and tribulation, as well as joy and happiness in my life. Were the times of trouble God's punishment for my doubts? Like most men I wavered between faith and doubt. Yet these did not match with the times when prayers were answered and when they were not. Was this all part of a master plan too complex for a man like me to understand? This is what the priests say. It makes it easy for God to always be right. A different thought occurs to me. Men will always be contradictions and because of this our lives will always move between joy and sorrow. Because of this we will always need prayers. Believing in something makes life's ups and downs more bearable. Whether or not there is a God controlling our lives matters little. We need God. It is that simple.

While I rested the Marshal rode to Nottingham to inform the boy King and his advisors of the great victory. When he returned I was sent to Pembroke to recuperate. The lovely Lady Isabel personally assisted in nursing me back to health. The Marshal had truly married an angel. I described the brilliant victory her husband had won at Lincoln. She smiled and sighed, "'Twould be a greater victory to have him here with me." I nodded and touched her hand. "My Lady, your father was a great man and your husband is a great man. Sadly others must lean on great men and women like you are the ones left to pay the price for the benefits we receive from their service."

"I know, Lewellyn. 'Tis selfish for me to wish him here," she said sadly.

"Nay, my lady, it be we lesser men who are selfish. We steal your happiness to benefit ourselves," I said unable to let her blame her true feelings wrongly.

A week later the Marshal returned home for another short stay. A messenger from London indicated Louis was ready to discuss terms. The Marshal was overjoyed and hoped this would mean the end of a bitter civil war. He joined the papal legate and several others on a peace mission to London. I was not well enough to join them. The meeting was to take place at Brentford. The Marshal went with high hopes and I wished him good luck.

Three weeks passed. My injuries had healed and I was anxiously awaiting the news. Early in July, we were roused by the cheers of the servants. The

Marshal had returned. As he dismounted I could see that things had not gone well. His face had regained the haggard look, cheeks sunken and eyes downcast. The Lady Isabel spoke first.

"What news, my lord?"

"There be no truce. Gualo sought more than Louis was ready to give. We were very close to an agreement. Before I could persuade Gualo to accept less, a messenger arrived from France and Louis was no longer interested in talking. I suspect reinforcements are being gathered in France. There is some good news. The French have given up the siege of Dover. Between the stout resistance of Hubert de Burgh and the harassment of Willikin, Louis has decided to cut his losses. If I am right and reinforcements are gathering in Calais, I believe they will seek to land somewhere other than Dover. I will be going to see Philip d'Aubigny tomorrow. Are you able to travel, Lewellyn?" he said and raised my level of excitement with the thoughts of new adventures.

"Yes, my lord. I am fully recovered," I responded cheerfully.

"Good I will need to send communications to many people." As he walked into the main hall he turned to his wife. "I am sorry, my love, I can only stay the night. You know you are constantly in my thoughts," he said as he stroked her beautiful golden tresses.

"You serve the greater good, my husband. I have always trusted your judgment in such matters. You are always in my thoughts as well," she said while looking out the window and gazing at three of their children playing in the yard below. She was a magnificent wife for a magnificent man.

We supped that night and sang some of the Marshal's favorite songs. I had composed a poem about the victory at Lincoln. The people were calling it the "Fair of Lincoln" because it had been so one sided. The Marshal smiled. "You have left out the story of the brave spy," he scolded gently. "Agreed!" said the Lady Isabel as she daintily wiped her chin after sipping some of the spiced wine she was fond of.

"A troubadour never writes about himself," I said solemnly waving the bone of a chicken leg that I had just finished. We laughed and enjoyed the evening. It was the life the Marshal had longed for, but was denied because of his commitment to honor and duty. We did not think about the fact that we would have to ride out of Pembroke in the morning heading for another meeting and another battle. There were rewards for this commitment and a full belly was certainly one of them.

It was mid August when we reached Dover to discuss events with Hubert de Burgh and Philip D'Aubigny. Louis was ensconced in London with less than half his original army. He was afraid to leave the safety of the Tower. He was still in possession of many of the eastern castles. The Marshal said laying siege to each of them would prove to be as futile as Louis' plan to take the west castle by castle. Numbers were now on the Marshal's side and so was time.

Each day saw new defections from the rebel cause. If Louis was not reinforced soon, he was finished. Spies in France reported a contingent of several hundred knights and a large group of foot soldiers were gathering in Calais. The ships of the pirate Eustace were ready to bring them to England. Philip D'Aubigny had organized a fleet to see it did not happen. Although many of the Cinque captains feared facing the evil Eustace, D'Aubigny had convinced them now was the time to rid the Channel of this scourge. Eustace had preyed on their commerce for years and had developed a considerable reputation. D'Aubigny said it was time for it to end.

On the 20th, we received word that the French would sail on the 24th and head for the mouth of the Thames. There they would sail up river directly to Louis in London and avoid the hazards of traveling overland through the Weald. In the evening, I went with the Marshal to a meeting to discuss final plans. Two of us were asked to serve the supper. Since the meeting was to include secret plans, regular servants would not be used for fear the plans would be compromised. It seemed as though my life had come full circle as I served the supper with Reginald, a trusted mate of Captain D'Aubigny. I was somewhat surprised that I still remembered the proper serving techniques from fifty years before. There are things you learn in youth you never forget. The table was cleared and ale was poured. Philip spoke first since he was the commander of the fleet. The others listened intently to his plan.

"The fleet is assembled and ready. My informants tell me the landing site is to be Greenwich." He belched. "I hope the information is as good as the ale." The men gathered around the table laughed. "Our fleet will be smaller than that of the French. Therefore, I propose a deception to give us some advantage in the fight. We will wait at Sandwich and allow the French to sail past us. I will launch the fleet and sail in the direction of France making sure we are observed by the Monk. It will appear to Eustace we are going to attack Calais. It is an old strategy. When you are outnumbered, you attack the port of the opposite fleet. He will have expected this, and left sufficient force in Calais to destroy such an attack. He will ignore us and sail on. My real goal is to gain the windward position. The wind will be at our backs. Our smaller craft will be able to maneuver better. Eustace will have to turn into the wind to face us. With his ships fully loaded this will be difficult. It may give us the advantage we need. We will fit our boats with ramming devices. If we can disable his heavier ships we may have a chance. With the wind at our backs, as we approach the enemy, we will throw quick lime into the air. It should blind any archers they may have onboard. In addition I am hoping the knights onboard will not be familiar with sea tactics and we may also blind them." The Marshal looked at Philip.

"A good plan. I will command from my cog," he said confidently. Both Hubert and Philip looked at each other. The Chief Justiciar spoke.

"My Lord Pembroke, we suggest you remain ashore." He glanced at Philip. The response from the Marshal was as expected.

"I think not. I have never commanded a battle from anywhere but the front." There was iron resolve in the voice. Hubert resorted to another argument.

"But my lord, with all due respect to your great skills, you are not used to fighting on a rolling deck of a ship. I respectfully request you remain ashore. As a younger man and sailor Philip will be better suited to command from the cog," he said pleadingly.

"Ah, the real reason is forthcoming—my age! I remind you of the attitude of the Count of Perche. He, too, thought this old man was defenseless. It was a fatal mistake. I will go." The two men looked frustrated. Then Philip spoke.

"My Lord Pembroke, neither of us, or any man in England, doubts your courage or skill with a sword, but may I point out another critical reason you should remain ashore. If my ruse fails and we are defeated then you are sorely needed here. It will be on your shoulders to repel the invaders as they come ashore. Only you can inspire the men in defense of the country," he added truthfully.

The Marshal considered the logic of the last argument, and with a dispirited look, reluctantly agreed. He had never declined a fight and it was very hard to decline this one, but he knew Philip D'Aubigny was right. The supper and the planning concluded, each man returned to his quarters to contemplate the days ahead. When we returned, the Marshal confided in me.

"Lewellyn, this may be the final battle. If they win, as I pray they will, Louis will have to agree to terms. I will have missed the last conflict. It troubles me. I feel my final act will be to avoid a fight." He looked down at his right hand and flexed it as though it was grasping an imaginary sword. Swinging his arm in a large arc, he cut the air with his phantom blade.

"My lord, you are not avoiding a fight. I remember many years ago when you chastised an inexperienced Adam d' Iquebeuf for charging into the melee for personal glory and thereby putting your plans at risk. The plan is a good one. All must play their part," I said meekly.

"My friend, and my conscience, you are right. 'Tis strange. I begged them not to name me regent because I was too old, but now I find it difficult to let others share the work. It makes little sense," he said perplexed by the conundrum. He ran his fingers through the long white hair and scratched the back of his neck. He slapped me on the back. It lacked the power to knock me forward as it had so many times before. I was glad it signified his willingness to accept his part, but it reminded me that age had stolen the vigor of this friendly gesture. We were no longer young.

The morning of August 24 showed the promise of a clear and breezy day. It was just the kind of day Philip D'Aubigny had hoped for. He was already positioned at Sandwich. From a cliff overlooking the bay, I anxiously watched the sea for a sign of the struggle. The Marshal was busy preparing for what would be needed if the sea battle now raging was a failure. He instructed me to come to him the moment I had news. It was late in the afternoon when I saw the Marshal's cog sailing toward the shore with a number of other boats. I knew some were ours, but there also were some that were not! I nervously watched the ships bob up and down with the action of the waves. For a brief moment I gave thanks for being on land for the last fourteen years. Finally I could make out the men onboard. They were waving our banners. The battle had been a success. I raced to tell the Marshal. We both returned to welcome the successful captains.

When we arrived at the docks we found them filled with cheering townspeople. As the ship drew nearer I could see the revolting, but welcomed, sight of a head on the end of a pike. It was the gory head of Eustace the Monk.

The Marshal was full of questions as Philip and Hubert walked with us through cheering crowds. He had to shout to be heard. "How was it?" he roared to the two men being overwhelmed by well wishers.

Hubert answered as we embraced among the throng, "Just as my friend here predicted. The Monk went past us at Sandwich. When he saw our intent he tried to turn. His boat was overloaded. It struggled to make the turn and so did the rest of the French fleet. There were seventy or more ships. We were far more maneuverable. Several overloaded ships foundered on the turn. The quicklime worked to perfection. When Eustace's ship was taken, several of the main ships carrying knights retreated back to Calais. The cargo-bearing ships were not so lucky. The sailors of the fleet recognized the value of taking their cargo and made quick work of the small crews sailing them. When we did not find the Monk onboard, we feared his use of the black arts to escape, but some of our men had served with him in the past and were wise to his tricks. Eustace had hidden himself under sandbags in the bilge of his ship. He tried to offer ransom for his life. The sailors who have lived in fear of him would have none of it. His head was removed in a single stroke. My lord, you have won a great victory. Louis will have to sue for terms."

"England has won, my friends. Let us return to the town. There will be much celebrating this night. God has given them into our hands. I express the thanks of your King for that which you have accomplished this day." The evening was spent in riotous celebration.

Faced with no supplies and no reinforcements, Louis requested a truce to meet with the Marshal and his council to discuss terms. The meeting was set for early September at Kingston. Some in our camp suggested we demand a total surrender. The Marshal spoke against this idea. He did not want a repeat of the previous negotiations. England needed peace. He said civil wars are best ended quickly and with as little animosity as possible. He offered amnesty to the rebel barons. Louis would be paid for the expense of removing his army. The terms were accepted. On September 12, 1217, the treaty of Kingston was signed. In three weeks the last French soldier took ship and returned to Calais. All were jubilant, and bells rang all over England.

In the months that followed, the Marshal set about appointing ministers to restore good government. By the spring, judges were sent out to restore the functioning of the courts. They were told by the Marshal to be mindful of the rights granted under the Magna Carta. This pleased the recently returned Archbishop of Canterbury, Steven Langton.

I recalled the words I had heard Queen Eleanor say to the Marshal long ago in a moment not meant for my ears, "William, behold the stars. The astrologers say they control our destiny. Had they been different, you might have been a king. A magnificent one!" Events now showed the wisdom of the great Queen's words. The stars had aligned to make it happen.

We received word Queen Isabella, Henry III's mother, journeyed to Angouleme to visit her young daughter Joanna, so named for her dead father. Joanna had been promised to none other than Hugh de Lusignan, the man who was jilted when King John married her mother. She was only seven and was being raised at his castle according to the custom. The one-time lovers met and rekindled the flame. The council was informed Queen Isabella had married Hugh.

It was not happy news for the council. She was immediately dispossessed. Marriage for a widowed Queen without their approval was unacceptable. It could create more rival claims to the throne. Even her son, King Henry, suggested she be excommunicated. I, on the other hand, being a singer of songs was happy the two lovers were reunited. To me love was more precious than titles. I was glad she found happiness for she had very little with King John. The rest of the year was spent rebuilding and gossiping about Queen Isabella's plight. Good times always accentuate the trivial.

Life was returning to normal. The Marshal's family was whole again. We were enjoying the benefits of the Marshal's good stewardship. The country was at peace and functioning normally as the Christmas season approached, but I noticed the Marshal was not looking forward to the season with his usual enthusiasm. I thought it was because we were spending another holiday away from Pembroke. As regent, the Marshal had taken up residence at the Tower of London. Christmas Eve he excused himself from his guests and returned to his quarters. I followed quickly to see if there was something I could do.

"Is there some difficulty, my lord?" I inquired, concerned with the unusual behavior.

"Only my age, Lewellyn. I am very tired." His cheeks were depressed and now showing the rigors of age. As I helped him with his dressing gown, I noticed his large frame had begun to lose some of its bulk. I began to worry.

"Are you ill, my lord?"

"Perhaps a little. 'Tis not unexpected after so much celebrating. I wish to sleep. Good night, my friend," he said as I left his chamber. The Lady Isabel had also excused herself and was entering their room. She gave me a concerned look and nodded as she went to her husband's bedside. I lingered in the doorway briefly and heard the Marshal say, "I am fine. Worry not, my wife." I closed the door and went to my room.

For several weeks he continued to lose weight, but kept to his busy schedule. His friend, Sir John, suggested he slow his pace. Surprisingly, the Marshal agreed and we all knew his health was truly failing. The Lady Isabel wanted answers. Physicians were summoned and from all over the kingdom. They came to offer remedies—one more bizarre than the other. One suggested he sit in a mixture of oatmeal and calf's blood. The Marshal refused to be subjected to their suggestions. He insisted God could not be countermanded. It was his time. He told them soberly, "I have cheated death many times, but this time he will win."

The Lady Isabel remained at his bedside as his condition grew worse. My constant tending of my sick lord was a source of irritation to the Marshal's eldest son. The young William Marshal who would soon become the Earl of Pembroke seemed threatened by the high regard I held in the household. The years he had spent away from the family had caused a different relationship to develop. His brothers and sisters were quite used to my role. He was not. He felt it was his role to tend his father as the future Lord of Pembroke. His mood was sullen and not friendly. I tried to understand. To live in the shadow of one's father, knowing you can never measure up to the incredibly high standard he has set, must be a heavy load to bear. We all hope our children will achieve greater things than we were able to attain. It is the natural order of life. Knowing that it is not possible would demoralize even the best of us. With this in mind I tried hard to stay clear of the future Earl while still performing my duties.

By the end of Lent the Marshal requested to be brought home. We traveled by boat, as much as was possible, to make the great man more comfortable. We made it to his estate at Caversham and decided he could go no further.

We all knew what the end result must be and tried not to burden the Marshal with sad faces. We did not offer false promises by saying all would soon be well. It would have been unseemly to do that to a man who honored the truth above all things. The royal council was summoned to the manor. They waited to see what the Marshal intended. Who would be named to replace him as regent? Would the Marshal be able to establish a proper succession in his present state? Many had doubts.

Gualo had been replaced by Pandulfo as Papal legate and was the first to arrive. Peter de Roches brought the boy King. The Marshal's entire family was present. The Lady Isabel and I continued to administer to the sick man. That evening, the Marshal requested all to attend him. I carried the message and the room soon filled. The Marshal spoke from his bed. He appropriately addressed the boy King first.

"Sire, I have served you the best of my ability. 'Tis no longer possible to continue. God has decided the issue. I must now pass your protection on to another." With that the Bishop of Winchester stepped forward.

"I shall serve his majesty. It is my responsibility now," he said in a firm voice. The Marshal was very weak, but the statement by de Roches roused his spirit.

"Not so, my lord Bishop! I was the one the King's late father appointed to be guardian. I only relinquished the charge temporarily, to fight a war. I shall give this some thought and make a decision tomorrow and may God help my judgment." He turned to the legate and said, "Take Lord Henry and return with him tomorrow." They all left the room. As I turned to go, I heard the dying man speak to his wife.

"Remain with me a while. I do not have long. I must complete my work tomorrow. I fear Sir Bishop is too eager to rise in power. It does not bode well for England," he said as he reached out a weak hand and rested it on hers.

The Lady Isabel stayed with her beloved husband through the night. She had me summon the council in the morning. When they arrived, the Marshal made a great effort to sit up. He spoke in a very weak voice.

"I have decided. I commit the Lord Henry to the protection of God." He looked at Pandulfo, the papal legate. "As the Pope's representative I commend him to your care." My eyes turned to the Bishop de Roches. There was an uncomfortable look on his face. The Marshal continued, "Sire, may God grant that you be a brave and honorable man." The young King replied, "Amen."

The Bishop started to speak protesting the choice. Again the Marshal drew on some inner reserve of strength and said curtly, "Be still, Lord Bishop!" He asked Pandulfo to leave with the King and dismissed the gathering of nobles. A very disgruntled bishop left without the boy he had hoped to dominate.

The Marshal asked me to summon his five sons. I returned with them quickly and each was told of the legacy he had arranged for them according to custom. He asked his son William to give sums for the prayers to be said for him. Gilbert, the most devout of the brothers, suggested more be given, but the Marshal squelched the suggestion and said God could not be bribed. He would face his maker as he had faced his kings—honestly and unafraid.

He summoned his daughters and requested that I play while they sang his favorite song. It was difficult, but we all managed to finish before several broke into tears. Sibilla was the most distressed. He requested I come closer. I knelt by the bed and tried to control my emotions. He leaned forward slightly and whispered for a few moments in my ear. My tears stopped and I stepped back. John d'Erly was next. There was a warm grasp of the tired hand and a nod of the head. He asked them all to stay and spoke to the Lady Isabel, "Kiss me for the last time, my love." She tenderly embraced and kissed her devoted husband. It brought tears to all present.

He looked at John and asked who the two handsome nobles who had just entered were. We all turned and saw no one. He laid back, closed his eyes and was gone. It was May 14, 1219, when my master, my teacher, my friend left us to struggle on alone.

I was sent to tell the King and his advisors. According to the last wishes of my lord, his body was to be taken to London to be buried in the Round Church of the Knights Templar. As the funeral procession passed from town to town the people were moved to tears. The "Good Knight" was gone. The world would not see his like again. When we reached London the procession grew. Behind the body stretched a long line of nobles, clergy and the common people of England. Such was the level of grief, that all, rich and poor alike, mourned his passing. From Prince to peasant, all came to pay respects to the man who had served them honorably for so many years, years when he sacrificed personal happiness for the benefit of all. Even his longtime foe, Philip of France, said to his court, "The Marshal is dead. He was the most loyal man I ever knew." He did not need to tell any of them which marshal he meant.

As we crowded into the Round Church of the Knights Templar on a small hill above the Thames, the Archbishop of Canterbury said the mass. He closed his eulogy by saying, "Here lie the remains of the greatest knight in all the world."

With those final words the old storyteller places his empty mug on the table. He bows his head, as if he is saying some type of silent prayer. The tavern is completely hushed for several minutes. The old man raises his head, scoops up the coins in his cap and places them in a leather pouch. The silence is broken by one of the gathering, "Old man, what did Lord Pembroke say to you on his deathbed?"

With very tired eyes, Lewellyn looks at the stranger, "That, my friend, shall always be between the Marshal and me." He lifts the precious lute and turns to the tavern keeper. "Good sir, the hour is late. Might I find a small place to sleep here this night?" The tavern keeper mindful of the windfall he has reaped because of this man accedes to the request immediately. As the patrons leave the premises debating the meaning of the evening, Lewellyn is given a place by the fireplace in the kitchen to spread his bedroll.

In the morning, the tavern keeper is awakened by a loud pounding on the door. As he goes to open it, he encounters a well-dressed knight.

"Keeper, my name is Sir John d'Erly. I come seeking the old troubadour called Lewellyn. I was told I would find him here."

Delighted and surprised to meet the man mentioned in last night's tale the keeper says, "He is indeed, my lord. He is sleeping in the back room." He mentions to the knight how the story from the previous evening had entertained his patrons. "Can this fanciful tale be true?"

Sir John nods and says, "The story is true. The new Earl of Pembroke is seeking Lewellyn to write it down. It be the reason I have journeyed these many miles." The tavern keeper is amazed.

They go to the kitchen. Sleeping peacefully with a smile on his face is the old man. Sir John thrilled with finding his man shouts, "Troubadour, I have come to fetch you home!" There is no response. "Lewellyn!" He shakes the sleeping man. There is no response for he is sleeping the eternal sleep. Sir John lifts the peaceful, lifeless body gently and says tenderly, "These times ask more of men than they think they can give."

Sir John takes the body of the old troubadour back to Pembroke for burial. Two years later, the Earl of Pembroke, the son of William the Marshal, sends to France to hire a young French poet called Jean Le Trouvere (the troubadour) to write L' Histoire de Guillaume le Marechal. *It becomes a medieval classic and fountain of information for future historians.*

Epilogue

The story you have just read is based on historical events. Most of the characters were real people and some of their comments are from surviving records. Translations vary, but the essence of the story is true. The Marshal was very real and did the things you have read. I shall endeavor to explain the reasons for his seeming disappearance from the history of a very colorful and important time. Most medieval historians acknowledge the "Good Knight" as the finest paladin of this or any similar period. Why has this magnificent fighting machine and a man of remarkable integrity taken a back seat to lesser knights and nobles? The explanation lies in several areas.

The first reason comes from events which occurred right after the Marshal's death. A power struggle developed between the men who wanted to control the youthful Henry III. In the last chapter you learned of the ambitions of Peter de Roches. He would emerge as the power behind the throne. The Marshal's suspicions proved true. The Marshal's sons lined up to oppose de Roches. It would be the losing side. None of them had the skills or support the Marshal had enjoyed. In trying to follow their father's wishes they encountered Peter de Roches' vengeance. Henry III, who owed everything, including his life, to the efforts of the Marshal, turned out to be a weak character. Manipulated by many in his long reign, he changed his loyalties frequently.

Stories of the time were generally written by those loyal to the winning side. Praising the losers could be hazardous to your health. The Marshal's five sons all met tragic or early ends. They each died without issue. The wealth and power of the Pembroke legacy passed to the daughters and was divided over time among other famous families. The name Marshal disappeared from the upper echelons of nobility.

The second reason was explained by our storyteller, Lewellyn. The time was filled with many larger than life characters. Eleanor of Aquitaine deserves all the attention scholars have given her. Richard was certainly as colorful as he was controversial. His role in history is mixed between reality and legend. He had great troubadours who would make modern political spin managers envious. Romantic novels, written by people like Sir Walter Scott, gave Richard an undeserved heroic position in the minds of many people. He was fortunate to precede a very unsuccessful king—his brother John. It made his military exploits seem better than they were in real terms. His good looks didn't hurt his legend either. You have to admire the statue that graces the yard in front of the House of Commons. John was the king everyone loves to hate, although some historians are now trying to put him in a slightly better light. Henry II's escapades were bound to inspire many great books and plays. His long and tumultuous reign provided many great stories. To use a modern saying, these people "sucked up all the oxygen in the room."

The third reason is a rather curious one. The final chapter ends with the selection of a French troubadour named Jean to write the epic poem about the Marshal. I used this unknown historical character to construct the story line. Some historians believe Jean was really John d'Erly. It is a question scholars will probably never solve. *Le Histoire de Guillaume Le Marechal* was written in the language commonly used in the 13th century court tales, Norman French. The epic poem, a wealth of medieval information and the source of much of this book, was unreadable by common Englishmen of succeeding centuries. It was translated into modern French by the scholar Paul Meyer at the beginning of the 20th century. Only a few people, seriously interested in the subject, have taken the time to translate this epic work. Recently there have been some books on the age of chivalry that have mentioned William Marshal and his amazing feats.

The most bizarre reason for the Marshal's disappearance from history is a seldom told story about an Irish priest who was said to have cursed the Marshal and his family. It seems he was angry about the Marshal's claim to some land in Ireland. Who knows?

For any or all these reasons, the Marshal has been denied a place in history that I believe he richly deserves. He was a man who rose from obscurity to be the virtual King of England. He did this by ability in an age where accident of birth dominated and trumped all other considerations. He was respected for his word and loyalty by friend and foe alike. He was a knight whose tournament records can be equated to modern sports heroes like Ruth, Gretzky or Jordan. He was that dominate over his peers. Without his presence on the world stage, history would have surely unfolded differently. What would have happened if

Eleanor had been captured by the Baron de Lusignan? What if the Marshal had chosen to kill Richard at Le Mans instead of sparing his life to honor the code? What would have happened to England if he had not been victorious over the French prince in1217? What if he had refused the regency? Would others, like de Roches, insist the terms of the Great Charter be honored? For all these reasons and one more—it's a great story—I tried to make this amazing man come alive in the chapters of this book. I wanted to be faithful to history, my chosen profession, but also give a feeling for the reader to relate to these characters. It is why I chose historical fiction rather than straight footnoted history.

The man whose effigy graces the floor of the Temple Church in London deserves better. Sadly, very few people know the story. The blockbuster novel *The Da Vinci Code* by Dan Brown calls the effigies—those of "unknown knights." Even the church's brochure for the few people that visit the site has the wrong date for his birth. I doubt the Marshal would really care, but he truly deserves the words Steven Langton, the great Archbishop of Canterbury, spoke at his funeral. "Here lies the greatest knight in all the world."